PETRICHOR

Jonathan D. Robbins

Honey & Da,

your names are my truth

petrichor [**pet**-ri-kawr]

1. the distinctive, earthy scent produced when rain falls on dry soil
2. constructed from the Ancient Greek words πέτρᾱ (*pétra*) meaning "rock" and ῑχώρ (*ikhōr*), the "ethereal fluid" or "blood of the gods" in Greek mythology

"Adaptive behavior of plants, including rapid changes in physiology, gene regulation and defense response, can be altered when linked to neighboring plants by a mycorrhizal network. Mechanisms underlying the behavioral changes include mycorrhizal fungal colonization... [and] interplant communication via transfer of nutrients, defense signals, or allelochemicals... The hierarchical integration of this phenomenon with other biological networks at broader scales in forest ecosystems indicate that underground 'tree talk' is a foundational process in the complex, adaptive nature of forest ecosystems."

> — Gorzelak et al. (2015). *"Inter-plant communication through mycorrhizal networks mediates complex adaptive behavior in plant communities." AoB Plants*, Volume 7.

"I am a feminist who believes that violence against women is one of the most prevalent, deeply rooted, and historical forms of oppression. Religious, economic, and governmental institutions are older than human rights institutions. It is inevitable that, in examining the causes of oppression against women, we encounter the root of that persecution, namely: Religious, economic, and governmental institutions... This sets the stage for a challenging and severe struggle."

> — Mohammadi, N (2023). *"Imprisoned Nobel Winner Narges Mohammadi tells Angelina Jolie Iran's people will prevail." Time.*

Act 1

Chapter 1
"Eeao"

One million years in the future, a kitten crash-lands on Earth.

She's fairly standard for a tabby, especially considering how other species have diverged. Big, pointy ears. Spine like a slinky. Vertical, black pupils embedded within lustrous, green eyes. Upon landing, she befriends exactly one living creature and, like a true feline, now intends to kill everything else. This friend of hers (well, the animal she's begun purring herself to sleep alongside every night) is a human. An old man, more specifically.

The old man calls her *"Eeao."*

The kitten doesn't understand why he's chosen this name for her, but she reveres his summons with instinctual devotion. It's the only truth she knows. She has no memory of a mother. No recollection of a home. Already, she's forgotten the tiny spacecraft that transported her to this planet. She has no concept of who she is or why she's alive or where she fits on the continuous, overlapping spiral of animal evolution. All she understands is the bond she's formed with her human; everything else flows from this habitual waypoint.

"Eeao!" he likes to call from within their cave, his high-pitched note ricocheting out into the dense rainforest, bouncing off leafy ferns and tangled, moss-covered branches—her name scatters feathers into fog.

When his call reaches her, she feels it vibrate through her claws first, usually stuck into the bark of a vine-strung *Ceiba pentandra* (North America's variant of the mighty, tropical kapok); already, she knows the juiciest prey nest only in the tallest trees. Within a fraction of a millisecond, his voice vibrates through her whiskers next; she's learned to recognize the subtle tingle it elicits, the way it races up the nerves of her springlike vertebrae, tickling her brain's tiny temporal lobes faster than the sound waves themselves can circle the cochleae of her inner ears.

She's by his side within heartbeats, always.

Her hypersensitive claws are not a newly evolved feline feature, but rather an individual adaptation unique to Eeao. She doesn't remember her brief space voyage, crash-landing, or the ensuing wildfire that singed the whiskers around her eyes and ears. She doesn't remember the atmospheric bursts that left her hearing mildly impaired. She thinks everyone else feels sounds in their claws before hearing them too.

Not the old man, though. He's oblivious to most noises.

"*Eeao!*" he startles when she jumps up from behind, perching herself on his bony shoulder. Still just a kitten, she's light, barely the weight of a feather. But the old man is *old.* And he's lived in solitude for most of his life. He isn't accustomed to entertaining such mischief; she bounces nonstop around his cave, knocking over his measuring pipes by day, clawing through his medicinal herb stash by night. He found the kitten just four moons prior, in the aftermath of (what he assumed to be) a lightning-born brush fire. Burnt and alone and barely big enough to breathe. Surely a newborn. But a newborn *what?* Unsure of her species, he scooped her from the rubble and has been tending to her ever since.

He still isn't sure what she is, or how big she'll get—already, she's doubled in size since he found her. In all his years, he's never seen a creature with fur. Feathers and scales and hard exoskeletons, yes. *But what is this soft material coating its body?* He doesn't have words to describe such a mammalian quality. It isn't like the coarse hair he ritualistically shaves off his own head every new moon. It's something else entirely. An organic silkiness novel to his fingertips, banded with intricate stripes of black and silver, a map of interwoven fractals ribboned across her body, her face a radial, kaleidoscopic pattern of identity.

She entrances him.

Her playful behaviors. Intelligent eyes. Baby-like voice.

She's less trouble than she is fascinating company. He recognizes someone in her—surely a person, *but whom?* On nights when hailstorms howl and thunder shudders his cave, the old man appreciates the way she nestles her warmth upon his chest, creeping her whiskers along his neck, purring rhythmically from ear to ear.

Plus, she keeps pests away.

The shiny-plated horned beetles that used to plow up the old man's herb garden are easy prey. Lumbering their chitinous bulk atop fragile, spindly legs, she assassinates the beetles one by one until none exist within a wide perimeter around their cave. Spiders disappear next. Even the aggressive, burrowing types, though they're twice her size, are no match for Eeao's pounce; she raids their nests and clears their cousins' webs until all eight-legged vermin are vanquished from the area. Ever-dissatisfied, she expands her palette: Endless earthworms, meaty bullfrogs, and slimy salamanders packed with protein nourish Eeao's growing muscles, transforming her body into an efficient killing machine, capable of snatching birds from treetops and plowing newts from mud puddles with equal artistry.

Just a few days ago, she discovered she's grown large enough to pin down a giant praying mantis on her own. They like to dawdle up from the local swamps, tall and emerald and much less durable than they appear. They're more than triple her size, with huge, fluttering wings that parachute from their backsides, reaching colossal wingspans nearly the entire width of the cave's mouth. Face to face, their bizarre, black, unblinking eyes nearly swallow Eeao's. She has to tear and bite her way through a furor of crunchy, iridescent green before coming out victorious, confirming her status as predator, its as prey.

But the mantises aren't easy prey.

Lately, they've begun traveling to and from the swamp in herds, a defense tactic they seem to have evolved over the beetles and spiders. Their plurality makes Eeao nervous. So many legs, so many eyes. If she takes down one, what will its companions do? Where does one mantis end and the next begin? She hasn't yet found the courage to confront the horde. But she's determined to eventually. She's been studying their movements, flock patterns, weaknesses, the joints where their twiggy pincers buckle...

The old man watches from his perch above the cave, amused, as the kitten skirts through the bushes below, tailing the herd. Unlike Eeao, the man isn't concerned with the giant mantises. Despite their monstrous sizes, he knows they pose no threat to him or his cave. They aren't toxic, venomous, poisonous, or even aggressive; according to ancient legend, the *Fae* eliminated all dangerous organisms from this jungle long, long ago... In fact, when he was a young boy, the old man used to keep several jumbo mantises as pets, allowing them groom his scalp each night for lice and mosquitoes with their long, discerning pincers. Elsewise, their plump hindlegs taste delicious deep-fried.

No, these praying mantises are harmless. The kitten hunts for practice. Or for sport. *How similar she is to humans*, the old man muses.

"*Tagi!*" a human voice calls out in the distance.

Humans. *Here come the dangerous pests...*

Chapter 2
"Tagi"

The old man descends the rocky lip of his cave.

He dons a poncho in preparation for company; made from assorted plumes and feathers, all woven and strung together with *areemo* twine (bark he stripped from the colloquially-named ficus tree and then softened into thread), the garb drapes over his shoulders like a billowing cloak, concealing his lean form in its dark, purple folds.

Other humans don't often venture up to his remote cave—a half-day trek from their lakeside nest in the lowlands—but whenever they do, they demand he clothe himself. Dignity, honor, pride. Shame, authority, manners. Human society conjures lots of ideas the old man finds useless.

But still, as with mantises, numbers intimidate.

The company visiting today consists of ten men, plus five women and a young boy in tow. They all wear brown tunics and skirts, fabrics spun from softened, fibrous *areemo* bark, along with layers of intricately woven *raea* feathers, silky in texture yet durable for function, flexible for movement, their plumage a black-indigo gradient. Their skin tones underneath come in gradients as well: Deep umber to tawny olive, many with pearlescent freckles scattered over marbled, blue veins, their skin a cacophony of camouflage.

The camouflage would work if it weren't for the bioluminescent yeast colonies coating their scalps; each trespasser is neon-capped.

The old man, formally named *"Tagi,"* can see the procession of humans coming from quite a distance. Their shaved heads dot the jungle, each a radiant speck of violet light through the misty trees. He counts sixteen heads and decides to put on his harness too, for good measure. The harness is made from *raea* quills—massive, flightless descendants of *Struthio camelus* (the ancient, common ostrich), which have since evolved decorative plumes that sprout from their backsides and enjoy stampeding in gaudy herds through the open fields near the lake. The quills, each longer than a man's arm, deep umbra in color, and firmer than rib cartilage, are bent and fashioned so that they criss-cross around Tagi's chest, shoulders, and back, buckling via carved notches above his hip bones.

The piece is further adorned with the plucked, sharpened spines of a *mabato* plant, which jut from the harness in all directions. He wears the bulky piece over his cloak, as they all do, for show, effectively transforming his torso into a living weapon, lethal from all sides. Really, he feels more like a spiny lake urchin. Yet if he wanted, he could easily skewer an adult *camraea* bird on each needle-like spine and still kill a grown man with a hug. He knows this because he saw his mother do it once. Long, long, long ago.

If he'd had a choice, Tagi would've burned this harness along with the rest of the possessions he destroyed back when he was appointed *Teerta* and exiled to this cave. He was barely an adolescent at the time. But, like a verbal name, this harness is another piece of human decor he's required to keep.

"*Tagi!*" the voice bellows again.

Do they think I'm deaf now?

The voice belongs to a young man called *Maetri*, and although the group hasn't yet drawn close enough for Tagi to make out their individual faces, he already knows Maetri is at the front of the march. They aren't supposed to have a formal leader. Sure, the nest has several chieflike captains who oversee certain societal affairs (the *Teerta*, himself, being one example). But the *Fae* don't allow centralized organization among humans—according to ancient legend, the last human who tried to establish a rulership was snatched into the sky during a *Kamaruna* ceremony and thrown in the *Aeo* to drown. And yet, as Tagi has come to notice over the last thirty or so moons, Maetri is more often than not leading a line.

Eeao darts into Tagi's view. Emerging from the jungle, she's drawn to the safety of home as the human visitors approach. She takes a quick moment to slink between the old man's bare calves, and then she disappears into the cave's dark yawn, intending to study the hominids' interaction from obscurity. She wants to size up this pack of traveling primates, learn their flock patterns, their weaknesses, the points where their twiggy limbs buckle...

Tagi wonders passively if the *Fae* have noticed Maetri's ambitious rise in leadership yet, whether they'll cut him down soon for noncompliance or continue to let it fester. *It would be too great a wish.* If Tagi has learned anything in his long, long life, it's that the *Fae* are as boring as sunrise after a night of *Kunjaruna* debauchery. Placing hope in them is as good as praying to ancient gods.

"*Tagi!*" Maetri calls a third time, now within a stone's throw. Indeed, front and center.

Tagi can see an angular crease of frustration across the man's sweaty forehead. The day is warm and wet, the air a thick, all-encompassing presence, the sun a pale orb shimmering through hazy layers of atmosphere, insisting to be seen, felt, appreciated. Winged insects swarm through the air; moths larger than birds flutter weightless, shifting and whirling through translucent clouds of mosquitoes and humidity. The humans have been hiking all morning, uphill. Still, Tagi waits silently within the mouth of his cave, forcing them to come to him. The new moon ceremony, *Kunjaruna*, isn't for another three-and-a-half weeks. As *Teerta*, he has no obligation to interact with humans today and, thus, intends to spend no extra energy on them.

"*Synto una*," Tagi says, their phrase for *good morning* (the English language died a million years ago).

"*Hmmph*," Maetri returns, taking a few moments to hack his machete through a tangle of vines that aren't even in his way. Tagi rolls his eyes; as *Teerta*, he also devotes his spare time to maintaining the jungle's network of trails, and it is upon one of his very own well-worn paths that these humans have had the luxury of traveling today. Each man in the party wields a clean machete. The women are able to walk side by side. Their hike today has been long, but easy. *And still they'll gripe.*

"What brings you all this way?" Tagi says, roughly translated. Behind him, perched in a shadowy alcove within one of the cave's arching walls, Eeao keeps her keen sight focused on the approaching party. She feels extremely outnumbered, but, sensing little tension from the old man below her, tries to mimic his calm resolve.

"You're being replaced," Maetri says. "You have eight moons."

Eeao flinches with Tagi.

"How do you mean?" Tagi's voice is calculated. But fear is a foul odor Eeao can smell on a creature's skin; Tagi suddenly reeks of it. Pheromones erupt from his pores like geysers aimed straight at Eeao's nostrils. The kitten's muscles freeze. Her fur prickles, revealing striped patterns of bioluminescence coating her skin as well—already, Tagi's own yeast colony has spread from his scalp to Eeao's undercoat. She's too young to realize the way this benign infection betrays her, the way it exposes her as a glowing statue of vigilance, shining against the cave's deep, black throat.

Still, the humans either don't notice her or they don't care; they're all infected with similar radiance, anyway. Right now, they're more concerned with the larger mammal. The men surround Tagi in an instant, ten of them forming a semicircle. The speaker, Maetri, a boulder of a man with a wild mane of dark, gleaming hair (grown long around the sides of his shaved scalp) and a glowing, mold-ridden beard to match, stands directly in front of Tagi, muscle-corded arms folded over his own spike-studded harness. Maetri's harness is much larger than Tagi's, with various sheaths and weapon-towing slings attached to either side. Today, Maetri appears to have packed light—for the long trek, probably. Still, he wields enough flintstone tools and daggers at either hip to butcher Tagi multiple times over if he wanted.

Blades. Machetes. Axes. These men and women are *punteeku*, hunters, and they each glare warlike fury in the late morning aura.

Other than his own spiked harness and several stone instruments stashed inside his cave, Tagi possesses no weapons. He's a healer, not a fighter. He's unprepared. *Replaced?* This isn't supposed to be happening. Not yet. *Am I already so old?* As *Teerta*, he's enjoyed invulnerability for most of his life. But now it seems time itself has turned against him, lured him into an ambush.

"I mean what I say," Maetri sounds testy, like he expects the old man to put up a fight or something. "This decree is confirmed by the other Chiefs. Your time as *Teerta* is ending. We've come with your replacement."

Maetri moves aside, and two women step into the semi-circle. A young boy stands between the women, clutching their hands for support. He looks small and sickly, dressed in a baggy *areemo* tunic too large for his skeletal frame. But the boy sticks out for another reason: Unlike everyone else in the crowd, the child's scalp-yeast coats him head-to-toe. Arms and face. Legs and ears. Every follicle on the boy is clogged with the luminous parasite—a symbiotic biome stretching across his skin's microbial landscape, varnishing his entire body in a shimmery, violet sheen. Though harmless, the translucent overgrowth results from a deficiency in the boy's autoimmune system (a recessive trait he inherited from some vine on his family tree). While most humans maintain yeast colonies only on their scalps, armpits, and groins, this boy's skin is overrun by a glowing, fungal enterprise.

But of course, at this point in the future, no one understands concepts like genetic inheritance or autoimmune function—or even yeast, for that matter. Some people believe this type of overgrowth results from a leakage in the brain. Others just view it as a mark, or a curse. Thankfully, Tagi, being a man of science, views the boy's skin condition as benign and unimportant—although he can tell from the boy's pale lavender color that his follicular sebum is lacking vital nutrients.

The boy is malnourished. Frail. Clearly unwell.

And now, all of a sudden, Tagi feels insulted by this feeble procession. There are hundreds of healthy humans down in the nest. His family—his people—generations upon generations—an historic culture and heritage of which he's always believed himself to be an integral part, even living way out here in isolation. They all know him. He's the oldest human among them. He's been their *Teerta* for almost a thousand moons. He's saved so many of their lives, he could line their afforded lifespans end to end and it would stretch the entire length of human history (or so Tagi imagines). But now here he stands, confronted by armed forces and a replacement boy barely weaned from his own mother's *nunee*, expected to just retire his role as *Teerta*, end his life's work, and surrender himself to the *Fae?* Without any formal ceremony or fanfare?

What happened to honor and dignity and shame and respect?

Tagi and Eeao blink in unison, neither capable of much else.

"You have eight moons to teach him everything you know," Maetri gestures at the boy, who does nothing but stare down at his own tiny, bare feet, plastered in dried mud and calluses, his ankles just scabby, glowing knots of bone. "Everything, *Tagi*. Understand?"

"When did the Chiefs agree to this? Why wasn't I present? Or is this the work of you and the *punteeku?*" the edge in Tagi's voice resonates through Eeao's body—it's a vibration pattern she doesn't recognize. Everything feels wrong. Her claws ache; she's ground divots into the stone beneath her paws, ten tiny indentations, a fossil record of her fear.

Maetri laughs at Tagi's questions, finding them absurd. He doesn't answer any.

"After the eighth *aruna*," Maetri continues, using their word for *moon*, "you are to come down to the *Aeo* and volunteer for *Kamaruna*. We have marked the day. The *Fae* will be waiting for you. Do you understand, *Tagi?*"

He thinks I am old and dumb and ready to die but I am not.

"I understand," is all Tagi can say.

Chapter 3
"Bowi"

The human child vomits every time Tagi tries to feed or water it, and the resulting puddles are far too acidic for Eeao's taste. If not for re-eating, why regurgitate? It seems to the kitten a cavalier waste of nutrients. Is the child trying to die?

This morning's visitors have long since departed, and Eeao does *not* appreciate the wasteful spawn they left behind. She lurks just beneath the cave's mouth, enveloped in warm afternoon haze, pacing back and forth to stretch her legs when inclined. But her green eyes remain trained on Tagi, who's tending to the child within the cool darkness of their hollow.

"Drink this," Tagi proffers another ladle, this one sloshing with an ambiguous, steaming fluid.

The boy's lips are dry, cracked, gray. He shakes his head, turning away. "*Pom... Pom...*" He keeps uttering the word, *drip*.

"You need to drink," Tagi says. "You could die if you dehydrate." The tea he's offering is a fresh brew of ginger and garden-grown *renomo*, steeped in rainwater drained through his own filtration device. It's yet another one of his herbal remedies for stomach illness (so far, nothing has worked to staunch the boy's vomiting).

"*He has a weak stomach,*" the boy's mother—or perhaps it was an aunt, or an older sister, one of the women holding him, someone who cared enough to know—had said while handing the child over to Tagi. And then they all left. No hugs. No kisses. No goodbyes. The vomiting started as soon as they were gone, right there at Tagi's feet. Bright yellow bile. Since then, the boy has been heaving nonstop.

Tagi maneuvers the ladle toward the child's nose.

"Smell it, the aroma will help."

The boy gives the fragrant tea a weak sniff, but the look on his face remains sour. He sits semi-reclined on Tagi's own feather bed, moaning and delirious, sweating through his stained tunic though he runs no fever. He holds his stick-thin arms crossed tightly over his concave abdomen, hands clenched, as if bearing a great weight. There's a well-utilized stone bucket on the ground beside him.

Tagi huffs, depleted. He drinks the ladle of tea himself. *Eight moons.* The thought is like a gnat lodged in his ear. But he knows he shouldn't dwell on it. Not with so much work to do. *Eight moons.*

He turns back to the boy, and like lightning a memory jogs Tagi's wrinkled, old brain—the child's sallow eyes, his jaundiced coloring, the pure bile he vomits. Tagi has treated this boy before, five or six moons ago. And on several other occasions as well. A semi-regular patient. Always the same symptoms: Nausea and vomiting. Always cured with the same, last-ditch treatment method: *Pomaeo* infusion.

"*Pom...*" the boy croaks through parched lips. "Drip..."

"Ah yes, yes, yes, of course, *pomaeo!*" Tagi flies into action, feeling foolish for not recognizing the boy sooner, for being more preoccupied with his own mortality than with treating his patient, his successor. "Let's see, where are my *camraea* quills..."

From her station at the cave's opening, Eeao perks her ears, watching in oblivion as the old man performs one of the many medical procedures he's refined over the course of his life as *Teerta. Camraea* quills: Long, hollow, needle-tipped. He sterilizes one of the blue feathers in a cauldron of boiling water, and then carefully scours it of all barbs and fibers, scraping down the calamus until all that's left of the quill is its smooth, flexible tube structure.

"You see, *Eeao*," Tagi narrates his steps aloud to the kitten, figuring he'll need to get used to teaching anyway, "we have now turned this quill into a conduit through which medicine can flow..."

Next, he hurries outside the cave to find a *pomaeo* fruit: Succulent, sack-like, engorged with water, sodium, and complex sugars. As children, he and his cousins used to climb trees and then drop these soft, massive melons onto the heads of unsuspecting passersby, dousing each victim in a wet, sticky *splat!* As an adult, he makes much better use of the fruit. He knows of a *pomaeo* patch growing in the jungle just a short walk from his cave; Tagi quickly returns with two enormous, green melons, one hauled under each arm.

Skeptical, Eeao stands sentry within the cave's mouth.

"Just one *pomaeo* fruit," Tagi explains to the kitten, "holds enough water to hydrate the Chief *momo*'s entire brood..." He brings the fruit over to the boy, and then retrieves the hollow, needle-tipped *camraea* quill he'd prepared earlier. Taking the quill's blunt end, he jabs it into the first *pomaeo*, cleanly piercing the fruit's firm flesh. He then holds the fruit up over his head, allowing the tube to dangle down in front of him. "In a moment," he continues to say, "gravity will draw the fruit's water down through the conduit, allowing it to drip from the quill's tip, watch..."

It's at this point that Eeao succumbs to curiosity and stalks closer for a better view.

"There it is," Tagi remarks, holding up the quill's fine tip in his other hand. Indeed, a green, translucent fluid has begun to bead and drip from its fine point. He turns to the boy, grinning. "And now, we prepare the injection site..."

Really, Eeao is only interested in the dangly quill tubing. She's got her vision locked on the string-like piece Tagi pierced into the fruit. She pounces. Claws puncture organic skin. The *pomaeo* melon bursts. Juice splashes everywhere.

"*Eeao!*" Tagi snaps. "Out!" He scoops her up in one hand and tosses her out of the cave—she lands on a cushioned bed of moss with a sharp *"Eeao!"*, confused and disturbed by the physics of what just happened.

Tagi begins all over again, glad he'd at least had the foresight to retrieve two *pomaeo*s. He hurries his pace as the boy begins another round of dry heaving. Finding an adequate vein on the boy's arm is near impossible; he's so thoroughly dehydrated, it's as though what little blood he has left has been sapped deep into his bones. A cloth tourniquet cinched tightly above the boy's elbow eventually coaxes a small, wriggly vein up to the surface of his forearm. With a poultice made from crushed *teeho* leaves, a natural antiseptic, Tagi gently cleans the skin on the boy's forearm. *Quick, while it's visible.* Quill needle poised, he pokes the pale, blue current before it has a chance to recede.

The boy doesn't notice the quill entering his vein—all three are so thin.

Now, with the needle inserted, Tagi rests the connected *pomaeo* fruit on a ledge in the cave wall, elevated over the boy's head so that its juice continues to flow through the tubing, drawn into the boy's bloodstream via gravity and his own pulse. Tagi then loosens and rewraps the tourniquet carefully around the boy's forearm, securing the inserted quill in place. And then the old man steps back, job complete.

For a moment he just stands there and smiles, as he usually does whenever he's finished with a patient (he can't help but marvel at the network he's created, this manipulated convergence of biologies). In a way, he's given the boy a new organ, an intravenous style of ingesting nutrients. In a way, he's cheated the systems of life and death, tricking the boy's body to accept sustenance rather than reject it.

Eight moons. Perhaps, Tagi thinks, the only one he's fooled is himself.

Meanwhile, the child is finally quiet. He lies there, pale and quivering, slipping into a welcome state of comatose. Slowly, the *pomaeao*'s juice drains into the boy's cardiovascular system, nourishing his depleted muscles with hydration and electrolytes. Tagi has no idea of the *pomaeo* fruit's ancient history, no clue that it was genetically engineered by his ancestors one million years ago in response to a global water crisis. He just thinks of the fruit and quill as environmental tools for human medicine, gifts of evolutionary symbiosis, fauna and flora cooperating as one. When this *pomaeo* fruit is dry, Tagi will infuse the boy with another one. And then maybe another. And then, if the boy's body responds as it has during past episodes, he should be cured of his nausea and vomiting by tomorrow morning. Simple as that.

But what if I let him die? The ensuing stab of shame guts Tagi. He's never once entertained the idea of letting a patient die. What would he even do? Just sit there and watch the boy dry heave to death? Slow. Agonizing. Pointless. It's almost a relief knowing that it wouldn't make a difference anyway, that the Chiefs would simply appoint another child to replace Tagi, and he'd be marched off to his death in eight moons regardless. This boy is replaceable enough, surely. *Why waste another life?* No, the decision is made for him. Tagi will care for the boy. Nourish him to full health. And teach him, too. *Someone has to be* Teerta *when I'm gone.* The ethics are obvious.

Outside the cave, daylight wanes. The sun sinks slowly across the sky, as though submerging through a hazy, rippling ocean of pink and coral currents. *How long can the sun hold its breath?* Eeao sits in a puddle of fading sunlight, one leg pointed skyward, furiously grooming sticky *pomaeo* juice from her undercoat. Spiky and wet, her fur will likely remain damp for days given the jungle's staggering dew point. Tagi doesn't feel bad for her. He's seen far worse consequences befall far more innocent behavior.

"Let that be a lesson," Tagi chides, joining Eeao outside. "You can't go pouncing at every little thing that moves." He likes to think the kitten can understand him. She likes to think maybe next time he'll help her execute a more successful ambush.

Their cave is situated against the base of a steep mountain range. Behind them, the land climbs upward, gnarled and bouldering, creeping with moss and vines. Before them, the rainforest stretches down toward a lake in the distance, affording them a wide, panoramic view that extends for miles. Really, the geography is that of a volcanic caldera, some forty miles in diameter, created 999,000 years ago, when the supervolcano beneath Yellowstone last erupted.

But of course, nowadays, no one knows the history of that apocalypse. To Tagi, the overall scene is a peaceful jungle ringed by towering mountains, the lake an enormous bloodstain marking its heart. His entire life has happened inside this overgrown, geographical bowl. He thinks this is it, the entire world. His people call it the *Uyi*. They think this is all that humanity has ever known: A lush, jungle biosphere within which the human species has always existed, planted here by the *Fae*. The encompassing mountains are an edge beyond which lie alien realms uninhabitable to humans. Or, at least, that's what the *Fae* legends say. And when testing a legend's veracity means scaling near-vertical cliffs so high they scrape the clouds (the lowest point around the caldera's metamorphic rim is a cliff wall over one hundred feet high), humans tend to believe the legends. As far as Tagi and his kin are concerned, only the *Fae* themselves dwell beyond the mountains.

Eight moons. The gnat burrows deeper into Tagi's eardrum. Wading across the other end of the twilight sky, opposite the setting sun, the silvery crescent moon shimmers, distorted through a dark mirage of shifting, atmospheric streams. Night is near. How many of those does Tagi have left?

"*Teerta?*" the boy stirs behind him.

Tagi startles reflexively, still unnerved by the echo of another human voice inside his cave. "Yes?" He returns to the boy's side, running his fingers along the intravenous tubing to make sure nothing's been tangled. "Is everything alright?"

The boy doesn't answer. Instead, he rasps, "Thank you." And then he falls silent, his hands resting at his sides, unclenched. Already, the fruit is emptying, and the boy's half-closed eyes are sinking in and out of focus.

"Sleep," Tagi tells him, unsure of what to do with the child's gratitude. He's *Teerta*, what else is expected? *Thanks are wasted words.* Tagi turns to leave the boy, but then pauses, struck by a thought.

"What's your name?" Tagi asks.

"*Bowi,*" the boy says. And then he's unconscious, overcome by fatigue.

Tagi nods, pondering the name. *Ba-owo-i.* In their language, translated from its ancient, alphabetic symbology, the syllables literally mean *beneath-ancient-ground.* An ominous name, yes. But as a person, what does it imply—*if anything?* Having changed his own name once, long ago, Tagi understands the power of semantic personhood...

He ventures outside the cave to rejoin Eeao, another creature he named. Evening mist rolls down the mountainside behind them like a tidal wave spilling over the caldera's southern lip, racing in slow motion to engulf their tiny bodies. Eeao, still combing sugar crystals from her sticky fur, feels a sudden urge to go racing off into the jungle directly ahead. So she does.

Tagi watches her disappear into the underbrush. He remains standing alone, thinking of the boy's name. Somehow, now that Tagi knows what to call him, *Bowi* seems much less replaceable than the nameless child he'd been just a few moments earlier.

Chapter 4
"Eeao"

Earth doesn't remember starlight.

Enveloped within thick, swirling clouds of methane, carbon dioxide, and evaporated ocean tides, the planet is a hothouse, maintaining a thermal maximum reminiscent of Earth's ancient Paleocene (the geological age born from the dinosaur-killing asteroid). As such, only two celestial bodies are bright enough to pierce the planet's warm, atmospheric deluge: The sun a pale disc, the moon a winking pearl.

Still, even when the moon is new and the sky chokes pitch-black, night on Earth is never truly dark. Bioluminescent flora (composite species of lichen manufactured by humans 1 million years ago during the *Genetic Revolution* [for the purpose of holiday decor], which utilize symbiotic fungal-algae cells to biosynthesize luciferin by day and then oxidize the chemical by night, resulting in the emission of bright, green light) have run amok and now dominate the planet's ecology. All seven of Earth's jungle continents are encrusted in creeping, psychedelic lattices of fungal oxyluciferin.

The radiant lichens climb tree trunks and bouldering mountainsides alike, ensnaring entire landmasses in tendrils of molten light. They fan across treetop canopies and coat long, woody vines of rainforest liana, which then twist and weave themselves into glowing, venous networks, blood vessels coursing through every tree and stone on Earth, nature's ichor emerald and lustrous. By now, some strains have even evolved their own fruiting offshoots, spore-bearing mushrooms that glow vibrant shades of teal and jade and auburn, each color the result of a different catalyzing photoprotein.

Nobody misses the stars. Everyone thinks nighttime has always looked like this.

Actually, the luminous vegetation works to Eeao's advantage. The short light waves produced by oxidized luciferin are perfectly suited to her feline visual spectrum, allowing her sensitive eyes to perceive the blue-green world of nighttime more clearly than the bleary, yellow-red mirage of sunup. Nightly, she darts between tree branches aglow, balancing her delicate weight so as not to disturb any leaves. Ears flat against her skull, fur pressed down over her own yeast-coated skin, she moves like a cloaked shadow through the jungle's vivid, nighttime brilliance.

Tonight, Eeao doesn't intend to follow the pack of humans that visited this morning. But she can't help herself. Curiosity, as with her innate attraction to Tagi-like beings, constitutes an entire region of her deeply evolved brain. She convinces herself she's hunting the nocturnal, round-faced birds that like to perch on corresponding treetops and *hoot* back and forth to each other, as if no predator could possibly reach them (humans call this owl-like species *arunaea*, or *moonbird*), when in reality she's just snacking along the way, slinking seamless from treetop to treetop, snagging white-winged morsels in single-pawed swipes, all while keeping an eye on the moss-lit path below, faintly aware of the lingering scent of humans...

At a certain point, all the aromas around her coalesce into a single olfactory stream of chemical wildlife, and she can't help but get lost in its surging current. She allows it to guide her movements, direct her line of sight. She maneuvers her hunting path to follow its drift, happily unaware that tonight's underlying flux of human odor is luring her closer and closer to their nest at the end of the trail.

Eeao doesn't realize how far she's gone until it's too late.

She's never ventured this far from Tagi's cave, out in this direction. To her, nighttime is a game of inhibition. A time for running fearlessly through the trees, pouncing with pride, expanding her limitless boundaries without care or caution. She considers herself to be this ecosystem's top predator, with unrivaled speed and prowess, as though no creature could possibly overpower her—

"EEAO!"

She's crushed underfoot as something tall trips over her. She scrambles to flee. Her assailer has a voice like Tagi's, but with less gravel, younger; the human curses under its breath, wiping dirt from a skinned knee. Eeao disappears into nearby shrubbery, hiding within the shadows cast by a glowing net of tangled vines. More humans approach. Eeao hunkers low to the ground, backing deeper into the vegetation—she wants to ensure her own camouflage while still maintaining vision on the beast that snuck up on her.

"What was that?" the young man gawks around in all directions, planted on his buttocks. He's fallen into a spongy bed of blue *wykyno*: Comprising more than half the *Uyi*'s shrub layer, these species of tendrillar, fungus-like plants sprout colorful leaves and generally make for comfortable landing pads.

"What's the matter?" several more humans arrive, young like him, but each mature enough to fend for itself if necessary. They're all dressed in feather skirts, shirtless except for spined *raea* harnesses that buckle across their chests and shoulders. Two are female, the rest male. Heads neatly-shaven, they all sport matching crowns of fungal luminosity.

"Something snuck up on me," the young man on the ground says.

Eeao shifts, snaps a twig, freezes in place.

No one notices.

"*Aevi* saw a *Meemmal*," one of the women snickers. They all share a laugh, except for the man in the mud, who hurries to stand up, flushing a noxious perfume of shame so pungent it burns Eeao's sinuses.

"No, really, I saw something," the man says with boylike insistence. A thin crescent of blood pools along the ridge of his scraped kneecap before trickling down his shin. "It was small, and it ran between my feet and took off, quicker than lightning. I've never seen anything like it—"

"Cut the *kahtopo*," someone slurs.

"Yeah, tell it to the *Fae*," another says.

They all laugh at him again.

The young man's face reddens. He continues to protest, but Eeao has lost interest. These animals are loud, brash, and stink of pubescent pheromones.

Bored, she ventures deeper into the underbrush, tunneling her way through moist detritus and fleshy stalks of non-green *wykyno*.

Unlike the lush, treetop greenness of the *Uyi*'s canopy layer, the jungle's understory is multicolored and diverse, consisting primarily of tendrillar *wykyno* species: Leafy, spiraling bushes, which rely on underground mycorrhizal networks to photosynthesize carbon, freeing them to sprout above-ground in a rich variety of shapes and colors. Red species generally create broad, fanning leaves, streaked with fiery orange veins. Yellows spring and loop in carefree defiance. Pink-shaded *wykyno* climb high into the rainforest's canopy like braided vines, whereas blue varieties remain on the ground, forming tall, iridescent stalks that bead milky sap along their vertical sides; although lighter, periwinkle types exist too, which tend to remain low and flowery, creeping edgewise through the forest in tangled, horizontal lattices.

Unbound from the chore of photosynthesis, *wykyno* aren't pigmented with chlorophyll like their verdant, plant cousins. Enabled by underground, fungal partners, these opportunistic plants are nature's latest experiments run wild—rebellious splashes of color amidst Earth's old-fashioned greenery.

Anyway, Eeao's needle-sharp claws tear easily through *wykyno,* fallen leaves, soggy branches, gullies of decomposition; the jungle is constantly rebuilding upon itself, rising from the trenches of its own, fallen remains. To Eeao, this soft vegetative graveyard is a playground, moldable and forgiving, a surface through which she can burrow. She pops out the other side of the shrubbery, mud caked into her still-wet fur. But she doesn't mind. She'll clean off later. The human voices are behind her, so she ventures onward, following the smell of something new and intriguing: Cooked meat.

Having learned from her earlier blunder, Eeao proceeds with more caution. She won't let a human step on her again. Stealing up the side of a towering kapok tree, the kitten gives herself some height; a shadow slithering up its mammoth trunk. From the tree's high branches, she assesses the jungle below. Most everything is draped in green incandescence, streaked with blooms of floral mutation, colorful constellations flowering beneath the blackened sky. Here and there, Eeao notices bright violet specks twinkling amidst the vegetation—human heads, the pack she'd just encountered. They're moving in some sort of formation, spreading out through the forest.

Are they hunting her?

Eeao doesn't feel like waiting around to find out. She leaps over to the next treetop, gliding soundlessly through the air, her landing momentum cushioned by the force of her claws sinking into wet bark. And then she leaps again, and then again, and again, navigating the jungle canopy like some ancient flying squirrel (the rodent species was exterminated, along with nearly all other mammals, around 800,000 years ago).

The sticky smell of smoldering flesh clogs the humidity. Eeao is hungry, and the intriguing scent is coming from somewhere nearby; she pauses a moment, twitching her whiskers and swiveling her neck to hone in on its directionality. She's getting close. Reassessing her visual surroundings, something catches her eye ahead: A massive gap in the forest, beyond which the ground appears like an undulating plane, moonlight glinting off of its surface...

It's the bloodstain she and Tagi have observed from their far-flung cave. The lake at the caldera's center. Now, closer than she's ever been before, Eeao is mesmerized by it. This black nebula of gently rolling matter. An ever-changing refraction of the moonlit sky above, shattering over and over and over upon itself.

Unaware that it's just water, Eeao feels compelled to approach the lake, investigate its magic. She leaps to the next treetop, and then on to the next, and then to another, and then she's reached the treeline: The vast, tangled ring of foliage (descendents of rubber and balsa, xate and cecropia, kapok and Dinizia, once-tropical species now ubiquitous worldwide) encircling the lake's narrow, pebbly shoreline. Loath to forfeit height, Eeao settles herself along a cecropia branch extending over the water like a curved arm.

Below her, blooms of glowing, genetically enhanced algae (designed during the *Genetic Revolution*, for the purpose of luxury koi ponds) bob up and down, rippling shades of carmine and crimson, lightwaves so long they're almost infrared. Clumped around the lake's frothy perimeter, the algae dissipates toward the water's center, giving way to a wide expanse of deep, dark black.

Anchoring her claws into the cecropia's moist bark, Eeao carefully leans her face over the branch's edge. Spray off a cresting wave tickles her whiskers, revealing the lake to be nothing more than a huge puddle of wet water. Jaded, she loses interest.

But then she catches that whiff of charred meat again. It's close. Very close.

She looks up, eyes darting, scanning the lake's panorama. Strange light patterns flicker in her left peripheral, shocking orange against nature's verdant mosaic. Amnesic to the wildfire she experienced the day of her crash-landing, Eeao knows fire only as a small, tamable concentration of heat that Tagi conjures every morning outside the cave: An elemental creature with proximal range and utility.

But the bonfire she now sees burning along the left side of the lakeshore is a plasmic monster, searing the night sky with a flaming tongue, belching plumes of smoke into the atmosphere. Dark specks dance along the ground, animals circling the pyre's engorged belly—humans? Eeao can't tell whether they're attempting to tame the fire beast or fighting to kill it. Several figures appear to be pulling a giant bird carcass from its scorching blaze: The smell Eeao has been hunting. But the sight of that seared carcass sparks a fear in the kitten's psyche, something innate and primal. She'll go no nearer to that bonfire, no matter how interesting it smells.

But what else can she explore?

The novelty of everything she's seen tonight compels Eeao onward. She tracks back into the jungle, and then follows the treeline parallel to the lake's curve, its glinting surface always on her right. A variety of new and interesting insects inhabit the trees down here, close to the water. Mosquitoes larger than her head. Dragonflies longer than tree branches. Hard-plated beetles and their squishy, ravenous larvae, worming across the undersides of *wykyno* fronds, gnashing their vortices of juvenile teeth. Eeao finds them all quite tasty, though lacking the succulent bloodiness of moonbirds... She tracks them by the sounds they make: Chirps, buzzes, synth-like sighs. The jungle is alive with symphonies of mating and meal calls. And Eeao is high up in the rainforest canopy, nosing around a cluster of massive cocoons, which hang like silken mummies from a viridescent liana vine, when she mistakes an enormous stick bug for a sprawling Dinizia branch—she leaps onto its skinny back, snapping the bug in half.

They both succumb to gravity.

"EEAO!"

The stick bug crumples like dry kindling, legs splaying helplessly on its way down.

Eeao tumbles, falling, plummeting, branches and leaves whipping past her face. But she's able to lock her sight on the oncoming ground. Swiveling her tail midair, counterbalancing her front half, she centers her four legs squarely beneath her body as the forest floor races upward, the Earth itself charging at her like an unforgiving predator.

She lands with a soft *thump!* in a lush thicket of xate.

Nothing hurts.

The kitten stands. She shakes herself off. She licks one of her front paws, uses it to comb her whiskers. She's all in one piece.

But she's not alone.

Chapter 5
"Momo"

A human is here.

Young—younger than the boy back in the cave. And it smells different. Female?

Eeao bristles, contracting the coils of her springlike body, readying for escape.

But nothing happens. The girl just stands there, barefoot and alone, clothed in a plush feather tunic and skirt. Like the boy, this child's yeast colony spills down her scalp, face, and limbs too—she looks like she's been doused in ultraviolet dust, her entire body enameled radiant.

Eeao blinks at the bioluminescing creature.

The child blinks back, eyes round and wide-set, eyelashes coated aglow.

They're in a small clearing, an open patch in the forest's understory. The ground is carpeted in velvety moss and budding mushrooms, fallen leaves and pebbles slickened by rains that never dry. Over the young girl's shoulder, through a gap in the trees, Eeao can see the lake's glittering blackness. Next to the girl, a bulky structure juts up from the forest floor. It's perfectly geometric, wide at its base, narrowing to a pointed top, wrapped in a stretched layer of *hympano* skin (a giant, leathery species of fungus).

Eeao thinks the structure is some sort of smooth, leafless tree. The girl knows it as her home; her mother claims to have constructed it herself. There are dozens more of these dwellings throughout this nook of the jungle, each erected in its own small clearing, all plotted strategically along the lake's elevated southern bank, the side that never floods. But of course, Eeao doesn't understand any of that. She just knows enough to realize she's fallen into a human nest.

The kitten takes a slow step backward, her skin a bristling, rippling aura.

The girl cautiously steps back as well.

For a moment, both are pleased by their opposite's mirrored response, and this, at least, soothes Eeao enough to flatten her fur. They remain still for several heartbeats. Quizzical. Suspicious. Eventually, enough time passes for Eeao's curiosity to overpower her initial anxiety. Why is the child clenching its fingers? What's in its hand? Why does it smell so nice? Tentatively, nose twitching, Eeao steps forward...

The girl points a finger and screams, "*Momo!*"

And Eeao is gone before the child can blink, darting back into the xate fronds that cushioned her landing, a shadow disappearing. The girl's mouth hangs open in shock.

"*Momo, momo!*" she cries louder. And then she disappears too, running inside the structure, entering through a tall, rectangular cutout near its base. Her skin's violet glow emanates from within the otherwise dark opening, betraying her presence inside the fungal edifice.

Eeao lurks within the xate, watching and listening, muscles triggered to spring at a neuron's notice.

"*Momo, momo!*" the child repeats the word again.

And then, somewhere overhead, a bird Eeao doesn't recognize mimics the child's voice.

"*Momo! Momo!*"

The parroted call echoes against the jungle canopy, rousing a chorus of chitters and caws from other birds—avians outraged at the terrestrial voice imitated in their treetop domain. Eeao quirks her head, astounded by the trickery.

"*Momo! Momo!*"

The child has gone quiet; only bird voices punctuate the night air—one of them like an alarm on repeat.

"*Momo! Momo!*"

"Momo! Momo!"

"Momo! Momo!"

Eeao rotates her face, looking around overhead, wondering if maybe she should go up there and silence the bird herself, when a new human voice pierces her awareness:

"Ayee! Ayee!"

It's out in the distance, approaching fast.

"Ayee! Ayee!"

Rapid footfalls, running through underbrush, splashing through mud; the violet radiance of a human scalp materializes into view, and Eeao has just enough time to scamper beneath an adjacent patch of xate before a full-grown woman comes trampling through the one she'd formerly been using as coverage.

"Momo!" the girl runs out of the structure, arms flung wide to embrace her *mother*.

The woman ignores the child, bypassing her entirely to enter the structure. Soon, soft cooing ensues from within, and a lullaby floats out through the rectangular cutout, mother tending to child.

Except the little girl remains standing outside, the song dancing in the air around her.

"Momo, come out here," she pleads, dwarfed beside the towering, conical abode. "I saw something out here."

Inside, the woman takes her time, as if the haste in which she'd arrived had been a fever dream experienced by everyone else but her. Outside, the girl waits vigilantly, eyes scanning bushes and trees, hoping for another glimpse of that weird, striped creature she'd seen. Her hope goes unfulfilled.

Meanwhile, Eeao is losing interest. She considers taking off to hunt whatever bird made that strange, echoing call, but then the woman emerges from the structure with a murmuring infant cradled in her arms. This catches Eeao's attention; she readjusts her focus, honing in on the human baby.

Its proportionately large head, dusted in patchy newborn fuzz, barely shimmers—oddly, its mother's microbes have still yet to colonize its fresh scalp. The woman herself is clothed in a woven skirt and a harness of *raea* quills over her torso, embedded with *mabato* spines similar to fashions Eeao has seen other humans wear. And although the harness leaves the woman's breasts exposed, she does not hold the baby up to nurse, but rather up against her shoulder, the infant's head nestled between two protruding spikes.

"What is it?" the woman asks the girl.

"I saw something," the girl says, visibly exasperated at having to repeat herself. "It was over here, and it fell from the sky, and it was pretty small, do you think it was a *Meemmal?*"

"How should I know, I didn't see it," the woman is preoccupied, affording the girl only a fraction of her attention while she burps the infant in her arms.

"*Momo,* I am scared," the girl says. And then, "I want to go find it!" She grabs her mother's elbow—the highest point on the woman she can reach—and tries to pull her into the jungle, presumably in search of Eeao, though by now the kitten has maneuvered into a patch of flat-leafed philodendron on the opposite side of the clearing. From her new vantage point, Eeao can vaguely see into the structure through its rectangular opening, making out a variety of tools inside, pots and buckets and spears organized neatly on the ground, along with three mats laid out for sleeping. A smell similar to the bonfire she'd encountered earlier drifts in lazy circles around the clearing, growing stale.

"You're supposed to be sleeping with your baby sister," the woman says in a scolding tone. "It's far past sundown. Why are you awake? I don't see an emergency."

"I cannot sleep without *Bowi*," the little girl complains.

"You need to learn how," the woman says.

"I cannot."

"You can and you will," the woman snaps, the ferocity of her earlier haste suddenly flaring. In her arms, the baby whines. She tries to soothe it, pitching her voice into a fluttering note.

The girl flinches, but remains defiant. "I want *Bowi* back," she says.

Bouncing the baby in the crook of her arm, the woman sighs.

"You'll see him every new moon, when he becomes *Teerta*," she tells the girl.

"But the new moon is so far away!"

"*Amutee una kotyna-ah*," the woman groans—a trite phrase that literally translates: *Allow the sun to move.*

This answer only irks the little girl more. She crosses her arms over her chest and frowns, creating a circuit of knotted skin in the space between her eyes. "Why does he have to be *Teerta?*" she says. "I want him to stay here and be my brother forever."

"He'll always be your brother," the woman replies, pressing the baby's cheek up to her own. She rubs her lips against the newborn's soft, pristine skin, feeling its perfection, its complete lack of yeast and concern. *Stay this way, please.*

"But why does he have to be *Teerta?*" the girl whines. Her full-body glow is a stark contrast next to the woman's cleanly defined scalp.

"Please, stop complaining, *Daeo*," the woman will not listen to it anymore. "It's an honor to be appointed *Teerta...*" She wants to say more. She wants to tell her daughter that she misses Bowi too, and that she never wanted things to end up like this, and that she wishes there was another way to save her son's life. But she knows there isn't another way.

She knows this was the only option to spare Bowi from *Kamaruna*, and that's the part she doesn't know how to tell her daughter.

The little girl sucks in a deep breath to protest some more, but the arrival of another animal silences her. This time it's a human male, with wild black hair and an untamed beard—the same man Eeao saw this morning, the leader of the human pack that delivered the boy to the cave.

"*Maetri*," the woman gulps, eyes flashing. Beside her, the little girl clutches her skirt.

"We need to talk," the man steps into the clearing. Mud cakes his beard and armpits, and clumps of it hang from his long hair, like he's purposely plastered his luminous parts. He managed to approach the scene silently too, unbeknownst even to Eeao; now, stalking calmly toward the woman and her children, it's evident how: He's bare except for a few feathers wrapped over his loins, free of the clanging weaponry and harness he wore this morning. As if he knows his presence here is threat enough. His tawny, speckled skin glistens, glossed in sweat, reflecting moonlight and jungle glow.

Eeao watches keenly, wondering if anything will end up dead.

"Okay then, talk," the woman says, shifting her baby to her other arm so she can hold the girl's trembling hand. Though Maetri is technically the father of all three of her children, none of them ever feel safe around him.

"No, *Nyno*," he sighs—it resonates a strange, growling timbre. "We will talk in private. Down at the *Aeo*. Now."

The woman, Nyno, clenches her jaw. Generally, she goes out of her way to avoid private encounters with this man. Even during the *Kosharuna* full moon, if she can help it; for a moment, she's reminded of the baby's soft skin, where it came from, how it happened. "Here, *Daeo*, take your sister," she turns to relinquish the infant into her other daughter's arms, taking comfort in the thought of her two girls sleeping safely tonight. But Maetri stops her from making the transfer.

"No," he says. "Bring the baby. Follow me."

Next to her, Daeo goes rigid. Still, Nyno knows better than to object. She puts her older daughter to bed, sheds her spined harness, swaddles her baby in a spare blanket for comfort, and then follows Maetri out into the jungle.

Her infant burbles against her thundering heartbeat.

Chapter 6
"Nyno"

Eeao has never before considered sex, let alone the human idea of gender. Being the only feline on Earth, sexual dimorphism is a new concept to her. But now, trailing behind the man and the woman as they trek down to the lake, she can't ignore the stark differences between them.

First, their smells: The female smells of maternal hormones, fear, and a touch of lake water, as though she's recently been down to bathe in its shallows; whereas the male effuses anger and paranoia, dried blood and groin sweat.

Next, their strides: The man takes broad, deliberate steps, each footfall landing heavily heel-to-toe; meanwhile, the woman glides on the balls of her feet, each step quick and carefully placed. Two seemingly different species, yet they navigate the rainforest's obstacles at equal speed. Where he charges straight through bushes and ferns, she high-steps over vines and protruding roots. When he swings his arms to clear the way, she clutches their baby to keep it supported.

Eeao slinks a safe distance behind them, all the way to the lakeshore, where she makes herself comfortable in the shadowy fronds of a palm tree overlooking the water. The man and woman halt just before the lake's lapping blooms of iridescent algae.

Out here, the open sky is an opaque dome, the lake a vanity mirror for the moon.

"Is it fixed?" Maetri asks Nyno. Steam hisses around them, dancing off the lake's warm surface.

"Almost," Nyno shivers despite the night's heat.

"Almost? Let me see."

Reluctantly, Nyno unwraps the baby swaddled in her arms. It gawks up at them, pale and bug-eyed, with a look of sheer, almost sibylline helplessness fixed on its face.

Maetri's eyes go wide for a moment, and then they narrow.

"It looks the same," he grunts. "There's something wrong with it."

"No, no, look," Nyno lifts the baby higher, holding its scalp up to Maetri for closer inspection. But the man only repels.

"Where?" he says, almost accusingly. "Where is its *patu?*"

"It's coming in, I swear—"

"It looks the same as it did the day it came out of you," Maetri sneers again. "It's patchy—dim—look!" He gestures at the baby's scalp like it's leprotic, its sparse patchwork of bioluminescent microbes failing follicular anchorage. "There's something wrong with it."

"Her *patu* will glow," Nyno insists. "She's had trouble feeding, it might take longer, she—"

"Has anyone else seen it?" There's shame behind Maetri's revulsion.

Nyno goes quiet; she can't seem to catch her breath. She's been hiding her swaddled curse for weeks. *When will the curses end?*

"Just *Paelo,*" Nyno finally answers. "And of course *Daeo.*"

"*Paelo* can't keep her mouth shut. Why did you show her?"

Nyno falls quiet again. She's too ashamed to answer Maetri's question, to explain that she only enlisted her cousin's help to cross-nurse the child due to her own recent inability to lactate. *There's something wrong here,* were the first words Paelo uttered upon examining her situation, followed by, *and not just with the baby.*

"*Paelo* is trustworthy, she'll keep quiet," Nyno says. "You're paranoid and you know it."

He seizes her shoulder with crushing ferocity.

"DON'T TELL ME WHAT I DO OR DON'T KNOW!"

Up in her palm tree, Eeao blinks, alarmed by the sudden violence. Below, the woman and child whimper. Skirt soaked from stumbling into the water, Nyno retreats several paces from Maetri, cowering, pain radiating beneath her shoulder cuff. She presses her baby tightly to her breast.

"Please, *Maetri*," she pleads. "Please don't hurt the baby. Please."

Maetri grunts, fists clenched at his sides, cords of muscle rippling up and down his arms, his shoulders, his neck. To Eeao, he looks like a charged predator, a danger to ground-dwellers; unthreatened, she watches with anticipation—judging by the man's bulk, she doubts he could scale her palm tree.

"Stop crying," he barks at the woman and child. Moisture beads along his forehead; sweat and humidity steam off his body. Nyno wills her tears to evaporate. She's never seen him physically harm any of her children, but she knows he's more than capable. Swallowing terror and pain, Nyno straightens her stance to face Maetri square-on. From experience, she knows the only thing he hates more than resistance is weakness.

"Perhaps if I take her to the *Teerta*," Nyno suggests, "maybe he can help—"

"No," Maetri cuts her off. "You'll show no one else. Not until I've figured this out."

"I've been watching her *patu* closely," Nyno insists. "Each morning when I awake, I can tell it has spread a little more. It's growing across her head, just very slowly."

"First you give me two children with too much *patu*, and now you give me a child with none," Maetri sneers.

"Please, trust me," Nyno begs. "Her *patu* will glow, just give her more time."

"It doesn't matter if I trust you," Maetri says, face shadowed within his mane. "Everyone else will notice, sooner or later. Probably at the next *Kunjaruna*. And they will not approve of a *Meemmal* like that." He points at their daughter in Nyno's arms, their child, a lump of bare, uncolonized flesh.

"Be patient, please, she is not a *Meemmal*," Nyno says, clinging to hope that her daughter's bioluminescence (or lack thereof) will fix itself in time.

The real tragedy is this: Nyno is clueless to the genetic factors involved. She doesn't realize that when she was a child, the sun beamed a photon into one of her ovaries, altering a single gene inside the particular ova that'd grow to become her third-born (the same gene, coincidentally, responsible for yeast-overgrowth on her first two).

Nyno doesn't realize the mutation that alteration caused. She has no idea her newborn possesses a supercharged immune system, resulting in skin sebum resistant to all strains of the glowing *patu* fungus manufactured to live within human hair follicles during the *Genetic Revolution* (for the purpose of fashion). Nowadays, after a million years of the yeast's unmitigated proliferation across generations of human scalps, no one understands concepts like autoimmune function or parasitic symbiosis, let alone genetic mutation. They all think the human scalp, the *patu*, glows naturally from within. Everyone believes the violet yeast to be an inherent feature of the human species, an innate power they all wield without effort, without thought. Well, not all of them.

Your baby is cursed, Paelo keeps saying.

"I already saved one child," Maetri mutters darkly. "I made your first-born *Teerta*. I did that. If it weren't for me, he'd be volunteered at the next *Kamaruna*."

"I know, and I'm so grateful to you, Maetri, I really am—"

"But when everyone finds out about that disgrace," he points again at the child's dim, streaky scalp, his upper lip curling, "the *Kamaruna* blood will be yours to repay."

With that, he leaves her petrified, standing ankle-deep in a scarlet swell of algae, his last comment lodged in her gut like a knife. Around her, nothing seems to move, the jungle and lake and moon all frozen in time. For a fleeting moment, Nyno allows herself to feel relief—this encounter with Maetri could've lasted longer, and ended much worse. To see him storm off and disappear so quickly, to see his *patu* recede and then eclipse into the jungle, is to remember that he too is just a small animal, with no more power over the world than she has.

And yet still, her shoulder throbs... *Tonight could have ended so much worse.*

From the crook of Nyno's good arm, her baby chirps a pure note, unaffected by anything. She looks down to see the infant staring past her, up at the sky, at the crescent moon, its sickle shape blurry and warped behind rolling currents of cirrus. Nyno follows her child's gaze; clouds glimmer overhead, basked in lunar radiance. Streaking silver across the black sky, they create a patchy effect similar to the microbial one beneath her daughter's plume of baby hair.

Aside from her streaky *patu*, the infant is perfect. All her children are perfect—*at least, they're perfect to me. What am I doing wrong?*

Enveloped in evening humidity, it's a long while before Nyno wills herself to move again. When she does, she finds her feet have sunken into the lake's muddy shoal; it pulls and sucks around her ankles as she trudges out of the shallow water. Each step feels laborious. She pauses to rest at the edge of the jungle, leaning against a palm tree that overlooks the water. Her baby continues to stare upward, gazing into the tree's shadowy fronds.

But by now, Eeao is far away, back home in her cave, nestled on Tagi's gently vacillating ribcage, having long since lost interest in the smelly humans down by the lake.

Chapter 7
"Tagi"

Every morning, Tagi rises in tandem with the sun, as though attached to it by gravitational strings.

He can't help it, never could.

Even on the darkest, rainiest mornings, he can feel the great star pulling itself up over the horizon, grasping hold of his earthbound weight for leverage, tugging him with brutal force into each new day. As a child, its inescapable hold would invade his dreams and jerk him awake. But in his old age, it's become something of a meditative experience. He likes to lie semi-conscious through the ashy hours of dawn, becoming increasingly aware of his own weight, the beating of his heart, the stickiness of his palms, the earthy smell of mist drifting in from his garden while sun beams meander slowly up the side of his face. It's a pleasant way to come alive each day.

This morning, however, a strange ache in his neck pervades all other sensations. And then, before he's even opened his eyes, a single thought crashes into his mind:

Eight moons.

Tagi jolts upright, sending Eeao into a scramble—she clatters into his collection of whittled cooking utensils, disoriented from waking up on the ground rather than their typical sleeping spot deeper inside the cave. Tagi rubs the knot out of his neck, wincing; he'd used his wadded-up poncho as a pillow last night. Eeao glares at the boy sleeping in their bed. For a few tense moments, Tagi worries their ruckus will have caused the boy to stir. But no, the child is thoroughly asleep. Tagi figures he'll probably remain that way for most of the day, and probably for the best; the child has much to recover. Dehydration. Malnutrition. Emaciation. There's a certain point of atrophy beyond which the human body can't recover, and Tagi knows this boy came within spitting distance of it yesterday.

"If the sun grabbed hold of you for leverage," the old man whispers under his breath, picking up the utensils Eeao knocked over, "you'd get yanked straight into the sky." He can't decide for whom the comment is meant.

Sitting beneath the cave's arching mouth, Eeao preens herself. She doesn't like that she can still smell *pomaeo* juice in her undercoat, no more than she likes the sickly boy who stole the bed she and Tagi usually share. This is not how things are supposed to be. She decides to manifest her displeasure this morning by stalking around the cave and glaring in the child's direction, even hissing at it once or twice, when inclined.

Moving quietly, Tagi approaches the sleeping boy. His slight, skeletal frame sprawls limp on the feather mattress, like a cadaver—a quick double-take confirms the up-and-down movement of respiration. Somehow, despite Tagi's bed being a mere clump of *raea* plumes bound by woven reeds and balanced upon a rickety, wooden frame, the scrawny child is dwarfed lying on it, making the bed seem luxurious. Tagi figures he'll allow the child to keep this bed and make a new one for himself, something smaller. Not that he'll need a bed for much longer, anyway.

Eight moons.

Gently, Tagi adjusts the boy's arm, turning it over to check yesterday's injection sites. He'd infused the boy with three *pomaeo* fruits in total, and so had poked the boy in three different locations up his left forearm. Before going to sleep last night, he'd coated the three pinpricks in a thin layer of *teeho* poultice to encourage healing. Now, Tagi is pleased to see the three spots are neatly scabbed, with only mild bruising left beneath the boy's otherwise glittering skin. If the child is still nauseous when he awakes, Tagi will infuse him with another fruit. Otherwise, he'll have the child drink by mouth to see if the juice settles in his stomach. Either event will require another trip to the *pomaeo* patch for more fruit. So off he goes.

Eeao follows Tagi out into the balmy morning. Fog steams up from the ground, curling around their bodies, the air a fluid through which they wade. On his way to the patch, Tagi stops first at his medicinal garden, which is nestled beneath a rocky outcropping adjacent to his cave. Dew trickles down the lip of the metamorphic overhang, which shields the garden from the environment's frequent downpours while also allowing in enough sunlight and air circulation to nourish its plants.

Ginger and ginseng. Mansoa alliacea. *Teeho* and *renomo*—the genetically-modified, fungal-resistant descendants of spiked pepper and chamomile, respectively. It's a small yet diverse garden, originally planted by a wise *Teerta* long, long before Tagi's time. And like all other *Teerta*s since, Tagi monitors the soil every morning, pressing his fingertips into the moist earth between each sprouting plant. Sometimes, he'll find dry patches in the plot and sprinkle them over with some of his filtered water, but those occasions are rare. Today, as with most days, his fingertips sink into the garden's wet, spongy bed and come out dripping. Satisfied with its state, he plucks a pair of fragrant mint leaves to chew on as he continues into the jungle.

"Want some *hynho*?" He offers a mint leaf to the kitten. She sniffs it and sneers, whiskers fraying. He smiles as the familiar, zingy flavor bursts between his teeth. "You're missing out." Eeao believes the old man's whiny speech patterns are the result of him not understanding how to purr properly.

Up ahead, two paths fork the jungle. The trail on the right winds down toward the distant lake; on the left, it hugs the inner curvature of the caldera's mountain range, disappearing into the distance. Tagi chooses neither path, instead pressing into the foliage between them. Soon, he's descending into the rainforest's dark understory, a verdant, shadowy world of tangled roots and chirping insects. Mud squelches between his bare toes, step by step. Somewhere close, a frog lets out a deep, bellowing *RIBBIT!* and Eeao can feel the ensuing vibrations resonate through the ground.

Hands out in front of him, Tagi claws through the lush vegetation, tunneling his way toward the swampy *pomaeo* patch he knows to exist within. Soon, he bursts into a small clearing overhung by a window of gray sky. Before him, the ground is a soggy, sprawling carpet of vines, riddled here and there with plump, green melons that protrude from the ground like tombstones. There's so much water stored within this *pomaeo* patch, so much life swelling within it, that Tagi can almost feel each fruit aching to burst. Eeao keeps her distance from the melons, wary of their explosive power, claws retracted so deep inside her toes they hurt. This time, Tagi plucks three ripe *pomaeo* fruit, managing to wedge one under each elbow while balancing a third between his two hands. He then carefully makes his way out of the patch, maneuvering gingerly to keep the fruit from rupturing.

Overhead, the morning sky darkens, filling with storm clouds that seem to materialize from nothing. On his way back to the cave, Tagi tracks the approaching thunder, counting his heartbeats between each flash of lightning and subsequent *BANG!*

He and Eeao scamper back into their cave just as the storm's first gusts descend.

"*Teerta?*"

"Oh!" Tagi is startled to find the boy awake and sitting upright in bed. He plops two *pomaeo* melons into his nearby water basin, and then brings the third over to the boy. Outside the cave's mouth, sheets of wind and rain cascade from the sky, torrents of precipitated atmosphere pummeling the earth. Inside the cave, the three mammals hunker together, dry and sheltered from the meteorological drama.

"*Bowi*, how are you feeling?" Tagi asks his patient. Though gaunt, the boy's brown eyes seem alert and colorful, jaundice dissipating.

"I'm thirsty," Bowi says. "May I drink?"

"Please do," Tagi hands him the fruit.

The boy rips into it, piercing the *pomaeo*'s taut skin with his fingernails to tap its bittersweet juice. He throws his head back as he gulps. Translucent green liquid dribbles down his chin; he laps at the fruit with a voracious thirst Tagi diagnoses as a good sign.

"Drink slowly," he encourages the child. "You don't want to upset your stomach."

"My stomach is fine now," Bowi says, pausing to catch his breath.

Tagi and Eeao both cock their heads—Tagi because he's dubious, Eeao because she expects the boy to spew at any moment. But Bowi manages to hold down the *pomaeo* juice. He even asks Tagi for another one to drink when he's finished the first.

"Wait until later in the morning," Tagi cautions. "If you drink too much all at once, you'll overwhelm your stomach."

"My stomach is fine," Bowi mumbles again, but he doesn't object further. Tagi suspects this is only because he's too tired. The boy sits slumped over himself, the sharp vertebrae of his arching spine outlined through his *areemo* tunic, like he's just a sack of bones spilled onto the bed. Boys are supposed to have boundless energy, nimble arms and legs for climbing and running, plump cheeks for smiling. This one looks like a day-old carcass dug out of a soggy fire pit. Tagi knows it will take moons just to fatten Bowi up to proper size—and that's only if his stomach really is fine.

"Your stomach is not fine," Tagi says, feeling awkward, like he's been forced to speak aloud a very obvious truth no one else in the cave wants to admit. "I recognize you. I have treated you before, several times. You're often very ill when I see you."

"Well now I feel okay," Bowi says, lying back, closing his eyes, drinking in the moment, the sensation of ease, what it's like to finally not be in pain. A peal of thunder shudders the cave.

"Hush, you are still very ill," Tagi wonders how cognizant the boy even is. "You've been unable to hold down food and water. You're chronically wasting away." *At a certain point, the body eats the mind.* "I want to help you get better, *Bowi*."

"You have," Bowi smiles, still tasting *pomaeo* on his tongue. "I'm better now."

"No. You may be feeling better for the moment. But I want to figure out what's wrong with your stomach so I can prescribe a cure that will work long-term. You can't survive your whole life by infusing yourself with *pomaeo* juice, you know."

"Why not?" the boy asks. "Can't you do it for me?"

Eight moons.

"Hush," Tagi snaps. "I won't always be around to help you. Besides, you need more nutrition than *pomaeo* fruit alone. You need a complex diet. You need to put meat on your bones and fat in your skull. You won't survive to adulthood if you're unable to eat."

Tagi's warning doesn't seem to phase the boy.

Children think the present moment lasts forever.

"I want to cure you," Tagi sighs. "I want you to grow up healthy and strong. Don't you understand?"

"I understand..." Bowi says. And then, echoing Tagi's sigh, "I just don't think a cure is possible."

Chapter 8
"Heersu"

The old man asks many questions Bowi doesn't understand. Did his mother *anunai* him as a baby? Has he ever *paramao* from the *Aeo*? Does his diet include any *reewo, talapako,* or *bareebo*?

"*Reewo, talapako, bareebo?*"

"Seasoning herbs your *momo* may have used while cooking," Tagi explains. Beside him, Eeao sits and stares at the boy like an angry gargoyle, her presence somehow taking up more space in the cave than anyone else's. Bowi assumes she's a legend he simply hasn't heard of yet. "I'm trying to figure out if there's something you might be allergic to, perhaps something your *momo* used to feed you on occasion."

"I don't know, I only ever eat *pomaeo*," Bowi says, feeling guilty for not having a better answer. Really, it's been so long since he's eaten solid food he doesn't remember what anything else tastes like. Perhaps, somewhere deep in his memory, he can faintly recall the taste of smoked *raea* meat, but he has no clue what herbs his mother would've used to season it. The boy shrugs.

Tagi rubs his temples, growing tired. The storm outside has raged into the afternoon, and so far he's failed to identify a reasonable explanation for the boy's chronic vomiting.

"Is it because I'm... *Patummal?*" Bowi ventures the word anxiously, glancing down at his yeast-coated hands.

"Of course not," Tagi frowns. "Your skin condition has nothing to do with it. *Patummal* is a misnomer, anyway. Yes, *-mmal* is a suffix indicating disease or corruption. But the *Patummal* condition is certainly not a detriment. That's just a silly myth. You should be just as strong and healthy as the rest of us... But you're not... And I need to figure out why..."

"I'm sorry," Bowi can sense the old man's frustration.

Tagi quirks an eyebrow. "What are you sorry for?"

Bowi flushes, embarrassed. "I don't know."

"Hush then, it's a wasted word."

Later in the afternoon, the storm finally recedes, howling, sucked back into the atmosphere by a quickening jet stream. The world outside their cave is left drenched and battered. Stripped tree branches litter the ground. Residual rainwater trickles off every leaf, frond, and vine. Most droplets, upon hitting the warm ground, evaporate instantly into steam. But those that don't, the lucky droplets that find cool, shaded rocks and lichen-covered patches of earth to seep into, are absorbed by the jungle, remade into life itself, a chemical transaction, resulting in one of the richest, most pleasing aromas found in nature.

"Are you strong enough to walk outside?" Tagi dons his black feather poncho, inhaling the scent.

"Of course!" Bowi jumps to his feet, as though he's been waiting all this time for permission to leave bed. Immediately, though, his head spins. He doubles over to keep balance, hands on his knees, bracing himself against the force of blood surging up to his brain.

Eeao ducks and covers.

"Are you sick again?" Tagi asks. He'd given the boy another *pomaeo* fruit to drink, but that'd been well before noon. He returns to the child's side. "Does your stomach hurt?"

"No," Bowi sounds relieved. "I just stood up too fast."

"Here, use this," Tagi hands him a walking stick; he has several ancient ones stored within the cave, dusty relics, gnarled canes used by old *Teerta*s before him. Though he's loath to admit it, Tagi takes particular pride in his physical fitness, and vowed long ago to never let himself fold over a cane. He walks every day with his back upright. He stretches each morning to stay limber. He performs an exercise routine each night before bed. Those old *Teerta*s, he's always thought to himself, simply hadn't taken care of their bodies the way he has. They'd let old age stiffen their joints and stoop their shoulders. But not him. He'll never.

Eight moons.

Now here he is, nearing the end of his life, walking perfectly upright beside his replacement: A child crutched up against one of his predecessor's old canes. Today, his own pride mocks him, swelling like a *pomaeo* fruit lodged in his chest.

"Where are we going?" Bowi asks as they step outside the cave, blinking in the sunlight; its warm rays shimmer down through the liquid sky.

"To my *Heersu*," Tagi says, leading the way. "I'm going to find out what's been making you sick."

Bowi likes the garden. All the different plants, sown with such forethought and consideration. Tagi tells him they're arranged according to their root structures, and that each species was planted by a *Teerta* long ago to grow in optimal symbiosis with its adjacent neighbors. *Bareebo* next to *talapako*, so that the latter's branches have room to expand. Shallow-rooted *renomo* surrounded by deep-rooted *reewo*, to prevent the former from drowning. Multicolored *wykyno* sprouts here and there, to maintain the soil's mycorrhizal health. All the plants bloom on different cycles too, drawing in a steady flow of pollinating insects no matter the moon. Something about this organization, the sheer sense of the garden's organic arithmetic, strikes Bowi with an epiphany: "We should make the whole *Uyi* a *Heersu*."

Tagi snorts. "Where would anyone shit?" He kneels in the soil to gather various samples of flora. "Come over here. I am going to have you taste different leaves and roots, to see if any of them have an effect on you."

Bowi totters closer. The cane he wields is nearly twice his height. It sinks into the garden's damp, spongy bed, making a loud *splop!* sound each time he yanks it out to take another step. "Maybe the whole jungle can't be a *Heersu*," the boy concedes. "But what if we teach everyone to plant their own? I can show my *momo*, and then she and *Daeo* can plant a *Heersu* too, and then—"

"Hush," Tagi snaps. "Only the *Teerta* is allowed to grow a *Heersu*."

"Why?"

"Because plants possess power," Tagi explains, trying to use terms the boy will understand. "The plants in this *Heersu* are beneficial. I can use them to heal people who are sick, or injured. However, not all plants are good. Some are toxic, lethal, like the red *cananeero* flower—I'm sure your *momo* has warned you about those. If everyone knew how to plant a *Heersu*, it's inevitable that someone would use the power to harm others. That's why the *Fae* entrust this power to only one person: The *Teerta*."

Bowi has trouble understanding the concept of inevitability. That anything can be guaranteed or predicted in such a chaotic, painful world seems to directly contradict his experience of life so far. But then again, he's still only a child—a fact of which he's all too aware. Bowi nods along to everything Tagi says, hoping the old man doesn't think him slow or incapable.

"This one is *talapako*," Tagi holds up a small, pointy leaf coated in fuzzy, green fibers.

Bowi takes the leaf, touches it to his tongue, scrapes some of its velvety green fibrils with his teeth. It tastes like dirt and something else that instantly evacuates his sinuses.

"Spicy, *eh?*" Tagi snickers. "*Talapako* is usually the culprit of upset stomachs."

"*Momo* doesn't cook with that," Bowi grimaces, eyes watering. "I've never tasted it before."

"Alright, let's try another."

Systematically, Tagi has Bowi sample every plant in his garden. Leaves, roots, bulbs, stems, petals, fruits, vines, seeds. Some are spicy. Others are bitter. Most taste like dirt, tinged with the faint acidity of rainwater. None elicit any notable reaction in Bowi. By the time evening falls, Tagi has exhausted the garden, no closer to curing the boy.

"Well, now we know what doesn't make you sick," Tagi figures it's his responsibility to remain optimistic. *Every wrong answer points to the right one.*

Overhead, Eeao has stationed herself in the canopy of a nearby tree (some hybrid gymnosperm descended from Asian ginkgos and South American conifers, radically adapted to the globe's current, tropical epoch). Around the kitten, lichen veins richer than jade glimmer to life, as though the sky's fading daylight drained into the jungle itself. A mere shadow in the tree's leafy branches, Eeao cleans blood and feathers from a recent snack off her whiskers—though her gaze remains fixed on Tagi and the nuisance child below.

"I don't think anything is making me sick," Bowi says. "I think I'm just... Always sick... And some days are worse than others."

Tagi gives the boy a puzzled look. From nearby vegetation, as though materializing from leaves, an eclipse of moths flutters into the air, each larger than the boy's head. They flit in all directions, wings speckled brown and silver, attracted to the jungle's emerging luminescence. Up in her tree, Eeao gnaws a feather in half. Its metallic taste deeply gratifies her. And down below, Bowi feels like he's acknowledged a shameful truth: His illness is his own fault.

"Come, let me help you," Tagi sighs, taking Bowi's hand, supplanting the cane with his own support. Hand in hand, they walk together back to the cave. *Perhaps*, Tagi thinks, *the illness is not in the boy's stomach, but in his mind.*

Later that evening, Tagi prepares a bland yet satisfying meal of simmered beans, minced *bareebo*, and lightly-salted grasshopper legs, stewing the ingredients in the cauldron over his firepit. It's a hearty recipe, known by many to provide comfort. Bowi enjoys the food; he chews quickly, working his teeth and jaw muscles to thoroughly devour each crunchy bite. The experience of eating feels somehow both novel and intimately familiar. He cries when he's finished—not because he feels sick, but because he feels relieved and satisfied and finally full. He falls asleep shortly afterward, more content than he's felt in all his moons.

While Bowi snores, passed out beside the extinguished fire pit, Tagi slips inside the cave to recline in his own bed. He sighs as he sinks into the feather mattress, the kink in his neck finally releasing into the familiar softness of his pillow.

Eight moons.

The kink returns immediately, along with the gnat. Tagi does his best to relax, but to little avail. Soon, Eeao appears from the dark, eyes aglow. She hops onto his chest; purring ensues. Tagi combs his fingers through her soft fur, grateful for her presence. But his thoughts continue to revolve around the boy as he drifts to sleep. Beneath his eyelids, the old man feels as though he's turning in circles, scouring the deep, foggy corners of his mind, sifting through soupy memories, hoping to puzzle together some sort of solution to the child's illness before it's too late.

Eeao falls asleep thinking of the boy too. She hopes he'll continue to sleep outside.

Chapter 9
"Daeo"

Daeo hates her life.

Being a little girl isn't easy.

Nothing is within reach. Everyone is too busy. Nobody slows down, though time itself seems to drag on forever. Everything is someone else's decision. And no one cares when bullies bully because, well, at least for this little girl, bullies are just another fact of life.

"Die *Meemmal!*" several older children dump Daeo into a swampy, bubbling bog. "Die *Meemmal!* Die, die, die!" the gang jeers while she flails her limbs through the geothermal mud, struggling to keep her head afloat. Since her brother departed to become *Teerta*, Daeo has become the sole target of their bullying. The bog they've thrown her into today is warm and deep; she can't feel the bottom with her feet. Muck slurps around her legs and torso, sucking her downward like quicksand. A sense of panic rips through Daeo's chest at first, but she dismisses the fear. She knows from experience that if she stays perfectly still, she can float here long enough for her mother to find her. Elsewise, the bullies will fish her out sooner or later to perform another prank.

"Okay, friends, that was fun," Daeo tries to smile through a mouthful of mud. "Now how about we throw me in the feather dump?" At this point, out of all the other cruelties they could subject her to, Daeo considers getting plastered in *raca* feathers to be the most preferable.

"Let's shove worms up her nose and hang her upside down from the *Taepo*."

"Not yet, she needs to stew for a while."

The snickering lot leaves her submerged in the bog, with just her little head poking up from its murky surface, incandescent and pitiful. In their absence, the wilderness sings down at her in mockery—macaws cackle and squawk from treetops; insects trill and whirr around her face; hoatzins the size of prehistoric velociraptors let out long, patronizing sighs, like her getting stuck in the swamp has inconvenienced them in some way. To Daeo, it feels like nature itself has forsaken her. She imagines that if Bowi were still here, things would be different—sure, she'd still be stuck neck-deep in swamp water, but at least he'd be here too, right alongside her, the two of them stuck together. His companionship made daily torture so much more tolerable.

"*Momo!*" Daeo waits until she's sure the older children are out of earshot before calling for help. "*Momo! Momo!*"

Her cries echo into the vast jungle, unanswered. She wishes *Kreeko* were still useful; that dumb, single-minded bird stopped caring about her as soon as the new baby arrived. Once upon a time, Daeo enjoyed the undivided attention of her mother, her older brother, and a gigantic trained parrot. Nowadays, she's all alone. Invisible to everyone—well, everyone except the gang of juvenile ruffians who target her every waking moment. Passively, Daeo wonders if this is how the tadpoles in this bog feel too, squirming around her in the muck, invisible to everyone except their rapacious older relatives, who sit along the bank and slurp at their newborns with long, projectile tongues. A buffet of random chance, the toads blindly thin their own herd. Metamorphosis requires luck.

But unlike the toads and tadpoles, Daeo's bullies are not indiscriminate. She knows they target her for two specific reasons: Size and skin. Both born prematurely, she and Bowi have always been runtier than their cousins. And, thanks to sheer chance, they also inherited that pair of recessive genes inhibiting their skin's antifungal defense; unlike everyone else's clean-cut radiance, limited only to areas of densely-packed hair follicles, Bowi and Daeo are both completely coated in fungal varnish.

Dazzling. Shimmery. Conspicuous.

Beneath the translucent layer, their skin is as normal as anyone else's—Bowi is freckled honey-tan, Daeo is pigmented dark as the new moon. But these days, no one cares about skin pigmentation. It's the fact that their skin glitters. The fact that their entire bodies glow. To everyone else, their full-body *patu*s look odd. Untidy. Socially unacceptable. Crass, even. People with this skin condition are referred to as *Patummal*, which roughly translates as *diseased*-patu. Not necessarily inhuman, like their patchy-scalped baby sister. But still strange enough to warrant the occasional *Meemmal* slur—even from adults.

It's another cost of being different. Another fact of life.

Nyno doesn't find her daughter until halfway through the day. She uses a fallen vine to reel the little girl out of the swamp. Slimy and waterlogged, Daeo's fingers and toes come out so wrinkled they look like dried *sokeeto* berries. Coated in muck, she barely shimmers.

"Why, *Daeo*? Why?" Nyno wipes green sludge from the girl's luminous face. They don't have time for this nonsense—the *Fae* have been sighted, descending over the horizon, approaching the *Aeo*. Having left her baby with Paelo to go out searching for Daeo, Nyno is particularly annoyed to have found her daughter playing in the forbidden swamp grounds, yet again. "Why don't you ever listen to me?"

"I'm sorry, *momo*—"

"How many times am I going to find you stuck out here? What are you even doing?"

"I was playing," Daeo lies. "And I fell in."

"Again?" Nyno is skeptical, but she figures the child has suffered enough and doesn't scold further. *She'll learn by some point.* For now, they're in a hurry. They need to be at the *Aeo* with everyone else, gathering for the *Fae*'s arrival. She swings Daeo up and over her shoulder like a slain *raea* chick and then races back in the direction she came, following the path she'd tunneled through the jungle's understory to get here. Legs burning, lower abdomen cramping, body still recovering from recent childbirth, Nyno trudges, fueled by a dissociative form of determination known only to mothers in distress.

Daeo bounces along on her back, cheek pressed against her mother's bare shoulder blade, swallowing intermittent waves of shame. She knows her mother doesn't believe her lie. But does she know the truth? Does she see her daughter's vulnerability? The way she sticks out like a glowing mushroom compared to all the other children?

How could she not?

To Daeo, mere existence is a responsibility that feels unfairly held against her.

Can't her mother tell?

"You stink like the swamp," Paelo wrinkles her nose when they return. "Where'd you find her?"

"Guess," Nyno rolls her eyes. Paelo doesn't have to. Nyno reclaims her swaddled infant from her cousin's arms, quickly peeking beneath the feather blanket to see the baby girl smiling up at her, perfectly content, a dribble of Paelo's milk glistening on her tiny chin. Nyno covers the baby's head again, and then presses the bundle to her chest. They're in the secluded privacy of Paelo's *capku* (the conical dwellings their people construct from *areemo* timber and mycelial *hympano* skin), so they're unlikely to be overseen. But still, Nyno prefers to keep the baby's bare head concealed at all times. Paelo's own newborn sleeps peacefully on a nearby feather mat, its perfect little scalp aglow. "Come on," Nyno says, "we need to get to the *Aeo*."

"We're probably late," Paelo says, picking up her baby. She carries it naked with her, bouncing the babe against her hip like a medal of honor, free and exposed to the open world. Meanwhile, Nyno's baby doesn't know daylight.

Smothered, she carries the infant like a stolen secret out to the *Aeo*, her guilt a palpable shroud, while her other daughter trails conspicuous, mucky footsteps in their wake.

Chapter 10
"Fae"

Airflow across the *Uyi*'s bowl-shaped geography shifts upon the *Fae's* arrival. Descending from the crater's northern mountains, their beating, synchronized wings blast cool gusts of wind across the lake's steaming surface, which then resonate outward, scattering mist and birds in semicircular ripples around the rainforest. Nyno shivers, her skin prickling from spray off the lake. She stands with her people, throngs of them, lined up and organized along the southern shore like ants. They watch as the swarming, winged humanoids approach.

To Nyno, the *Fae* have always looked unnatural. Like they don't belong down here in the *Uyi*'s ecosystem of plants and animals, but to some other, outer realm. Somewhere outside of nature. She's tried all her life to imagine the world beyond the mountains, the land of the *Fae*, the nature to which they belong, but the picture she conjures is nothing but a horrifying vacuum of blank, empty space. These human-insect beings are a form of life she cannot comprehend.

"xxxxxxxxxxxxxxxxxxxxxxxxxxxxxxxxxxxxxxxxxxx"

The clacking buzz of their wings, amplified off the water's vast, rolling surface, drones against Nyno's skull with ceaseless, palpitating force. Beside her, Daeo cowers with hands over her ears. In Nyno's arms, the baby squirms; she hopes she's bundled her snugly enough to shield her from this hellish noise. Meanwhile, Paelo continues to bounce her own newborn on her hip, seemingly deaf to the sound, while her child's mouth hangs open in a soundless scream Nyno can't hear over the approaching roar.

"XXXXXXXXXXXXXXXXXXXXXXXXXXXXXXXX"

The swarm flies in a sideways, pyramidal formation, the entire multitude led by one, expanding upward and downward, left and right, bodies staggering outward for maximal aerodynamics. Nyno can never tell how many there are, or whether the formation's leader holds any sort of distinction—all *Fae* look the same. Translucent, brittle skin stretched over green and blue organs; naked, their insides are wholly visible, a constant pumping and shifting of parasympathetic activity on crystalline display. Their sizes vary somewhat. But on average, they each stand double Nyno's height, with twin sets of dragonfly wings that extend from their shoulder blades and span nearly the width of an entire *capku*. Their four wings, each formed by glittering tessellations of veiny membranes, beat at such high frequencies they create a blurred halo-effect around each *Fae* body, facilitating forward and backward propulsion, as well as side-to-side pivoting and a hover more elegant than levitation.

Nyno has heard countless *Fae* myths among fellow birthing *momo*s, ideas that insectoids are genderless, or asexual, or that they reproduce somehow by re-fertilizing insect larvae with *Meemmal* seed. She knows their wild conjectures are just gossip. She doesn't think they'll ever know anything more about the *Fae* than what they can see with their own eyes.

And as things are, confined within the *Uyi*, Nyno is probably right. She and her people have no access to historical records, no knowledge of microbiology or genetics, the ways their ancestors augmented human DNA one million years ago to produce the insectoid species now known as *Fae*. Actually, Nyno and her people believe it to be the other way around, that humankind is a younger, inferior offshoot of *Fae*—a wingless subspecies, as some ants sprout wings while their lesser cousins remain dawdling through the soil.

For a moment, Nyno pictures Daeo back in the swamp. *Aren't we all stuck down here?*

As the swarm makes its final descent toward the southern shoreline, the details of their faces come into view. Bulging, compound eyes wrap around the front sides of their otherwise human heads, reflective and unblinking, each an infinite array of tiny, UV-sensitive lenses. In Daeo's worst nightmares, she comes face-to-face with those menacing, alien eyes. But in reality, she knows she has nothing to fear; *Fae* never land during their visits to the *Uyi*, and they aren't generally interested in children. Today, they come only to prune *Kamaruna* volunteers: The oldest and weakest among the human population. It's a ritual that takes place at midday every half-moon.

Today's *Kamaruna* have already been selected—six individuals of varying ages, each chosen for some sort of handicap. One is a young man with an irreparably broken leg. Another is a stick-thin woman, unable to bear children. Not even the oldest is much older than Nyno. A few volunteered themselves. But usually, the selection process for *Kamaruna* is a matter of mob mentality, wherein the nest's strongest, fittest humans gang up and choose whichever six they deem least valuable. Or most convenient. It's framed as benevolence, or mercy—they tell children the *Kamaruna* volunteers will be happier where they're going.

The chosen volunteers now sit huddled together on the shoreline, each bound in cords of *areemo* twine, their ankles tied to large, heavy stones. Maetri is among the barrel-chested men and women guarding them, spare twine dangling from his meaty hands. Lately, Daeo has begun to wonder why the *Kamaruna* volunteers need to be tied up if they're going to such a happy place.

"XXXXXXXXXXXXXXXXXXXXXXXXXXXXXX"

The swarm is now directly overhead, hovering in their distinct formation, just higher than the treeline. From somewhere within the humming horde, six individual *Fae* break rank and descend toward the gathered *Kamaruna* volunteers. No words are exchanged. No communication is made. For all Nyno knows, the *Fae* might not even have vocal chords. But what each *Fae* does possess are two powerful, humanoid arms, which the six ambassadors now use to seize the bound *Kamaruna* volunteers and lift them into the sky. Some squirm as they're hoisted. The barren woman hangs limp, already surrendered. As the *Fae* rejoin their formation, and as the formation ascends back over the lake, Nyno follows with her eyes the six, dangling stones. She knows the tethered humans will never touch dry ground again.

At a certain point, midway over the lake, the formation pauses, hovering. And then Nyno watches while the six volunteers are dropped into the *Aeo*, one by one. No one can hear their splashes; the distance is too great. But everyone on the southern shoreline breathes a sigh of relief when the *Fae* discard the final volunteer and continue on their way, flying back over the northern mountains, disappearing like nothing happened.

Everyone in the *Uyi* continues life as usual.

But Daeo is left particularly unsettled after today's *Kamaruna* ceremony. There's something about it she doesn't understand. Just as Nyno can't fathom the *Fae*'s world beyond the mountains, Daeo can't fathom the sort of happiness found at the bottom of a lake.

Today, Daeo decides she will no longer tolerate the unfathomable. From now on, she wants to know everything.

Chapter 11
"Bowi"

Bowi feels useless.

Then again, he's felt useless for most of his life.

For as long as he can remember, he's never measured up to expectations. Daeo with her boundless energy, her constant need for more attention. *Momo* and her miscarriages, her never-ending struggle to create more children (because he was nowhere near enough). The bullies, always looking for more places on his *Patummal* body to bruise. The *Fae* and their perpetual demand for more and more *Kamaruna*. Perhaps, then, it's perfectly natural that, now sitting here in Tagi's cave all day, every day, doing basically nothing, he should feel utterly, shamefully, morbidly useless.

"You're not doing nothing," Tagi says when Bowi voices his concern. "And you're certainly not useless. You're healing and learning. There's nothing useless in healing, and there's nothing useless in learning."

Bowi remains incredulous. But at least he knows Tagi is right about one thing: His health has improved significantly. Over the quarter-moon since arriving at Tagi's cave, he hasn't vomited once. Nutritionally, he's enjoyed a cornucopia of tasty, novel foods, all prepared in Tagi's stone cauldron. Morning and evening, the old man whisks garden-grown ingredients and juicy insects into his boiling, savory brew, always managing to concoct some unique, finely-tuned recipe to delight Bowi's taste buds. And sure, now that Bowi stops to think about it, he realizes he's learned a few things from just sitting around and eating too—like the subtle difference in taste between *bareebo* and *reewo*; the twelve different ways to cook *raea* meat; the proper etiquette for de-legging grasshoppers versus mantises. Day by day, the underlying pigment is returning to Bowi's cheeks: A lithe, speckled copper. And as more time passes, he is beginning to forget the sensation of nausea altogether.

"What does it feel like, when you get sick?" Tagi asks one morning, cleaning leftover breakfast out of the cauldron with a tool he made from *mabato* bristles.

"I don't know..." Bowi says after thinking for a moment. "Sometimes I just wake up early in the morning and feel pain in my stomach..." He doesn't know how to explain the searing sensation, the way it jerks him awake, propelling him to empty his insides.

"And it never mattered whether or not you'd eaten the night before, correct?"

"Uh-huh..." Bowi doesn't want to remember the details. He doesn't want to go back to those moments in his mind, alone and heaving behind the *capku* in the early light of dawn, trying to keep quiet while his mother and sister slept—not because he didn't want their help, but because he didn't want them to know he needed it. Yet Tagi keeps asking him to remember. His stomach feels fine right now, why can't he just enjoy this reprieve? Or worse—what if remembering triggers the sickness to return?

"How many moons have you seen, *Bowi?*"

"One hundred and twenty-one." Theirs is a number-oriented, herding society, wherein children are taught sequences and arithmetic as soon as they can speak.

"And at what age did your illness begin?"

"I don't know... I've always had it."

"What did your *momo* do to help you when you were sick?" Tagi needs Bowi to paint some sort of picture for him. Right now, extracting relevant information from the boy is like trying to pick *sokeeto* berries blind, and Tagi hasn't even found the bush.

"*Momo* would give me water, or *pomaeo* juice when she could find some. And she'd fan air on my face to cool me down. Sometimes she'd make me tea, like you make."

"*Renomo?*"

Bowi nods, "Except I don't like drinking it when it's hot. Only after it's cooled down."

"Noted," Tagi sighs. "I hope to never offend you again with a piping-hot brew. Now then, did your *momo* ever try giving you—gah—*Eeao*!"

The kitten is stuck halfway up Tagi's back, her claws caught in the feathery fabric of his poncho. She'd miscalculated a jump aimed for the perch of his left shoulder. Tagi reaches around and plucks her from his back. Now, caught by her nape in Tagi's grasp, wriggling for freedom, she finds herself held captive, up-close between two bulging human faces.

"What is it?" Bowi leans closer, mystified. He hasn't seen much of Eeao these past few days; the feline has been making herself scarce to them, spending long stretches of time outside, hunting in new parts of the rainforest. She thinks Tagi must be beginning to miss her. She hopes one day he'll follow her on one of her excursions, and together they can look for a new cave to inhabit, somewhere the intruder child won't be able to find them. Really though, Tagi has barely noticed her absence—until now.

"To tell you the truth, I don't know what she is," Tagi chuckles, and then to the kitten, "what are you, little *Eeao?*"

"*...eeao...*"

"You don't know?" Bowi is shocked. He always assumed the *Teerta* and other Chiefs to be as omnipotent as the *Fae.*

"Well, let's consider her objectively," Tagi says, stroking his forefinger beneath Eeao's chin, both to pacify her and to bring her face into view. She blinks up at him with jaded, diamond eyes. "She can't be an *aea*, since she doesn't have feathers or a beak."

"Or wings," Bowi adds.

"Those too," Tagi nods. "Which means she also can't be a wasp, or a dragonfly, or a bee either. And she doesn't have fins for swimming, so she can't be any kind of *aeo*. Perhaps she's a strange, new type of *onynsa*?"

"No way!" Bowi laughs at the idea. "She doesn't have enough legs to be *onynsa*. And she doesn't have scales, so she can't be *lyreea*."

"Good observation," Tagi says, dancing his knuckles along Eeao's arching spine—a trick that instantly gets her purring. "Well, I've given you my best guess. What's yours?"

Bowi takes a moment to analyze the kitten, taking particular note of her facial symmetry, the whiskers regrowing around her nose, the striped patterning of her fur, the infantile quality of her voice. Back on the first day he arrived in Tagi's cave, he'd been so delirious he'd assumed her slinking figure to be a dream, or hallucination, or some trick of shadow and light too vivid for his mind to configure. Now, she seems as natural to him as anything else.

"She's kind of like us," Bowi remarks after some thought.

"How do you mean?" Tagi flips Eeao around to face himself. They lock eyes. He can tell how conflicted she is, caught between the urge to flee and an inescapable craving for evermore affection.

"Well, she has hair like ours, kind of," Bowi trails his fingers through the kitten's coat. It's the first time he's been able to touch her. Somehow, she feels exorbitantly softer than any texture he's ever felt; her fur glides beneath his fingertips like solid water. Using his fingernails, he combs some of her fur aside, revealing a patch of luminous, violet skin beneath. "And she has a *patu*, like us."

"She certainly does," Tagi is, once again, pleased with Bowi's consideration. The boy is thoughtful, slow to speak, and yet when he does, his observations come as unexpected insights. *He will make a good* Teerta, Tagi thinks.

Eight moons.

"But I don't know what this is for," Bowi points at Eeao's tail, which she's begun to flick back and forth in agitation. He's never seen an animal with such an appendage—he can only compare it to a snake's body, or a *raea*'s long, S-shaped neck. The way the kitten seems to curl it in and out of itself mesmerizes his eyes.

"This is her tail," Tagi says. "It's actually quite remarkable, the way she uses it for balance. I've seen her walk along skinny tree branches with ease."

"How?"

"Well, her tail seems to be made mostly of muscle. If she starts to tip one direction, she'll use it to counterbalance herself. Watch, see how she balances as she walks across my shoulders, see? It's kind of like holding your arms outstretched to balance on one foot."

Bowi watches, amused, as the kitten paces back and forth along Tagi's shoulders, flicking the tip of her tail. She pauses to sniff at Tagi's dusty scalp. But when the boy reaches up to touch her again, she scampers away, leaping off Tagi's shoulder and disappearing from the cave altogether.

"She leaves as quickly as she arrives," Tagi muses.

"I like her," Bowi says, staring out the cave's opening.

"Too bad she doesn't seem to like you."

This comment stings Bowi.

"How can I make her like me?"

"Well, you can't *make* anyone like you," Tagi begins slowly, stretching his mind for the right words. *What does it mean to be a social animal?* As a hermit, he feels deeply unqualified to speak on such matters. This dialogue alone might be the longest non-*Teerta*-related conversation he's had with another person since childhood. Yet here he is, responsible not just for teaching Bowi how to be *Teerta*, but how to be human. *My words will stick with him for the rest of his life.* "It's all about learning to communicate. Learn how *Eeao* likes to be held. Learn what she likes to eat. Learn how she likes to play. If you learn how to communicate with her, she'll start to communicate with you. And then maybe she'll start to like you."

Bowi sits in silence for a moment, pondering Tagi's answer. Finally, he asks, "How can I communicate with someone I can't speak to?"

"Speech isn't the only form of communication, you know," Tagi laughs at the notion. "Come with me." He helps Bowi to his feet, possessed by an idea. *Might as well begin teaching.* "I'm going to teach you the most important thing you will ever learn."

"Where are we going?" Bowi asks, following Tagi into the cave's farthest corner.

In the darkness, their bioluminescing *patu*s provide them just enough light to see their immediate surroundings. Multicolored striations line the walls of this deep cavity, once-flowing rivers of sedimentary minerals transfixed by time and geophysics. Warped around his peripheral, the lining along the walls makes Bowi feel like the cave is swallowing them whole. And then, all of a sudden, Tagi guides him around a corner he didn't realize existed.

And they emerge into a hidden, subterrestrial world.

Chapter 12
"Ynsyna"

Strange, geometric figures riddle the cave walls.

"I don't get it," Bowi is overwhelmed by all the intricate carvings—even the ceiling of this immense cavern is inscribed with characters, though he has to squint and crane his neck to see them.

"This is *ynsyna*," Tagi explains with a sweep of his arms. Combined, their *patu*s illuminate the walls sufficiently, though Bowi's full-body sheen augments the light of Tagi's receding hairline by tenfold; for once, the old man feels the boy possesses something he lacks. "*Ynsyna* won't help you talk to *Eeao*, but it will allow you to communicate with all the *Teerta*s who have come before you, no speech necessary. They've chiseled their words here, inside the cave itself. Their wisdom is preserved eternal."

Bowi still doesn't understand why Tagi thinks the carvings are so great, or what they could possibly have to do with wisdom, but he knows better than to scoff. Clearly, Tagi knows a valuable secret about this cave, and the boy is eager to learn whatever he can. At first glance, in the violet light of their *patu*s, the squiggly markings could be overlooked altogether, mistaken for some naturally occurring pattern of erosion, or mold. It's only upon closer inspection that Bowi identifies repeated symbols, specific figures, order amidst chaos—the characters are arranged in neat sequences, which run parallel to the cave's striated layers. Their creation, undeniably deliberate.

"So old *Teerta*s made these before you were alive?" Bowi tries to imagine how many of them needed to have existed in order to create so many meaningful carvings. Suddenly, the cave feels hauntingly ancient, its history longer than Bowi can conceive. The air around them, once rich with the earthy aroma of fungi and calcification, now smells overpoweringly of time's damp, ominous musk.

"Well, not just old *Teerta*s," Tagi lowers his voice modestly. "Some of the *ynsyna* is mine. Come, look, over here." Bowi follows the old man to the other side of the cavern, their bare feet echoing on the cool stone floor. Sharp, glistening stalactites jut like fangs from the cave's yawning roof, while their sister stalagmites incise upward, jaws poised to snap shut around them. From somewhere deeper still, Bowi can hear the faint, trickling *drip! drip! drip!* of subterranean water, its source hidden from sight. In his head, it sounds like the Earth's digestion at work. This thought makes the boy queasy, and for a moment he loses his orientation. How large is this cave? He can't see the other end of it through the dark. Bowi halts, tugging Tagi's poncho.

"What's the matter? Are you hurt? Unwell?" Tagi flies into *Teerta*-mode, possessed by the ancient, generational lore surrounding them. He encourages the boy to lean against a nearby stalagmite, and then begins fanning air on his face, as his mother used to. Dwarfed beside the colossal spire of calcite, Bowi curls into a fetal position. It takes clenching every muscle in his body to resist the nausea roiling up his stomach—like fingers clawing for escape. Beads of sweat line his forehead and neck. The taste of bile spikes the back of his tongue.

"I don't want to be sick, I don't want to be sick," his cries echo within the earth, ricocheting back at him with cruel acuity. "Please, *Teerta*, I need to lie down."

"Come, let's get you back to bed," Tagi easily lifts the boy. "The air is fresher near the cave's opening."

As usual, Tagi is right; air circulation is much better in the outer cave, which Bowi now realizes is just an antechamber to the larger *ynsyna* cavern within. Tagi places the child in his bed. Cool against Bowi's sweat-slickened skin, the airflow relieves his discomfort considerably. Just in case, Tagi fetches a *pomaeo* fruit—he already has a stash of five bobbing in his water basin.

"What happened?" Tagi asks upon returning to Bowi's side. The boy reclines at a forty-five degree angle, his neck and upper back propped on woven, feather cushions Tagi made several days ago. "Does your stomach hurt?"

"It did, but I'm starting to feel better," Bowi breathes heavily, his contracted muscles releasing one by one as his abdominal pain dissipates. "I don't know what happened, I just... I started feeling sick when we went deeper into the cave. I felt like I was going to vomit."

"Hmmm..." Tagi wrinkles his bushy, white eyebrows. He sees two possibilities: First, that Bowi's sudden-onset remission correlates chemically with their entering the *ynsyna* cavern; or second, that the timing is just coincidence. Regardless, he decides they'll wait to re-enter the inner cavern until another day, prioritizing first the child's health. He gives Bowi a *pomaeo* to drink. "Do you think you can keep it down?"

Bowi pokes his fingernail through the fruit's skin, and then takes a few tentative sips. He smiles as the cool juice coats his esophagus and stomach, further alleviating his pain. "Yes, I will be okay," he says.

"Good," Tagi returns the smile, but behind it a bubble of anxiety swells. *Eight moons.* Does he have enough time to teach the boy everything a *Teerta* needs to know, and cure him too? At this rate, it could be moons before Bowi even goes back inside the *ynsyna* cavern. Somehow, through the foggy layers of his wrinkled memory, Tagi seems to recall being afforded a much longer period of time training with his old *Teerta*. And he didn't even have an illness to overcome. Even now, just below the ring of his tinnitus, he can still hear the raspy, impatient whisper of his old *Teerta* from long, long ago: *No time to waste.*

"Let's get our minds on something else," Tagi snaps from his thoughts. "It's time to begin your first *ynsyna* lesson."

Bowi gulps. "I don't want to go back in there," he points down the cave's throat.

"Don't worry, we can stay out here, near the fresh air," Tagi assures him. "Watch, you won't even have to get out of bed." The old man hurries to retrieve the walking stick Bowi used the other day. Turning it upside down, he now uses it to draw a triangle on the cave floor, dragging its pointed end through the soft dirt. *I suppose I will end up using a cane after all,* Tagi thinks wryly to himself, drawing six more shapes beside the triangle: A circle, an inverted triangle, a square, a diamond, a waxing crescent, and a waning crescent.

"See these?" Tagi directs Bowi's attention to the symbols he's drawn on the ground. "All speech stems from seven core sounds. And these symbols represent those seven sounds. *Ynsyna* is the practice of building words with these visual symbols. Does that make sense?"

Bowi nods blankly.

"Okay, look at this first one," Tagi points at the triangle, "it represents the sound: *-ae.*" He over-pronounces the vowels, enunciating with his mouth the symbol's intended sound. "Say it with me: *-ae.*" Obediently, Bowi parrots Tagi. "Good. So whenever you see this triangular shape, I want you to associate it with that sound. This next one, the circle, represents the sound: *-oh.*" Again, Tagi widens his mouth to form a big O-shape as he demonstrates the sound for Bowi. He proceeds down the line of characters, explaining to Bowi that the inverted triangle stands for the *-ah* sound, the square for the *-oo* sound, the diamond for the long *-ee* sound, the waxing crescent for the short *-ee* sound, and the waning crescent for the soft, subtle *-yih* sound (a high-pitched tone unique to humans of this geologic era, evolved in concert with the planet's rising humidity and lubricating effects on vocal cords).

"The last one is tricky," Tagi warns. "It can sometimes appear as a silent sound, and other times like a melodic note."

"How can a sound be silent?"

"Well, let's look at the word *ynsyna*. It can be broken down into three core sounds: *yihn-sihn-ah*. Pronounce it with me, Bowi: *yihn-sihn-ah*." Tagi draws on the ground two waning crescents, followed by an inverted triangle, left to right. "However, the first two sounds are dominated by modifying sounds, *-nn* and *-ss*, both of which force the tongue to pronounce the core sound in different ways," Tagi modifies the two crescent shapes, drawing a slanted dash across one and a squiggle-dash combo through the other's center.

"Modifying sounds are different from core sounds," Tagi continues. "Core sounds come from the voice. Modifying sounds are created by the tongue and mouth, like *-ll, -ck, -hh, -dd, -gg, -th*, and such..." He proceeds to draw twenty smaller symbols in the dirt, each representing a sound made with the tongue or lips. "Altogether, these are the building blocks of language: Seven core sounds and twenty modifiers. I expect you to memorize all of them."

"All of them?" Bowi gawps.

"It's not difficult, once you begin learning," Tagi says. "You see, language comes from nature. It's as fundamental as the air we breathe, the ground we walk, the trees around us. At the very root of language, you'll find the four core elements. You know what those are, right? First, *Aeo*," he draws in the dirt a triangle followed by a circle, unmodified, their word for *water*. "Next, *Aea*," he draws a triangle beside an inverted triangle, again unmodified, their word for *sky*. "What's the third element, Bowi?"

"Uyee," Bowi blurts the word for *fire*, relieved it's a question he can answer. Tagi draws in the dirt a square, a waning moon, and a diamond, no modifications.

"And last, *Uyi*," Tagi writes out their word for *earth*: a square, a waning moon, and then a waxing moon. "These are the four purest words in language, unmodified by anything superficial. As long as you can remember *Aeo, Aea, Uyee,* and *Uyi,* you'll always know the seven core sounds."

Tagi smiles, feeling triumphant with his first lesson.

Meanwhile, Bowi is too accommodating to tell the old man he barely understood any of it. He just grins and nods along, hoping Tagi doesn't try to pepper him with yet more information.

Later on, while the dewy showers of evening bathe the jungle indigo, and Tagi goes out to light the *uyee* beneath his cauldron for supper, Bowi studies the symbols still scratched into the ground.

Triangles. Squares. Circles.

Curves, squiggles, dots.

At first, they all seem to jumble together in the dirt, and Bowi strains his eyes trying to make sense of them. But he remains determined. In between bites of food that night, he pronounces the seven core sounds under his breath, imagining their shapes over and over again in his head. He traces each modifying symbol on his forearm with his index finger as he falls asleep later, envisioning them against the blackness of his mind, humming a quiet melody to himself, a tune to help him remember the purpose of each unique character.

When he awakes the next morning, he can sing them all with ease.

Chapter 13
"Eeao"

All attempts to lure Tagi away from the boy have failed.

For the first time in her five-month life, Eeao is beginning to feel alone. Of course, every thinking animal must grapple with feelings of isolation at some point—aloneness is, after all, the end result of consciousness. But for Eeao, this realization strikes an unhealed bruise.

She can't ignore the bond forming between Tagi and the child; it's a sort of kinship she's never known. The sounds they make to one another. The steaming slop they eat side-by-side. Their shared interest in those vile, exploding melons. Their similarities are precisely what differentiate them from her, and this knowledge taunts Eeao relentlessly. Like a dangly, uncatchable nuisance, their relationship prickles her fur and makes her mewl with envy. She can't even sleep on Tagi's chest anymore—he's placed his newly constructed bed too close to the child's for Eeao to feel comfortable. The past few nights, she's taken refuge in an isolated, moss-blanketed cranny above the cave's entrance, from whence she's able to secretly glare down at them both as they sleep.

Not that she sleeps much at night, anyway. As Tagi has shifted his attention to the boy, Eeao has shifted to a more nocturnal lifestyle. She hunts beneath the waxing moon, expanding her knowledge night by night of the jungle's iridescent canopy and its immense variety of cuisine. *Arunaea,* white-faced moon birds. *Kynaea,* hard-beaked macaws. *Camraea,* hoatzins with turquoise-blue plumage and succulent, bloody chests. Humans know them by words; Eeao knows them by smell.

The kitten is growing, changing, evolving every day into a skilled, mammalian mercenary.

She thinks she's mastered the jungle, seen everything nature has to offer, until one night, on the scent of some fresh *camraea* hatchlings in the marshy lowlands, she pokes her nose through a dense tangle of philodendron and finds on the other side a vast, open field dotted with humongous, feathered bodies.

The monstrous creatures graze, roving two-legged across the field with their serpentine necks low to the ground, plucking at sprouting verdure with tiny, beaked heads. Eeao can tell immediately the giant birds are dumb, scattered about at random, tail feathers pointed to the near-full moon. They reek of avian pheromones and their own guano. But their intimidating sizes make the kitten uneasy. Younglings strut through the grass on tall, stilt-like legs, while their larger relatives leave dinosaur-sized footprints in the soil. One wrong step could leave Eeao flatter than a lily pad.

Springlike, Eeao ascends the branches of a nearby cecropia to secure a better view of the impressive creatures. Within the grassy field's soil, glowing mycelial threads knit intricate fungal networks, underlighting the birds in an eerie, green cast. From her elevated vantage, Eeao sees each massive bird as a dark spot upon the luminous meadow.

But there are other spots too, smaller, violet-capped, moving quickly across the other side of the field. Humans? Or some other type of predator? Whatever they are, Eeao is far outnumbered. She climbs higher, settling eventually on a short, sturdy branch hugging the tree's center.

Soon, the approachers are within earshot.

"If they're perfectly healthy, why make them volunteer for *Kamaruna?*" a human voice rises over the nighttime din of crickets and rustling feathers. Eeao perks her triangular ears, honing them toward the speaker.

"Because they *aren't* perfectly healthy, don't you get it?" another voice, lower in pitch. It sounds vaguely familiar to the kitten—a human she's heard before?

The approaching figures halt, too far away for Eeao to see the details of their faces. There are five in total, all about the same size, huddled close together. Around them, the flock of enormous birds continues grazing, undisturbed.

"*Patummal* is a blemish, a weakness," a new voice chimes. "We are meant to keep the nest strong, yes?"

"Yes, of course," the first voice. "But I don't understand—how does *Patummal* manifest as a weakness? *Veetri* is *Patummal,* and he's one of our strongest—"

"*Veetri* steals *Kunjaruna* glory every new moon," the low, familiar voice says. "And he only gets away with it because he's a Chief's firstborn *babi.* You know that to be true."

"Otherwise," a female voice, more deliberate than the rest, "I'd say *Veetri* is one of the fattest leeches in the nest."

They all fall silent. Meanwhile, Eeao is bored of their meaningless gibberish. Rustling through the leaves around her, a steady breeze carries on it the juicy scent of fresh *camraea* hatchlings.

"But what about *Patummal* children?" the first voice finally speaks again. "How can we make young, otherwise healthy children volunteer for *Kamaruna?*"

"They *aren't* healthy, remember?" the female voice snaps. "*Patummal* are as bad as *Meemmal.*"

Eeao slinks soundlessly across the cecropia's upper branches, and then glides off into the night, eager for the taste of young, helpless blood.

Chapter 14
"Maetri"

Much like herding *raea*, herding people is more a game of perspective than power. Maetri has been learning the art since childhood, alongside his brothers, watching closely their father, Paetri, the *Uyi*'s Chief *raea* wrangler.

The key, Maetri has learned, is to identify the average motivation across all herd members, and then extort it.

Food? Safety? Comfort? Survival?

What's the most common force driving each individual's decision-making?

When it comes to *raea*, the simple beasts want only to feed and congregate, knowing somewhere in their pebble-sized brains that survival hinges on the whole herd sticking together. To keep the herd healthy, simply provide large fields. To direct the herd's movement, simply frighten one bird in a desired direction, and the rest will follow. Like a single body, the herd moves as one. Similarly, humans share common goals. And as long as they think those goals are being met, people don't tend to care (or even notice) who's leading.

Tonight, Maetri herds his cousins through conversation, bouncing ideas off his sister like two coordinated wranglers corralling an oblivious flock of *raea*.

"The sacrifice would be *Tarma-ako*," says his sister, Kleeo, using an umbrella term meant to describe the *greater good*. The humans are huddled amidst a flock of nearly two hundred *raea*, which meander around them peacefully, their heads bobbing up and down to graze the field's perpetually shorn vegetation. Aside from their rustling army of tail feathers, the night is quiet—a type of quiet that makes humans whisper.

"*Tarma-ako* or not, we're only five people," their cousin, Aevi, has always been pessimistic. Younger and a full head shorter than the rest of them, he wears a harness studded with *mabato* spines so long, everyone gets poked in the face when leaning in to hear him. "If this is your way of ousting *Veetri,* you'll need the entire nest's support."

Kleeo rolls her eyes, "Enough about *Veetri*. This isn't about ousting anyone."

"This is about doing what's best for the entire nest," Maetri directs the conversation back to the pacifying banality of mutually shared interests. "If we begin volunteering all *Patummal* for *Kamaruna*, we secure more moons for us and our children."

"*Some* of our children," Syno quirks an eyebrow, the bloodlust on her freckled face unmistakeable. Maetri knows she won't be a problem—at least, not right now.

"*Most* of our children," Kleeo corrects her. "Only one in twenty babies is born *Patummal.*"

"Oh, is the prevalence really that high?" Aevi says sarcastically. "I still don't see how this is going to help anyone."

"The benefits are long-term," Maetri says. "Far-reaching. Think about it: Generations from now, our population will be organized in such a way that there's always a class of inferiors to volunteer for *Kamaruna*. No more fighting between clans. No more skirmishes and betrayals. No more human lives cut short. For the first time, we control our fate, not the *Fae.*"

"Okay, but you still need the full nest's support," Aevi says stubbornly. "Or do you intend to strong-arm the mandate? One final skirmish to end all skirmishes?"

"Not a bad idea," Syno snickers. "When do we start?"

"No," Maetri shakes his head. "We convince them with words. *Patummal* are the same as *Meemmal*—we can all agree on that, right?"

"Uh-huh."

"Sure."

"Well, no, not technically…"

"Yes they are."

"No, they're not."

"Why not?"

"Well, what's your definition of *Meemmal*?" Tapati sighs. "Because by some standards, *Aevi,* you're the biggest *Meemmal* in the *Uyi.*" The oldest cousin in the group, Tapati has begun to suffer nightmares recently—terrible, sweaty, suffocating dreams where he's tied up and lifted into the air for *Kamaruna*. He awakes each morning with the bitter taste of *Aeo* on his tongue. He's more eager than any of them to escape impending fate. And yet, like a true elder, he loves to resist anything anyone else says.

"Fine," Aevi sighs. "If you want a practical definition of the word, *Meemmal* are the invader beasts we hunt during *Kunjaruna.*"

"Sort of human, just without a *patu*," Syno adds, tapping a finger on her glowing, clean-shaven scalp.

"Sort of human?" Maetri chews on the words. "What do you mean by that?"

"Well… I mean, *Meemmal* look like us."

Maetri scoffs, "What? You think *Meemmal* look like us? Really? I mean, sure, they have the same general shape as us—two arms, two legs, a head, torso, voice, teeth. But they don't look like us at all. You'd never mistake me for a *Meemmal*, just as I'd never mistake any of you. Our *patu* is what makes us fully human," he reaches up to part his unruly mane of hair down the middle, exposing the glow of his violet scalp.

"Just as *Meemmal* have no *patu*," he continues, "*Patummal* have too much. You look at me, and you know immediately I'm not *Patummal*. I have the skin of a full human." He points now to his bare arm; his skin, a four-toned patchwork of marbled pigments, not a speck of yeast visible. He thinks humans have always looked this way.

Everyone does. None of them know about the *Genetic Revolution*. Or that their speckled skin tones are an ancient bioengineering accident that rippled uncontrollably through the human population.

"We all bear the patterned skin of true humans," Maetri continues. "On our arms, our faces, our chests, our backs. But *Patummal* don't. Their skin is overrun by *patu*. They are not fully human. They are as different from us as *Meemmal* are."

"You're forgetting an important distinction," Tapati sighs. "*Patummal* have *momo*s. They come from our own nests, from our own bloodlines—they are born from sacred *Kosharuna* ceremonies. Two of my own nephews are *Patummal.* Whereas *Meemmal* come from beyond the mountains, outsiders. They're a different species altogether. It's one thing to sacrifice a captured *Meemmal* to *Kamaruna*. But it's another to sacrifice a *Patummal* child, conceived lawfully during *Kosharuna.*"

"You're wrong," Maetri says, eliciting dubious looks around the huddle. Even Kleeo has no idea where her brother is taking the conversation anymore. "*Meemmal* are not a different species altogether. They have to come from somewhere, right? Well, sometimes they are born here. In our nests. To our *momo*s."

"That's crazy," Syno snorts. "No one has ever given birth to a *Meemmal.*"

"You're wrong," Maetri says again.

"And you're full of *kahtopo*," Aevi slurs.

"Enough of this," Tapati brushes Maetri aside. Their spined harnesses rattle as they pass one another. "I have better things to do with my night than listen to your nonsense, *Maetri*. Come," he nods to the others, "*Dynjo* is deep frying mantis legs tonight and I don't want to miss the first batch—you know how she burns them." Aevi and Syno follow their older cousin, snickering and elbowing each other on their way. Soon, their violet heads vanish into the misty jungle, leaving Maetri and Kleeo alone in the *raea* field.

Kleeo gives her brother a patronizing glare, "What was that nonsense about? We almost had them on our side. Now they think you're insane."

Maetri doesn't care. "I have a new idea."

Chapter 15
"Nyno"

Night by night the moon waxes luminous.

Yet Nyno fears her baby's *patu* is waning.

She examines the infant's scalp obsessively each morning and evening, holding her daughter so close she tickles her head with her eyelashes. But somehow, after two moons of streaky growth, the child's *patu* is now fully receding, fading away altogether. Where once several glimmers of violet banded the crown of her head, opaque skin now grows. She's becoming less and less radiant as time progresses, like an ember cooling.

What am I doing wrong?

Nyno hopes she's going crazy, that this is all just some delusion projected by postpartum imagination. But Paelo confirms the worst.

"Its head looks like a bad *pomaeo*," the younger woman says, holding up a dull, moldy melon for comparison. "It's cursed. Like a *Meemmal.*"

Nyno covers her baby again, burning with shame. It's late-afternoon, and they're seated cross-legged within Paelo's cluttered *capku*. A peppery incense burns within little clay jars strung from the thatched, steepled ceiling. Outside, Daeo is busy at work stacking small rocks, one on top of another, for no reason in particular.

"Wh-what should I do?" Nyno is beyond desperate.

"You could start by feeding it yourself," Paelo says, clutching her own infant to her free breast. "Between your leech and mine, my *nunee* are about to fall off."

"You know how much I appreciate you," Nyno swallows a lump of guilt. "I try to nurse her every night myself, I really do. You saw me nurse *Bowi* and *Daeo* when they were born. I had no problems back then. But my body just isn't producing this time, I don't know why."

"You keep saying you appreciate me," Paelo observes, "but I keep wondering when I'm going to start feeling that appreciation."

"You'll feel it in a few moons," Nyno reminds her of their deal. "I still need time to finish making your cloak."

"And the quilt, and the harness," Paelo lists. "And the tunics and soft-clothes for little *Haelo* to grow into. I don't want to make clothing ever again, do you understand me?"

Nyno nods. Really, if given a choice, Paelo is one of the last people she'd ever turn to for help. Imprudent, insulting, and socially inept, Paelo is hated by virtually everyone in the *Uyi.* Plus, she's *Patummal,* a born pariah. But it's because she's so disliked that Nyno knows she won't go gossiping to anyone about her secret. Paelo keeps to herself, hunting and venturing in solitude, shirking community and clothing alike. She only agreed to conceive her own child recently in order to remain off the *Kamaruna* list—rumor has it, she pinned the man down during *Kosharuna* and broke one of his ribs in the process. And now it seems (or at least, when Nyno fulfills her end of their deal) she's going to start wearing clothes too.

"*Momo momo!*" Daeo pokes her head inside the *capku*'s opening. And then, in a single, exasperated breath, she says, "I want to do something important I am tired of being useless."

Nyno quirks, finding the statement odd. "Who says you're useless?"

"I do," Daeo says. Behind her, her tower of rocks has toppled over.

"*Eejo-o kumpa-eptek,*" Nyno recites a core principle. *No one is useless.*

Daeo knows a platitude when she hears one. Rolling her eyes, the little girl turns to Paelo and decides to ask something bold: "*Paelo,* why do we look the same?" She holds her glittering arm next to Paelo's.

Paelo snorts. Nyno gasps, stunned by her daughter's crass question. Of course, both women know the little girl is referring to their matching skin conditions—Paelo and Daeo both glow head-to-toe—but speaking openly about one's overgrown *patu* is a severe taboo.

"Go gather fifty *mabato* spines," Paelo diverts topics with a wry smile. "Your *momo* will need them to start making my new harness."

"Okay!" Daeo darts off.

"Wait—be careful, they're sharp!" Nyno calls after her.

"She knows that," Paelo scoffs. "Your daughter may be *Patummal*, but she's not stupid."

"You don't know my daughter," Nyno sighs, exhausted by everything. She places her bundled newborn in a cradle made of twisted, interlocking *raea* quills. After a restless morning, the child is finally drifting into a nap. "Feed mine when she wakes up, will you?" Nyno says, rising. She dons her spined harness, and then ducks out of the *capku* to follow Daeo.

"Where are you going?" Paelo sounds affronted.

"To gather more feathers for your cloak," Nyno lies.

Crafting, both material and otherwise, is a skill that comes naturally to Nyno. She learned to make her fingers fly when she was just a little girl, watching her older sisters weave feather and thread into intricate, durable textiles. Nowadays, everyone knows of Nyno's particular finesse. People across the *Uyi* speak of her keen eye for detail, her nimble dexterity, her knack for sourcing the highest-quality *areemo*. She's been giving quilts as gifts for as long as anyone can remember—the last born of her own mother's brood, stripping *areemo* bark into thread was the only craft Nyno's mother had time to teach her before she volunteered for *Kamaruna*. Really, the deal Nyno managed to strike with Paelo should work to Nyno's advantage; making clothes is what she'd be doing anyway.

So what am I doing wrong?

A narrow, overgrown path snakes from Paelo's *capku* down to the *Aeo.* Trickling through the rainforest's leafy canopy, sunlight kindles the afternoon mist, transforming walls of moisture into curtains of dazzling, microscopic emeralds. Daeo hasn't traveled far before Nyno catches up to her. The little girl is beginning to wade off-path, into the jungle's tangled detritus, toward a spined *mabato* plant jutting up from the enmeshed vegetation. Taller than a full-grown man, the *mabato* is coated in green, woody thorns, which protrude from its engorged, central stalk, making the juicy plant impenetrable to most animals—including Daeo (each spine is about the length of her extended arm).

"How am I supposed to do this?" Nyno can hear Daeo talking to herself as she approaches.

"Let me show you," Nyno calls, hurrying her high-step across the dense flora.

Daeo startles, and is then immediately embarrassed to see her mother.

"I can do it myself, *momo.* I know how."

"You're going to do it wrong," Nyno says. "You need to know the right method for plucking *mabato* spines if you want them to be usable."

"I know the method," Daeo rolls her eyes. "I have seen you do it enough times."

"Oh." Nyno halts. Her daughter's reply feels like a slap. *How old is* Daeo *now?* "Show me then, if you're so good at it," she challenges the girl.

Daeo pauses, but refuses to doubt herself. Never before has she had an opportunity to impress her mother like this. Usually, the woman is busy with anything else. But now, for the first time in what feels like ages, Daeo has her *momo*'s full, undivided attention, and she doesn't want to ruin it. She steps back to assess the *mabato* plant as a whole, identifying the gaps between each bloom of thorns, the chinks in its teal, organic armor. Then, to Nyno's amazement, the girl carefully reaches her scrawny arm through one of the prickled gaps, wraps her fingers firmly around the base of one particularly long spine, and then twist-pulls in a single, sharp motion like she's been doing it all her life. The spine comes free of the plant, carrying with it a notch of cartilaginous stem tissue attached to its base. Daeo tries to hide her own amazement.

"Nicely done," Nyno says. "But you're twisting in the wrong direction. Look, see how the thorns cluster in circles, and they all slant this way? If you twist to the left, the spine will come out with more of the stem intact. Watch." Nyno joins her daughter beside the plant, and then deftly protracts a spine herself. The elongated thorn comes out with a larger chunk of stem attached to it. Nyno holds it beside the spine Daeo pulled for comparison. "See? This one will be much easier to affix to a harness."

Daeo nods silently. And then she reaches into the plant's spiny foliage for another try. This time, she twist-pulls to the left, and out pops a spine identical to the one her mother pulled.

"You got it," Nyno smiles. And for a moment, she remembers the way her own *momo* cheered when she first learned to strip *areemo* bark. That day, her mother's smile grew so big it took up her whole face. Nyno doesn't remember many details about her mother's appearance, but she remembers that smile, bright as the full moon. Four days afterward, her *momo* would sink to the bottom of the *Aeo.* So much time has passed since that day. *How many moons have you been my daughter?* Nyno now wonders, looking down at Daeo, realizing she'd stopped counting her children's moons sometime during her string of miscarriages. *What else have I forgotten? What else should I teach you?*

"Okay, I can do this by myself now," Daeo says.

"Oh, right," Nyno steps back. Suddenly, her daughter seems far older than possible. "Well, then, when you're done, bring the spines back to me and I'll show you how to embed them into a harness frame, okay?"

"Okay," Daeo sounds indifferent.

"And you don't need to collect fifty of them. Twenty is enough to start."

"*Paelo* wants fifty," Daeo says stubbornly. "I will bring back fifty."

Nyno crosses her arms over her chest, folding them through the spaces created by her own spined harness. "Fine," she says. "We'll use the extras to begin making your first harness."

Daeo's eyes blossom. "Really? I am big enough?" Traditionally, children of the *Uyi* are only allowed to wear soft-clothes, for safety purposes. Despite begging for moons, Bowi had always been deemed too small for his own harness. The idea that she might now get to wear one herself, making her the only spined child in the *Uyi*, seems to Daeo too good to be true. Is this her salvation from the bullies?

"Well, not yet, but soon," Nyno says. "As soon as you're big enough for your first *Kosharuna*, I'll let you wear the harness."

Immediately, Daeo remembers what she fears most about growing up—even the spiniest harness isn't enough to protect a girl during *Kosharuna*. Her salvation is snuffed.

"But first, before I make you your own harness, you need to promise me something."

Daeo sags under life's awful weight, "Whaaat?"

"Oh please, don't act so dramatic. All you need to do is promise me you'll stop playing in the forbidden swamp grounds. *Wyntiko?*"

Daeo blinks, daunted. How can she promise something outside her control?

"It's about time you grow out of those games you used to play with *Bowi*," Nyno continues, emboldened by a reclaimed sense of maternal incumbency. "The swamp is no place for a growing girl. Why do you keep playing out there anyway? You always get yourself stuck. Did you lose something in the swamp? Is that why you're always out there? I can't imagine you really find it all that fun. I want to keep you safe, *Daeo*."

Daeo grits her teeth, scrambling mentally to escape this interrogation. She decides to pivot with another daring question: "*Momo*, when I grow up, will everyone hate me like they hate *Paelo?*"

Nyno chokes, startled again by her daughter's bluntness. "Wh-why would you ask that?"

"Because I am *Patummal*, like her..." Daeo runs her fingers along her face, arms, legs. Can't her mother see?

Nyno grits her teeth, scrambling mentally to escape this interrogation.

"*Momo! Momo!*" A mocking cry comes to her rescue. Nyno recognizes the parrot, *Kreeko*, instantly.

"I need to get back to *Paelo*," she sighs, already beginning her trek back to the *capku*, zigzagging out of the knotted underbrush. "We'll finish this talk later." And then, over her shoulder, "If you lost something in the swamp, maybe I can help you find it!"

Daeo watches the neat, tidy glow of her mother's scalp disappear back up the path toward Paelo's *capku*. Eventually, her *patu* is swallowed altogether by gleaming curls of mist. But in Daeo's mind, aside from Bowi, her mother's care is the only thing she's ever lost.

Act 2

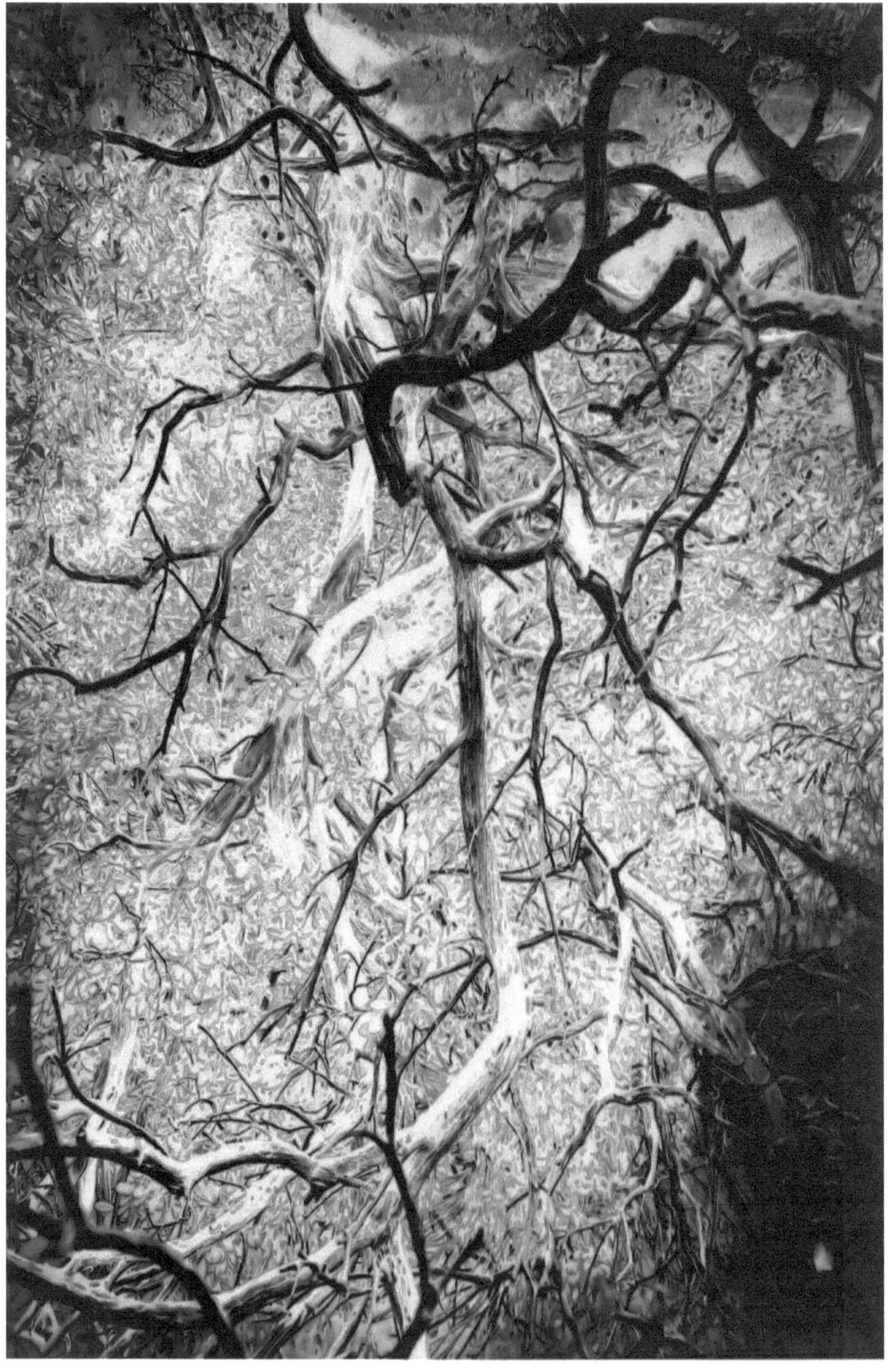

Chapter 16
"Kosharuna"

Yet that's not entirely true.

There's something else Daeo has lost, or is in the process of losing. She just doesn't realize it's started yet. She expects childhood to continue indefinitely. A time period that will probably last about as long as forever. A tier of existence she'll never escape and, when she honestly thinks about it, doesn't really want to.

But already. Huge chunks of it are gone. And there's no going back.

Tonight will be her first *Kosharuna* without Bowi. Normally, they'd hide together in their mother's *capku*, alone while she'd leave to fulfill her adult duties. Cuddling, he'd sing songs to her throughout the night, wonderful, musical tales of adventurers on quests through the jungle, and the fantastical creatures they'd encounter. He'd make it all up in his head, imagining myth into truth as he sang. She knew none of his stories were real. Or even plausible. The heroes in his songs were always too perfect, too clever, too convenient. But the logistics never mattered. The siblings could escape any inescapable snare so long as Bowi's melodies captivated Daeo's attention. His voice was what kept her safe from the screaming and wailing outside.

But tonight, she's all alone for *Kosharuna*.

Well, not completely alone—she's been left in charge of her newborn sister while their mother leaves to participate in the ceremony. Little comfort.

"I'd stay with you if I could," Nyno always says before exiting. "But I can't." And then she's gone. Only to return well past midnight, typically bloody, bruised, or limping.

For reasons that seem sacred and unquestionable, participation in the full-moon *Kosharuna* ritual is mandatory for all adults in the *Uyi*. Daeo has no idea what goes on exactly during the monthly ritual. But from what she hears outside, she imagines it must be horrific. Sounds of it bombard the *capku*'s outer layer, barks and hollers from men gone savage, men strong enough to smash through the *capku*'s leathery walls and trample her underfoot if they wanted. Daeo has never actually seen Maetri harm her mother, but she knows that he does. And she knows that it happens outside. All over the *Uyi*. During *Kosharuna*.

The *capku*'s opening flap is threaded with ringed *areemo* knots, which can be fastened to tie the entrance shut. Daeo inspects them thoroughly after her mother leaves, ensuring each link of twine is snug and secure. Indeed, she's safely sealed. Behind her, the baby burbles sleepily. Something like jealousy strikes Daeo then—the infant has no idea what's about to happen.

The night outside is already hostile and stormy, the full moon suppressed behind black, electrified clouds. Horizontal rain pelts the *capku*'s southern side. Gusts of wind rattle its conical structure, which tugs against its fungal-rooted anchors like a swaying tree. But Daeo takes no comfort in the white noise. She knows that in time it won't matter, that the adults will proceed with *Kosharuna* regardless, and the men will simply take the wind's howl as a challenge. Sooner or later, *Kosharuna* will drown out the storm.

Either that or the *Fae* will:

"*XXXXXXXXXXXXXXXXXXXXXXXXXXXXXX*"

Daeo hears their arrival, the sound of them hovering in the rainy sky. For further reasons beyond Daeo's understanding, the *Fae* sojourn to the *Uyi* every *Kosharuna* to observe the human ceremony. Daeo figures it must have something to do with the full moon, she just doesn't know what.

If Bowi were here, this would be the point at which he'd begin to sing.

But tonight, Daeo doesn't have a brother. She has only herself. For a fleeting moment, she reaches within to find her own voice, but falters—when she tries to recall her favorite song of Bowi's, she can't remember any of his words or characters. She can't even remember his voice. She has no distraction, no defense, no plan. She knew this night would come eventually—why hadn't she prepared? Helpless, she falls to the floor in a fetal position, directly in the *capku*'s center, reduced to a whimpering tremble as the shrieks outside begin.

Daeo knows they come from women. She can't recognize any one voice among the screams—they ring from all directions and blend together in a hypnotic, tortured chorus. But she thinks she can hear her mother out there, a resistant note, grating against the rest. It sounds desperate. Powerless. Surrounded. Soon, the wailing chorus swells to consume it, and then every voice bursts into its own distinct note, all of them grating against each other in a sort of chaos that forces tears from Daeo's eyes. She tries to shut them, but behind her eyelids she sees her mother's scream as an aural image, her face transfigured by terror, pain, blood.

It's happening—right outside—her mother—so many women—everyone screaming—Daeo can't escape the sound.

This is the part of the song when Bowi's hero would arrive.

But there are no heroes tonight. Just her own two hands to cover her ears.

Beside her, the baby stirs in its cradle, roused by the ruckus. Flashes of lightning and the pervading glow of outdoor lichen penetrate the *capku*'s translucent walls. The glossy feather blanket tucked around the infant's tiny, squirming body used to belong to Daeo—whose eyes fall on it now. Vision blurry with tears, reality distorted, Daeo remembers how soft that blanket used to feel. She used to sleep with it every night. Her mother had originally made it for Bowi, but then gave it to her when she was born. Up until two moons ago, it'd been hers ever since...

Daeo is compelled now to touch the blanket, to wrap it around her glowing body, to bury her face in its plush, familiar folds. Instead, she picks up her blanket-wrapped sister, who is now fully awake and beginning to cry as well.

"Oh—no, no, no, shh—shh," Daeo whispers through her own convulsing sobs. "Everything is okay, everything is okay, everything is okay." She's talking as much to herself as to the baby.

And somehow, like the baby understands her words, she stops squirming. She settles her patchy head in the crook of Daeo's elbow. Blinking, Daeo realizes this is the first time she's ever held her sister. Yet their molding to one another feels so natural. So welcome. So instant.

"Everything is okay, we are okay, you are okay, I am okay," Daeo keeps whispering, though she barely believes it herself. Outside, male voices tear into the wailing chorus—shouts and yells, snarling peals of laughter. Thunder roars against the *Fae*'s all-encompassing buzz. But when Daeo opens her eyes again, the baby is smiling up at her, content. To her innocent, blanket-covered ears, the frantic voices and chaotic noises are just bursts of irregular soundwaves, air syncopating at random intervals. It all means nothing. The warm support of Daeo's body is the only truth the baby knows right now.

And in a sudden rush of realization, Daeo no longer feels alone.

She is for this child what Bowi was for her.

Comfort. Protection. Unity. Trust.

"You are my sister," Daeo says, breathless, understanding for the first time what it means to be an older sibling. Is this really the first time she's looked at the newborn? Their mother always keeps her hidden. Now, the baby's eyes gaze up into her own, pupils deep and dark as fresh soil, ready to absorb. Her curly wisps of hair are black like Daeo's. The left side of her face is a checkered pattern of tan and olive freckling, while the skin on her right half is all dark brown. A calico cross between Bowi and herself. She is beautiful, her camouflage captivating.

Envy—love—rapture—Daeo wants to hold her sister in this blanket forever.

Finally, the outside noises begin to fade away—not in volume, but in Daeo's perception. She is here. She is safe. She is not alone. At some point, her body begins to rock gently back and forth, movement born from parasympathetic impulse. And in the back of her mind, one of Bowi's familiar melodies emerges from the fog. She has him here with her too. They're all together.

Still clutching her baby sister, who's begun to drift back to sleep against her chest, Daeo lulls herself into a meditative stupor. Back and forth, back and forth. Eventually, she's unconscious. Asleep. Curled up with the baby on the ground.

Nyno doesn't notice them when she returns, much later. Her head is splitting, aching from concussion—someone's fist collided with her left eye at some point during the ceremony. She tastes blood, but not much. Her vision is still fuzzy, nighttime colors vivid and dancing in her periphery. She's just cognizant enough to retie the *capku*'s entrance shut behind her. She knows sleep is the only remedy for the *Kosharuna* mushroom she ingested during the ceremony. Within heartbeats, she's unconscious on the ground too, sprawled only an arm's length away from her sleeping daughters.

Outside, the full moon drifts across the sky. Its light gradually overpowers the dissipating storm clouds. The night falls silent. The *Fae* have long since departed, and the misty sky is otherwise vacant. Every human is asleep. The *Uyi*, though luminous and green, sounds empty of life. Like the jungle itself has slipped into a coma, numb after such a riotous night.

Daeo awakes to the pale aquamarine of dawn. Her jaw aches—she's been clenching her teeth all night. Her back is sore from sleeping on the ground. But her baby sister is still sound asleep in her arms, which makes her smile. Carefully, quietly, she places the sleeping infant back in the cradle of *raea* quills. It's the same cradle she and Bowi used to sleep in as babies too, but only Nyno knows that. Daeo notices her mother when she turns around: Still unconscious on the ground, there's a dark welt beneath her left eye socket, and her lower lip is cracked with drying blood.

Standing over her, Daeo wonders if her mother is now pregnant again. After all, *Kosharuna*, the children are told, is how babies are made.

Tension in her bladder prompts Daeo to venture outside to the waste pit. It's early, the sun not yet visible through the trees. But she isn't nervous as she unties the *capku*'s opening; Daeo knows no one will be awake this early, especially not after last night. Except perhaps Bowi, Daeo imagines. She remembers he'd often rise early after *Kosharuna*, before the sun, and slip outside the *capku*. She never knew what he was doing all those dawns, but now she wonders if he's awake too, up in the *Teerta*'s cave, breathing in the same morning dew that fills her nostrils now...

There's a small walking path behind her mother's *capku*, which leads through the jungle to their concealed waste pit. Daeo makes her way in that direction, but something catches her eye, something skirting through the treeline overhead. It's moving quickly, high within a kapok's understory. Silver and striped, the creature seems to glide across the lichen-crusted branches like something from a dream. Then it pauses for a moment, and Daeo catches a lucky view of its face. Pointy ears. Bulging, green eyes.

Radial symmetry. It's the same animal she's seen before, that night not long ago.

And then Eeao is gone.

And Daeo is left staring.

Chapter 17
"Tarma-ako"

Technically, Tagi is only required to visit the human nest during *Kunjaruna*, the new moon. That's when his services are valued by those in power.

Otherwise, casualties from the *Kosharuna* full moon must seek out his help themselves—generally, bloodied women will trudge up to his cave the day after, desperate for daubs of his medicinal *reewo* poultice, or his expertise resetting broken bones (Tagi has a particular knack for relocating wrists and shoulders). He hopes for a decent turnout after this most recent *Kosharuna*, an opportunity to show Bowi his wide range of first-aid tricks. He's even pre-readied a stack of dry, flat boards for making splints.

But the next morning, no one arrives.

"Odd," Tagi rubs the sagging folds of his neck, disappointed. "Normally there's a line."

"Why don't we go down to the nest?" Bowi suggests from within the cave, still waking up.

"The *Teerta* is only required to go down during *Kunjaruna.*"

"Okay... But can't we still go anyway? What if someone is too injured to walk all the way up here?"

Tagi shrugs. "I'm not required." He then turns to proceed with his morning activities. Bowi watches the old man stoke the fire pit beneath his cauldron, and then toss fresh-ground *reewo* into its simmering broth. Eeao is nowhere to be seen, but Tagi isn't concerned about her. To him, independence is a virtue.

"What is your tongue craving this *una, hmm?*" Tagi asks, obscured behind his steaming brew. "I could fetch us some fresh *camraea* eggs to boil? Or perhaps toss a pair of grasshopper legs into the stew? It's important to eat protein every *una* when you wake up, *Bowi.*"

"Somebody's always hurt after *Kosharuna*," Bowi says. "Maybe we should go check?"

"They'll come if they need me," Tagi shrugs again.

"What if they're too injured?"

Tagi rolls his eyes. "If they can't make the hike here, or if they don't have anyone to carry them, then... Well... How should I say it... Nature is as nature does? *Tarma-ako*."

"That's awful!"

"That's life."

Seven moons, says the gnat.

Tagi ignores it. "Think about your own situation, when you first came here," he continues. "How many people helped carry you up to my cave?"

Bowi shuts his mouth. It's true, he did require assistance from several others to complete the hike. But would his health ever have deteriorated in the first place if he wasn't required to wait for *Kunjaruna* just to receive *pomaeo* infusions? Perhaps he'd have been stronger if a certain *Teerta* had come down to hydrate him more frequently? "What about people who don't have anyone to carry them?" Bowi argues instead, skirting the proximal discomfort of his own experience.

"If no one will carry them then... They aren't worth carrying."

"But how can you judge that?"

"I don't need to judge," Tagi says, dicing several *voreeko* (long, gourd-shaped vegetables, with the consistency of zucchini) and tossing them into his stew. "I trust the nest knows that if someone is worth carrying, they will be carried up here."

Bowi pauses. He's still sitting on the feather mattress Tagi made for him, looking out at the morning—a vignette of foggy verdure framed by the cave's jagged mouth. "What if no one knows the person needs help?" he's thinking about his mother now, all the *Kosharuna*s he witnessed her crawl back into the *capku*, alone, weeping silently to herself. She even handled her miscarriages by herself—though, one time, Bowi followed a trail of blood to the waste pit behind their *capku*... The feral terror he witnessed that day still echoes through his body.

Meanwhile, Tagi decides in favor of the grasshopper legs. He stalks quietly toward a zebra-striped shrub, where several of the giant insects lounge on broad, veiny leaves. "When you've seen as much as I have," he says, low under his breath, "you learn that suffering is inevitable. It's everywhere, in everything. *Tarma-ako*. From the moment life begins, so does decay."

"What does that even mean?" Bowi lowers his voice too.

"It means..." Tagi pauses, holding up one arm, hand poised like the mouth of a snake. Then, without warning, he strikes at the bush, quicker than Bowi can blink. Several grasshoppers flutter into the air, bouquets of green-speckled wings shimmering like leaves blown through mist. But in Tagi's hand, he holds up a captured grasshopper. Using his forefinger and thumb, he snaps off its plum-sized head. "It means you save what you can save, and let go of what should be let go. For the benefit of the whole."

"But what if—"

"There are no what ifs," Tagi is growing impatient. "This cave is our station. It's our duty as *Teerta* to remain here and study *ynsyna*. Simple as that. Besides, you don't really want to hike all the way down to the *Aeo* today, do you? In this heat? *Kahtopo*," Tagi waves his hand dismissively. He then begins de-legging his decapitated grasshopper, prying its long hind legs from its torpedo body with surgical precision. As he tosses each stick-like appendages into his brew, the feet remain poking up through the stew's bubbling surface. Bowi watches them dance around the cauldron's lip. Eventually, as the stew cooks, the six legs sink lower and lower, softening until disappearing altogether into the steaming concoction. Already, Bowi can smell the protein-rich addition—a savory, nutty aroma that triggers his appetite.

"Is *tyrkuna* almost ready?" Bowi asks, referring to *breakfast*.

"*Ah-ha*, not so keen to hike down to the nest now that you smell my cooking, *eh?*" Tagi teases.

Bowi doesn't find the comment amusing. Looking down at himself, he sees little more than a meager, bloated belly protruding from his own skeletal frame. "Forgive me for waking up hungry," Bowi returns.

"Yes, yes, the stew is nearly done, no need to get defensive," Tagi realizes his misstep.

Bowi rises from bed, throwing on his oversized *areemo* tunic. Its sleeveless cutouts droop over the sides of his bony arms; he tries in vain to cuff the fibrous material over his shoulders, to give it a snugger fit, but the fabric doesn't fold neatly. An ember in his firestorm of internal shame, his mother had always insisted on making all his clothes extra large, saying it would encourage his body to grow. As if this futile tunic she made countless moons ago ever did any good. At least now his belly is beginning to fill out its baggy midsection.

"I still think we should go down to the nest today," Bowi says, emerging from the cave to join Tagi beside his cauldron. "After we eat *tyrkuna*."

"Enough about the nest," Tagi shoos the boy away. "You'll spend the day here learning *ynsyna* and that's that."

"I already know all the *ynsyna*."

Tagi laughs. "Oh really? You think you know all the *ynsyna?*"

"Yes."

"There's more to learning *ynsyna* than just memorizing all the characters."

"Like what?"

"Like what?" Tagi mocks. "Alright, you little expert. Build your name. Right there in the dirt. Spell it out using *ynsyna*. Go on, show me how much you know."

Panic wallops Bowi in the chest. He feels stupid, ignorant. He'd spoken too fast.

"That's what I thought," Tagi smirks. "It's wonderful that you've memorized all the characters—and I even like that little tune you created to sing them—but next you need to learn how to use the characters to build words. *Ynsyna* is a method of communication, after all. Here, keep stirring for me, I'll show you how to build your name."

Tagi hands Bowi his ladle (a polished, wizened piece of mahogany), and then retrieves the staff he used the other day from inside the cave. He drags its pointed end through the dirt again, drawing two symbols on the soft ground: A circle and a crescent moon.

"What does this one sound like?" Tagi points to the circle on the left.

"*-oh.*"

"Good. And this one?" he points to the waxing crescent.

"*-ee.*"

"Good. Now, say the two sounds together."

Bowi pauses to think. "*-ohwee?*"

"Yes, very good, but shorten the *-ee* to emphasize the first syllable," Tagi says. "See how when you say the two sounds together, your mouth naturally forms the *-ww* sound to bridge the connection? That means we don't need to use the *-ww* modification mark to build your name. However, we do need to modify the beginning sound with the *-bb* modification mark, so that it sounds like *-bohwee.* Remember what that one looks like?"

Bowi nods. "A vertical line, through the top of the symbol."

"Correct. And we draw it up here, on top of the *-oh*, like this," Tagi bisects the circle's upper arc with a small, vertical dash. "There. Now it says *-bohwee*. That's what your name looks like."

Bowi stares, analyzing the characters in the dirt. Their distinct composition, the pattern they form side by side, sort of looks to Bowi like a fat beetle with a single, tiny antenna protruding from its head. He tries to assign some bit of his identity to it, to enmesh this visual symbol with the intimate sound of his mother calling his name, but the sensory crossover feels awkward and entirely inadequate.

"That's it?" Bowi asks, handing the ladle back to Tagi.

"What? Not satisfied with your own name?"

"No, I mean, I just expected..." Bowi trails off. "I don't know what I expected..."

Tagi spoons out a chunk of boiled *voreeko*, and then brings the ladle to his lips, blowing before tasting. "Mmm," he chews in satisfaction. "Well, I expect you to fill your belly with this delicious *tyrkuna*, and then spend the rest of the day practicing *ynsyna*. Sound agreeable?"

"Fine, I'll stay here and learn *ynsyna*," Bowi shirks away in defeat. He fetches two stone bowls from within the cave, and Tagi fills them generously with steaming brew. Aromatic steam erupts in Bowi's face, enticing his palette. His stomach yawns dreamily. Still, he can't escape the mental image of his mother suffering, alone, blood everywhere...

As he and Tagi sit down beneath the cave's arching mouth to eat, he comes up with a proposal. "How about if I stay here in the cave, learning *ynsyna* like you want me to," Bowi says, "will you go down to the nest today? Please? I really think you should go and check to make sure everyone is okay after last night. There could be someone bleeding and—"

"Why are you so insistent?" Tagi chuckles. "Have I not made myself clear? The *Teerta* is only responsible for the nest during *Kunjaruna*. It's *Tarma-ako*. Drop it."

"But why? It's not like you're busy. You're never busy. You spend all your time up here in your cave, tending your *heersu* and carving your *ynsyna*, but—"

"EVERYTHING I do is important," Tagi snarls, suddenly enraged. "Just now, you couldn't even build your own name. You know nothing. Your knowledge is but a drop in the *Aeo* compared to mine. Therefore, I suggest you bite your tongue and listen to me when I speak. I'm trying to teach you the things you need to know, child. Now, I've said it several times already, but I'll say it once more: WE ONLY GO DOWN TO THE NEST DURING *KUNJARUNA*. Is that clear?"

Bowi nods, too frightened to do anything else. Tagi has never spoken to him so aggressively. The contrast is shocking. Somewhere nearby, a frog lets out a languid, wet *croooak*. In his hands, Bowi's bowl is still half-full of stew, and he hasn't even taken a bite of his grasshopper leg, which floats submerged in the broth like a twisted, chitinous noodle.

Yet despite his prior appetite, Bowi's stomach clenches. He can't eat anymore. His heart is stuck on his mother. Her face fills his mind's eye. He sees her freckled cheeks, her mismatched eyes, her bloody nose, her cracked lips, the bruises around her neck. And then Daeo, what is she doing? She's all alone. How is she coping? *Someday*, his mother used to tell them, *you'll both be big enough to participate in* Kosharuna *too*.

Bowi still doesn't even know what happens during *Kosharuna*, or how his now being *Teerta* will affect future participation. But he's very familiar with the sensation bubbling up his esophagus now.

"*Tarma-ako*," Tagi mutters, returning to his bowl. "A compound word—tricky, but I'll teach you how to build those too."

Like a dormant volcano suddenly awoken, Bowi vomits *tyrkuna* all over his name.

Chapter 18
"Tagi"

Never one to let a perfectly-seasoned grasshopper leg go to waste, Tagi finishes Bowi's bowl of stew while he ponders the boy's resurgent illness.

From a physical perspective, his symptoms don't make much sense. The boy isn't allergic to anything—meaning, he didn't suffer any adverse reactions to the variety of specimens Tagi tested on him. Roots, vegetables, herbs, minerals. Tagi's most recent round of tests, which he'd administered to Bowi several nights ago, included all varieties of fungi found around the *Uyi* (except for the ceremonial *aruna* mushrooms, of course). None of the organisms made the boy sick upon ingestion. Instead, the boy has happily gorged himself on everything (meal and specimen) Tagi has presented to him. Now, given this new bout of vomiting after such a long period of remission, Tagi suspects the boy's ailment may be purely psychological.

So the question remains... Why?

After laying Bowi down to rest inside the cave, and then venturing into the jungle on several errands, the old man is now returning, trekking through the underbrush surrounding his marshy *pomaeo* patch. He has two melons in tow, one under each arm. Above him, beyond the jungle's vaulted, chittering canopy, the clouds are mild and vaporous, the sun a wan beacon buoyed in cerulean fog. Macaws the size of men squawk down at him from treetops, clucking their monstrous beaks and rustling their scarlet plumes in a way Tagi imagines they intend to be threatening. Really, he finds the looming *kynaea* more ridiculous than anything else. He knows they wouldn't dare swoop to ground level; their bulky wings aren't suited to pierce the jungle's dense understory.

According to a passage of *ynsyna*, back inside the cavern, carved by some ancient *Teerta* who was obsessed with bird species, most of the *Uyi*'s flighted avians are aerial hunters simply because they're too big to penetrate the rainforest's impervious shrub layer. *Even the hungriest* kynaea, one part of the engraving reads, *is powerless against the worm that remains grounded.* In Tagi's mind, all these birds are useless background jabber, airheads worth only the feathers they drop. The only three bird species that matter to him (and to most other humans of the *Uyi*) are the meaty, flightless *raea*, their smaller, egg-laying cousins, the *camraea*, and the ever-vigilant *momo* parrots. Otherwise, bird utility ends there.

On one of his earlier errands, Tagi went around collecting fresh *camraea* quills, which he now plans to scour into new transfusion needles. Returning to his cave, he kindles the fire pit beneath his cauldron to begin the scouring process. Within the cave's darkness, Bowi continues to moan.

"Still nauseous?" Tagi calls, clambering up the outside lip of the cave's mouth. The boy's response is incoherent.

Perched above the cave, wedged between the bouldering mountainside and the jutting trunk of a tall, broadleaved fern, hangs Tagi's water-filtration device. Essentially a bowl-shaped rain garden reconstituted into a mycofilter, it consists of a suspended net basket, made from tightly-knit *areemo* fibers. Housed within the basket is a bed of soil, blooming with pastel-colored mushrooms and other, origami-like folds of mycoflora. Beneath the hanging basket, thin strands of mycelial roots dangle, fungal tubules that have burrowed through the nutrient-dense *areemo* netting in search of evermore material to repurpose for their own growth. Little do they know, Tagi is the one repurposing them: Positioned beneath the basket, a stone basin catches the purified rainwater that drips periodically from their hydraulic root tips. Filtered through layered soil, *areemo* fiber, and bionetworks of mycoremediation, the rainwater Tagi collects from this filter is the purest in the *Uyi*.

But of course, Tagi can't take full credit for the ingenuity. Instructions for making the device, right down to soil and mycoflora specifications (which were originally developed during the *Genetic Revolution*, in response to that aforementioned water crisis), are inscribed within his ancient cave. Over the course of his life, Tagi has recreated the device more than a dozen times, refurbishing it whenever the mushroom roots devour too much of their home basket. He has yet to show it to Bowi.

Seven moons.

Tagi sees his own reflection in the basin's crystal water. The lines under his eyes, the wrinkles around his mouth, the long bridge of his weathered nose. When did his eyebrows become so white? Tagi sighs, heaving his stone basin toward the rocky ledge over the cave's upper lip. He tips the basin over the edge, pouring filtered water into his cauldron below. Water cascades, splashing, spilling into his well-positioned stone kettle. The fire underneath sizzles from overspill, but Tagi's aim is refined enough that he manages to fill his cauldron without quelching the fire pit beneath. Once finished, he maneuvers the half-full basin back into place beneath his mycofilter, and then he leaps down from the perch. His knees and feet spring with nimble alacrity upon landing. He's barely winded from the physical exertion of moving a heavy, water-filled basin. He feels as young as ever.

Who was that face in his reflection?

Seven moons.

Inside the cave, he hears Bowi begin another round of vomiting. *Once he begins, he's unable to stop.* Standing over his cauldron, Tagi brings a ladleful of filtered water to his lips. It's still cool. He lets it trickle into his mouth, down the back of his tongue, water so brilliantly pure it tastes like mist evaporating after a thunderstorm. He fills his ladle again, and then joins Bowi inside the cave while his cauldron continues heating.

"It's going to be okay, *Bowi*," Tagi sits beside the boy, who's hunched over his makeshift bed, drooling vomit into the same stone bucket Tagi gave him on his first day. Sweat drips down the boy's forehead; patches of his tunic are soaked sour from perspiration. Tagi wets a spare *areemo* rag with water from his ladle, and then uses it to wipe Bowi's mouth clean. "Lie back," he coaxes the boy to recline.

"My stomach," Bowi groans, clutching his arms around his abdomen. Too weak to resist Tagi's nudging, Bowi lies down in bed.

"Relax your muscles," Tagi says, taking Bowi's hands and unwinding them from around his sides. He then drips cool water from his ladle onto the boy's forehead.

Bowi winces as water trickles past his eyes. "What are you doing?"

"Trying to cool your body temperature," Tagi says. "I think you are panicking, *orynam*, and, as a result, overheating. It's a self-destructive feedback loop." Empty of water, Tagi trades his ladle for a wide piece of dried frond (which he uses as flooring inside his cave), and then uses it to fan air onto Bowi's glistening face. "Focus on the cool sensation," Tagi says. "Let it relax your body. Shift your awareness from the pain in your stomach to the cool air on your face..."

All of this feels futile to Tagi. Paradoxical to his pharmaceutical nature. Sure, he's read a few passages of *ynsyna* about these kinds of ailments—ancient accounts of illnesses that exist only in the mind, resistant to traditional forms of treatment, symptoms contingent on mental wellbeing. But he always considered those anecdotes akin to old-wive's tales. Soft science, conducted by *Teerta*'s with an inferior understanding of cold, hard medicine. In all his moons, Tagi has never met an illness he couldn't blame on external, organic forces. Yet now, in front of him, Bowi's groaning gradually softens to a whimper. The boy's eyes remain closed, but his affect relaxes. Soon, he begins to shiver.

"Too cold?"

"No," Bowi says. "It feels good. I think it's helping. Thank you."

Tagi smiles warily. *Indeed, all in his mind... So now what?*

After a while, Bowi's shivering turns to snoring, and Tagi hears his cauldron begin to boil. He spends the rest of his day scouring the quills he collected earlier, transforming them into hypodermic needles in case Bowi needs a *pomaeo* infusion later. *His illness might reside in his mind, but it could still very well kill him.*

At some point toward evening, as sundown triggers the *Uyi*'s lichen crust to oxidize and luminesce, a mellow drizzle brings Eeao scampering home. She appears from the misty trees, darting across intertwined branches, fur wet and spiky, a shadow in the glowing canopy. Tagi spots her immediately.

"*Eeao,*" he calls up to her.

"*Eeao,*" she responds, gliding to ground level and slithering between his ankles in swift, fluid motion.

He's glad to hear her familiar chirp.

She's glad to find him without the boy.

Once Tagi's finished scouring enough quills to infuse Bowi every day for the next seven moons (if need be), he refills his cauldron to begin preparing supper. He doubts Bowi will have an appetite when he awakes. And even if he does, *pomaeo* juice should be the prescribed medicine. But just in case (and because it's what he's gotten used to doing), Tagi boils an extra *camraea* egg and stews enough *voreeko* to feed them both.

While the old man cooks, Eeao prowls around the cave's entrance—she can smell the boy sleeping inside, but she wants to rid the zone of any further pests. She satisfies herself on a couple of crunchy, alien-headed ants (hefty descendents of *Gigantiops*), pouncing too quickly for the oversized insects to spring away. Each shiny black ant, when pummeled into the ground, is larger than Eeao's entire face.

"*Teerta?*" Bowi rouses when Tagi starts ladling fresh stew into his bowl.

"*Bowi*," Tagi sets his bowl on a rock ledge, and then hurries into the cave to check on the boy. "How are you feeling? Ready to try some *pomaeo* juice?"

Bowi pushes himself into a sitting position. His *areemo* tunic drapes around his body like a blanket. In the dim light of their *patu*s, the boy's face is gaunt, posture depleted, eyes already yellowing. "I don't know. I feel okay. But I think you should infuse me, just to be safe."

"Why don't you try drinking?" Tagi presses, intent on making progress.

"I don't want to puke again," Bowi says. "I'm scared."

"No need to be scared," Tagi pats the boy's back, trying not to sound impatient. *Keep him calm.* "If you throw up again, then I'll infuse you. But I don't think that'll happen. I think you'll enjoy the flavor of *pomaeo* juice. You've had a nice, restful afternoon sleeping, and now your body probably wants some nutrition. Think of how sweet it will taste."

That last comment seems to stir something in Bowi. Elementally, beyond the anxiety burning his stomach, the boy is dehydrated, his throat hoarse and raw from vomiting all day. When he speaks, his tongue is so dry it cleaves to the roof of his mouth like an overcooked piece of *raea* jerky. He's desperately thirsty.

"Okay. I'll try drinking."

"Very good," Tagi smiles, pleased with the boy's compliance. *Perhaps he's still young enough that his mind can be remolded.* The old man fetches one of the two melons he plucked earlier today, both of which he left bobbing in the water basin he keeps inside his cave. Bringing it back to Bowi, the child's eyes fixate hungrily on the fruit.

"Here," Tagi hands it to him. "Drink slowly. One sip at a time."

Bowi holds the *pomaeo* in his lap. He's familiar with the conflict before him—voracious thirst battering a fortified dam of nausea. He yearns for juice, cool water, anything to wash the day-old grime from his mouth and soothe his fiery stomach. Yet fear lingers; at any moment, whatever he drinks might come rushing back up. Knowing this simple act could trigger immediate punishment, Bowi hesitates with the fruit in his hands.

"Go on," Tagi encourages, biting back his impatience. "You can do this."

Bowi nods resolutely, and then pierces the fruit's skin with his thumbnail. Pale, green water spurts through the puncture-hole. Cool as it dribbles down his fingers, the juice smells sweet and inviting. Bowi raises the melon to his lips, and then draws a tentative sip. Flavor bursts on his tongue, pleasant and reassuring, diffusing through his mouth and sinuses.

The first sip goes down easily.

After several slow breaths, Bowi takes another, larger sip. From the back of his mind, a melody drifts into his consciousness, the new one he's created to help him memorize the *ynsyna* characters. He begins humming the tune as he takes his third sip.

"Keep drinking," Tagi says, stepping out to retrieve his own bowl. "I'm going to eat my stew before it gets cold."

Bowi continues humming and sipping while the old man finishes his supper outside the cave. The combined pleasures of flavor and melody absorb Bowi's senses, overpowering his lingering nausea. Finally, he feels at ease.

Meanwhile, his hum produces a high-pitched vibration throughout the cave that tickles Eeao's stubby nose whiskers. She's immediately suspicious. What is the child doing? Why is it making that funny noise? As though drawn by an alluring siren, she approaches the boy carefully.

Bowi's fifth sip is his longest one yet. He's getting bolder, more eager. The pain in his stomach is gone, like a flame doused. He's overcome it. Soon, his sips become chugs. He can't help it. He's humming and drinking, drinking and humming. And it feels wonderful. Around his ninth chug, he notices Eeao sniffing his foot. Sitting on his bed, one leg dangling over the side of the mattress, he watches while the feline takes particular interest in a scab on his heel. To Eeao, the child smells vaguely familiar, like a faraway place she can just barely remember visiting... This is the closest she's ever observed him.

To Bowi, the kitten is a bizarre, twitchy fiend. He stares at her with interest, but remains still, resisting the urge to reach down and touch her fur. Fiend though she is, her wide-eyed face is charming. He lets her sniff up to his ankle, and then to his shin. Her whiskers tickle his bare, goose-pimpled skin. He smiles, continuing to hum.

"Perhaps she's starting to like you."

Neither Eeao nor Bowi noticed Tagi's reentrance, and now his sudden voice startles them both. Eeao bolts to the elevated safety of her moss-blanketed cranny. Bowi's smile collapses.

"Aww," the boy sighs. Now all he can see of the kitten are her luminous, green eyes staring down at him from her lofty crevice.

"It's alright, she'll come back to you in time," Tagi says. "You're learning her language."

"Am I?" Bowi doesn't feel so confident. Then again, he's nearly finished drinking an entire *pomaeo* melon and his stomach feels great. "Well... Maybe I am doing something right."

"Keep it up," Tagi smiles, wondering if perhaps he should touch the boy's shoulder reassuringly, or offer him some kind of congratulatory hug. Something about this moment feels like an accomplishment for both of them.

When is affection appropriate?

Instead, the old man decides to go back outside, extinguish his fire pit, and clean out his cauldron. The evening's earlier drizzle has since stopped, but the night is surprisingly chill, cooled by a gusty, south-bound wind. Tagi can smell heavier rains coming. Mistrustful of the air around him, he hurries into the jungle to relieve himself. Indeed, halfway through his business, the weather betrays him. Lightning and thunder. Raindrops the size of *pomaeo*. By the time he returns to his cave, soaked and shivering, Bowi is asleep again, the boy's parasympathetic nervous system busy repairing itself. Standing on tip-toes, Tagi peers into Eeao's dark cranny.

"Thank you," he whispers to the purring kitten.

He thinks she wants to help Bowi too.

Eeao thinks they're fattening the boy up to eat.

Chapter 19
"Eeao"

Because why else keep the child alive?

It's the only logical conclusion Eeao can fathom.

Save for its burgeoning caloric value, the child offers little use elsewise. It eats all day and sleeps all night, never lifting a finger to hunt or explore on its own. Surely the old man is toying with their food, intending to butcher it for a later feast.

This new epiphany restores Eeao's sense of confidence around the cave. Her resentful slink rebounds to a high-footed strut. She resumes sleeping on Tagi's chest every night, and discovers she thoroughly enjoys eyeing their sumptuous prey as it snores beside them. It's a long game they're playing, the old man and the kitten. A sport of cunning calculation. The slaughter will be well worth the wait. With each passing day, the kitten's respect for the old man's artistry deepens.

Meanwhile, to keep her senses sharp, mind agile, and belly full during this waiting period, Eeao continues her solo hunts through the *Uyi*, traversing the wide jungle valley by day in search of whatever amusing treat she can find. Lately, she's gotten a taste for *kynaea*, the giant descendants of macaws. She found a lucky catch several days ago, recently dead from natural causes, the feathered carcass still fresh and tangled in its own treetop nest. It made for a delicious buffet—she returned to it several times that day, cleaning its entire skeleton of anything edible. Now, she wants to try hunting a live one.

She often sees them soaring across the rainforest's lofty emergent layer, high up where the treetops fade into clouds. Their colorful wingspans—cobalt and jade, garnet and gold—stretch five times the length of her own kitten body. How they manage to keep their pterosaurian bodies aloft,

Eeao has no clue. But she isn't deterred. She's gotten a taste of their blood and she wants more.

One day, after carefully observing the birds' aerial patterns, the way their long tails flutter vulnerably upon landing and takeoff, Eeao makes it her mission to catch one. She devises a plan. Perhaps if she can position herself on the right tree branch, and jump from the right angle, she'll be able to leap with just enough force to snag one of their tails midair and bring it crashing to the forest floor with her. The fall won't phase her; she's survived higher. And once grounded, the bird yanked completely out of its element, wings rendered useless, her size disadvantage won't matter anymore. The feast will be hers. She's sure of it.

So she finds a sparse patch of jungle around noontime, an area with clear sky overhead and plenty of low foliage to keep her concealed. Several *kynaea* fly in lazy circles. The kitten creeps through thickets of xate and vibrant orchids, hidden from the sky though it stretches open above her. One of the birds, cloaked in gleaming sapphire feathers, alights in a nearby kapok tree. Eeao locks onto her target. She beelines across the forest floor, making straight for the tree's massive trunk. Dangling from its lower branches, several moss-covered liana vines sway in the afternoon breeze. Tunnel-visioned, eager for blood and feathers, Eeao springs for one of the vines, intending to climb it into the kapok's lowest rung of branches. But when her claws connect, they sink into something unfamiliar.

The vine slips off the tree, curling in on itself. Eeao feels a hard, scaly surface beneath her toe pads—like lizard skin, but thicker, fleshier. She realizes it's not a vine as they fall together—the way it wraps itself around her body midair, moving freely on its own.

They hit the ground.

She's tangled, coiled.

A muscular vice contracts around her ribcage, squeezing the air from her lungs.

"*Eeaoooo—*"

Her skeleton collapses in on itself, as though liquified. She can't breathe. The force around her is too strong, gripping too tight. And then, to her horror, an emerald face appears, levitating in the air before her. No, not levitating—it's attached to a long, winding neck, which seems to snake out of view.

Except it's not out of view.

It's what's wrapped around her.

Locked in place, unable to move her limbs, the creature's face fills Eeao's vision. A forked tongue flickers from its mouth, glossy and black. Two yellow eyes bulge like knots on either side of its angular head, both equipped with vertical-slit pupils even narrower than the kitten's. Its skin smells of shrewd, reptilian pheromones and dank, putrid death.

Soon, Eeao fears it will smell of her death.

The kitten panics, scrambling desperately against the boa constrictor's hold.

But she can't access her paws.

She can't kick. She can't claw. She can't bite.

Finally, the jungle has ensnared her.

Eeao is prey. And she's unfit for escape.

Chapter 20
"Daeo"

Just like last *Kamaruna*, Daeo fidgets with questions as today's half-moon ritual proceeds. Why do the *Fae* always take six? Who chooses the volunteers? Why would anyone want to live at the bottom of the *Aeo*?

"xxxxxxxxxxxxxxxxxxxxxxxxxxxxxxxxxxxxxxx"

But unlike several weeks ago, Daeo decides today she won't stay silent.

"Momo?" she tugs on her mother's *areemo* skirt despite the approaching *Fae*.

"Shh," Nyno hisses, glancing down at her daughter before reaffixing her gaze skyward, like everyone else on the lakeshore. They'd barely arrived in time to join the shoreline gathering (Daeo had tripped and fallen into their waste pit, allegedly by accident, of which the cleanup had caused them to run late, again) and Nyno is not in the mood for any more of her daughter's nonsense. The cracked lip she received last *Kosharuna* is now a puss-filled infection obstructing the line of her smile. Her fingers are cramped from vigorous, nonstop weaving. Her pelvis aches from who knows what. And pressed against her harnessed chest, she feels her bundled baby squirming, its lips puckering toward one of her impotent nipples. *I have enough problems as it is.*

Next to her, bouncing in its own mother's arms, Paelo's naked newborn shrieks blood-curdling homicide.

"WAAAAAAAAAAAAAH"

Today, the child's cry reaches a new sonic frequency, audible even over the cacophonic *Fae*—a result of its developing vocal chords and repeated exposure to trauma.

"WAAAAAAAAAAAAAH"

"XXXXXXXXXXXXXXXXXXXXXXXXXXXXXX"

"MOMO?" Daeo tugs again, unfazed and unrelenting.

"*SHH!*" Nyno hisses more sharply. And then, to the ruckus beside her, "*Paelo*, can you silence your baby?"

"WHAT?" Paelo shouts.

"*MOMO?*" Daeo tugs.

"*WAAAAAAAAAAAH*"

"*XXXXXXXXXXXXXXXXXXXXXXXXXX*"

The *Fae* are directly overhead, beating the air into a circulating torrent.

"*MOMO? MOMO?*"

"*NYNO*, WHAT DID YOU SAY?"

"*WAAAAAAAAAAAH*"

"*XXXXXXXXXXXXXXXXXXXXXXXXXXX*"

Nyno can't take it anymore; without thinking, without speaking, before Daeo can tug one more time on her skirt, she shoves her newborn into Daeo's arms. And then Nyno bolts. She breaks through ranks of the dutifully gathered, fleeing back into the jungle, toward her *capku*, her face streaked with salty, uncontrollable tears.

Paelo shrugs.

No one cares.

The six volunteers are lifted into the air.

"*XXXXXXXXXXXXXXXXXXXXXXXXXXX*"

Daeo blinks, shocked at her mother's flight. She feels suddenly abandoned, dwarfed by the squirming bundle in her arms, surrounded by adults twice her size, everyone watching while six others die. But the baby seems to remember Daeo's touch; her squirming stills. Daeo stares down into the infant's uncovered eyes while the *Kamaruna* ceremony continues. Her irises are mismatched, one golden-green and one endless black, mirroring the juxtaposed colors of her face. In her mind, Daeo can see her brother's face in her sister's, as well as her own. Daeo gently sways back and forth on her heels until her sister's eyelids droop shut, content. And then they both are. Together.

When Daeo looks up again, the *Kamaruna* ceremony is over. *Fae* bodies dot the horizon, disappearing back over the northern mountain range. Everyone on the lakeshore is dispersing too, returning to their routine activities, conversing back and forth like nothing remarkable happened. No one even seems to have noticed Nyno's early departure.

Meanwhile, the baby remains placid in Daeo's arms—though her weight is quickly becoming a problem. Peering around, Daeo doesn't see her mother anywhere. Even Paelo ditched her.

"Whyyy?" Daeo groans. Her mother has never disappeared like this before. The girl's biceps burn, unused to carrying this extra weight. But she doesn't want to set her precious cargo down on the sandy bank. So she trudges as quickly as she can, carrying her sister back into the jungle, following the path to her mother's *capku*, hoping to arrive there before her arms tire out.

Eventually, about halfway home, Daeo runs out of energy and collapses alongside the path, managing to fall into a cushioned patch of spiraling, yellow *wykyno*. To the infant, landing in the plush, non-green organism is as comfortable as landing in her feather-padded cradle. Nevertheless, Daeo only pauses long enough to restore blood flow to her cramping muscles. She's never seen anyone else leave a baby lying on the ground before, and she feels guilty for having done it at all.

Picking her sister up again, Daeo repeats, "You are okay, you can make it, you are okay, you can make it," over and over as she continues, more to reassure herself than the already-pacified baby. Propelled by this mantra, Daeo arrives at her mother's *capku* without having to stop again.

"*Momo?*" Daeo pants, pushing open the entrance flap. She finds her mother inside, sprawled sideways in her narrow sleeping mat. "Are you okay?"

"I'm sorry, *Daeo*," Nyno groans, remaining on her side, motionless, eyes closed. "I didn't get enough sleep last night."

Daeo knows why—in the midst of a midnight thunderstorm, it'd been up to her mother to re-thatch a surprise leak in their *capku*'s roof. *Life never stops*, was what she'd said when Daeo awoke briefly from the commotion. It didn't take Daeo long to fall back asleep. But she knows her mother must've spent the rest of the night thatching. The roof overhead now looks taught and fresh. The floor beneath, however, will be muddy for the next few days.

Daeo hedges around the muddy spot, figuring she'll cover it herself later with dry fronds if her *momo* doesn't get to it first. And then she sets her baby sister down in her cradle of *raea* quills.

"Is it asleep?" Nyno asks without looking.

"Yes, she is asleep," Daeo says.

Nyno breathes a sigh. She figures she has at least until this afternoon before the baby stirs for another feeding. The idea of squeezing in a nap before taking the baby again to nurse from Paelo seems like an immense reprieve she can't allow herself to waste.

"*Momo?*" Daeo is suddenly beside her. "I have a question about *Kamaruna.* During the ceremony, why does—"

"Not now," Nyno's eyes remain shut. "I'm napping. Go pick more *mabato* spines for me."

"But—"

"Go."

Daeo sighs. "Okay, *momo.* How many?"

"Many," Nyno says with finality, right before escaping into slumber.

Chapter 21
"Eeao"

Fuzzy, colorless spots cloud Eeao's vision.

Occasionally, as the suffocation process advances, the snake's triangular face shifts into focus, its mouth widening hungrily in front of the kitten's eyes. But for the most part, Eeao's eyesight has been rendered inoperable—an intake of sensory information that, much like her air supply, no longer flows to her brain.

She's still alive, but barely.

Wrapped in the boa's muscular coils, her body hangs useless and limp, internal organs squished around the width of her spinal cord. Neural impulses send random twitches through her face and whiskers, which poke up through the helicoid creature, a patch of gray, striped fur encompassed in green, concentric rings. But otherwise, she can't move at all.

Slowly, almost delicately, the boa constricts tighter. The superior predator has won.

Eeao feels herself succumbing.

Lost in semi-conscious miasma, she forgets the details of her peril. What vine? What snake? What jungle? All that's left in the dark void of Eeao's mind is a small shred of her organic cognizance, a cascade of neurons blinking offline.

And then suddenly, her awareness erupts to encompass everything.

She sees the snake consuming her body.

But then she sees the snake succumb to the beak of a hungry *raea* bird.

Which succumbs to another predator.

And then another.

And another.

Until everything succumbs to the jungle.

And then the jungle blooms.

In a flash, Eeao sees it all—energy flowing through lines of successive organisms, never ending, never slowing, everything disintegrating back into a jungle that so readily rebirths.

But then something strange happens.

The tightness around Eeao's chest releases. Her lungs expand.

The kitten sucks in a deep breath, and then gasps for another.

Emerald coils untangle around her, the scaly body gone limp.

Blood spurts in all directions.

The snake is dead.

Nothing makes sense.

Circulation reflows through Eeao's limbs as she falls free, but she's too weak to stand. Blinking, writhing, panting for evermore air, she looks around desperately, unable to focus her swimming vision, every neuron in her brain screaming awake.

What happened? What killed the snake?

One by one, Eeao's senses return, starting with scent—she smells something human.

Chapter 22
"Daeo"

Initially, Daeo heard the kitten's capture through the trees—a strange, deflating squeak. She'd already collected an armload of carefully-protracted *mabato* spines from a nearby plant; on a hunch, she decided to bring one along to investigate.

Now, standing over the snake's wriggling, impaled carcass, she's glad she brought the spine.

She instantly recognized Eeao's face poking out of the boa's knotted helix; it's the mysterious creature she keeps seeing! Familiar, yet so alien. Undaunted by the man-sized snake (known as *syreea* in their language, she's used to seeing much longer ones strung out across barbecue pits), Daeo snuck up behind the reptile and skewered it through the head (boa-wrangling is, traditionally, one of the first practical skills taught to children of the *Uyi)*.

Now, as the freed kitten unfurls in the golden light of noon, it looks even more bewitching.

Daeo crouches down to help untangle her from the bloody, green scales. Slowly, the feline's body comes alive beneath Daeo's fingertips. Silken and docile, Daeo handles the creature with as much delicacy as her abrupt, impatient nature can manage. Again, she sees something familiar in the creature's face. Its tiny teeth. Its black nose. Its projecting ears. The way its striped forehead wrinkles like a quizzical brow. Something about the animal's countenance reminds Daeo of her mother, her brother, her baby sister, even Paelo. Somehow, compared to the *Uyi*'s variety of other fauna, this creature feels something like kin.

Within time, the kitten's wits return. She shakes her head. She piques her whiskers. She blinks rapidly, contracting the various membranes of her multilayered eyelids. When she realizes she's escaped one animal's clutches only to have fallen into another's, she bolts, slipping through Daeo's fingers like running water.

"No!"

Surprised, Daeo grabs to reclaim the kitten.

"Come back!"

But Eeao deftly evades her; she leaps for a dangling vine (having clearly learned nothing from her last attempt), and scampers up into the kapok's understory. Already, she wonders if her sapphire *kynaea* is still perched where she'd last seen it.

"Please come back!" Daeo cries in vain. Truly, abandoned by everything. "Please!"

Eeao ignores her. Eager to reestablish her status as a predator, she scans the tree's upper limbs, parsing the intricate, leafy realm with her laser vision. She feels bested by both the snake and the child, and now craves new prey to dominate. Alas, her targeted *kynaea* has since flown off, along with the rest of its kind. The sky above is clear and quiet, albeit glossed over with thickening mist. But surely there's something else to hunt, somewhere. Silencing her other senses, Eeao listens carefully, ears atwitch, surveying the jungle's aural dimension for any sign of proximate prey.

"Pleeeeease?"

The off-key pitch of Daeo's whine jams Eeao's auricular frequencies. She scowls down at the girl, crinkling her whiskers. As far as the kitten is concerned, this young human only saved her from the snake in order to make a snack for itself. This sound it's making now must be some sort of sonic assault. Eeao flattens her ears back against her skull, resisting the beast's attack.

"Please come down," Daeo continues calling. "I just want to be friends." She doubts the creature can even understand her. But sad children say sad things. Especially when no one is listening. "I do not have any friends. My brother is gone. My *momo* is too weak to feed my baby sister and... And I just want to know if life gets better at the bottom of the *Aeo*. Because I need something to get better. So please... Please come down and let me talk to you. I need someone to talk to. Please?"

All the words come out in a rush. And in the ensuing silence, Daeo feels stupid.

Eeao gazes down at the child for several heartbeats. From their corresponding perspectives, interwoven twigs and mossy branches frame their faces. Daeo thinks she sees understanding in the feline's eyes, a sentient look of compassion. Really, it's boredom. The kitten springs from her lofty perch to an even loftier one. And then she's gone, scampering ever higher.

"No!" Daeo cries, running at the tree. She jumps for a low-hanging branch, but can't reach it. She jumps again. Failure. Huffing, determined, Daeo backs away from the kapok to devise a new strategy. Without tripping over the boa's fresh, curled carcass, she walks around the kapok's colossal trunk, squinting up into its topmost branches. It takes her a moment, peering through all the foliage, but soon she spots the kitten again—a silver streak, darting across one limb that extends into an adjacent, leafy balsa. From the ground, Daeo stalks the feline's movement.

It doesn't take Eeao long to notice she's being tailed. Grunting, panting, and whining to herself, the little girl doesn't seem to understand the concept of stealth. Perhaps the child is just a dumb groundcrawler? Scraping and clawing at whatever it can reach? Eeao is beginning to feel less threatened. Thanks to her height advantage, the kitten feels significantly larger than the girl. Smug, she slinks her way across the rainforest's upper domain, trying to ignore her bumbling follower, but then she gets an idea:

Why not guide this child back to the cave? Double their feast? This one is about the same size as the other. They'll be fat enough for eating any day now. And this way, she and the old man won't have to share—sure, they'll go back and forth between the two carcasses, ripping out entrails and such, but sharing two of them will be so much easier than playing tug-of-war with just one.

Decided, Eeao pivots ninety degrees toward home, rebounding off the lichen-veined trunk of a North American jelutong (a relatively new species of tree, which evolved from its original Asian relative and migrated transcontinentally via *Fae* networking around 400,000 years ago).

Daeo has never traveled this far on her own. Yet she can't slow her pace. Compelled by burning curiosity and a strange, gutting sense of loss, she doesn't pause to think. She keeps her neck craned, eyes trained on the silver blur above. What if she never sees the creature again? After holding it in her own hands, after being so close, she can't bear the idea of losing it again.

She needs something to hold onto. Something to reclaim.

The land slopes upward, and Daeo soon finds herself clambering up the side of a lush, overgrown embankment. She tugs on verdant creepers and multicolored tendrils of *wykyno*, using the dense, tangled flora for leverage. At a certain point, she goes deaf to the internal sound of her own ragged breaths, and instead becomes gradually aware of the jungle's ambient noises.

Shrieks and trills cascade from above, a treetop chorus of ethereal, overlapping melodies. Large, winged insects fill the air with a constant, percussive buzz. Wind whistles frantically through hollow reeds and tree branches. Frogs croak a deep, bellowing bassline. Around her, the *Uyi*'s natural symphony comes to life. And from within the labyrinth of mystifying sound waves, Daeo thinks she can hear her brother's voice, singing...

"Daeo?"

She really can hear her brother's voice.

The kitten stops, perched atop the rocky, moss-hung lip of a cave. And standing just within the cave, leaning against a tall, wooden staff, is Bowi.

"*Tynji!*" Daeo gasps the word *brother*. She nearly trips over her own feet.

"How did you get here?" Bowi's face blooms into a smile, radiant as the sun. He drops the staff he'd been holding and runs to hug her. They embrace, clashing, falling together into a flowering bed of heliconia, dazed and laughing. Daeo feels like she's in a dream. Surrounded by the shrub's toucan-colored blossoms, they smile at one another.

"But seriously, how'd you get here?" Bowi asks.

"I followed that—" Daeo points to where she'd last seen the kitten, but Eeao is gone, watching them instead from her cranny hideout. "Where did it go?" Daeo looks around, flushed.

"What are you talking about?"

"I followed a little... I think it was an animal?" Daeo feels like she's trying to describe something imaginary. "I do not know what it was, I have never seen anything like it before, but it was silver and striped, and I followed it here and found you."

"Oh, are you talking about *Eeao?*"

"What?" Daeo quirks.

"It's this little critter that follows the *Teerta* around," Bowi tries to explain. "She's really cute, but hard to catch. It sounds like you're describing her."

"Maybe," Daeo shrugs. "Probably."

"Probably," Bowi nods, smiling again. He doesn't really care how she got here. He's just excited to see her. Even counting his mother, Daeo is the person he's missed most from the nest.

Cupping her hand against his face, Daeo almost doesn't believe the boy before her is her brother. His skin is more vibrant than she remembers, and warmer, too. His smile is more toothy—he never used to show his teeth while smiling, did he? It hasn't been long, but suddenly their moon apart feels like an entire lifespan. Daeo likes the way he looks now. His new lifestyle must be beneficial. She wonders how the *Teerta* has been treating him. And then she wonders if Bowi likes his life better this way... At the *Teerta*'s cave... Without her...

"What are you doing here?" Tagi appears around the bend of a nearby walking trail. Sitting atop his head, balanced with one hand, he carries a round, woven basket filled with freshly picked vegetables and berries.

Daeo freezes, feeling caught. She's seen the *Teerta* before, but she's never interacted with him personally. He's almost like a celebrity to her. Or a god. A dignified entity with enough knowledge and authority to consider her worth nothing.

"This is my *tynjo, Daeo*," Bowi introduces his *sister* to Tagi.

Tagi scrunches his stern, wizened brow. "That's not what I asked, but nice to meet you. Anyway, I'll ask again: What is she doing here?"

The siblings share an anxious look. Daeo hopes her brother will handle this conversation, given his familiarity with the *Teerta*. But Bowi remains mum—how should he know why his sister showed up?

"Eeao!"

A gray flash lands on Tagi's shoulder.

"I followed that!" Daeo points at Eeao.

Tagi chuckles, begrudging the kitten now purring in his ear; Eeao hopes the old man appreciates the bounty she's brought home. "You followed *Eeao* all the way to my cave?" Tagi runs his fingers along the kitten's arching vertebrae. "That's quite a long way from the nest."

"I lost track of time," Daeo admits, glancing up at the sky. Layers of pink cirrus blanket the mid-afternoon sun. Has her mother noticed her absence?

"Well you shouldn't be here," Tagi says.

"Why not?" Bowi interjects.

"It's dangerous out here, in this part of the jungle," Tagi lies. Eeao leaps from his shoulder, stalks off to patrol the area. "This is no place for a little girl to be exploring on her own. She needs to return to the nest. Now."

"Okay," Daeo sighs, but then realizes, "I do not know how to get back."

"See that path," Tagi points toward the trail behind him—a narrow but well-trodden walkway, walled by overarching vegetation. "Follow that straight, without turning on any detours. It'll lead you down to the *Aeo*. From there, you'll be able to follow the shoreline to the nest. *Wyntiko?*"

"Okay..." Daeo eyes the path reluctantly. The directions sound simple enough. But she wants to spend more time with her brother.

"I can walk her home," Bowi offers.

"No," Tagi shakes his head. "Absolutely not, *Bowi*. You will stay here and practice *ynsyna*. This afternoon I'm going to teach you about compound words, which are perhaps the most integral part of our language. We cannot stall your progress."

Seven moons.

"But does she have to go now?" Bowi persists. "Maybe we can play a couple games of—"

"There's no time, look at the sun," Tagi scoffs. "If she doesn't start walking now, she won't get home until later tonight. Won't your *momo* be worried? No, she must go now. You'll see each other soon enough, when we come down to the nest for *Kunjaruna*. Now come along," Tagi takes Daeo's hand, and then helps her out of the heliconia patch.

Accepting Tagi's guidance, Daeo waves goodbye to her downcast brother.

Tears well in Bowi's eyes.

But Daeo isn't sad.

She knows how to find her way back.

Chapter 23
"Tynji"

Maetri and his brothers all hate each other.

Which is how they've survived this long.

"*Veetri*, load my *syn-syn*, will you?" their father, Paetri, hands a long, clay pipe to his eldest son. They're all seated within Paetri's massive, lavishly decorated *capku*. As the *Uyi*'s Chief *raea* wrangler, Paetri is afforded many luxuries rarely seen in other homes. A carpet of silken, woven *wykyno* tendrils lines the floor. Feather tapestries bedeck the conical ceiling, forming a multicolored mosaic that spirals over their heads. It mirrors the way Maetri and his eight brothers circle their father now.

Veetri, a leaner, less hairy, *Patummal* version of Maetri, takes his father's pipe and carefully dusts a fine powder into its bowl. Consisting of crushed *zymee* and *keeryno* leaves (contemporaries of marijuana and tobacco, respectively), the hash powder Veetri concocts is unrivaled across all the *Uyi*. It's also their father's guiltiest pleasure. All his younger brothers hate him for it.

Veetri hands the loaded pipe back to Paetri. "Here you are, *kosha-kymara*," he says in reverence, using a compound word literally meaning *sperm donor* (their language has no intimate word for *father).* Converting moons to solar years, Paetri is little more than a decade older than his firstborn.

Wordlessly, Paetri lights his pipe from a smoldering incense pot beside him. And then he begins puffing. The young men watch in silence as smoke fills the vaulted *capku*. They all know why they've been summoned for this private gathering. Maetri just wishes their *sperm donor* would hurry up and get on with it.

"As you all know," Paetri finally speaks, "I'll be volunteering at the next *Kamaruna*."

Silence. Maetri tries not to roll his eyes. They've all been waiting patiently for the old man to volunteer (after the *Teerta*, Paetri is second-oldest in the *Uyi*), but no one has patience for this type of martyrdom. *Just tell us who gets the* raea *herd*, Maetri thinks, flexing his jaw muscles. He's spent his entire life shadowing his father, learning the art of *raea*-wrangling, all for this life-extending inheritance. Whoever wins the title of Chief *raea* wrangler will be able to postpone his *Kamaruna* volunteer date by many, many moons. *The birds should be mine.*

"Which means tonight will be my very last *Kunjaruna*," Paetri continues, languidly rolling his tongue across each word. "I will be sitting on the sidelines for this one, but I hope you each slay a *Meemmal* tonight. I am proud to have produced all of you. Over the course of your lives, you've each impressed me in your own unique ways, all nine of you. Sure, some may look at my offspring and say, twenty-three daughters versus nine sons, perhaps I did not do as well as I could have? *Bah*—I am too proud to care. Anyway, after next *Kamaruna*, you will each inherit a possession of mine. To *Kotri*, my youngest boy, I leave behind my *capku*."

Kotri looks astounded to be receiving anything.

"To *Keetri*, my next youngest," Paetri drawls on, "I leave behind the furniture inside my *capku*."

Keetri and Kotri nod to each other—this is starting to make sense.

"To *Kaetri*, my next youngest, I leave behind the *hympano* outer lining of my *capku*—you could use it as flooring, I've seen the sty you live in."

Kaetri says, "Thank you."

"To *Peetri*, my next *babi* in line," Paetri rarely uses the intimate word for *son*, so Peetri perks up, "I leave you the waste pit behind my *capku*, to bury once I'm gone. I hope this is a responsibility you can actually handle."

Peetri says, "Thank you."

To his next three sons, Paetri gifts his whittled knife collection (for butchering *raea*), his whittled pair of shears (for skinning *raea*), and his favorite lasso (for wrangling *raea*). What, exactly, they're each supposed to do with their individual gifts without the coveted herd itself, they haven't a clue.

"To *Maetri*, my second-born," Paetri now smiles because, despite all the *kahtopo*, he actually respects his hairy renegade. "You've already given me sixteen grandchildren between four *momo*s, so to you I leave behind the rest of my *Kosharuna* women. May your bounty be as plentiful as ever."

The older man winks. Maetri seethes.

"And lastly, to my first-born *babi*, *Veetri*," Paetri now smiles at his single *Patummal* son. "To you, I leave behind my pipe. May your lungs be ever-clogged."

Paetri hands him the pipe, still smoldering.

Veetri blinks.

Everyone blinks.

Paetri laughs, slapping his eldest on the back, "And you can have the *raea* herd too."

Veetri beams.

Maetri bites through his lip. He tastes blood, a lifetime of bitterness.

"Alright, you leeches," Paetri sneers, "that's all I have to say. Now get out of my *capku*, all of you, get out, go, go, go, I'm sick and tired of you!"

The nine brothers exit one by one, each hating the other more than ever.

But after tonight, Maetri hates his *kosha-kymara* most.

"Congratulations, *tynji*," Maetri flashes Veetri a bloody smile. He's sick and tired of waiting. From now on, Maetri will take whatever he wants.

Chapter 24
"Kunjaruna"

A byproduct of spliced firefly DNA, each *Fae* body is equipped with a bioluminescing organ. It protrudes from between their shoulder blades, a green nodule just beneath the juncture of their four translucent wings, and functions via nitric oxide gas and internally produced luciferin. Unlike humans, whose bioluminescing scalp yeast grows externally and glows at a constant rate, an adult *Fae* is able to control their light apparatus through respiration. By simply opening a tracheole within their dorsal airway, oxygen flow can be managed to and from the luciferin-producing organ, allowing insectoids to flash and blink at will. They strobe this accessory for in-hive communication—like coordinating massive, nighttime aerial maneuvers.

Bowi sees them coming tonight: A twinkling, pyramidal formation, hovering over the northern mountains. Glowing green against the black, moonless sky, the approaching *Fae* reflect crisply off the *Aeo*'s dark, rippling surface. To everyone gathered on the opposite shoreline, it looks like two swarms slowly converging, one on top of the other.

"Are we late?" Bowi asks, struggling to keep up with Tagi's pace. They began their hike down to the *Aeo* just moments before the glowing horde appeared on the horizon. Bowi figures the adults on the lakeshore have probably ingested their *Kunjaruna* mushrooms by now.

"Not at all," Tagi can't hide his excitement. This will be Bowi's first *Kunjaruna* as *Teerta*-in-training, and he's eager to give the boy some first-hand experience. *Seven moons.* "We are right on schedule."

"But the *Fae* are about to land," Bowi says, high-stepping over a large root jutting across their path. Little clay jars rattle from his sides, strung together and tied to his hip belt with *areemo* twine. Tagi is rigged with a string of jars too. They contain various poultices and healing herbs, along with bandages, scoured *camraea* quills, and strands of sterilized *raea* plume fibers for stitching. The weight of their medical cargo is strenuous, but Bowi refuses to grow weary.

"The action won't start until later tonight—remember, our *punteeku* still need to run all the way around to the other side of the *Aeo*," Tagi says, referring to the nest's army of *hunters*. "It usually takes them until midnight to slay all the *Meemmal*. Once they return to our side of the *Aeo*, that's when we treat their wounds."

Bowi nods. So far, his experience as *Teerta* has been a lot of sitting and waiting.

Meanwhile, across the *Aeo*, the *Fae* descend upon the northern shoreline. They carry with them, bound and dangling from ropes, fifty humans of varying ages. Grown and flown over from the *Fae*'s next-closest human nest, near the former Great Lakes (which have since merged into a singular, massive Great Lake), these fifty humans are airsick, exhausted, and terrified. They're every bit as *Homo sapien* as the *Uyi*'s current primate population. Except none of their scalps glow. Their skin is bare, dull, uncolonized by *patu* yeast. Instead, unbeknownst even to themselves, their nail beds and cuticles teem with a different type of microscopic, parasitic yeast endemic to their separate environment—closely related, but non bioluminescing (developed long ago during the *Genetic Revolution*, for the purpose of specialized mani-pedi treatments). They have no idea how important their fingers and toes are to the *Uyi*'s present ecosystem.

"*XXXXXXXXXXXXXXXXXXXXXXXXXXXXX*"

The *Fae* drop their cargo on the northern lakeshore, and then gracefully ascend to a safe, superior altitude from whence to hover and watch. They form an ominous, glowing pyramid in the sky. Down on the pebbly lakeshore, the fifty humans scramble to their feet, dazed and bewildered by their alien surroundings (much like people of the *Uyi*, these humans from the Great Lake have never seen the world beyond their local nest). At first, some of the humans begin to relax, believing nothing could possibly be worse than the terrifying flight they'd just endured. The ground is foreign, but solid. The lake is unfamiliar, but calm. The weather is balmy, but peaceful. Radiant jungles climb the mountain ranges all around them, glittering green against the black sky.

But why are the *Fae* still hovering overhead?

"*XXXXXXXXXXXXXXXXXXXXXXXXXXX*"

What are they waiting for?

"*XXXXXXXXXXXXXXXXXXXXXXXXXXXX*"

Some of the humans begin to make themselves comfortable, reclining on the sandy bank, yearning for rest. A woman reunites with her child. A man breathes a sigh of relief.

That's when they're ambushed.

"Die *Meemmal!* Die! Die! Die!"

One hundred muscular, harnessed, violet-capped humans charge the northern lakeshore, descending on their unsuspecting prey with typhonic force. Flintstone machetes hack apart limbs. Stone axes glance off faces. Men are decapitated. Women are gutted. Children are impaled with *mabato* spines. Bodies hang from harnesses; the *Uyi*'s strongest men and women compete to see who can skewer the most.

It's a game. It's a riot. It's a bloodbath.

"Die *Meemmal!*"

Really, it's germination.

"*XXXXXXXXXXXXXXXXXXXXXXXXXXXXXX*"

By the time Bowi and Tagi arrive at the *Aeo*'s southern shoreline, the women and children who remained behind during the hunt are now reassembling to greet the returning *punteeku*. They bang on drums made from rubbery *hympano* skin stretched over hollowed-out balsa trunks. Some prance around with wooden flutes, piping shrill melodies into the air. The sonic environment they create is invigorating, though lacking organization. Bowi scans the crowd for his sister or mother. He can't see either. Faces and arms weave into a congregated mass, but he can't identify anyone he loves among them. Several women greet Tagi upon their arrival, and they're quickly ushered to a wooden booth constructed along the treeline—the *Teerta*'s *Kunjaruna* station.

Bowi recognizes the booth. He's laid upon it many times before, to receive *pomaeo* infusions. Now, he feels strange standing on the other side of it.

"Categorize the poultice jars in these cubbies, down here," Tagi points at the cutout shelves behind the booth. "They'll be easier to access that way—you'll note the *ynsyna* labels, carved within the cubbies."

Bowi reads by the light of his skin, recognizing the *ynsyna* characters inscribed on each shelf and then matching them to their corresponding medicine jars.

"Quick, they're coming!" Tagi sounds almost gleeful.

Bowi looks up—indeed, a procession of violet scalps emerges from the luminous jungle. Having made their way around the lake's circumference, the *punteeku* return to cheers and adoration. Even on this moonless night, Bowi can clearly see blood dripping from their spined harnesses. Some of them are limping. Others cup hands over seeping wounds. Yet they all roar maniacal laughter, enjoying the euphoric come-down effects of the *Kunjaruna* mushrooms they all ate at the start of the night. In their midst, hanging from harnesses and draped across shoulders, they carry the bodies of fifty slain *Meemmal*.

"They clean up after themselves," Daeo had once observed.

Bowi desperately wishes to see her now. He hasn't seen his sister since the day she found their cave, and he's been anxiously awaiting *Kunjaruna* just to hug her again. Does she know where the *Teerta*'s station is? Their mother always sent Daeo to bed when she took Bowi to get infused. Will Daeo know where to find him tonight? Will their mother bring her?

Bowi doesn't have much time to wonder. The wounded surge their booth like a tidal wave, and Tagi talks so quickly it takes Bowi's entire attention span just to follow the old man's instruction: "Hold the skin taut vertically to close the wound, like so, and then thread an arm length of plume fiber through the *camraea* needle, like so—no, no, no, through the notch of cartilage at the bottom, like so, yes, and then we begin stitching laterally across the wound, like so..."

Bowi doesn't know what's happening. He just does what he's told. Blood covers his hands. Flesh is all he can see. Someone took a spine through the thigh. Someone else took one through the ribs. They all continue laughing while Tagi stitches them back together, everyone seemingly numb to the pain. Bowi can't tell if their wounds were inflicted by the *Meemmal* or each other. Somehow, he doesn't think those dead outsiders were ever equipped with *mabato* spines...

The unwounded *punteeku* continue past the *Teerta* booth, parading their *Meemmal* carcasses into the jungle. They puff out their chests while passing flocks of admirers. They gloat while licking human blood from their lips. Bowi recognizes Maetri among them. He knows where they're going next—to the forbidden swamp grounds, where they'll dump the *Meemmal* bodies into the bottomless muck.

Bowi remembers what that feels like.

Chapter 25
"Nyno"

In Nyno's experience, *Kunjaruna* mushrooms are the worst.

A close cousin to psilocybin (all three *aruna* fungal strains originated on the Antarctic continent hundreds of millions of years ago, only evading human discovery until they finally melted out of the south pole's deep permafrost, nearly one million years ago), they imbue the ingester with a psychedelic, near-spiritual adrenaline rush, followed by a pica-like craving for iron. Of course, Nyno doesn't understand the science or history behind the tiny, brown mushrooms. She just knows the throbbing headaches and heart palpitations she suffers whenever she eats one.

So naturally, when Maetri pulled her aside prior to this evening's *Kunjaruna* ceremony and told her to stay hidden inside her *capku* instead, she was elated. She didn't argue. She didn't ask questions. She didn't care that he'd grabbed her by the shoulder and barked the order at her. She was just happy for any excuse to opt out of a communal mushroom trip.

It's the little blessings in life, Nyno tells herself, rubbing her bruised shoulder with one hand while changing her newborn's soiled soft-clothes with her other. *It's the little reprieves.* Tonight, rather than chanting and running around in a psychedelic frenzy with the other birthing *momo*s, Nyno plans to enjoy a rare, early night in bed. *Finally.*

"*Momo*," Daeo nags. "We need to go to *Kunjaruna*."

"No," Nyno says, raising her voice over her baby's piercing shrieks—for some reason, the infant has been fussy all evening. *Of course.*

"Whyyy?" Daeo joins the fussing.

"Because tonight we aren't required to join," Nyno says, patting the baby's back, hoping for a burp. Outside their *capku*, she can faintly hear *Kunjaruna* festivities beginning down by the lake—laughter and mayhem, the steady pounding of large, resonant drums.

"But I want to go," Daeo says.

"Whyyy?" Nyno can't fathom.

"Because *Bowi* will be there. He is with the *Teerta*. Remember?"

"Oh," Nyno had forgotten. *How could I have forgotten?*

"Come on, *momo*," Daeo grabs her skirt. "We need to go see *Bowi*."

"Stop it, *Daeo*," Nyno pushes the girl away, causing the baby to unleash another cry. Nyno continues bouncing it against her chest, desperate for peace. "*Maetri* ordered us to stay inside tonight, and that's what we're going to do. Now get ready to sleep. Please?"

"But... But..." Daeo wants to cry and tantrum. She wants to throw herself at her mother. She wants to beg and scream for what she wants. But tonight, she decides against all of those things. Instead, she resolves to sit on her feather sleeping mat and glare at her mother in stony silence.

Many moments pass like this.

"*Shh... Shh...*" Nyno sighs, turning her fussy baby around to pat its back again. This cycle continues for a while. Nyno finds no success. "Oh come on, why won't you stop screaming?"

"I think she wants to be unwrapped," Daeo breaks her silence.

"What?"

"You always keep her wrapped up like that, even when she sleeps," Daeo points at her tightly-bundled sister. "I think you should unwrap her. She might be happier."

Nyno stares at Daeo. The baby keeps screaming, crying, gurgling on its own saliva. In Nyno's arms, it writhes like a reanimated mummy, tearing at its bonds. Nyno and Daeo blink at the same moment.

"I think you should go to sleep," Nyno finally says.

"I will when she does," Daeo retorts.

Nyno doesn't know how to respond. She would've never spoken with such contempt to her own mother, way back when she was a child. *How old is* Daeo?

Eventually, all three of them drift into uncomfortable slumber...

Much later, in the midst of a terrifying nightmare she'll mostly forget, Nyno hears a noise.

She jolts awake. Someone is entering her *capku*. Still hallucinating fragments of a strange dream (ghastly flurries of miniature *Fae* beings), she scrambles out of bed, jumping to her feet.

"*Shh*," a female voice.

By the light of their scalps, Nyno vaguely recognizes the woman's face. *Is that* Maetri's *sister?* The visitor stands within her home's entrance flap, holding it open halfway; a curl of mist creeps past her into the *capku*. Peering around, Nyno is grateful to see her two daughters remain sleeping. The woman waves her hand, beckoning Nyno outside. Nyno dons an *areemo* tunic.

"Bring your baby," the woman whispers.

Nyno's heart jolts. Anxiously, she tightens the swaddling around her sleeping infant. *What is this about?* Stepping out into the night, the air is overwhelmingly humid, almost too thick to breathe. Nyno can see dawn coming, a faint, watery graying of the black horizon. Meanwhile, the jungle's neon-green luminosity forces her to squint. After her eyes adjust, Nyno sees two others standing outside her home: Maetri and someone else, another woman she recognizes but cannot name.

"Well, let's see it," the unnamed woman wiggles her eyebrows. Based on her broad shoulders and blood-smeared face, Nyno can tell she is not a birthing *momo* like herself, but a *punteeku* like Maetri—a strong woman who hunts during *Kunjaruna*.

"Shut up," the first woman hisses, also clearly a *punteeku*. All three are harnessed, with bits of entrails and dried gore still dangling from their spikes.

"What's going on?" Nyno glances toward Maetri. In the presence of these three, she feels vulnerable—they could murder her with a group hug. Her heart thunders so loud against her ribs she worries it'll wake the baby. "What do you want from me?"

"Show them the *Meemmal*," Maetri says.

"The... What?"

"The baby, *Nyno*," Maetri reaches, grabbing at the bundled child in her arms.

Nyno tries to hold on, but she's too weak, her fingers too tired, limp as boiled grasshopper legs. She releases hold of her baby. And then suddenly she's free. Standing unburdened. The baby in Maetri's possession. Aid. Assistance. Such instant, blind relief.

Thank you.

With a flick of his wrist, Maetri unravels the infant's swaddling. The feather blanket Nyno made for Bowi long ago flutters to the ground. Gawking, the other women recoil from the nude infant, disturbed by her receding *patu*: A single stripe glimmering faintly down the back of her scalp. Her final shred of humanness.

Nyno has never seen the child so bare. Even on the night of her birth. Now, naked and squirming awake, the baby doesn't even seem like her own anymore. Something is happening in Nyno's brain, a neural pathway rerouting itself. *It really does look like a* Meemmal.

"How did that happen?" wiggly eyebrows leans toward the baby again, too fascinated to help herself. The baby murmurs uncomfortably in their clutches. "How'd you pop out a *Meemmal?*" her eyes dart toward Nyno now, almost accusingly.

"Shut up, *Syno,*" the two women seem to dislike each other.

"We don't know how it happened," Maetri says, depositing the newborn back into Nyno's arms. The baby quiets, though Nyno feels like she's been re-encumbered with an immense, resentful weight. "But we know the signs. Her first child, the boy who's gone to replace the *Teerta,* is *Patummal.* And her second child is *Patummal* as well—they're both completely covered in *patu.* Now ask yourselves, has a birthing *momo* ever produced two *Patummal* children, consecutively, as *Nyno* has? No. It's too rare an occurrence. She's an example of an extreme situation. But she's a real, statistical example nonetheless."

"But what does that have to do with—"

"Her situation doesn't end there," Maetri continues. "Because after producing two *Patummal* children, she produces this: A pureblooded, bare-headed *Meemmal,* with no *patu* whatsoever. This is the first time in history someone has given birth to an outsider inside our nest. It's too remarkable to be coincidence. Too obvious to be chance. This connection between the *Patummal* condition and the *Meemmal* condition is unmistakable. It's a deterioration of physical being, an inferiority of humanhood.

"In *Nyno*'s offspring, you can see the progression from *Patummal* to *Meemmal* clearly illustrated. It isn't *Nyno*'s fault, she didn't choose these conditions for her children. But after seeing this evidence, the link is clear. She's unfit to reproduce. We must remove her status as a birthing *momo.* She'll procreate no longer."

The two women nod.

And, like her earlier nightmare, Nyno can't comprehend any of this. What is she without the purpose of procreation? What value does she offer the nest? Without her status as a birthing *momo*, she'll be volunteered at the next *Kamaruna*, surely. Terror rips through her chest like a sharpened *mabato* spine. How can her life end so quickly? *WHAT HAVE I DONE WRONG?*

"We'll create a new station for *Nyno*," Maetri is still talking. "Upgrade her status to Chief of textile sourcing. From now on, she'll prove her worth to the nest by outfitting everyone in the finest, most high-quality clothing the *Uyi* has ever seen."

Again, Nyno can't believe her ears.

"We're creating an entirely new Chief title, just for her?" Maetri's sister looks incredulous.

"Come on, *Kleeo*, you've seen *Nyno*'s work," Maetri snarls. "The harness on your own back was fashioned by her hands. All three of our harnesses were."

"Wait, you're the one who's been building these new harnesses?" the second woman, Syno, gasps. "These are the most durable spines and *hympano* I've ever worn. All the *punteeku* want harnesses like ours. *Nyno*, you could become a legend."

I'm still dreaming, Nyno decides. *That's what's going on.*

"I see," Kleeo nods, smiling slowly. "Brilliant solution, *Maetri*."

"Then it's settled," Maetri says.

"Wh—what are you talking about?" Nyno finds her voice only as the baby in her arms begins to cry. It's still unwrapped, naked, dull scalp coated in black, fuzzy hair. "What's settled?"

"Volunteer your *Meemmal* at the next *Kamaruna*," Maetri says, gesturing at Nyno's newborn. "Show everyone the evidence. It needs to be done. And then after that, you can enjoy your new life. You're a Chief now, one of the *Uyi*'s most important people." He pats her shoulder, like she's accomplished something. And then the three *punteeku* depart, their harnesses rattling as they venture back into the lucent jungle, leaving Nyno alone with her baby.

For a long time, Nyno doesn't move. She just stands there beside her *capku*, silent while her child cries in her arms. Soft, whimpering sniffles. Like the baby doesn't know what it's crying about, but wants to cry anyway. *I know why you're crying,* Nyno thinks, her mind slowly processing the conversation, the decision, the dialogue during which she said nothing...

Like a snail oozing its way across the lakeshore, the sun creeps over the horizon, leaving behind a trail of smudged, molten daybreak. Around Nyno, the sun's ultraviolet rays trigger the jungle's bioluminescing crust to deoxidize. The baby continues to cry, but Nyno refuses to look down at it. Instead, while dragonflies and mosquitoes blossom like larva from droplets of morning dew, Nyno retrieves the feather blanket Maetri dropped on the ground. She shakes crumbles of dirt from its soft fibers. This is the same baby blanket she made for Bowi when he was born. It's the same one she wrapped around Daeo's tiny, luminous body. Now, after this last baby, she'll never again wrap it around another.

Enjoy your new life, Maetri's voice lingers. *Chief of textile sourcing.*

Nyno rewraps the infant. *How can you be a* Meemmal? *How could I have given birth to an outsider—*

No. She won't let herself think about it anymore. She won't look at it. She won't speak to it. She'll listen to its cries no longer. Maetri is right. It's a *Meemmal*. It must be a *Meemmal.* Why else would it lack a *patu?* This is not her fault. It was never her fault. It's the only explanation that makes sense.

I've done nothing wrong.

Regardless of how it happened, Nyno will do what she needs to do next, as she's always done. And right now, she desperately needs to sleep. So she returns to her *capku.* She sets her baby back in its cradle, deaf to its voice. She glances at Daeo, who's still snoring, and subconsciously blocks that sound as well. And then she goes back to sleep.

This time, Nyno dreams of nothing.

Chapter 26
"Bowi"

For several days after *Kunjaruna,* Bowi can't clear the smell of blood from his nostrils. Metallic, coppery—though he lacks such corollary terms to describe the bitter, astringent odor, he knows the smell to be mineral in nature. It follows him wherever he goes. *Kataka:* Their term for *blood,* life's red essence. Built with *ynsyna,* the word looks like three modified triangles, all pointing downward.

Down, down, down.

Blood. Bowi remembers this smell—that day he found his mother miscarrying in the waste pit.

Bowi awakes, vomiting.

"Did you have a nightmare?" Tagi hurries to his aid. It's been five days since the new moon. Generally up before the boy each morning, Tagi has never before seen Bowi projectile vomit simply upon waking. Normally there's a build-up, or a triggering event. *What happened in his sleeping mind?* Tagi pats the boy's back.

From her elevated cranny, Eeao scowls—she wants the child to die, of course, but does it have to be so messy on its way out?

"I don't know," Bowi moans, drooling strings of stomach acid over the side of his bed. Somehow, stronger than the taste of bile and mucus, he can still smell blood.

"Don't worry, *Bowi,* it's going to be okay, lie back now and try to relax," Tagi coaxes him onto his pillows, fanning his face with a dried frond like last time. He'd intended to reintroduce Bowi to the *ynsyna* cavern today. So much information to read. So much knowledge to absorb. *Seven moons.* He'd expected the boy to be healthy and ready to learn today. "Everything is going to be okay, *Bowi.* Your stomach is empty now, you've expelled all the bad energy, so just lie back, relax, and try to—"

Bowi lurches forward to vomit some more.

Instead of studying within the cavern, Tagi spends the entire day soothing Bowi. He finds little success. Fanning barely helps this time—the day is too hot and humid, the air itself too solid. The boy heaves periodically, like the leaky, hydraulic root tips of Tagi's water filter. Seemingly automatic. His stomach just won't hold onto anything. There's no use trying to feed him. Even a ladleful of water is too much to keep down. He's dehydrating, sweating, ejecting everything inside him.

"Please," Bowi croaks, now close to evening, "I need a *pomaeo* infusion." He begs for relief, for today's torture to end.

"Yes," Tagi agrees. "It's time for an infusion."

Eeao, bored and disappointed after waiting all day for the child to pass, saunters outside to stretch her legs and sniff around for nocturnal prey.

Meanwhile, Tagi feels defeated. Why didn't any of his soothing techniques work? He retrieves a fresh *pomaeo* from his water basin. *Hadn't we been making progress?* Today produced nothing but failure. Whatever headway they'd made this past month now feels like placebo—the closest term they have for such a phenomenon is *fynza-eera*, or *false hope*, named after the sweet, tingling sensation one feels after ingesting poisonous *cananeero* nectar.

"Alright, *Bowi*, hold out your arm," Tagi returns, carrying a *pomaeo* melon in one hand and a length of scalded *camraea* tubing in the other. Isolating a vein on the boy's arm isn't as difficult as it'd been last time. *At least he's somewhat healthier.*

Bowi watches as the quill's hypodermic tip punctures his skin. It doesn't hurt. If anything, watching the process makes Bowi start to feel better. This, he knows, will rehydrate his body, quell his stomach, keep him alive...

"Thank you," the boy sighs. He can feel the *pomaeo*'s cool juice entering his bloodstream. It makes him shiver—a full-body sensation that loosens the grip of his nausea.

"Good, now lie back," Tagi says, placing the connected *pomaeo* on an elevated ledge. Soon, a flow is established, directed by Bowi's pumping heart.

The boy smiles, but the old man turns away, grimacing. This is not a practical treatment solution. Infusions like this aren't meant to be conducted repeatedly, long-term. It's supposed to be a quick fix. An emergency procedure. Not an holistic alternative to eating and drinking altogether. Tagi fears that if the boy continues to rely on this hydration method, he might become dependent. If not physically, then psychologically. And at that point, Tagi has no idea how long he'll be able to survive. He's seen no account like Bowi's in the *ynsyna* cavern. No *Teerta* has ever measured the length of time someone can survive on *pomaeo* juice—let alone the nutritional differences between oral ingestion and intravenous infusion.

Then again, as far as I know, he may survive just fine... And yet, judging by the boy's fragile body, Tagi doubts it.

"We'll have you eating again by morning," Tagi says optimistically, poking at his fire pit with a long stick. Night has plunged the sky into murky blackness; rather than reflect the terrain's nocturnal luminance, tonight's hazy atmosphere absorbs light like a sodden sponge. Tagi intends to prepare himself a small supper of boiled eggs before bed. After tending to Bowi all day, he's famished.

Inside the cave, the boy breathes steadily, humming *ynsyna* letters to himself. For him, today was nothing but torture. His throat feels scratchy and raw. Fuzzy, acrid grime coats the enamel of his teeth. His stomach and abdominal muscles ache from repeated abuse. But at least now he's connected to a *pomaeo,* his water-engorged savior. Bowi watches it, resting on the ledge over his bed, slowly deflating. His intravenous tube spirals down from the melon; plunging into his arm, it gently pulsates in rhythm with his heartbeat. He feels the electrolytes already at work, coursing through his veins. Finally, he can close his eyes and relax.

When he's finished eating, Tagi returns to find Bowi still awake inside the cave.

"How are you feeling?" the old *Teerta* asks.

"Better," Bowi says. A breeze wafts cool mist into the cave. The night is still humid. But at least the temperature is comfortable, and Bowi is too. "Will you give me another infusion in the morning?" the boy glances up at his draining *pomaeo*, now shriveled and flat.

"No," Tagi says. "In the morning, you will be ready to eat again."

"But what if—"

"There are no what ifs," Tagi cuts him off. "Don't even think about it. Don't even entertain the option of waking up sick. Tomorrow you will wake up, you will feel wonderful, and you will eat *tyrkuna* with me. That's that. *Wyntiko?*"

Bowi nods acquiescence. Perhaps the old man is right? Perhaps tomorrow morning will be different than this morning? Perhaps tomorrow he won't awake to the smell of blood... Bowi wrinkles his nose, remembering the scent again. He's afraid. Where were his mother and Daeo during *Kunjaruna?*

"*Teerta?*"

"Yes?" Tagi answers, lowering himself into his own bed nearby. With the fire pit extinguished, the cave seems deeper and darker, lit only by their violet *patu*s.

"What's the point of *Kunjaruna?*"

Tagi blinks, surprised by the boy's question.

What an odd thing to ask.

"To protect the nest from *Meemmal* invaders, of course," Tagi says.

"But why do the *Fae* bring *Meemmal* invaders to the *Uyi* in the first place?"

"They don't bring *Meemmal* to the *Uyi*," Tagi explains, finding the boy's questions difficult to conceptualize. "Yes, they arrive with *Meemmal* in tow, on the night of *Kunjaruna*. But it's an inevitable thing, like *Kamaruna*. They can't help it. They don't bring anything anywhere. It's simply a function of their existence."

"What does that mean?" Bowi continues to watch his deflating melon. Its shiny, otherwise green skin, bathed in the purple glow of Bowi's, appears almost black, like the shadow of an object that isn't there.

"Well, it's sort of like how *Kosharuna* is, for us humans," Tagi says.

"I don't know how *Kosharuna* is."

"You don't know how—oh... I suppose you are a bit young," Tagi rolls his eyes. *How tedious, having to explain sex to a child*. He never imagined he'd be in such a position. He only ever participated in *Kosharuna* once before being appointed *Teerta*, and even then he'd only watched from the sidelines. "Alright, do you know how baby *camraea* chicks are born?"

"Yes. They hatch from eggs."

"Okay, but do you know where those eggs come from?"

"From... The *camraea*'s tail?"

"Ugh, you don't know anything," Tagi rubs his eyes wearily.

"Are you talking about what men do to women during *Kosharuna*?"

"Yes," Tagi claps his hands, relieved. "Precisely. That's exactly what I'm talking about. See, you're smart, you know how *Kosharuna* works. It's an inevitable thing, an automatic function of human nature. Well, the *Fae* have natural functions too, which sometimes align with ours. That's what's happening during *Kunjaruna, Kamaruna,* and

Kosharuna. Our species are cooperating, functioning for a greater purpose. Together. Sort of like *Tarma-ako*. Make sense?"

"No."

"Ugh, you'll understand when you're older," Tagi groans, rolling on his side to face away from the boy.

But Bowi isn't so sure. He feels like he's already been alive for so long, already seen so much. Yet he still can't make sense of anything. When will his understanding catch up with everyone else's? When will life finally start to make sense?

When Bowi awakes the next morning, he still smells blood.

Chapter 27
"Eeao"

After the old man's cave, Eeao's next-most-frequented territory is the nearby swamp. Primarily because it's her favorite place to expel waste. She can always smell the boggy marshland, no matter where she is in the *Uyi*. That fetid stench of decomposition and rot, plant decay and fungal rebirth—spores carry on the wind, biosignals alerting her to the presence of regenerative organisms hungry for excrement.

Consciously, she just likes that the swamp's stink conceals her own scent. Feces left unhidden, she knows, are the quickest way to become somebody else's. Plus, the sand around the swamp clumps in a particular way that satisfies her species' ancient proclivity for litter boxes.

Truly, Eeao loves the place.

The swamp, however, does not love Eeao. A complex ecosystem of mycelial organisms extending deep beneath the Yellowstone caldera, this geothermal marshland evolved over hundreds of thousands of years to achieve perfect symbiosis with the *Uyi*'s above-ground rainforest. Mycorrhizal tubules fuse with plant roots below the mud. They eat what the jungle sheds, and then deliver converted energy back to the flora in return. They mine the volcanic terrain with fungal fingers, neutralizing the caldera's hydrothermal activity while efficiently channeling mineral and fossil nutrients up to the trees. Eeao is an alien in their realm, a biological foreigner, an animal species exterminated from this land many, many millennia ago. And the bacteria inside her digestive tract, many of which cling to her feces, are particularly toxic to the *Uyi*'s underground mycorrhizae.

Today, the amount of gut bacteria she's littered around the swamp passes an ecological tipping point. The mycelial superorganism beneath will tolerate her shit no longer. Deep underground, hyphal roots release defense chemicals, triggering the trees above to excrete a combination of airborne volatiles—a pheromone-mimicry system, meant to attract carnivorous birds. Soon, if the distress signal works, predators from outside the *Uyi* will arrive to annihilate the invader...

In the meantime, Eeao continues to defecate where she pleases.

Today, however, she's in the midst of burying her waste when the stampeding arrival of many, tiny humans interrupts her.

"Die *Meemmal!*" the children squeal. "Die! Die! Die!"

Eeao prickles, perturbed. She can see the herd of children on the other side of the swamp, their glowing heads obscured behind overstrung vines and plumes of heated gas belched up from the bog. One of the children appears to be struggling, waist-deep in the shallow, mucky water. The others watch from dry ground, pointing and laughing. Eeao creeps closer, concealed within the tangled *wykyno* tendrils that sprout along the swamp's outer edge.

"Okay friends, that was fun," the child stuck in the swamp sounds frail and pathetic. But Eeao recognizes the voice—it's the same little girl who killed the snake. Intrigued, Eeao slinks up the mossy trunk of a drooping willow to secure a better view.

"Die *Meemmal!* Die! Die! Die!" the children continue chanting, some of them jumping up and down, kicking mud with their feet. "Die *Meemmal!* Die, die, die!"

"If you help me out, you can roll me in *bareebo* seeds," Daeo hopes to entice them.

"No." She fails.

"We rolled you in *bareebo* seeds yesterday."

"*Raea* feathers?"

"Boring."

"Eggs?"

"We do that all the time."

"Let's think of something new."

"Let's think of something really, really gross."

"Let's tie her upside down over a waste pit and—"

"Hey, what's that?" a tall boy with freckles striped across his face points into the willow tree. They all look up and see Eeao. Daeo recognizes the kitten immediately—and then she feels embarrassed, trapped down here in the mud like a *Meemmal*.

Eeao doesn't care about Daeo's situation. She'd just gotten comfortable on one of the willow's sloping branches and is now annoyed she has to move again. With a flick of her tail, she disappears before any of the children can say another word.

"It's gone!" the tall boy shrieks, astounded.

"Get it!"

Like a single, amoebic body, the children race toward the willow tree, splashing and sloshing in a frenzied stampede around the marsh. Some of them slip and fall into the muck; they cry and tantrum, shocked at how quickly their circumstances changed. The ones who make it to the tree are disappointed to find no trace of the strange, alien creature.

"It got away," the tall boy informs his fallen friends.

"Help us!" they cry from the bubbling muck.

Daeo watches, amused, as the other children begin sinking. They thrash and kick and spit and scream, ignorant to the trick of just staying still. But her amusement turns to envy once the others start tossing vines into the swamp to fish out their friends.

"Over here!" Daeo waves her arms, hoping one of them will inadvertently throw her a vine and reel her out too. No such luck. Soon, the bullies are all reassembled on solid ground, half of them sullen and drenched in green sludge.

"Let's go find that thing!" one of the dry ones suggests.

"I saw it go this way!" the tall boy takes charge, leading the gang in a direction that feels right to him.

Daeo watches their heads disappear. But she isn't disappointed—one particularly far-flung vine happened to land close enough for her to just barely reach with her fingertips. She waits until she's sure the other children are gone for good, and then she carefully extends her torso toward the vine. Wrapping her fingers around it, she gives it a tug. The vine remains steadfast—sturdier, even, than the feel of her mother's hands. Bottomless, infinite, Daeo kicks her feet through thick nothingness while using her upper body to pull herself from the mire. It's slow and painstaking. The process takes more effort than Daeo realized she had. Once back on solid ground, she falls into a multicolored thicket of spongy *wykyno*, panting.

"I did it," Daeo smiles to herself, gazing up at the rainforest's green, leafy canopy. "I did it." She can still taste the swamp's foul stench. But this is the first time she's ever escaped the bog on her own. Even Bowi had never managed to pull either of them out. She feels proud of herself, lying there in the shrubs, ringlets of blue and pink *wykyno* spiraling around her face. She wonders what else she can accomplish on her own. And then she sees an irregular shape, high within the trees—diamond, silver, striped.

Eeao gazes down at the girl, recognizing something she respects: The will to live.

Chapter 28
"Daeo"

The kitten vanishes, but Daeo isn't dismayed.

Without wasting time to clean up, she sets off toward the cave. She doesn't care about trailing swamp gunk. She's been anxious to see Bowi again, especially after their mother kept them apart last *Kunjaruna*. But between *raea* manure, mantis cages, b*areebo* seeds, and countless dunks in the swamp, she's been detained every day since; Daeo's "friends" simply won't leave her alone. But now, finally free of them, and with the sun still only climbing toward noon, Daeo has the entire day ahead to spend with Bowi—if she can find him again, that is. She quickens her pace, hoping he'll be just as excited to see her too.

Backtracking toward the *Aeo*, she relocates the same path she traveled last time. It switchbacks through the foothills of the *Uyi*'s southern mountain range, eventually ending up at the *Teerta*'s cave. Daeo completes the journey by noon, expending her final bit of energy in a mad sprint to the cave when she finally sees it materialize through misty foliage ahead.

"Bowi! Bowi!" Daeo calls, running up to the cave. She halts in the clearing outside and doubles over, winded. The cave looks deserted. The firepit exhales a thin, winding stream of smoke, like it's been recently extinguished. A huge, black cauldron sits empty beside it. *"Bowi?"* disappointed, Daeo wonders if he's even here.

"Tynjo?" his voice makes her jump.

"Bowi!" Daeo runs to him. He's shrouded within the cave, lying on one of two wooden beds inside. She tackles him anyway.

"What are you doing here?" he asks, laughing and blinking like he can't tell whether or not she's a dream.

"I wanted to see if I could find you!" Daeo beams, feeling proud of herself again.

"Why weren't you at *Kunjaruna* the other night?" Bowi asks. He still can't believe she's really here, in his arms—can the life he left two moons ago simultaneously exist here inside this cave? "I looked for you and *momo* at the ceremony, but I didn't see you."

"*Momo* made us stay in the *capku*," Daeo says. "She has been acting strange lately. Well, stranger than usual. But now I know where you live, so I can come see you whenever I am able to! Like today! I am sorry I did not come sooner, I have been trying to, but—"

"I don't think the *Teerta* will like that you're here again," Bowi says nervously. Tagi left only a short while ago to pluck fresh *pomaeo*—he'd infused Bowi with their last one earlier this morning.

"Why?" Daeo asks.

"I don't know," Bowi admits, hiding the bruises on his arm. "But he won't like us playing around. He wants me to focus on learning *ynsyna*."

"What is that?"

"It's a method of communication," Bowi says, feeling very knowledgeable. "I need to learn it, which means I don't have time to play games anymore."

"Why do you need to learn it?"

"So that I can know everything all the old *Teerta*s knew," Bowi explains. "They carved all their knowledge inside this cave. All their medicines and techniques and stuff. Once I understand *ynsyna*, I can go deeper into the cave and learn everything I need to know to become the next *Teerta*."

"Where are the carvings?" Daeo asks. "I want to see them."

"They're deeper inside the cave," Bowi points into the darkness, remembering the last time he ventured down the cavern's throat. He's already been vomiting since sunup. Now he feels his stomach raging once more.

"Show me!" Daeo grabs his hand.

Bowi recoils—not from his sister, but from his own blitz of nausea.

"Come on, show me," Daeo insists. She sets off by herself, venturing toward the cave's darkest point. Bowi watches her glowing figure sink into the blackness. And then she disappears around the far corner.

"Wait!" Bowi calls, jolting after her.

He finds her standing in awe, mystified by the cavern's towering speleothems and limitless, black ceiling. Their violet *patu*s cast light throughout the expanse, but only enough to perceive the cavern's impressive structure yawning before them. Closer at hand, Daeo notices a unique variety of subterranean organisms flourishing in the darkness—flaky, non-luminous lichens crawl out from rocky crevices, surviving off ancient, subterranean mineral deposits, while mushroom caps larger than lily pads cluster in damp corners, stacked one atop another like broad, fungal staircases. Dazzled by this strange, lightless world, Daeo can't decide where to focus her vision. And somehow, like her excitement is contagious, Bowi can't help but feel a thrill too; his stomach flutters, but this time it's a welcome sensation.

"Look here," Bowi runs his fingers along the wall closest to them. Carved impressions of *ynsyna* characters dance beneath his fingertips. "This is *ynsyna*. The cavern is covered in it. See? Different combinations of these symbols build different words."

"How?" Daeo walks closer, squinting at the lines of geometric shapes.

"Each symbol makes a different sound, in your head," Bowi explains. "And when you put them together, they create words. Listen, I made up a song to memorize all the characters."

He clears his throat. In the silent interim, Daeo hears a faint, distant *drip! drip! drip!* emanating from the cavern's black depths. To her, it sounds like the *Aeo* is leaking, somehow, all the way out here beneath the mountains.

And then Bowi begins to sing.

Daeo doesn't understand his alphabetical gibberish. But she relishes his familiar voice, his effortless melody, the soft delicacy of his volume, like he doesn't want to be overheard but can't help himself. She smiles, basking in his notes ricocheting around the cavern.

Bowi smiles too as he finishes his song. He likes the cavern's acoustics, the way it amplifies his voice. His sonic energy continues to echo for several long moments, traveling deep into the dark, endless earth. The lingering effects of his power, the ripples of himself, provide Bowi a compelling, euphoric sense of self-actualization.

He wants to sing every word carved inside this cavern.

"*Bowi!*" Tagi calls from outside.

Bowi gasps, "The *Teerta* is back!" He grabs Daeo by the elbow, yanks her around the corner with him. They spill into the bright, outer cave just as Tagi's spry silhouette appears in the cave's mouth.

"What's going on here?" Tagi nearly drops the three *pomaeo* melons he's holding. Initially surprised to find Bowi out of bed and accompanied by someone other than himself, he quickly recognizes Daeo's identical *Patummal* varnish. "What are you doing here again?"

"She was just—"

"I came to see my *tynji*," Daeo speaks for herself.

"Oh, did you now?" Tagi deposits the melons into his water basin. They *splosh!* with echoing piety. Eeao struts into the cave beside him, ready to use her claws if necessary. "I already told you, this cave is no place for children. Your *tynji* is studying to become the next *Teerta.* He has no time for fun and games."

"I do not care about fun and games," Daeo says. "I just want to be with my *tynji*. I can help him learn. He showed me the cavern and—"

"You went inside the *ynsyna* cavern?" Tagi turns to Bowi now, teetering between reprehension and delight. "How are you feeling?"

"I'm feeling much better this time," Bowi realizes with a smile. "I think I'm ready to learn what's written inside there."

"This is wonderful news," Tagi says.

Six moons.

"Let me stay and learn *ynsyneemo* too," Daeo interjects. "Please teach me, I can learn really fast, I promise I can." Really, she'll do anything to stay here forever and hide from her "friends."

"Learn *ynsyneemo?*" Tagi chuckles. "Little girl, you still speak *ragran-eena*, child's tongue. You don't even know how to pronounce contractions. And you think you can learn *ynsyna?*"

"*Momo* says it is just a speech impediment," Daeo defends herself. "It does not mean I cannot learn. I learn new things every day."

"She is really smart," Bowi concurs.

"Oh *kahtopo*," Tagi groans. *She got the boy into the cavern, didn't she?*

"I am only twelve moons younger than *Bowi*," Daeo presses. "I can hunt snakes on my own. I know how to pluck *mabato* spines without poking myself. And I am strong enough to escape the swamp, all by myself. I am plenty old enough to learn whatever *Bowi* is learning—"

"Alright, alright, enough talking," Tagi waves one hand at her while rubbing his temples with the other. "I'm considering your case, child. But if you talk my ear off, I'll be inclined to deny your wish. Now shush."

Daeo shuts her mouth. She stands with her hands clasped behind her back, hopeful, while shooting Bowi a nervous glance. But Bowi knows how much the old man values progress. And after vomiting for the past three mornings straight, ever since his bout after *Kunjaruna*, neither he nor Tagi can deny this rapid recovery. Clearly, Daeo's presence has a positive impact on Bowi's health.

"Alright, you can stay for the afternoon," Tagi concedes after letting the tension linger. "But only if you remain quiet. Your *tynji* is the one studying to become *Teerta*, not you. Understand?"

"I will not speak," Daeo promises. "I will only listen."

"Good child," Tagi twitches one corner of his mouth into a skeptical grimace. Eeao continues to eye the children warily, her whiskers downturned and quivering, mouth thirsty for blood. "Now then," Tagi continues, "Bowi, why don't you grab a *pomaeo* and have yourself a drink, if your stomach can handle it?"

Bowi nods eagerly, his mouth salivating—he's tasted nothing but bile for the past three days.

"Good," Tagi says. "Then after you've had your drink, we'll begin your first *ynsyna* lesson inside the cavern. *Wyntiko?*"

"*Wyntiko.*"

"I am hungry too," Daeo says.

"Of course you are..."

Begrudgingly, Tagi boils an extra egg for the little girl while preparing his own midday meal. "Remember, this isn't a nursery," he tells her while handing over a peeled, boiled egg. *As if it was that much extra work to make.* Still, he adds to the girl, "From now on, if you come here, I'll expect you to have already eaten. No free meals. *Wyntiko?*"

"*Wyntiko,*" Daeo nods gratefully. And then she gobbles down her egg, taking the *Teerta*'s words as a blanket invitation to visit whenever she wants, so long as she doesn't ask for anything.

Meanwhile, Bowi guzzles hungrily from his punctured *pomaeo*. Green juice dribbles down his chin, staining his *areemo* tunic. But he doesn't care about the mess. The only sensation that matters to him now is the cool liquid soothing his stomach. He leans back against the cave wall, his mind wandering while his body comfortably processes the influx of electrolytes. "How are *momo* and the baby?" he turns to Daeo, the question only now dawning on him. *Pomaeo* juice glistens on his chin. Yes, his old life still exists. Just not here...

"I think they are okay," Daeo says. Though really, she's unsure; her mother rarely lets her hold the baby, let alone see her. If Daeo were to answer her brother's question honestly, she'd tell Bowi that she's scared for their mother's health, and she wishes she could hold the baby more, and she worries that the baby is sad, and she doesn't understand why their mother always keeps the baby wrapped so tightly. Instead, she overlooks all those concerns and simply says, "*Momo* started calling the baby *Meemmal.*"

Tagi bites a simmered mantis leg in half. "That's odd," he says, teeth crunching.

"Why?" Bowi asks.

Daeo thinks, picturing her little sister's two-toned face in her mind. The baby is always so quick to smile. "I think it is because she has no *patu.*"

"What?" Tagi laughs at the absurdity. "That's impossible."

Daeo just shrugs. "Well, it is true."

The old man clicks his tongue. *Children and their wild imaginations.* Coming from a *Patummal* child like Daeo, a little girl enameled entirely in *patu,* he isn't surprised by her exaggerated ruse. "Bring the baby to me," Tagi says between chuckles. "I'll figure out what's wrong with its *patu.*"

Daeo nods eagerly. Yes, carrying the baby all the way to the *Teerta*'s cave by herself will be a challenge. But at least now she knows someone will finally help her family.

Tagi and the children finish their lunches without another word. And then they enter the *ynsyna* cavern to begin Bowi's long-awaited first lesson.

Chapter 29
"Meemmal"

Nyno is unwell.

Postpartum complications aside, sleep increasingly eludes her. She has no appetite. Her head throbs nonstop, like someone stabbed an invisible *mabato* spine into her cranium and left it there to fester. She lies in her *capku* day and night, the entrance flap drawn, all light reduced to the wan glow of either murky sunshine or night's evergreen luminance filtered through the structure's translucent, fungal walls. Yet no matter how tightly she shuts her eyelids, Nyno can't shut out the reality of her other senses.

The baby emits weak, intermittent cries from its cradle, just an arm's length away.

Nyno makes no movement toward it.

At first, after receiving Maetri's orders, Nyno continued bringing the baby to Paelo for nightly feedings. But lately, she's lost sight of the point. Why burden herself with the task of visiting her insufferable cousin? Why uphold her end of their deal if she'll no longer require Paelo's service in just a few days? Why increase everyone's misery? Somehow, even the infant's hungry cries are more tolerable than Paelo's cruel voice. And easier to ignore—Nyno rolls back and forth on her sleeping mat, side to side, hands over her ears to block out the baby's screams.

Under her breath, she's begun calling it a *Meemmal*. Deeming it as such makes its cries less grating, less alarming. Soon, the baby's voice fades into background noise, just another part of nature's symphony, like the screech of *raea* slaughtered in nearby fields. A daily occurrence. Just another lifeform converting energy. Nothing to worry about.

Kamaruna *can't come soon enough,* Nyno tells herself. In her mind, things will get better once the baby is gone, once the *Meemmal* is no longer her burden to bear. It's what she must believe. Because *Kamaruna* will happen regardless. Everyone will see. And then after that, her new life...

"Don't fret," Kleeo's idea of comfort is productivity; today, Maetri's sister has brought Nyno a bushel of freshly-harvested *hympano* (the leathery, fungal organism their people use for canvassing). She dumps the raw, tawny material in the center of Nyno's *capku.* "Your new station as Chief of textile sourcing will bring you great fulfillment. Here, I've brought you a gift, something to inspire new work. You're welcome."

Nyno is too tired for this.

"Are you going to shut that thing up?" Kleeo wrinkles her nose at the infant, who whines from its cradle like a weary, long-ignored alarm.

"*Huh?*" Nyno rolls over on her sleeping mat.

"Get up," Kleeo stands over her. "Come on, get up. When was the last time you went outside, *huh?* Put on your harness. And bring the *Meemmal.* I'm taking you on a walk."

Nyno doesn't appreciate the pushiness. But she's too weak to resist. Kleeo drags her from her sleeping mat, and then helps her into an *areemo* tunic and spined harness, appropriate attire for a mid-morning stroll to the *Aeo.*

"Don't cover it," Kleeo says when Nyno starts swaddling her baby. "Let people see the *Meemmal.* They'll all see it tomorrow, anyway."

The baby blinks up at the sun. It shines full-force on this rare, clear, brilliant day—like there's a solar intelligence up there, compensating sunshine for the deprived child.

Nyno feels strangely exposed in the daylight, walking outside with her secret uncovered. Eyes linger, heads turn. Passersby on routine errands—women with pregnant bellies and satchels of *bareebo* seeds, men heaving water basins and *raea* carcasses—pause their activities to stare at Nyno and the tiny *Meemmal* squirming against her breast. No one has ever seen anything like this. An outsider, born in their nest? Everyone's reviled by the scandal. Gossip ensues.

Kleeo seems to enjoy the attention; she wears a smirk as they walk the *Aeo*'s shoreline, still attracting looks. Nyno finds a spot to sit in the sand, and then tries to make herself as small as possible. She sets her baby in a flowery, pink cushion of *wykyno* beside her. Naked, bare to the world, the baby's eyes rove back and forth, absorbing, observing, finally seeing the world for the first time in her short life. Warm algae laps at Nyno's toes.

"Your hair is getting long," Kleeo remarks, running her fingers over the prickly black-and-blonde hairs sprouting from Nyno's otherwise radiant scalp.

"*Wakar*," Nyno mumbles, referring to their culture's head-shaving custom. "I keep forgetting."

"Let me do it for you," Kleeo offers.

Nyno sits still while Kleeo coats her *patu* in *raea* lard. The flintstone blade she uses to shave Nyno's hair is long and copper-colored. It makes a *pffft! pffft!* sound as Kleeo gently drags it across Nyno's scalp. At moments, Nyno wishes the woman would just sink the blade into her jugular. A quick ending. An easy way out of this mess. *Mercy like that doesn't exist.* When the shave is complete, Kleeo rinses Nyno's head off with lakewater.

"There, so much brighter," Kleeo runs her fingers over Nyno's *patu* again. This time, her scalp is silky smooth, at least twenty percent more luminous than before.

Nyno feels compelled to say, "Thank you." Beside her, the baby whimpers. Is it cold? Warm? Overwhelmed? Part of Nyno yearns to reach out and gather her child in her arms, to protect it—*my baby*—but then a larger part of her shoves that thought away.

"There's life after death, you know," Kleeo says, offhandedly. The two women sit side by side before the lake. Nyno stares down at the sand, unresponsive. Her eyes scan millions and millions of microscopic particles. Tiny shells and fragmented bits of fossilized, eroded organisms. But to Nyno, the sand is just inanimate matter, ground dissolved by water. Nothing remarkable. Nothing alive.

"It's true what they say," Kleeo continues. "There really is life at the bottom of the *Aeo.*"

Nyno doesn't look at her. "Why are you telling me this?" she asks.

"Because it seems like you don't believe it anymore," Kleeo says. "We all learned the natural principles as children. *Kamaruna* happens twice a month. *Tarma-ako.* We do it for a reason."

"I know."

"And yet you don't want to volunteer your *Meemmal* baby tomorrow," Kleeo says. "Don't deny it; I can tell you don't really want to. You're sad. But there's nothing to be sad about. You're sending the *Meemmal* away to become new life. Better life. You're doing what the *Uyi* requires, for the benefit of all. Don't you understand that?"

"Of course I understand," Nyno replies automatically. "And I do want to volunteer—"

"*Shh,*" Kleeo silences her, pressing her fingers against Nyno's lips. "You don't need to lie to me. I know how sad you are. I know you're grieving. I was once a birthing *momo* too, many moons ago. But I suffered only miscarriages. I became sad at first, depressed over the wasted life, and scared for my own future worth. But my cousin, *Syno,* is a female *punteeku,* and she told me that blood is never lost, only transformed. All life dies to live again. The cycle always continues; that's the only thing we can ever be sure of.

"So instead of remaining sad, I became strong, and I joined the *punteeku.* I fight every *Kunjaruna* to prove my worth and push the cycle forward. But you're lucky, *Nyno;* you don't have to become strong and fight to stay alive. You already have a valuable skill: Textile sourcing. So lean into it. Let go of old blood and create life anew. It's all for the best."

Nyno isn't facing Kleeo, but she can hear sincerity in the woman's voice. Instinctively, her gaze drifts to her baby. Surrounded in white and coral *wykyno* tendrils, the bare child looks ethereal, like a marbled pearl encased within some strange, otherworldly mollusk. Precious. Pristine. *Let go of old blood and create life anew?* Nyno forces her eyes away. She stares out over the water, the *Aeo*'s blue, rolling surface a mesmerizing void. *How many people are down there?* Her vision sinks into the watery expanse, unfocused and lost. *There's life after death, you know.*

Across the vast lake, the northern mountains steeple toward the sky. From Nyno's vantage point, the cliffs seem to jut out of the water, like the ridged fin of some giant eel rising from the deep. Tomorrow, the *Fae* will descend over those mountains and gather six volunteers for *Kamaruna*. Tomorrow, a stone will be tied to her baby's ankles.

"It's all for the best," Nyno forces the words from her own mouth. Salty and dry.

"Exactly," Kleeo traces a finger along the back of Nyno's soft scalp, admiring her handiwork again. "You have to keep telling yourself that. Because it's true."

If it's so true, why do I have to keep telling myself—

NO. Nyno turns her mind off. She swivels her torso to pick up the *Meemmal*, which is starting to fuss again. Its lips are cracked and flaky. Its face is clammy and yellowing. The outsider is hungry, thirsty, asking for life.

"Just give it some water," Kleeo advises. "But don't waste any food."

Chapter 30
"Kamaruna"

Daeo awakes early the next morning to an empty *capku*.

"*Momo?*" she peers around groggily. Even the baby cradle is vacant. Strange... She'd intended to get an early start this morning, steal out of the nest with the bundled baby and carry her up to the *Teerta*'s cave. If she can sneak out early enough, even the bullies won't be awake to impede her.

But apparently her *momo* woke up first.

"Find the baby, take her to the *Teerta*," Daeo motivates herself while she dresses. She's so focused on her current objective, she doesn't even realize today is *Kamaruna*. Her mother stores an *areemo* poncho in the wooden trunk next to her empty sleeping mat. It's baggy on Daeo's slight body, with enough folds to conceal the baby once found. "Perfect," Daeo is confident with her plan.

Outside, the morning is windy and dark, dawn smothered behind soaring plumes of cumulonimbus—a stark contrast from yesterday's sunshine. Drizzling rainfall accumulates into streams, which trickle through the jungle's leafy canopy like leaks in a massive, thatched roof. Daeo scurries down the path toward their waste pit, pulling the poncho over her head to keep dry. Muddy and slick, she pays careful attention to the ground's downhill gradient as she travels.

The waste pit, which is essentially just a trench covered by a large, soggy frond, is unoccupied when Daeo arrives. She pauses to relieve herself, and then doubles back toward the *Aeo*, thinking perhaps her *momo* went down to bathe the baby, or to collect water for *tyrkuna*. Something predictable.

Several adults loiter around the lakeshore when Daeo arrives. Mostly young men looking to catch *mongaeo* (meaty, amphibious newts, which lumber ashore by the dozens every sunrise). On this rainy morning, everyone wears broad-brimmed hats made of *hympano*. As Daeo scans the gloomy shoreline, they all look like tall, capped mushrooms that've somehow sprouted legs. Unfortunately, her mother is not among them.

By process of elimination, Daeo chooses to check Paelo's *capku* next. Where else could her *momo* have taken the baby? Certain of her logic, she trudges back into the jungle, expecting to find the two women sitting around Paelo's fire pit, complaining about the rain or their *nunee*s or something innocuous and trivial.

"How should I know where your *momo* is, *eh?*" Paelo scoffs, offended by the question. She's currently nursing her own newborn, alone by her fire pit, which sizzles and spits beneath the percolating rainfall. Judging by her temper, Daeo figures the woman hasn't been awake long. "I haven't seen your *momo* or that *Meemmal* curse in days."

Daeo frowns. "Why does everyone keep calling my sister a *Meemmal?*"

Paelo cackles. "I wouldn't call that thing my sister if I were you."

Thunder erupts; the atmosphere crackles.

"*WAAAAAAAAAAAAH*" Paelo's baby emits its well-practiced shriek.

"Oh shut up," Paelo shoves its face into her other breast.

Out of options, Daeo returns to her mother's *capku*. It's still empty when she arrives. Drenched and shivering, Daeo trades the heavy poncho for a dry tunic. She sits in the abode's center, encircled by her sleeping mat, her mother's sleeping mat, and the baby's cradle. Where could they possibly be? Daeo's imagination is exhausted. The constant patter of rain against the *capku*'s outer surface is almost like a warm blanket, all-encompassing and steady. Certain that her mother will return with the child at any moment, Daeo allows herself to drift into a meditative nap, sitting cross-legged and hunched over herself, like a red *cananeero* flower about to bloom...

Meanwhile, Nyno is struggling to force a *Kamaruna* mushroom down her baby's throat. The child keeps regurgitating it, giggling like this is all some sort of sick joke. *Please let it be?* Today's five other volunteers have dutifully chewed and swallowed their assigned mushrooms. They're all old enough to understand the reverence of this moment. Some of them are even excited—they've waited their entire lives to experience these sacred, fungal effects, reserved only for those standing on the brink of *Kamaruna*'s precipice. But Nyno's baby simply won't ingest the tiny, white mushroom. She feels flustered now, being so near to the end, yet unable to complete this final task. *Just eat it!*

"What's the problem?" Maetri approaches Nyno. They're all gathered near the forbidden swamp grounds, the six *Kamaruna* volunteers plus a muscly gang of *punteeku* overseers, present to ensure everyone adheres to custom. Maetri's father, Paetri, the former Chief *raea* wrangler, is among today's volunteers. Kleeo and Syno are among the *punteeku*, casually spreading rumors among their fellow hunters that Nyno's bizarre *Meemmal* offspring is really the product of a secret affair she had with the well-known *Patummal*, Veetri. They claim he's the one who seeded the abomination.

"There's no problem," Nyno tells Maetri, hiding the chewed-up, regurgitated mushroom in her left palm.

"Good, then give me the *Meemmal*," Maetri takes the naked infant from her.

And at that moment, Nyno knows she will never hold her last-born again. She watches silently while Maetri binds a cord of *areemo* twine around their baby's kicking feet. Attached to the cord's other end is a jagged, gray stone—an anchor. His fellow *punteeku* bind the other volunteers too; the stone Veetri reverently ties to his father's calloused ankles is so large it's practically a boulder. Nyno wants to look away, but the baby holds her gaze.

It's smiling. It's waving a hand. It thinks it will return to its mother's arms.

She thinks nothing's wrong—

In Nyno's palm, the slimy, uneaten *Kamaruna* mushroom feels heavier than it should, like a larva growing rapidly. Another secret. Nyno is desperate to get rid of the fungal fruit, but she's afraid someone will notice if she drops it on the ground. It needs to disappear. So she slips the *Kamaruna* mushroom into her own mouth and swallows.

Forbidden. Sacred. Impulsive.

The mushroom tastes like soil and rainwater.

The baby will not break eye contact.

Her mismatched face matches Nyno's.

What have I done?

Daeo awakes to the rhythmic beating of drums.

"*Kamaruna?*" she rubs her eyes, realizing the day. Outside, she hears the murmur of crowds gathering down by the *Aeo*. But she's still alone inside her *capku*; her mother never returned. Forgetting the poncho, Daeo hurries out into the rain.

"*Momo?*" she calls into the trees.

Thunder suppresses her voice.

As it subsides, the distant drums increase tempo.

"*xxxxxxxxxxxxxxxxxxxxxxxxxxxxxxxxxxxxxxxxxxx*"

And now the *Fae* are descending. *Kamaruna* has begun.

Daeo sprints down the path toward the *Aeo*, bare feet splashing through mud and rain. Is her mother looking for her? Or has she already gathered with everyone else?

Compelled by a nebulous, gut-wrenching panic, Daeo dives down a shortcut, sliding through a mud-slickened tunnel in the jungle's gnarled understory. She comes crashing out the other side like a cannonball shot onto the lakeshore, her momentum propelling her into the outermost rank of onlookers.

"Show some respect," Paelo happens to be among them.

Daeo scrambles to her feet, apologizing to the people with whom she's collided. They dust sand from their knees and cluck their tongues at her. One woman winds her arm back, preparing to swat Daeo on the head, but the little girl is too quick; ducking low, she squeezes between two sets of knees and darts into the crowd.

"XXXXXXXXXXXXXXXXXXXXXXXXXXXXXX"

Fae fill the sky. Their formation materializes from the billowing clouds like a massive, shimmering hailstone. Their insectoid wings roar louder than the thunderstorm. Like ants, the humans stare upward in awe. *Kamaruna* is underway.

Nyno stands closer to the lake, alongside the *punteeku* who guard the six volunteers. Maetri might be next to her, or Kleeo—she doesn't know. She barely knows where she is or what's going on. Her mind, warped by the tiny, pearlescent mushroom she recently swallowed, is now hyper-focused on one thing: The soft sand between her toes.

It's strange. A substance that seemed thoroughly dead yesterday now blooms and writhes with graphic life just beneath her feet. Staring down, Nyno sees tiny, shelled creatures crawling around on spidery legs, hiking across treacherous peaks and valleys of sand particles, each pebble a polished gemstone in its own right. She sees microscopic worms she'd never noticed before burrowing through moist, fungal detritus, worlds of interlaced hyphae pulsing water like blood. She sees spores taking root, seeds sprouting fingers, tiny plants leaching mineral nutrients from the ground through intravenous, mycorrhizal networks. Millions and millions of individual lives, all existing concurrently beneath her own, everything interconnected by the pulsating, symbiotic rhythms of life... *Nothing ever ends.* And if all this life exists within the seemingly dead sand beneath her feet, what lives beneath the *Uyi*'s soil? Its mud? The swamp? The *Aeo?* What really happens to the *Kamaruna* volunteers? Why must they be bound? Don't they know where they're going? The beauty of what they're becoming?

There's life after death, you know.

"XXXXXXXXXXXXXXXXXXXXXXXXXXXXX"

Daeo sees her mother standing further down the shoreline, among the burly-armed *punteeku*, her head downcast. And then she sees the six volunteers rise into the air. She sees that one of them is a baby. She sees its two-toned face, half like Bowi's, the other half like her own. She sees that it has no *patu*. She sees that it's crying, squirming, a tiny speck caught beneath the buzzing *Fae* horde.

But Daeo is too far away to do anything. She's arrived too late. Standing helpless on the lakeshore, face frozen in a voiceless scream, Daeo watches her baby sister soar high over the *Aeo,* drop into the water, and disappear forever.

Act 3

Chapter 31
"Ynsyn-eera"

Nyno is numb.

The effects of the *Kamaruna* mushroom last long into the night. Following the initial, mind-expanding rapture she experienced during the ceremony, Nyno spends the rest of the afternoon plummeting into a bottomless lake of bleak, infinite, psychedelic emptiness.

Nothing matters.

Nothing ever did.

Nothing ever does.

The overwhelming ecstasy elicited from witnessing life's cyclic nature churn so clearly before her eyes has sapped more psychic energy from Nyno's brain than she can physiologically muster. Now, spent, drained, wrung of all sense of herself, she wishes she could just sink into the ground and recycle her own wasted body. *This is why* Kamaruna *mushrooms are reserved for the end*, Nyno thinks. *I should be dead.*

"Get up," Kleeo finds Nyno still lying on the lakeshore that evening, violet scalp coated in sand. The rain ended long ago, and now the half moon hangs in the hazy sky like a chipped fingernail, waiting to snag something. "You've been lying here all day. It's time to get up and move on."

Nyno's eyes feel like jagged stones lodged in her skull. She tries to blink up at the moon over the *Aeo*, but her eyelids are stuck, glued to her dried eyeballs. Wading out of her own delirium, Nyno realizes she probably should get up, lest someone suspect she ingested something she shouldn't have...

Kleeo whispers, "I saw you eat that mushroom."

Nyno freezes.

"Relax," Kleeo snickers, pulling Nyno to her feet. "Once you start breaking rules, you realize no one else follows them either."

Nyno exhales a long breath. It feels like the first she's released all day. Her mouth tastes bitter and stale, like *sokeeto* berries left out to ferment. "I need water," she croaks.

"I'll get you some," Kleeo guides her back toward the jungle, the treeline wreathed in radiant lichen. Several others watch from the lakeshore, mostly women collecting water to boil, or bathing children before bed. *Do they all know what I've done?* Nyno doesn't remember what to be more paranoid about—eating the *Kamaruna* mushroom or birthing the now-dead *Meemmal*. In her fractured, fungus-addled mind, every terrible thing that's ever happened to her is happening all over again, all at once, right now.

"I have fresh water at my *capku*," Kleeo assures her. "It's not far."

Clutching feebly to the woman's arm, Nyno follows her into the jungle. The rainforest's luminous crust seems to pulse an emerald heartbeat, its rhythm chasing her own. She can barely look anywhere—her vision crackles with electric vibrance. Greens and blues melt together, while yellow and violet lightwaves fragment into kaleidoscopic shards that scratch against her retinas. She can't look directly at anyone's *patu*. Twigs claw at her arms and legs like cold, dead fingers. Serpentine vines dangle like nooses. *Wykyno* tendrils unfurl from the ground and cling at her feet, threatening to ensnare her, pull her under, absorb her life.

"Help me," Nyno doesn't realize she's crying.

"We're almost there," Kleeo's reassuring embrace reminds Nyno of her mother...

Several lifetimes transpire within Nyno's fevered psyche by the time Kleeo deposits her on a log bench outside her *capku*. The angry blaze of a fire pit consumes Nyno's visual field. She sinks into the damp, moss-covered log, which seems to expand around and behind her torso like an extravagant, cushioned chair.

Slowly, swirling colors congeal into solid, recognizable forms. A beige, triangular *capku*. The silvery, waxing moon. A pot of boiling water. A line of *areemo* strung between two bushy trees, upon which articles of clothing have been hung to air dry. Several humans bustle nearby, their *patu*s visible through the foliage, neighbors going about their nightly business.

"Drink," Kleeo hands her a ladle of cooled water.

Nyno sips, feeling oddly suspicious of the liquid. She tries to ignore her fear.

"Thank you," she says weakly.

"You'll feel better soon," a fleeting smile crosses Kleeo's battle-scarred face.

Nyno blinks, wondering if she imagined the smile. "You've eaten a *Kamaruna* mushroom before, too?" she asks quietly, thinking back to Kleeo's earlier comment.

Kleeo nods. "*Tapati* collects a secret stash. All the *punteeku* have tried them. We do it for fun."

Nyno is surprised by how unsurprising this information now seems. Just a few days ago, her station as a birthing *momo* felt inevitable and unchanging. A fact of life. It was all anyone had ever expected her to do. It was all she'd ever expected herself to do. It was supposed to be her life's sole purpose. She didn't think anything else was possible. Now, suddenly, she has an entirely new life ahead of her. *And all it took was for one man to say a few words...*

Is reality really nothing more than orchestration?

"Hey, *Nyno!*" Paelo's voice alters everything.

"What do you want?" Kleeo springs up in defense.

"I want what she owes me," Paelo steps into the fire pit's orange glare, pointing at Nyno. The *Patummal* woman stands alone, free of her infant and outfitted in a thorny harness. An accusing scowl sits angrily on her blindingly-bright face. "Just because you got rid of your *Meemmal* baby doesn't mean I didn't do the work of feeding it for the past four moons. We made a deal, *Nyno*. You owe me new gear and clothing, remember?"

Nyno closes her eyes, wishing to be anywhere else.

"She doesn't owe you anything, filthy *Patummal*," Kleeo spits in the dirt between them. "For all we know, it was your toxic milk that turned her child into a *Meemmal* in the first place. Everyone knows *Patummal* blood is bad."

Paelo scoffs, accustomed to this type of slander. She crosses her arms over her chest, mentally preparing a comeback, but the arrival of several neighbors causes her to reconsider—two male *punteeku* emerge through a wall of xate fronds, while a female in a spined harness circles in from the other side of the clearing. They each exchange glances with Kleeo, unspoken signals. Dancing firelight illumes the freckled constellations of birthmarks splayed across their arms and chests, faces and legs, skin uncolonized by *patu* yeast.

Paelo eyes them nervously. Compared to their minimal scalp-coatings, Paelo knows she sticks out like a big, glowing target. "Look, I just want what I'm owed."

"Leave my *capku*, dirty *Patummal*," Kleeo spits at her again. "And don't talk to *Nyno* anymore. She owes you nothing. She's a Chief now. Do you understand?"

Nyno's eyes are still closed; she listens while Paelo mutters something under her breath, and then her footsteps recede into the jungle. Indignant. Scornful. Nyno knows her cousin won't give up so easily. *Do I blame her?*

"Thank you," Nyno tells Kleeo after the other *punteeku* have dispersed. "But I don't mind crafting items for *Paelo*. I do owe her, and she is my—"

"*Shh,*" Kleeo silences. "It won't matter. She'll be gone soon anyway."

Failing to understand Kleeo's implication and too tired to request clarification, Nyno assumes she must've simply misheard the comment. For a while, the two women sit in silence beside the crackling fire. Kleeo stokes the pit's dried timber every now and then, whenever the flames begin to fade.

Like a resentful child waking from a nap, Nyno's stomach begins growling. "I need to eat," she says, realizing she has neither eaten nor seen Daeo all day. *What have I done?* "And then I need to return to my *capku.*"

Kleeo seasons and roasts a *raea* thigh for the two of them to split (Nyno manages three bites; Kleeo finishes the rest), and then she assists Nyno home. The walk isn't long—turns out, Nyno's *capku* is just a short trek downhill from Kleeo's. They pause outside the entrance flap; Nyno can see Daeo's little, violet form glowing faintly inside the *hympano* wall of their home. Something like guilt settles in her gut. *What do I keep doing wrong?*

"You have *ynsyn-eera* now," Kleeo says before departing, using a term Nyno has never heard before. Translated from its root words, it literally means *knowledge-hope.*

"*Ynsyn-eera?*" Nyno asks.

"You've taken the *Kamaruna* mushroom," Kleeo explains, a grin shadowed beneath the ridge of her forehead. "You've seen the life that comes after death. You know there's nothing to fear. You know it's all for the best. *Ynsyn-eera.*"

Lightly, Kleeo brushes her lips against Nyno's forehead. Surging tears disrupt Nyno's vision; the last person to grace her with such a gesture was her own *momo*, the day she volunteered. And then Kleeo is gone, disappearing into the jungle's verdant luminance. Nyno can feel the rush of her vacating air.

Daeo jolts awake as soon as her mother enters the *capku*. After having exhausted herself of tears this afternoon, the young girl had fallen into a deep, comatose slumber. Now, smacked by the weight of waking reality, cortisol spikes her blood like lightning.

"Where have you been?" she asks her mother.

"*Shh*," Nyno responds instinctively, retying the entrance flap shut. And then she remembers—*there's no need to keep quiet;* the baby is gone. *Ynsyn-eera.*

"*Momo*," Daeo's eyes brim with tears; sleep has replenished her reserve. She holds in her arms the baby's blanket—Bowi's blanket—her blanket. "Where have you been? Why did you not come home? I needed you to come home..."

"I'm home now," Nyno sheds her *areemo* tunic. It falls to the ground beside her sleeping mat, caked in mud and sand from the lakeshore.

"Why... Why did you volunteer my *tynjo?*" Daeo can't see through her tears. They just keep coming, surging from some reservoir beneath her face, blurring her vision, refracting her world. Soon, she can't see anything. She feels her *momo*'s arms wrap around her trembling body. She feels herself lifted into the air. She feels herself brought into bed with her mother. She feels her mother's tears on the back of her neck.

"*Ynsyn-eera*," Nyno whispers into her daughter's ear, almost like a lullaby. "*Ynsyn-eera.*"

Time passes.

Nyno continues repeating the phrase.

Ynsyn-eera. Ynsyn-eera. Ynsyn-eera.

They do not move. Tears spill sideways down their faces, creating two little sets of puddles on Nyno's sleeping mat. Their bodies are pressed together, but Daeo doesn't feel warm.

More time passes.

Daeo's tears slow, but they don't stop. Meanwhile, the back of her neck is no longer damp. Her *momo* has fallen asleep, though she continues to murmur: *Ynsyn-eera... Ynsyn-eera...* Quietly, cautiously, desperate not to rouse her mother, Daeo slips free from the cold arms around her. They slide off her skin like chopped, unfeeling vines. Without looking back, Daeo unties the *capku*'s entrance flap and steals out into the night, clutching her baby sister's blanket to her chest.

The air is thick and balmy. Hot mist steams up from the ground, puddles of rainwater eager to evaporate. The jungle smells like it's boiling. Still, Daeo shivers, hugging her feather blanket tight. It smells like her baby sister—sweet, slightly sour. It feels like her baby sister—soft, silky, warm. She imagines she would do anything to wrap it around her sister once more...

After running for some time, Daeo finds herself comfortably lost in the towering rainforest. Surrounded by staggering tree trunks and spongy stalks of *wykyno*, climbing vines and blooming orchid faces, luminous lichen carpets everything like a green, spreading disease.

Amidst the scenery, underneath a thicket of tangled, flowering philodendron, a dull, non-green object catches Daeo's eye. Upon closer inspection, she presumes it to be a simple rock, poking up from the ground. It appears maroon and mostly smooth, marbled with veins of crystalline black. Really, it's a million-year-old chunk of petrified wood (*Pinus contorta*), which has been eroding there for ages, formed from the trunk of a tree that witnessed Yellowstone's last eruption, when the supervolcano incinerated most of the continent...

But of course, Daeo doesn't know that.

To her, a rock is a rock. Or is it?

She plies it up from the ground. She wraps it in her baby blanket. It's small, but roughly the same weight her sister once was. Now, holding the fossil in her arms, wrapped in woven feathers that once belonged to her *tynjo*, her *tynji*, herself—it feels good. It feels right. It feels safe.

Her tears stop. She's not alone.

Ynsyn-eera.

Chapter 32
"Tagi"

Sometimes, Tagi dreams of his mother.

He never called her *momo* as a child; she volunteered for *Kamaruna* before he began speaking. *Mankata*, or *late-bloomer*, he was a child of very few words. As a little boy, he spent most of his time listening and observing, sitting and watching, staring and thinking. He experienced the world differently than everyone else seemed to. People thought him dumb for many moons—until one day someone noticed him mending a spider's broken leg with a twig and a sticky wad of *hympano* gum. Everyone marveled at his quiet thoughtfulness, the novelty of it, though the repair was admittedly impractical and short-lived (his mother squashed the spider with a rock the next day).

In retrospect, he used to believe that episode was the reason for his selection out of all the other children at the time to succeed their old *Teerta*; back then, he'd been too naive to truly understand their reasoning. But although he never shared any words with his mother before she disappeared into the *Aeo*, he still remembers her face vividly.

Tonight, she flashes through his dreams, cheeks and forehead smeared with blood—

"*Momo*—" he startles awake, seized by a full-body muscle spasm.

Eeao flies off his chest, bristling.

"*Teerta?*" Bowi stirs too.

Early dawn filters into the cave through a glassy wall of mist. Outside, *kynaea* and other birds sing a new day into existence. Tagi can faintly feel the sun climbing over the horizon, tugging on his already frayed nerves. His eyes dart about the cave, reorienting his conscious mind.

Eeao skulks to her shadowed cranny, peeved.

"*Teerta?*" Bowi is by his side. The boy's sister hasn't visited again for several days, but he's been nausea-free ever since their venture into the *ynsyna* cavern. Now, with Bowi gazing down at him in concern, Tagi feels almost as though their roles have reversed.

"I'm fine, I'm fine," he brushes the boy aside, swinging to his feet. "Just a strange dream. Nothing to worry about. I'm hungry. Why don't we start making *tyrkuna?*"

"What was the dream about?" Bowi asks.

"Nothing," Tagi flies about the cave, pirouetting on his toes, stretching his limbs, engaging his morning calisthenics; he takes pride in his ability to rise each day with vigor. "Will you help me light the *uyee* outside?"

"Were you dreaming about your *momo?*"

"What?" Tagi nearly falls over.

"I heard you call for your *momo*, in your sleep," Bowi says.

Tagi begins to say something, but then stops himself. He looks angry.

Bowi backtracks, "It's okay, I mean, I dream about my *momo* too... Sometimes..."

Tagi doesn't say anything; he just stands there, glaring at the ground. A solitary *Gigantiops* ant totters across the cave floor on bulky, groping legs. Soon, it begins crawling over the calcified boulder of Tagi's big toe.

"I miss my *momo*," Bowi says after some time, anxious to fill the silence.

At that, the old man snorts. "Why?"

Bowi blinks. "Because... I *braea* her," he says, using their word for *love*.

Tagi doesn't say anything.

"Didn't you *braeu* your *momo?*" confusion wrings pigment from Bowi's face.

Tagi continues to watch the herculean ant trek across his foot. "*Braeam* is a strange feeling," he finally says. "I've been alive for a long time. There were several people toward whom I may have felt some sense of it, once. But my *momo* certainly wasn't one of them."

Shocked, Bowi considers asking the man why, but then stops himself. If it's possible for someone to not love their own mother, he'd rather not hear the story behind it. Not while missing his own so much, anyway.

Up in her cranny, Eeao preens the inside of her leg, vigorously combing her fur as flat as possible.

Tagi snorts again, wiggling the giant ant off his foot and then squashing it beneath his bare heel. The resulting puddle is crunchy and acidic. *Perfect.* Tagi retrieves a clay vial, one of many he stores along a rock ledge inside his cave. The one he selects contains a special fuel: The crushed-up, liquefied bodies of various ants and termites. Carefully, using a chip of flintstone lying on the cave floor, Tagi scrapes the ant he's just pulverized into the vial. Its remains sink into the rest.

"I'll help you start the *uyee*," Bowi says, following Tagi outside to the fire pit.

Ringed by fist-sized, blackened stones, the pit of charcoal sits centered in the clearing outside the cave's mouth. Bowi fetches an armful of *areemo* kindling, which the *Teerta* keeps stored in a dry, enclosed alcove beside the cave. Meanwhile, Tagi makes his way over to a flowering *cananeero* bush several paces away. Fiery, red bulbs unfurl from fleshy stems taller than the old man's shoulders. Vivid and bountiful, shooting upward from leafy, central stalks, they smell intoxicatingly sweet, enticing to humans and insects alike. But Tagi isn't ignorant to their toxic allure. He plucks several flowers from their stems, careful not to spill any of the chemical nectar brimming within their elongated pistils. And then he carries the scarlet bouquet back to his fire pit.

Bowi is there waiting for him, having already constructed a small teepee of *areemo* kindling atop the charcoal heap. Tagi crouches beside him and sprinkles the red *cananeero* blossoms in a pile beneath the dried kindling.

"Would you like to do the honors?" he hands Bowi his vial of gelatinous insect fuel.

Bowi nods; to him, this pyromancy is as normal as drinking water. He pours some of the mashed ant guts onto the pile of red petals. Formic acid from the ant-termite cocktail mixes with the *cananeero* nectar, which contains a defensive chemical the plant naturally evolved to fry non-pollinating invaders. Soon, Bowi and Tagi are enveloped in plumes of chalky, white smoke as the heated chemical reaction ignites the kindling. Most humans of the *Uyi* believe the *cananeero* bush grows its flame-making flowers simply for the purpose of relighting their fire pits after rainstorms. Few realize the plant has goals of its own.

"Wonderful," Tagi watches the blaze roar to life. "I'll begin cooking *tyrkuna*."

The sticky-tart aroma of steamed *voreeko* soon saturates the morning humidity, permeating the rainforest's breezy currents of mist. Down-wind, Daeo can smell the appetizing food as she hikes nearer to the cave.

"*Bowi!*" she calls, spotting their violet *patu*s around the smoking cauldron.

"*Daeo!*" Bowi sprints to greet her, elated. "Where have you been? I've been waiting for you to come back."

"The swamp," Daeo grins through gritted teeth. Bowi immediately understands.

"What's that?" Tagi points at her with his ladle, referring to the lumpy bundle of feathers in Daeo's arms. "Did you bring food to contribute to this *tyrkuna?* Because otherwise, I've only cooked enough *voreeko* for two."

"No, this is just something I am carrying for my *momo*..." Deao hugs her baby blanket tighter, offering no further explanation.

"Well then I hope you've already eaten," Tagi tells her flatly. He isn't annoyed by her presence, per se. But he isn't overjoyed by it either. Generally, he barely has enough patience for his own company. But he can't deny the difference she makes for the boy—his eyes lighten, his voice quickens, his laughter rolls. She offers Bowi a type of medicine an old *Teerta*s simply can't give: *The psychological comfort of childhood*. Yet at the same time, to Tagi, the little girl is little more than a reminder of the nest—societal forces—imposed timeframes—another *Kamaruna*.

Six moons.

"How are *momo* and the baby?" Bowi asks.

"Better," Daeo lies.

"*Bowi*, hand me your bowl," Tagi begins serving breakfast. Neither he nor Bowi saw the baby's *patu*. Neither of them remember Daeo's *Meemmal* comment. Neither of them detect her lie.

And Daeo is grateful they don't question further. Because lately, she's begun to feel complicit in her sister's demise. Why didn't she run faster? Why didn't she wake up earlier? Why did she take a nap that morning instead of continuing to search for her mother? These, Daeo assumes, are the questions that'll naturally arise if she ever tries to explain to anyone what happened that day.

So she sits quietly on the ground while Tagi and Bowi eat their *tyrkuna*. She tries to believe everything really is better. And whenever her stomach growls, she hugs her baby blanket as tightly as she can, pressing its concealed chunk of petrified wood into her empty gut.

Chapter 33
"Bowi"

Apparently, the moon is just a giant mushroom.

Or, at least, that's according to the fourth *Teerta*, who believed so strongly in the moon's fungal origin that he inscribed his ancient theory as fact right here on a subterranean wall for Bowi to read a million moons later. That's why their word for *moon* (*aruna*) is the same as their word for *fungus*.

The next line of the fourth *Teerta's ynsyna* claims the *Fae* originated as lunar spores, which traveled via celestial, atmospheric currents all the way down to the *Uyi*. From this ancient voyage, bipedal life arose in the rainforest caldera. Because really, according to the fourth *Teerta's* next line of *ynsyna*, the universe at large is just a giant, semi-aqueous grotto. The moon is a distant, shimmery mushroom, caught up in the sky's lapping waves. The sun is a colossal, bioluminescing beast, which swims endlessly across the far reaches of the murky cave, routinely disappearing and reemerging over the rocky horizon walls. And as for the *Uyi* itself—it's just a tiny bubble of vegetation blooming somewhere along the cave's infinitely cratered floor.

Bowi is fascinated learning this clandestine knowledge. The first three *Teertas* had focused their writing primarily on elemental matters, like soil maintenance, weather patterns, water sanitation, fire chemistry, etc. In comparison, the speculative theories of the fourth *Teerta* utterly enthrall him.

"It makes so much sense, doesn't it?" he says in epiphany, relaying the information to Daeo, who's currently venturing deeper within the *ynsyna* cavern, neck craned upward. She's careful not to stray too far from her brother, who's camped near the edge of the cavern's entrance, today studying the fourth block of *ynsyna*. But she can never help exploring a bit on her own. She's particularly interested in the cavern's incising speleothems, their glistening, conglomerated surfaces. Humming her brother's alphabetic melody to herself, she runs her fingers along several slick, pockmarked stalagmites, comparing their textures to the marbled fossil in her blanket. Around her, beyond the reach of her bioluminescing *patu*, the cavern seems to sink forever into eternal darkness.

"Actually, none of that's true," Tagi calls from the cave's antechamber. He's busy at work, carving blocks of dried wood into new splints—they'd emptied his entire inventory yesterday, repairing a slew of *Kosharuna* casualties, all women. He'd been pleased to see a line form, if only for the teaching opportunities. But now, short-stocked and falling behind on other *Teerta*-related duties, Tagi feels like he has a mountain of work ahead of him. Anyway, he isn't too busy to eavesdrop on their chatter. "I wouldn't give too much credence to what some of those early *Teerta*s wrote."

"Why not?" Bowi feels defensive.

"Humans were dumber animals back then," Tagi explains. "They relied on more simplistic analogies to conceptualize the universe. The *aruna* isn't really a giant mushroom." He chuckles at the notion. Beside him, Eeao sits loyally, perking her ears whenever one of the children speaks—she can tell they aren't hunting inside the cavern, and a musty, fungal stench radiates from within, so she figures Tagi must have put them in there to die. Perfect.

"So then what really is the *aruna*?" Daeo groans, sick of disillusion.

"No one knows, but it's probably something much more complex," Tagi says, whittling away a slab of wood to create a narrow finger splint. "Probably something more akin to a transcendent animal, like the sun, given its routine, coordinated movement. It doesn't swirl about erratically, as a mushroom bobbing in water would. And it certainly doesn't glow on its own; it reflects the sun's light. That's what creates the *aruna*'s cycle. You know about that, right?"

"Yes," Bowi rolls his eyes, disappointed. He liked the mushroom idea more. Somehow, in his young mind, reality always finds a way to become boring.

"So then what are the *Fae?*" Daeo asks.

"*Hmm?*" Tagi grunts from outside the cavern.

"You said the *Fae* came to the *Uyi* as spores from the *aruna*," Daeo recounts.

"I didn't say that," Tagi clarifies. "*Bowi* read that theory from the misguided fourth *Teerta*. Now, perhaps if you stop asking so many questions and allow your brother to continue reading, maybe he'll find the information you seek, *wyntiko?*"

"*Wyntiko,*" Daeo sighs. Keeping tally, she's learned the old man usually snaps by her third question.

As Bowi continues deciphering *ynsyna* characters aloud, stumbling over vowels and mispronounced words, the next line informs him that, along with the looming, two-legged *raea* birds, humans are an inferior, evolutionary offshoot of the *Fae.* Whereas the winged *raea* line developed feathers and elongated necks for pruning the forest canopy, the human line developed nimble arms and bigger brains for crafting tools and managing the *Uyi*'s lesser organisms. All mobile beasts, the next line of *ynsyna* claims, from *aea* birds to *onynsa* insects, are the mutated descendents of *Fae* seed merged with earthbound vegetation, to varying degrees.

"But how did that happen?" Daeo figures she's waited long enough to renew her tally.

"How did what happen?" Tagi loathes ambiguity.

"How did the *Fae* merge with plants to create animals?" Daeo worries this will count as her second question.

"That's just how nature works," Tagi says, shaving a branch of mahogany into a leg brace. "Over time, everything degrades. Your body is made up of countless particles, so tiny you can't even see them, you can only see the whole they create. Well, nature is the same way. There are emergent processes at work all around us, in the trees, in the *aeo*, in this cave, all of them so miniscule and gradual that we don't even notice they're happening. But they still happen. We know because we see the outcomes. And the elaborate process that created us, the *raea, onynsa, lyreea,* all the animals—it happened so slowly that no one noticed until everyone was already here."

Bowi and Daeo ponder the old man's answer. To Bowi, the damp cavern around him seems dead and barren, long devoid of anything emergent—save for knowledge. What kind of invisible developments could be happening down here in the dark? What kind of organisms lurk beneath the ground?

"Is aging one of those processes?" Daeo presses her luck with a third question. She's thinking about her sister now, a baby who was once alive—hadn't they all been that small once? Isn't that what her mother told her when she was pregnant? *You grew inside my belly, too.*

"Yes, aging is a fine example," Tagi says. *How many moons?* "Now hush."

Bowi turns his attention back to *ynsyna*. After detailing the physiological similarities between human and *raea* anatomy, such as two-footed mobility, upright backbones, and angled shoulder blades (between which ancestral *Fae* wings once protruded, allegedly), the fourth *Teerta*'s final passage explains that a long-ago cataclysm killed off a third branch of evolved, four-legged descendents, as evidenced by the *montada-yryku.*

"What's *montada-yryku?*"

Daeo is glad Bowi asked the question this time.

"Ah, montada-yryku!" Tagi exclaims, shooting to his feet. "I've been waiting for you to get to this part. Let me show you."

Startled, Eeao bristles as Tagi drops his tools and hurries into the cavern. She figures he's just gone inside to check on the children's fermentation, but did he have to be so sudden about it?

Daeo rejoins Bowi just as Tagi enters the cavern. "Come," he links arms with the children, and then guides them along the *ysyna*-etched walls, in the opposite direction from which Daeo had been exploring.

Their feet patter across the damp stone floor, echoing against the cavern's vaulted ceiling. Bowi thinks it almost sounds like people are walking above them, mirroring their movements. But the space overhead is pitch black. And their combined *patu*s provide only enough light to see a body-width or two in all directions. If there are other creatures nearby, scampering through these mountainous depths, Bowi imagines they must be as light-deficient as *Meemmal*s, and therefore invisible in the dark. Suddenly, he feels blind. Out of place. A vulnerable creature of light choked within suffocating blackness. How easy would it be for a non-luminous creature to watch them from the dark? Their *patu*s glow like bait. He clutches tightly to the arms on either side of him.

"Are there any other animals down here?" Daeo voices his concern.

"Hush," Tagi won't even allow her one question this time; he's too eager to show them *montada-yryku.* Translated literally, it means *death-housed-in-rock.*

"Here we are," the old man eventually slows his pace, halting before a vertical slab of cave wall. They're deep underground at this point, and the temperature is hot. He stands back from the wall's sheer face, slanting his scalp to cast more light on the scene as the two children step closer.

Displayed before them, entombed in a thick layer of sediment, is the backward-arched skeleton of some alien monster. Its twisting vertebrae curve upward, ending at a narrow yet massive skull. Thick, razor-fangs protrude from its impressive upper and lower jaws, which are clamped around the neck of another skeleton—some smaller creature, similar in anatomy to its predator, with four limbs sprawled in cardinal directions. Really, these are the fossilized skeletons of *Canis lupus* and *Cervus canadensis* (an adult wolf devouring a young elk), suspended in geologic transfixion, captured when the Yellowstone supervolcano erupted and buried them together in a fold of liquified rock. Now, a million years later, preserved and exposed within the eroded cavern wall, the ancient, mammalian bodies hang on rare display for Bowi and Daeo to ogle.

"Fascinating, aren't they?" Tagi smiles.

"What are they?" Daeo beats Bowi to the question.

"Primordial animals, long extinct," Tagi says. "This big one was eating the other."

"How did they get stuck like this?" Bowi asks. It doesn't seem possible, the way the rock wall perfectly encases their bodies. Like a mud imprint, yet through solid stone.

"Remember those slow, invisible processes I was telling you about?"

Both children nod.

"This is what happens when one of those slow processes suddenly happens all at once," Tagi says. "The *Uyi* is always moving, you know. Right beneath our feet. The ground is always shifting, one way or another, very slowly. It never stops. But sometimes, *urynkata* shake the ground with so much force that mountains roll like waves. Well, millions and millions of moons ago, long before the first *Teerta* was even born, these two animals here were buried by an *urynkata*," he gestures at the fossils, using a word for *earthquake*. "And then over time, after a long while, the mountains settled around them. And then after another long period of time, flowing water and other forces eroded the rocks around their bodies to create this cave. And now here we are, lucky enough to view this beautiful glimpse of prehistoric life caught in action."

Tagi pauses, allowing the children to soak in the wondrous sight. Often, just gazing at these fossils gives him goosebumps; he can see all the painstaking care and effort previous *Teertas* must've taken to excavate this marvel. Meanwhile, Bowi finds the skeletons creepy and Daeo has begun to daydream about food. They both hope Tagi has finished his lecture.

"So this represents the third branch of life that evolved from the *Fae?*" Bowi asks, referencing back to the fourth *Teerta*'s chronicle.

"Yes, the big one," Tagi points at the fanged predator. The wolf's empty eye socket stares out at them, unblinking, the skull's profile embedded into the cave wall. Bowi tries to imagine what the creature might have looked like when it was alive, outfitted in flesh and blood. Would humans herd these cousins the way they currently herd flocks of *raea?* Or would these fanged monsters rule over the *Uyi* instead?

"It has teeth kind of like *Eeao*'s, just bigger," Daeo observes, still thinking of food. She admires the ferocity with which the wolf skeleton is holding its prey. To die in such a position of power, she imagines, must've required quite a cataclysm. "It has four legs too, like *Eeao*. Do you think *Eeao* will grow up to be one of these?"

Tagi laughs, "Certainly not. She's much, much too small. And the shape of her head is completely different from both of these skulls. See how narrow and elongated they are? See the size of these jaws? There is no relation whatsoever. I already told you, these animals are long extinct, remember? Why would you ask a question I've already answered?"

Daeo shrugs. "Then what is *Eeao?*"

"Irrelevant to the point," Tagi sighs. He's already grown sweaty and uncomfortable in the underground's stale heat, and he can tell the children have seen as much as they're capable of appreciating. Daeo is about to ask something else, so he stops her, "Enough questions. Let's get back to reading."

Chapter 34
"Eeao"

Outside the *ynsyna* cavern, up in her cranny, Eeao keeps vigil.

Staring down the cave's black throat, waiting for the old man to rejoin her, Eeao doesn't understand why he insists on following the children into the mountain's odorous depths. To her sensitive nose, the inner cavern reeks of fungal toxins and unidentifiable decay. There's also a sharp, high-pitched whine emanating from somewhere within—a threatening sound the humans don't seem to hear, even as it prickles Eeao's whiskers. She sees no logical reason to journey into such discomfort; can't the old man just wait outside with her until the children starve? Or suffocate? And then he can run in and drag out their bodies? Wouldn't that be easier? Why is he making the hunt so unnecessarily complex?

Then again, Eeao is beginning to suspect the little girl might not be prey after all. Over the past few days, the female child has ventured to and from the cave on her own, seemingly beyond the old man's control. And in retrospect, though she'll never know the child's true intentions that day, the kitten can't forget the way she once saved her from a snake... Eeao finds herself respecting the girl's behavior, though it makes little sense to her. How is the girl child so autonomous while the boy child remains so dependent? Why are humans so strange? Why can't they just eat the small ones?

Flummoxed by primate social dynamics, Eeao shakes her whiskers. She leaps down to the cave floor. Early afternoon sunlight beckons her, so she saunters languidly outside, disrupting lazy sheets of suspended dew as she leaps into the low-hanging branches of a tropical tamarind tree growing sideways from the rocky foothill. A flurry of blue *kynaea* wings erupts from the tree's upper branches, scattering into the air. Eeao follows them, springing upward into an adjacent tree, senses primed.

Today's hunt takes her northward, along the caldera's eastern ring of soaring cliffs. She favors some trees over others, sinking her claws into ones she knows have soft, malleable bark. All these stationary, leafy bodies are just stepping stones to her. Ladder rungs in her larger game. She has no idea the trees are actively working against her, collaborating with their fungal underlords, effusing chemical pheromones into the air. She's unaware of their advertising efforts, their broadcast to avian carnivores:

JUICY PEST, RIPE FOR EXTERMINATION!

As far as Eeao knows, trees are nothing but scratching posts, and birds nothing but prey.

Following the tantalizing scent of air-bound *kynaea*, the kitten journeys across a long, intricate network of tree branches, the leaves around her bursting with pheromones benign to her feline nose. Eventually, she locates her prize—a twiggy nest, held snugly between two intersecting branches and the trunk of a kapok tree, full to the brim with chattering, bug-eyed *kynaea* hatchlings. Fresh. Warm. She can still smell the amniotic fluid of cracked eggs wafting from their scruffy feathers. Each chick is nearly Eeao's size, but she isn't threatened. They point their beaks skyward, hungry and helpless, ignorant to the true cost of a meal.

Where is their mother?

Eeao doesn't care; she assails the nest, pouncing from above— her claws puncture two juicy chests upon landing. She snatches a third in her mouth, instantly snapping its neck with a swift jerk of her head. The two untouched chicks behind her continue screeching, blind to the violence around them. Whether they're still crying for food or for help, Eeao can't tell. She silences them, slashing both their bellies open with a single forepaw. There, much better.

Covered in blood and immature entrails, Eeao feasts.

By the time she's engorged her belly, the sun is sinking into the mountains on the other side of the rainforest. Several times, an adult *kynaea* rustles by, swooping through branches overhead as though to survey the nest. Sunset glimmers through its azure wingspan. Eeao doesn't care if it's the mother. She knows even adults of this species are too dumb and lazy to defend their own young. Satiated and unthreatened, the feline makes herself comfortable on the nest's edge, a soft patch of enmeshed feathers and twigs, unstained by the gory mess she created. There, she basks for a while in a sheen of sunlight piercing the adumbral treetops; gold glosses her silver coat. Beside her, five bloodied, dismembered carcasses lie silently atop their own eggshells.

When evening washes the sky pink, Eeao rises to stretch her legs. She's reveled here long enough. It's now time to slink back to the cave and pester the old man for a spare grasshopper leg—or whatever else he's cooking tonight. The kitten's ever-growling stomach is an entire cavern of its own. But before Eeao turns to depart, something in her upper periphery snags her attention. She looks up, and through a tear in the rainforest's green umbrella she notices a strange formation soaring just below the clouds...

V

She sniffs at the air, gaping her mouth to engage her specialized vomeronasal organ. A strange, avian whiff emerges above the typical evening smells, tickling the olfactory bulb of her brain. It's an unfamiliar species. Focusing her vision, she tries to make sense of the formation overhead—she can vaguely identify flapping wings, long necks, a distinct row of sharp, pointy beaks. And then the formation glides out of view, obstructed behind canopied foliage.

Ominous.

Eeao quirks her head.

But her interest fades as quickly as the formation flies away; she's hungry for a spare grasshopper leg. The kitten springs from the ravaged nest, making her way back toward Tagi's cave while the trees around her continue their extermination effort, dispersing pheromones into the wind.

Chapter 35
"Kreeko"

"Momo! Momo!"

Without a human baby to monitor, the parrot, Kreeko, feels idle and confused. Perched in the fruitful dipterocarps tree that grows sentry-like over Nyno's *capku,* she scans the ground intently for any sign of the baby. Nothing. She swivels her head this way and that, scouring the *Uyi*'s aural frequencies for any sound of the child she'd last imprinted to. More nothing. Perturbed, she resorts to emitting random false-alarms late into the night—the only other thing she knows how to do.

"Momo! Momo!"

"Ayee!" Nyno hisses, stumbling groggily from her *capku* to silence the bird. A few nights ago, she'd hoped the parrot's intermittent calls would be nothing more than a fluke. But as more time passes, the bird cries more frequently. *She's angry with me.*

Actually, the parrot doesn't know how to be angry. She just notices that something is wrong. She's been bonded to Nyno since the day she hatched (*momo* parrots are given as eggs to all first-time birthing mothers). For Nyno, receiving the egg was a rite of passage. For Kreeko, imprinting on Nyno and her subsequent babies was an evolved inevitability. The parrot can't help herself. By now, her species has been cooperating domestically with human mothers for hundreds of thousands of years—so long that they've developed an entire lobe of brain matter dedicated to communicating with young, hairless primates. These humans are her flock. Their babies are her passion. What is a parrot without passion? More nothing.

"Momo! Momo!"

"Ayeeeeeeee," Nyno groans, rubbing her eyes. The night is still early, but she's barely slept in days. *What am I doing*

wrong? Desperate to silence the bird, she pokes her head back inside her *capku*. "*Daeo?* Are you awake?"

"No..." Daeo grumbles, turning over on her sleeping mat. She doesn't appreciate any of this. Between the effort it takes to evade her bullies and hike to-and-from the *Teerta*'s cave every day, the little girl values her sleep.

"*Daeo*, please come outside," Nyno pleads. "I need you to rebond with *Kreeko*."

This, Daeo figures, must be a dream. Either that or a sick joke. She ignores her mother and resumes snoring, hugging her chunk of petrified wood like a baby doll.

"*Daeo!*" Nyno shakes the girl.

"What?" Daeo snaps.

"Please, just come outside with me. We need to do something about *Kreeko*."

Begrudgingly, Daeo leaves her fossil and baby blanket to follow her mother outside.

Evening greets them, muggy and stagnant. Along with, "*Momo! Momo!*"

"She won't stop," Nyno says. "Hold out your hand, get her to come down to you."

Daeo does as she's told, certain the parrot will just ignore her. This type of command only works if the parrot is directly bonded to the commander, and it's been moons since the bird was hers. But to Daeo's surprise, the parrot spreads her ruby wings and glides to the ground, alighting next to them in a crimson flurry. A remembered instinct? Standing upright on her stubby, feathered legs, Kreeko is as tall as Nyno's shoulder, with a beaked head the size of a bulky *hympano* toadstool. Yet despite her dinosaurian size, Daeo has never been frightened of the parrot (human children, too, are born with an evolved fondness for the maternal, avian species).

Now, Daeo reaches out to stroke the lustrous feathers along Kreeko's neck. It seems like forever since she last touched the creature. But something feels different this time; these feathers are not as soft as her baby blanket. The parrot holds Daeo in her beady, black gaze. Neither can tell what the other is thinking. Neither feels comfortable. Both know something is wrong.

Suddenly, in the reflection of the parrot's pupils, Daeo feels older than she ever has. She wants to retaliate—to run back inside the *capku* and bury her face in the plushness of her baby blanket—anything to rebel against time.

"There," Nyno breathes a sigh of relief. "Now she can rebond with you and—"

"*Momo! Momo!*"

Kreeko erupts in a whirlwind of feathers, flapping her wings, fanning her tail. Nyno and Daeo jump back to avoid her kicking talons. Seething scarlet, the parrot resumes her indignant perch overhead.

"*Momo! Momo!*"

"Something is wrong," Daeo says.

To Nyno, her words sound like an accusation.

"*Momo! Momo!*"

"It's okay, everything's okay, nothing's wrong," Nyno insists. "Come here, *Daeo.* Please, just hold out your hand again. We can get her to rebond with you, I know it's possible. *Dynjo* did it with hers and—"

"No," Daeo turns to go back inside the *capku.*

"*Daeo!*" Nyno calls after her. The girl doesn't respond. "*Daeo!*" *How old is she?*

"*Momo! Momo!*"

Daeo ignores them both and disappears into the *capku,* leaving her mother to feel like the one who's been abandoned. Standing outside, Nyno can see her daughter's tiny silhouette glowing faintly from within the structure's fungal sheath. A lone tear brims along Nyno's left eyelid, refracting her vision so that for a moment, a heartbeat, she sees three silhouettes glowing inside, one next to the other next to the other. *There should be three children—*

NO! She wipes her tear, shoving her thoughts with it.

"*Momo! Momo!*"

Nyno shoots the bird a vicious glare.

"*Momo! Momo!*"

These words are an accusation.

"*Momo! Momo!*"

A false accusation.

Nyno shifts her gaze downward, scanning the ground for a rock, a stone, anything hard and heavy to hurl up at the parrot. She's no longer a birthing *momo—maybe I never should've been one to begin with*—which means Kreeko is now unnecessary and can be silenced once and for all.

"*Momo! Momo!*"

Screaming, sobbing, flailing in a surge of unexpected rage, Nyno scoops up an armful of gravel and starts pelting whatever she can at the bird. Most of her projectiles fall short and rain back down on her. But she does manage to glance a pebble off the branch just below Kreeko's perch, which sends the bird fluttering into the night, squawking and stymied.

"*Mo—Mo—Mo—*"

Nyno feels accomplished; the bird flies off, vanishing into a nebulous spathe of green fog. She hopes to never see the parrot again. She hopes it never flies back. She hopes it leaves forever and takes all her memories away with it. Yet deep inside, she knows she hopes for too much. She always hopes for too much.

What do I keep doing wrong?

The sound of an approaching drumline pulls Nyno from her thoughts, alerting her to late-night activity. But *Kosharuna* was two days ago. There isn't supposed to be a festival tonight. Why would anyone start banging drums this late after nightfall?

Unless...

Voices accompany the advancing drummers. Nyno tries to listen, but all she can hear are frantic calls, vague cries repeating vague phrases over and over. *Momo! Momo*—No, they're saying something else. Words coalesce as the mob approaches.

"*Arynmo! Arynmo!*" Emergency.

"*Meerso! Meerso!*" Hurry.

"*Oko mee-uyisa!*" The world is ending.

Nyno has barely enough time to process what they're saying before several drummers crash into her clearing, their pace faster than their beat. Burly *punteeku*, they swerve around Nyno and her home, hefting their massive, tree-trunk drums on their shoulders as they run. Female *punteeku* march behind them, chanting the alarm.

"What's happening?" Nyno recognizes Kleeo's distinct speckling amidst the surging bodies.

"*Arynmo!*" Kleeo doesn't slow her pace. Nyno tries to trudge alongside the sweaty, spined woman, but Kleeo pushes her backward. "*Meerso!*" she yells at Nyno, "Hide inside your *capku!* Put on your harness! *Oko mee-uyisa!*"

Nyno's legs freeze beneath her body. She doesn't know what to make of Kleeo's warning. In their society, direct orders are only given to children; she doesn't have to do anything Kleeo tells her to. She's as free as anyone to follow the *punteeku*, wherever they're going, and see for herself what the *arynmo* is.

But she's never actually heard someone say the forbidden phrase aloud: *Oko mee-uyisa. The world is ending*—these words are heavier than the *Uyi* itself. People don't joke about world-ending affairs; at this point of animal evolution, the fear of apocalypse is a primary survival instinct. The subject itself is taboo. Life is too precious—or at least, it should be. This isn't melodrama. To warrant these words, everyone's in danger.

"*Momo?*" Daeo pokes her head outside the *capku*, disturbed by the ruckus.

"Go back inside, *meerso!*" Nyno cries. *What have I done?*

Meanwhile, perched in the branches of a balsa tree overlooking the algae-ringed *Aeo*, Kreeko has secured herself a front-row view of the *arynmo*. Glittering off the water's black surface, the nearly full moon's reflection is distorted by an invasive congregation of avians floating around the lake's shoreline. These creatures arrived earlier this evening, flying over the *Uyi* in a massive V formation, and already they seem to be multiplying. Their migration route doesn't typically take them over the *Uyi* (the last time they visited was more than eight thousand years ago), but this season they can't help themselves. Lured by faux-pheromones, puppeteered by fungi, they stream into the *Uyi* like an answered prayer.

Local humans have only heard of these beasts through legends: Terrifying, fanged birds with enough strength and ferocity to rip a man's head clean off his shoulders. Really, they're the oversized descendents of *Branta canadensis* (Canadian geese), with rows of dagger-like, conical papillae lining the insides of their beaks (evolved in concert with their increasingly carnivorous diets). Needless to say, the relationship between humans and geese has only gotten worse over the last million years. But tonight, the *Uyi* welcomes their flocks with open water.

Kreeko watches curiously as another V formation descends from the night's vaporous atmosphere, alighting with countless others around the *Aeo*'s shoreline. She can hear the din of human turmoil below, drums fading deeper into the radiant jungle. She can sense the primates' fear. But why are they so afraid? Sure, the arrival of this new bird species is odd, but why raise such an alarm? Kreeko doesn't ponder the situation for long; an itch beneath her left wing commands her attention. She preens, pecking between the long, rosy feathers extending from her ulna.

And then she's gone in an ambush of feathers, mauled into the lake by two of the geese.

In legends, humans call these monsters *paen-aemo*, or *above-and-below*.

Kreeko drowns while the amphibious birds devour her.

Chapter 36
"Maetri"

Of course, the world isn't actually ending.

Reality is just the dimension beyond perception; Maetri reminds himself of this principle daily. He remains calm while his fellow *punteeku* panic. He sleeps while they march through the night, sounding alarms, warning mothers and children of the dangerous creatures amassing in the *Aeo*. He doesn't care. He'd rather save his energy for an actual *Aruna* festival. Or for hunting one of the beasts himself.

Clad in his sturdiest harness, he walks down to the *Aeo* the next morning and kills one of the geese for everyone to watch, skewering it through the heart with an extra-long *mabato* stake. The other birds don't seem to care. Too busy guzzling the *Aeo*'s virgin waters, swallowing schools of fish and tadpoles, they bob razor-beaked heads in and out of the water, paddling their enormous, feathered bodies around the lake while Maetri drags their kin's massive carcass ashore by its thick, sinuous neck. Judging by the feel of it, he estimates the beast to be twice his own weight. Cloaked in dull feathers of black and brown and white, the godzilla goose exists in stark contrast to the *Uyi*'s indigenous host of colorful fauna.

Young boys watch Maetri from the treeline, hiding within tangled shrubs and *wykyno* vines. Maetri can tell they're awed by his bravery. They've never seen anything like this. No one has. Just yesterday, these creatures were no more than terrible beasts of myth, tales told to frighten children, bizarre petroglyphs found on prehistoric boulders. Now, to actually see flocks of *paen-aemo* descend from the sky like corrupt formations of *Fae*-mutants—Maetri isn't surprised so many people fear the end of the world.

In fact, he plans to profit from it.

Around noon, he creates a bonfire on the lakeshore and barbecues the giant goose he's slain for everyone to witness. He passes out charred cuts of meat for people to taste.

"Ancient poultry!" Maetri advertises a massive, barbecued leg over his head, parading it like a prize. "A million moons ago, the *paen-aemo* terrorized our ancestors—but today, we feast on them!"

A few people cheer hesitantly. The weather is balmy and mild, so the feast lasts into the afternoon. Humans and geese eye each other uncomfortably throughout the ordeal, neither species threatened enough to provoke a serious confrontation, but each intrinsically dubious of the other nonetheless. Still, Maetri's confident grandeur on the lakeshore inspires curiosity among his own kind. Mothers and children begin to venture outside their *capku*s again, tentatively joining the rowdy *punteeku* around Maetri's lakeside bonfire.

Everyone wears a spiked harness today—even children run around wearing adult-sized armor, just in case. Popular legends indicate their spined fashion motif originated as an ancient defense mechanism against these winged monsters. The legends aren't wrong. The barbecue is, however, eventually interrupted when Veetri suddenly comes barreling out of the jungle, screaming: "They're mauling the *raea!* They're mauling the *raea!*"

Perfect, Maetri thinks. He's been waiting for an opportunity like this. His older brother only inherited the flock a half-moon ago. And now, already, without even having to lift his own finger, supernatural forces have intervened to undermine Veetri's new position as Chief *raea* wrangler.

Almost like a curse. Almost like a blessing.

Delicious. This will be such an easy situation to manipulate; Maetri feels giddy just imagining the possibilities. *What luck!* He smiles while everyone races off to the *raea* fields, eager to either help Veetri save the herd or else witness the massacre.

So what if he loses half the flock? So what if everyone goes hungry?

Again, Maetri doesn't care. To him, the momentous arrival of *paen-aemo* is a cosmic sign that the world is changing, as it always is, like floodwater racing inexorably toward the next cascade—everyone goes over the precipice, it's just a matter of knowing how to fall. Maetri feels like he's been falling for a long time. A second-born son, the current of life rarely flows in his favor. But now, watching his older brother and everyone else descend into panic, once again, he realizes he's the only one with feet ready to land.

Another catastrophe, another tool.

He'll use these *paen-aemo* monsters for all they're worth.

Unfazed, Maetri finishes his barbecue in peace. He'd already spent a good deal of time babying a particularly tender rib to culinary perfection, and he won't let the appeal of mass hysteria stop him from savoring such a sublime cut of meat. Once he's eaten the rib, he babies and eats two more. And then he follows languidly in the trampled path left by the masses, patting his bloated belly every now and then to aid mild indigestion.

By the time he joins everyone else at the *raea* fields, the herd is decimated. Those that remain alive skirt around the edges of the grassy landscape, cowering together in frantic clusters, tail plumes hiked like hoop skirts over their ridiculous, stilt legs. In the middle of the field, an angry, honking gang of *paen-aemo* has taken up residency, twenty strong in total. They stand in an outward-facing ring, guarding their pile of bloodied *raea* carcasses like a pack of hyenas claiming territory. Meanwhile, humans huddle within the surrounding jungle, readying some sort of counter attack. Maetri knows in his gut that whatever they try will fail.

Indeed, after a tedious (and ultimately pointless) waiting period, Veetri and nine other *punteeku* charge at the geese in a coordinated assault, equipped with spiked harnesses, *mabato* spears, and flintstone machetes. They rattle their weapons as they run—*hoping to intimidate?* Maetri scoffs; the geese erupt like pterodactyls at their attackers, snapping their serrated beaks and thrashing their taloned feet. The clash is messy. Beaks crunch shoulders. Spears lance necks. Talons slash faces. Spined harnesses snag webbed feet. Several backup *punteeku* run in to assist, but they end up just pulling their comrades' marred, bloodied bodies from the feathery entanglement. Reassembled and thoroughly defeated, the humans retreat.

"A fight like that is hopeless," Maetri laughs at Veetri and the others limping back to the shaded treeline. At this point, they're just grateful the geese aren't launching pursuit.

"*Kahtopo,*" Veetri curses. Blood gushes from his bicep—one of the geese took a mouthful out of his arm. He sits on the mossy ground and allows several women to inspect his injury, all the while keeping his eyes trained on the geese, which have by now regrouped in the field's center, huddling victoriously around their pile of pillaged meat.

"Well this is a problem," Maetri flaunts in front of Veetri, blocking his view.

"Would you like to do anything helpful?" Veetri simmers.

"You're the one who's Chief," Maetri mocks. "I'm at your service, *tynji*. Tell me what to do. Or should I do what you just did? Run out there like an idiot and get mauled?"

Several people laugh.

Someone whispers a *Patummal* slur.

"Be quiet, I'm trying to think," Veetri snaps. He used to think his life would improve once he inherited his *kosha-kymara*'s fields. He used to think that once he became a Chief, the *Patummal* slurs would finally end. Every day since childhood, he's longed to be seen for more than just his overgrown *patu*. He never thought life could possibly get worse once he inherited power—let alone this catastrophic. Yet here he is. Faced with catastrophe. Punished by forces beyond his control. "*Oko mee-uyisa,*" Veetri mutters to himself.

A woman soon arrives with several canteens of clean water. She and a team of helpers quickly get to work cleaning wounds. Ten injured men sprawl on the ground, seeping blood and tears. "You should go to the *Teerta,*" one of the women advises upon seeing Veetri's severed bicep.

Heeding her advice, several *punteeku* assemble and assist Veetri to his feet, but Maetri stops them. "You can't just leave your *raea* herd unattended, *tynji,*" he says. "More of them will be killed." Sweeping his arm across the field, he commands everyone's eyes. Sure enough, the humans watch as six more geese alight, joining their bloodthirsty companions in the field's center. *Twenty-six strong.*

"More will come from the *Aeo,*" someone warns.

"They're invading our resources!" another cries.

"We can't let them!"

"The *raea* are ours!"

"Leave me in charge of protecting the herd," Maetri offers. "I can shepherd the remaining *raea* into the eastern fields, and then I'll devise a rotating guard to ensure they're protected from further harm. Give me the word, *tynji,* and I'll manage it while you recover."

Veetri hates the proposal. Sure, Maetri has more experience with the eastern fields than anyone else in the nest, but Veetri isn't blind to the passive-aggressive games his younger brother plays. This is a power grab. An insurance ploy. Another strategic move in a much larger game—one in which any extra leverage could mean life or death at the next

Kamaruna. But what other choice does Veetri have? Everyone else is either bleeding or cowering.

"Alright," Veetri concedes, his pulse spurting from his open arm. "*Maetri*, gather *Syno*, *Kleeo*, and the rest of the female *punteeku*. Have them herd the remaining *raea* into a single group, and then funnel the herd through the eastern pass. Tell *Tapati* to stay behind with a larger force of men; have them create a barrier so the *paen-aemo* can't easily follow. And make sure everyone is spined—this will get uglier before it gets better."

"I couldn't have given a better order myself," Maetri grins.

Actually, under Maetri's command, the situation gets better pretty quickly. With the advantage of more time to think and plan than his brother had been afforded, Maetri sends fleets of *punteeku* in strategic directions, each group assigned to a different task. Some herd *raea*. Some surround the *paen-aemo*. Another runs ahead to ensure the eastern fields are clear and accessible for the incoming herd. The operation turns out to be rather simple, and the *paen-aemo* turn out to be lazier than anyone would've guessed based on the terrifying legends—most of them just gawk and *honk!* passively on their way to and from the *Aeo*.

"The amount of *raea* they slaughtered should keep them satisfied for the next few days," Maetri says while coordinating future contingencies with several other *punteeku*. "Right now the situation looks good on the eastern fields. With any luck, the *paen-aemo* won't find the herd there. But I've established a rotating guard just in case. When will *Veetri* be well enough to resume his role as Chief?"

"The *Teerta* treated and bandaged his arm," Kleeo informs the group. "But his wound was severe. Several tendons were torn. And the skin wasn't cleanly cut, but ripped. It could be several moons before he's able to use his arm again. If ever..."

"Well then, it's a good thing I'm here," Maetri says.

Everyone agrees.

Someone chuckles a *Patummal* slur.

Chapter 37
"Mabato"

For a handful of days, Nyno won't let Daeo leave the *capku* unattended. She escorts her daughter on covert trips to and from the waste pit. She accompanies her on harried walks down to the *Aeo,* where they bathe each other as quickly as possible in sight of the menacing *paen-aemo.*

The odious birds infest the lake, more numerous than algae blooms. But they leave the impenetrable jungles virtually untouched, only alighting in open fields and marshlands when hungry for the occasional land animal. For this reason, Daeo doesn't understand why her *momo* is so fearful of the invaders—what are they even invading? She's frustrated she's no longer able to visit Bowi and the *Teerta* when she wants.

But at least she's immune to her bullies; they watch from shady thickets, prowling through foliage from afar like animals as she travels to and fro with her mother. Daeo knows her "friends" are too cowardly to accost her in front of her own *momo.* She hugs her blanketed fossil in one arm while holding her mother's hand with the other, sticking her tongue out at the ruffians whenever she catches them staring.

In the adult sphere, word has spread quickly that Nyno is now a Chief. People respect her in ways she never dreamed possible.

"*Nyno,* we have fresh armloads of *mabato* spines for you," Syno and another female *punteeku,* both wielding thick bundles of spikes on their shoulders, pass Nyno and Daeo on their way to bathe in the lake. "Where do you want us to put them?"

"Umm... Drop them off outside my *capku,*" Nyno says. "I'll process the spines later."

Giving commands. Directing orders. Exerting power over *punteeku*. Daeo's bullies watch enviously from the outskirts while she remains safely beneath her mother's broadening wingspan.

Yet despite her newfound power, Nyno feels worse than she ever has in her life. She barely has an appetite anymore. Her body mass is diminishing by the day. She rarely talks to anyone, even Daeo—they exist together in stony silence, neither wanting to know what the other is thinking. She hasn't slept in four days; ironically, subconsciously, she just lies awake all night waiting for Kreeko to call. Nothing.

"If you make me my own harness, I can go places on my own again," Daeo suggests when they return home, her voice bubbling with hope.

Nyno barely hears her. She finds the *mabato* spikes Syno had gathered stacked in a pile behind the *capku*, waiting to be embedded into new harness frames. They're all of varying lengths, stacked upon each other in a thorny, jumbled pyramid. As of today, Nyno has received one hundred and twenty-three requests for new harnesses—all from *punteeku*.

"If you make me my own harness," Daeo continues temptingly, "you will not have to take me to the waste pit anymore."

One hundred and twenty-four.

"No," Nyno mumbles.

"Why not?"

"The *Uyi* is no longer safe."

"Which is why I need one."

"You're too small; it won't make a difference."

"Other *momo*s are giving their kids harnesses."

"Their kids are bigger and stronger than you are," Nyno dismisses her, rummaging inside the *capku* to gather her inventory of woven *areemo* straps. Ever since the night

Maetri named her Chief of textile sourcing, she's been weaving continuously. She exits again with her arms loaded so full of braided straps, Daeo can't see her face behind all the material.

"The *paen-aemo* are not even that dangerous," Daeo persists. She's annoyed that such clownish birds brandish such psychological power. Then again, why does it feel like her mother's attention only exists as a reactionary measure? "If I stay beneath the trees, they cannot attack me."

"Not dangerous?" Nyno huffs, dropping her *areemo* heap next to the pile of spines. "Two men were mauled and killed just yesterday, down by the *Aeo*. I'm not letting you out of my sight."

Daeo can't ignore the hypocrisy, the drastic shift in her mother's parenting.

"I will not go to the *Aeo,*" the little girl insists, bargaining like a hostage. "I only want to go to the waste pit by myself." And to the *Teerta*'s cave, of course. But she's still keeping that a secret from her *momo*. She figures this streak of overprotectiveness, only inspired by the advent of *paen-aemo*, is just a phase the woman will soon get over, just like all the other *momo*s. Once she can get away for long enough, Daeo figures, her mother will get busy with other things and forget about her again. And then life can return to normal—or, at least, to a level of normalcy that permits regular visits to Bowi.

"Please?" Daeo stands eye-level with Nyno, who sits cross-legged on the ground, cracking her knuckles, preparing for the meticulous task of sorting every spine by length.

"No."

"But you said you would make me a harness."

"I did?"

"Yes."

"No I didn't."

"Yes you did!"

"When?"

"Two moons ago!"

"Well, things have changed since then," Nyno tosses a runty, futile spine aside.

"Yes, things sure have changed," Daeo says angrily.

To Nyno, this sounds like another accusation.

"No, I remember now," she says, recalling their past conversation. "I said I would make you a harness after your first *Kosharuna*."

Daeo's stomach drops—she'd forgotten that caveat. How inconvenient.

"But that is not fair—"

"Not fair?" Nyno cuts her off, now angry too. "I was making harnesses for adults twice my size before I was even allowed to wear one. I had to wait until my first *Kosharuna*, just like everyone else."

"But—but—"

"What? You think you're ready to participate in *Kosharuna?* Have you started bleeding yet? Perhaps you can take my place in the ceremonies, now that I'm no longer a birthing *momo*. How does that sound? Are you ready to be a *momo?* Are you ready to birth your own *babo?*"

Daeo glares. Nyno knows she's being cruel to the girl, but she doesn't care. She devoted her entire adult life to her children, sacrificing herself for them—*I did everything I was supposed to*—yet her own daughter eyes her with ferocious contempt. Nyno feels victimized, bitten by a child she created with her own blood and tears. *Is she even my child anymore?*

"You don't know what you're asking for," Nyno finally turns away from the girl, focusing again on her stack of variegated spines, matter she can regulate. "Once you grow up, there's no going back."

"I cannot control my age," Daeo snarls. "And neither can you."

"Hush!"

"I hate you!"

Slap!

Nyno doesn't realize what she's done, but the palm of her hand stings. Daeo flinches away with a red cheek.

"I'm—I'm sorry," Nyno stutters.

Daeo doesn't respond. Her face burns, but she's felt pain worse than this. She whirls around and storms into the *capku;* though on her way, struck by an impulse, she snatches up that runty *mabato* spine her mother had discarded, hiding it quickly within the folds of her blanket. It fits comfortably next to her chunk of petrified wood.

Nyno doesn't notice the swipe. She's too caught up in her own head, organizing spines, replaying conversations, filtering memories. Once, shortly before her own *momo* volunteered for *Kamaruna*, Nyno remembers seeing her mother cry. She'd found her behind their old *capku* that night, weeping because she'd just lost her status as a birthing *momo*. It was the first time she'd ever seen the woman in tears. Now, Nyno feels like crying herself.

What have I done wrong?

Inside the *capku,* Daeo throws herself onto her sleeping mat. She buries her face in her baby blanket and screams a muffled note of pure agony. Why does life always flow against her? Why does everything constantly go wrong? Daeo considers wallowing in misery for the rest of the afternoon, but the idea of wasting time in such a manner sickens her. She has energy. She has motivation. She has a novel, plastic brain. Still a child, she's not yet a boring, knuckle-dragging adult. And she's not going to let these advantages slip by, unused, another day longer.

Sitting atop her sleeping mat, she withdraws the miniature *mabato* spine she hid inside her blanket. She holds it before her. Sure, she could go out and pluck a longer, sharper one herself, if she wanted. But she has a different purpose in mind for this poky tool. She snaps off its lower end, shortening the spine further. Now, it fits cleanly in her hand, the pointy end protruding two finger-lengths from her enclosed fist like a dagger. Using her fingernails and a shard of flintstone she eventually finds on the ground near the *capku*'s entrance flap, she sharpens the *mabato*'s fine point, whittling until it draws a bead of blood from her fingertip with only minimal pressure. Satisfied with her creation, she tucks it into the waistband of her *areemo* skirt, fitting the dagger snugly against her body. She doesn't imagine she'll ever use it to harm anyone.

But her *momo* is right, the *Uyi* is changing. And she needs some sort of protection. Something she can use to defend herself—if the *paen-aemo* harass her, of course. Armed with her baby blanket, secret fossil, and a makeshift dagger, Daeo feels safe enough. Whatever it takes, she will return to the *Teerta*'s cave.

Nothing can stop her.

Chapter 38
"Momyna"

Tagi has seen many strange things in his thousand-some-odd moons.

He's seen scaly tree iguanas regrow entire limbs—his *momo* kept one as a pet when he was a young child, from which she'd routinely butcher and barbecue a hind leg. He's seen gnarly, festering wounds heal with only minimal help from a few stitches of fine, sterilized *raea* fibers. He's seen men rape women under the bright light of *Kosharuna,* sanctimonious unions from which howling children emerge.

He's seen so much strangeness over the course of his life that it all seems normal.

But Tagi has never, ever seen anything as strange as the *paen-aemo.*

"Oko mee-uyisa," he can't help but mutter at the spectacle, bewildered more and more each morning. They clog the *Aeo*'s shallow littoral zone, forming a ring of bobbing, feathered bodies around the lake's mid-perimeter. From the view of his elevated, distant cave, they look to Tagi like some aquatic parasite infecting the lake, teeming from the outside inward. He watches their presence grow daily as more and more V-shaped flocks descend, lured by the *Uyi*'s chemical advertisement...

"Why is this happening?" Bowi would rather investigate the situation than catastrophize it. He's seen many strange things in his life too but, unlike Tagi, he's not yet old enough to know the comfort of what's normal. "Do you think the *Fae* brought them?"

Tagi shakes his head. He has little to say about this phenomenon. During the next *Kamaruna,* he and Bowi watch from their distant cave as the *Fae* proceed with the half-moon ritual like nothing's amiss, as if the *Aeo* isn't infested beneath them. The *paen-aemo* don't seem to mind the *Fae* either; they part casually as the insectoid swarm descends, paddling their webbed feet to swim aside. Clearly, the two species are familiar.

Humans around the *Uyi* suspect the *Fae* and *paen-aemo* to be cooperating in some sort of cross-species alliance. Really though, the *Fae* resent the *paen-aemo* and would prefer they stick to their migratory route. Geese aren't supposed to intersect with *Fae* business; aside from their obnoxious *honk!*ing, *Fae* are mildly allergic to one of the water-resistant oils the birds secrete from their feathers (their exoskeletons itch upon contact). They feel sorry for the ground-bound humans who now must deal with the web-footed pests. But they don't feel bad enough to do anything about it.

Genetic hybrids of mammal and insect origin, *Fae* aren't able to detect the avian pheromones saturating the *Uyi*'s biosphere. They don't yet realize that the *paen-aemo* are a symptom of a much larger problem. They think their arrival is a simple fluke. A coincidental disturbance. A silly mishap. They're much more concerned with much more important matters.

Meanwhile, Eeao can smell the *paen-aemo* all the way from her hideout within the cave. To her, they reek of danger. Fellow carnivores, she can tell by the fetid stench of their guano they could do her harm. She's been laying low since the V formations first entered the region. As much as it pains her, she's decided to take a hiatus from hunting, at least until she grows bigger, only venturing outside the cave's immediate proximity on brief, bidaily occasions; the old man feeds her scraps of food often enough. Sometimes though, for an adrenaline rush, she still likes to sneak down to the swamp and leave her mark on nature—but she reserves these jaunty expeditions only for early mornings, when she has optimal energy to escape potential attacks (she's already evaded two close encounters with snapping, fanged beaks). Otherwise, so far, she continues to thwart the *Uyi.*

"Is there any information about *paen-aemo* inside the *ynsyna* cavern?" Bowi asks Tagi over *tyrkuna* one morning, a few days later. After reading chronologically for the past moon or so, Bowi is on track to begin the thirty-first *Teerta*'s block of *ynsyna* today. In total, Tagi told him, there are over ten thousand ancient *Teerta*'s to read through (there are actually more than twice that number, the old man just quit reading after a certain point of repetition), so Bowi figures it won't matter if they skip around a bit.

"Some of the early accounts speak of *paen-aemo*," Tagi says, peeling the shell and membrane off a hard-boiled *camraea* egg. The orb is half as wide as his face. "They're the reason our people wear spiked harnesses, you know."

"Makes sense." Bowi finds all the old legends cliche.

"I always thought they were just a myth," Tagi says, biting off the top of his milky, yolk-filled globe. "We have proof that other beasts roamed the ancient past. We have the *montada-yryku,* preserved inside the cavern. But we only have stories and petroglyphs of the *paen-aemo*. We've never seen any actual evidence of their existence. That's all the *Teerta*'s wrote of them, just the same old legends. But now, to actually see them alive... And here... These beasts are more ancient and fearsome than the *montada-yryku, Bowi,*" Tagi says forebodingly. *Five moons.* "Life is going to get much more difficult with them here."

"How?" Bowi asks, finishing his own egg. Despite Daeo's absence the past few days, he's found the arrival of the *paen-aemo* more exhilarating than frightening. Tagi even let him stitch up Veetri's chomped bicep the other day, holding his hands from behind to guide his fingers, all while the accompanying *punteeku* relayed a vivid account of their battle on the *raea* fields. If anything, the steady flow of *paen-aemo*-related injuries has helped break up the monotony of *ynsyna* lessons.

"Survival is hard enough," Tagi tells the boy. "Remember how much work it's taken just to keep you alive?" The old man offers a wink to lighten his pointed statement.

Bowi shrugs. He still has a continental bruise around the various injection sites on his left forearm, shaped sort of like the *Aeo*. He feels spots of pain along his esophagus, areas burned raw by reflux, exacerbated every time he swallows. He doesn't like it when Tagi uses his own condition to make a point.

"What's your point?" Bowi decides to say.

Tagi cocks an eyebrow. He takes a long moment to finish eating his egg. "My point," he eventually says, "is that it's a childish thing to enjoy the excitement of chaos. These birds are a menace. They've already killed several people down by the nest. They've injured many more. *Kahtopo*, they maimed the Chief *raea* wrangler, his arm is practically ruined—no offense to you, of course, your stitching just needs much more... Practice..."

Bowi winces, realizing the old man's point.

"The spectacle may seem like fun now," Tagi continues, "but in nature, spectacles always have consequences. I'm only able to teach you what I know. I can't teach you about the *paen-aemo*. I can't help you as the *Uyi* changes in response to them. All I can do is teach you my knowledge of the past. And after that... After I'm gone... Well, I wish you *atrypa*."

Atrypa: A word for *luck*.

They clean their *tyrkuna* bowls with filtered water from Tagi's above-cave basin. And then it's back into the *ynsyna* cavern for Bowi—he figures even if he did somehow manage to read every single word carved inside the cavern, it would require him to read constantly, without sleep, for the rest of his life. History seems far too extensive for just one person to know.

"Why is there only one *Teerta?*" Bowi wonders aloud, taking a break from the thirty-first *Teerta'*s laborious lecture on moon-faced *arunaea.* Right now, studying an otherwise unremarkable species of screech owl feels wholly irresponsible.

"Knowledge is objective," Tagi says, preoccupied as he scrapes mildew deposits from the cavern's damp walls into a clay vial—there's a particular species that grows down here, which he periodically collects and infuses into the soils of both his *heersu* and mycofilter. "If there were two *Teerta*s at once, their opinions and emotions would inevitably clash, corrupting the objectivity of their knowledge. No, the purest way to preserve knowledge is to pass it down directly, one by one, teacher to child."

Something about Tagi's logic seems intuitively wrong to Bowi, but he doesn't know how to articulate the error. "Can a girl ever become *Teerta?*" he asks, thinking of Daeo now.

"A girl *Teerta?* Of course, why not?" Tagi chuckles, finding the question naive—his old *Teerta*, the one who'd trained him long ago, had been a venerable, spitfire of a woman. Imagining the *Teerta* as a male-only role seems counterintuitive, if not ludicrous, to Tagi. "Whenever it's time for a new *Teerta*, the Chiefs appoint whichever child they deem... Best-suited for the role. They don't usually care about sex. Unless it's time for *Kosharuna...*" He says the last part without humor.

Bowi's thoughts shift now to his mother. What would she have been like as a *Teerta?* What would their lives have been like if she'd raised him here, in this cave, with all this knowledge, right from the start? Then again, if she'd been appointed *Teerta* as a child, she'd never have been allowed to participate in *Kosharuna.* She'd never have become a birthing *momo*. If she'd learned *ynsyna*, he would've never been born. Why does Tagi's earlier logic still seem so erroneous?

"If two people disagree about something," Bowi asks, "is it ever possible for them both to be right?"

"*Kahtopo!*" Tagi curses—he's accidentally scraped a bit of mold into his mildew vial, contaminating its contents with the wrong fungal strain. Ruined, he'll need to clean the vial out and begin all over again. "No. If one person is right, the other person has to be wrong. Simple as that. One or the other. That's how logic premises work. Now get back to reading."

Bowi obeys, but he decides to skip ahead, bypassing the rest of the thirty-first *Teerta*'s ramblings on *arunaea*—no one, he figures, should ever concern themselves so deeply with a single bird species, much less one that says *hoot*. Tagi doesn't notice his lapse.

The thirty-second *Teerta* begins their block of *ynsyna* by detailing the stages of human pregnancy. Bowi is immediately engrossed, fascinated by the writer's fearless objectivity regarding such taboo matters.

"*Mo-myih-nah?*" Bowi stumbles over a word he doesn't recognize.

"*Momyna*, the study of motherhood," Tagi says, returning with a clean vial. "You're on number thirty-two?"

Bowi nods.

"She's an interesting *Teerta*, if I remember correctly," Tagi screws his face up in thought, puzzling through his memory. He's read the accounts of almost ten thousand *Teerta*s over the course of his life in this cave, and he takes pride in his ability to recall each of their unique studies—or at least, all the interesting ones. "She provides the first scientific account of the human birthing process. A bit gory, if you ask me. But detailed. Insightful. Lots of information about labor and delivery, ovulation and conception, stillbirth and abortion. Feel free to skip her if you want—"

"No," Bowi gasps, shocked that Tagi would suggest skipping perhaps the most interesting *Teerta* yet. "I want to read her words." He's still thinking about his mother. He's thinking about blood in the waste pit. He's thinking about the thirty-second *Teerta*, who was once alive long, long ago. He's imagining that if she were the current *Teerta* instead of Tagi, maybe she would've helped his mother that day. All those days. All those miscarriages. And now, he's thinking about the kind of *Teerta* he wants to be. He's thinking about what's important. "*Momyna* sounds important to me," he says. "I want to learn more about it."

"Well then by all means," Tagi throws up his hands, figuring he should at least admire the boy's dedication to thoroughly read every *Teerta*. "But I warn you, *momyna* is a grisly study."

"Makes sense." Bowi finds the warning cliche.

Chapter 39
"Nyno"

Inevitably, after lying awake for eleven nights straight, Nyno's biological need for sleep overtakes her.

When it happens, she falls not into satisfying hibernation, but into a fleeting lapse, a transitory slip, a prolonged moment between blinks.

One day, pausing to rest her swollen, achy fingers, surrounded by heaps of spines and straps and other working materials, Nyno lets herself become so still that she begins to notice the sun's movement in her peripheral, arcing across the canopied sky, time cartwheeling past her. And then when she blinks, it's replaced by the waxing, crescent moon.

Just like that. Days slip into nights.

Yet no amount of rest soothes her carpal tunnel.

And no amount of completed work seems to lessen her ever-piling load. News of her new station continues to spread around the *Uyi*, taking hold of the human population like a virus, compelling evermore necessity for evermore clothing. Another twenty-six *punteeku* request new harnesses. Eighty birthing mothers demand *areemo* satchels, and another forty-three petition for new soft clothes. One first-time *momo* tries to requisition Nyno for a second baby cradle, the kind fashioned from interlocking *raea* quills, and Nyno is thrilled to deny her.

"That's not my job," she grins, almost maniacally. "I'm only responsible for clothing."

The young, dejected mother turns away, juggling twins in her arms.

"I bet you don't miss those," Kleeo snickers. Her friendship with the new Chief of textile sourcing has become something of a habit; she visits Nyno's fire pit every other morning to swap gossip and deliver new harness requests from the *punteeku* (the lake-dwelling *paen-aemo* horribly complicated their latest *Kunjaruna* run, kindling yet more demand for new, durable harnesses).

Daeo hates it when Kleeo visits.

"Refill my *aeo* canteen, dirty little *Patummal*," though technically her aunt, Kleeo barks orders at Daeo like she's her commandant.

Daeo tries to hide inside her mother's *capku* whenever the woman comes around, but it seems as though Kleeo can smell her. Nyno thinks Kleeo's just teaching her daughter the *punteeku* way of respect. Daeo thinks her aunt wants her dead and cooked in a stew. She keeps the small, *mabato* dagger she whittled several days ago safely tucked inside her waistband as she emerges from the *capku.*

"Fill my canteen too, please?" Nyno says. She'd fill it herself, but she's currently seated on the ground, fashioning long *raea* quills into a harness frame, and the calamus cage criss-crossing her lap makes it impossible for her to readily stand.

Daeo does as she's told, plucking up all her courage just to approach Kleeo. The woman wears both a glare and a smirk. Holding her breath, Daeo takes the *hympano* canteen from her aunt's meaty, calloused hands. And then, retreating behind the *capku* to refill from her mother's water basin, she overhears the two women chatting:

"Please don't call my *babo* a dirty *Patummal*," her mother says.

"But that's what she is," Kleeo snorts. Daeo can't tell if the woman is disgusted or amused.

Nyno can't tell either. "*Daeo* is a good girl," she continues. "She isn't awful like *Paelo* and some of the others. She's smart, and she's kind, and she does what she's told. Or at least she tries to. She isn't like other *Patummal.* She's a good girl."

"All *Patummal* are dirty snakes," Kleeo sneers. "You'll see."

Nyno doesn't know what to say. Impulsively, she wants to defend her daughter. What *momo* wouldn't? She loves her child. Daeo is the only one she has left...

But now, listening to Kleeo, she remembers the argument she had with Daeo the other day. She remembers the way the girl glared at her. She remembers the contempt in her daughter's eyes. The spite in her voice. *I hate you.* Remembering those words, Nyno feels victimized all over again. She knows her daughter is changing—*so much is changing*—but what kind of child would glare at their own *momo* with such venomous hatred? *I've done everything I'm supposed to,* Nyno thinks. *Why does she hate me for it?*

Daeo returns. Both women fall icy silent. Daeo delivers their refilled canteens. Neither thanks the girl. So Daeo slips back inside the *capku* to resume hiding.

"Will you pass me that bowl of *hympano* paste?" Nyno gestures from beneath the frame she's constructing, pointing at a clay jar on the ground beside Kleeo. Kleeo brings it over to her. Out of all the steps it takes to build a harness, gluing *mabato* spikes into the evenly-spaced divots she's already carved into the frame is Nyno's favorite. Most builders just jam the spines into the divots; each *mabato* spear carries a knob of cartilage attached to its bottom, which generally wedges snugly into a tiny, hollow slot. But by daubing *hympano* paste around the bottom of each spine before securing them in place, Nyno's harnesses prove far more durable than traditional contemporaries.

"Even your *hympano* paste is special," Kleeo observes, watching Nyno drizzle a bit of thin, glue-like substance along each cartilaginous ridge. Normally, the chemical paste humans procure from the *hympano* fungus is much more gum-like and viscid, typically used for patching leaks in *capku* walls. "Do you make that paste yourself?"

Nyno nods, "I add salt and temper it overnight, in a stone pot over the fire pit."

"How'd you discover that trick?" Kleeo sounds impressed.

Nyno shrugs. "Once when I was young, my *momo* wanted to see if *hympano* cooked well. It turned out awful, stickier than anything—completely inedible. So when I grew up, I made it again, but with a different purpose in mind."

"*Hmph*," Kleeo says, sounding less impressed.

Kleeo never stays long, which is the only reliable thing Daeo likes about her. Nyno, too, is glad when the woman leaves; she has an errand to run this morning, one which she'd prefer to complete in private.

"Promise to stay here, will you?" Nyno tells Daeo as she gathers a bundle of freshly made soft clothes beneath one of her arms.

"Where are you going?" Daeo raises an eyebrow, sitting halfway within the *capku*'s entrance flap.

"Out," Nyno says vaguely, now throwing the spined harness she's just constructed over her shoulder, balancing it with her free hand so as not to poke herself in the face. "Will you promise to stay here and mash ants while I'm gone? We're running low on fuel."

Daeo rolls her eyes. This is the first time in eleven days her *momo* is leaving her alone. There's no chance she'll stay here.

"Promise you'll stay here," Nyno insists.

Daeo just nods, which, at this point, is good enough for Nyno. Struggling to haul her new-made cargo by herself, she ventures down the *Aeo*-bound trail. After trekking a short distance, however, she veers eastward, crossing through a wide thicket of tangled philodendron and fiery-orange *wykyno*. The day is searing hot, the atmosphere thin and misty around her. Lavender streaks of cirrus pattern the otherwise sun-white sky. Competing *kynaea* and *camraea* birds trill overhead, their colorful melodies cascading from treetops like trickling streams of rainfall—though in the distance, Nyno can still hear raucous *honk!*s spurting from the clogged lake.

On the other side of the leafy thicket, Nyno finds the forking, uphill path toward Paelo's *capku*. Trudging, she arrives to find Paelo alone, slouched on a log beside her simmering fire pit. The younger woman watches suspiciously as Nyno approaches, wobbling beneath the weight of her delivery.

"What do you want?" Paelo always sounds like she's just woken up.

"I'm delivering what I owe you," Nyno says, dropping her bundle of soft clothes on the ground before Paelo. With her hands freed, she holds up the new spined harness, comparing its size to Paelo's shoulder width. "Yup, this should fit you perfectly."

Paelo just scowls, "You forgot the quilt and tunics."

"I'm bringing those next," Nyno explains, still catching her breath. "It's a lot to carry. I'm making two trips."

Paelo chews the inside of her cheek. She scans Nyno up and down with her cold, gray eyes. "You're wasting your time," she mutters. "I won't need any of it."

"Wait, where's your baby, *Haelo?*" Nyno looks around, suddenly realizing the newborn's absence.

"She's gone."

"What?" Nyno's lungs freeze. She drops the harness.

"Are you stupid?" Paelo sneers. "Haven't you heard? My *Patummal* milk turns babies into *Meemmals*. So *Haelo* was taken and given to another *momo*. A normal *momo* with a normal *patu*, who will make sure *Haelo*'s scalp stays bright and her skin stays clear. And as for me—I won't get to enjoy anything you owe me because I'm being volunteered at the next *Kamaruna*."

"WHAT?"

"That's what I get for helping you," Paelo smiles bitterly. "But since I'm the *Patummal* one between us, I'm the *momo* who gets dropped into the *Aeo*. Your curse has truly become mine."

"This doesn't make sense," Nyno is panting again, still unable to catch her breath. The idea that her younger, perfectly able-bodied cousin might succumb to *Kamaruna* at such a young age, right after birthing her very first child, sickens her. It just doesn't seem natural. Or fair. "That's not what happened—you didn't turn my baby into a *Meemmal*—her *patu* was already fading—she was born like that—she was already becoming a *Meemmal*—it wasn't your fault—"

"Shut up," Paelo cuts her off. "Just shut up, will you? You sound like an idiot. Don't you see what's happening? Haven't you noticed yet? I've seen it coming my whole life. The *punteeku* always use whatever reason they can to volunteer *Patummal* for *Kamaruna*, just so the rest of you with normal skin can live a bit longer. Well, now they're going full-swing with it. First they claim my milk is poisoned, now they're saying the *paen-aemo* arrived just to punish the nest for appointing *Veetri* as Chief *raea* wrangler."

What am I doing wrong?

"Everything's blamed on whoever's *Patummal*," Paelo seethes. "Everything becomes a new reason to get rid of us. You really never noticed what they're doing, *Nyno?* You're stupid if I'm the one who has to tell you this... Whatever. At least now my curse is gone and I can enjoy sleeping peacefully through my last few nights as a living, breathing human. Now, if you'll excuse me, I'm trying to enjoy my last few days too, but right now you're disrupting that. So please, if you don't mind, fuck off."

Nyno staggers backward. They both feel weightless after unburdening so much.

"I—I've been nothing but gracious to you," Nyno is breathless. "I kept our deal. I made you clothing and a harness. I've been fair to you. How dare you speak to me like that?"

"*Pfft*," Paelo scoffs. "I just told you I'm about to die, but you're more upset that I spoke unkindly to you?"

Nyno blinks.

"Fuck off," Paelo says again.

Nyno feels slapped, victimized.

"I said fuck off!" Paelo is yelling now.

Nyno turns to leave, tears of shock blurring her vision.

"And enjoy your last few moons with your *Patummal babo*," Paelo's venomous scream continues. "I'm sure they'll find a way to volunteer her next!"

Really, both women are sobbing.

All Patummal *are dirty snakes. You'll see.*

Nyno runs.

Chapter 40
"Daeo"

Ant-mashing is a menial task generally offloaded to small children. It doesn't matter the variety—any creepy-crawler in the *Formicidae* family will do. Just crush their bodies into a soft, chemical jelly, collect the contents via jar or vial, and the job is done. Even termites suffice as suitable fuel for *cananeero* nectar. It's a nasty business. Yet despite the tedium, this customary form of child labor is what truly keeps the *Uyi's* fire pits burning. Daeo recognizes the importance of the work. But she has no intention to help her mother today.

She sits outside the *capku* for a short while after her mother leaves, waiting in case the woman decides to return for something forgotten. Finally alone, it takes all her willpower just to keep from bolting.

Passing time, Daeo scans her eyes around the ring of foliage surrounding the *capku's* clearing; a sole *cananeero* bush punctuates the greenery, capturing her focus. Inflorescence arranged in a corymb, its flowering, red stalks expand outward in all directions, some extending into the ring, reaching toward the fire pit like limbs eager to light.

Though poisonous to humans, Daeo has always found *cananeero* flowers beautiful. Composed of silky, overlapping petals, which secrete beads of golden nectar and whorl vibrantly around glistening, stigma-stamen antennae, the scarlet blossoms unfurl like sticky-rich landing pads for buzzing pollinators. Several wasps currently solicit the bush's highest rung of blooms, lazily penetrating pistils. To them, evolutionary ecology is just an everyday food-exchange.

Meanwhile, lower down the *cananeero* plant, Daeo notices a fumbling leafcutter ant meandering its way up one of the stalks. Bypassing leaves and nodules of stem tissue, it appears determined to reach one of the sweet, crimson bulbs at the very top of its quest. Daeo wonders if it wants to die. She watches while the ant climbs higher and higher, eventually traversing one flower's underside, crawling upside down just to reach the sugary nectar above. When the ant finally pulls itself up and over the flower's lip of petals, onto the *cananeero's* red landing pad, it charges forward, splashing through amber beads of nectar, beelining for the bulb's protruding, aromatic tongue.

But the ant is already burning by the time it reaches the nearest stamen. Tiny, microscopic wisps of smoke plume from its six, blistering feet. It stumbles, falling down into the flower's pistil and nectaries, where the rest of its body begins to incinerate, chemically reacting with the *cananeero's* potent juices.

From Daeo's perspective, the invaded blossom slowly shrivels to encapsulate the ant, eventually emitting a thin, white trail of smoke from its center before collapsing in on itself, stem and bulb crumbling to the ground, smoldering beneath its bouquet of upright sisters. *One erupts to save the rest,* the old adage goes. Daeo doesn't remember where she first heard the proverb. But she knows it wasn't from her *momo*.

She's gone before the fallen flower has time to extinguish itself.

Ranging westward through the rainforest's permeable underbrush, Daeo treks steadily uphill, grasping hold of tendrillar *wykyno* fingers to pull herself over bouldering embankments. Rather than risk exposure by walking the main trail to the *Teerta's* cave, today she's utilizing a short-cut through overgrown terrain. Her surroundings are lush and evocative, inviting her ever-onward.

Unaccompanied, Daeo remembers again what freedom feels like. But she isn't alone—wedged between her elbow and hip, she carries the weight of her sister, a fossil wrapped in their baby blanket. And pressed against her other hip, strung within her waistband, a makeshift dagger walks astride her like a friend. In her ears, the jungle's orchestral clangor organizes itself to the beat of her footsteps.

Eeao notices Daeo's arrival before anyone else—Tagi is out tending the *heersu* and Bowi is deep inside the *ynsyna* cavern, beginning his afternoon studies. Patrolling the cave's mouth, the kitten first recognizes Daeo's pleasant scent drifting along a current of humidity before spotting the girl's luminous profile through the trees. She prances out to greet Daeo, enticed by the child's familiarity. After many long, monotonous days hiding in and around the cave, the kitten is excited by the girl's return; up until now, she'd assumed the extra child to have been eaten by the carnivorous invaders. She darts between Daeo's ankles, purring intimately to communicate her respect.

"Hello *Eeao*," Daeo smiles. She bends down to scoop up the kitten, but Eeao springs away too quickly, luring her inside the cave. "*Bowi?*" Daeo calls into the blackness.

"*Daeo!*" his call echoes from the inner cavern. A heartbeat later he's racing around the corner, scooping her into an embrace. Wrapped in his arms, Daeo feels him squeeze her baby blanket and dagger tightly between them, but he doesn't seem to notice them on her. "Where have you been?"

"Have you not noticed?" Daeo jokes. "*Oko mee-uyisa.*"

"*Momo*'s kept you on lockdown," Bowi understands immediately. Yet again, he hadn't seen them during the last *Kunjaruna*—most children and *momo*s remained in hiding while the *punteeku* marched around the *Aeo*, battling *Meemmal* and *paen-aemo* alike. For a moment, jealousy colors Bowi's vision—he misses their mother's protective arms. "How are *momo* and the baby?" he asks.

Daeo pulls away from his embrace. "They are fine," she lies. "How are you?"

"I'm great!" he beams. "I've been learning so many things! Did you know that some *momo*s can give birth to three babies at once? And in order to give birth, a *momo*'s entire pelvis literally splits open. Isn't that crazy? Oh, and look what I've been learning about today!" he holds up a chunk of igneous rock, roughly the same size as the petrified wood wrapped in Daeo's blanket. "The forty-sixth *Teerta* studied rocks and caves and stuff, and according to his *ynsyna*, a super long time ago, this rock was once liquid!"

Daeo can tell Bowi finds all this information genuinely exhilarating. She just couldn't care less. "*Bowi*, I want to ask you something."

"You want to know how a rock can become liquid?" Bowi assumes, still marveling at the jagged, crystallized stone in his hand. "Well apparently, long ago, there was a huge explosion and everything melted and—"

"No," Daeo interrupts him. "I want to ask you something else—"

"Ah, so you've returned," Tagi's voice booms into the cave. He enters carrying a variety of leafy, harvested vegetables, which he drops promptly into his water basin to preserve freshness. "I was wondering when you'd show up again. *Bowi*, will you please process these vegetables—the *renomo* and *bareebo* should be stored in dry containers after you wash them."

"Yes, *Teerta*," Bowi flies into action.

"I am happy to see you again," Daeo bows politely to the old man.

Tagi eyes her, dubious. "Yes, well, I hope you're just as happy to hear that, in anticipation of your return, I've prepared a special assignment, just for you."

"Really?" Daeo bubbles, feeling special.

"Really," Tagi nods.

Really, he's devised for her a near-impossible task that should, in theory, keep her too busy to pester him with any more questions for the remainder of his life.

"Your brother recently discovered *momyna,* a topic he finds particularly interesting," Tagi tells her. "So now, it's your turn to discover what interests you."

Daeo's eyes widen. *Baited,* Tagi thinks.

"I want you to take a moment and think of something you find interesting," he instructs the girl. "It doesn't have to be anything special. Just something you want to learn about. Whatever it is, big or small, identify it with one word. Then, once you've decided, tell me what that word is."

Daeo looks down in thought. Something she finds interesting? Something she wants to learn about? Countless words swirl through her mind—*aeo, fae, momo, kamaruna, Meemmal, punteeku, ynsyn-eera, kosha-kymara, cananeero, Patummal...*

Eeao slinks between the girl's violet-coated ankles, still purring.

"Decide on a word yet?" Tagi hadn't expected Daeo to take such an indulgent moment.

"*Patu,*" she finally answers.

"Wonderful," Tagi doesn't care. He grabs a walking stick and etches a symbol in the dirt. "This is what the word *patu* looks like, built with *ynsyna.* Learn it. Memorize it. Then, while your brother continues reading inside the cavern, I want you to search the walls ahead of him until you can find an instance of this word. Once you find it, tell me and we'll go read about it. Sound fun?"

No, the task itself doesn't sound fun to Daeo. Squinting down at the two modified characters Tagi scratched into the ground, she can barely make sense of the squiggles. Visually parsing through millions of *ynsyna* lines scratched onto cave walls just to find this particular arrangement of letters could take a lifetime—a fact of which Tagi is well aware. As aforementioned, he doesn't care whether or not Daeo ever finds her word; he just wants to keep her quiet and busy.

Five moons.

But today, following her brother inside the cavern to resume his studies, Daeo isn't disparaged. She can almost feel her word in here, somewhere in the dark, *patu,* a secret longing for revelation.

Chapter 41
"Eeao"

Believing the old man's ground-scratches to be some sort of territorial mark, Eeao sits on the word *patu* while Tagi and the children vanish into the *ynsyna* cavern. She's still fascinated by the little girl's return. How can such a small, defenseless creature with such a high-pitched, impish voice continue to roam the jungle freely?

Doesn't she smell the danger? Isn't she afraid?

Staring into the cave's depths, listening as the interwoven voices of Tagi and the children ricochet around its darkest corner, Eeao is beginning to think perhaps she's been wrong about the small ones all along. Perhaps the old man doesn't intend to eat them at all. Perhaps the children possess a power she'd previously overlooked—certainly the little girl, at least. The little girl isn't a dumb, aimless liability like the little boy. And she's not a vicious, preying beast either. She has a purpose. She has a will. In fact, considering her reconnaissance capabilities and authority over snakes, Eeao is starting to think the girl might be the most competent human of the trio...

And now, all of a sudden, epiphany hits Eeao like a mudslide: The little girl is their alpha.

All afternoon, Eeao sits reverently while the humans toil within the cavern. She still doesn't understand why they're so obsessed with the rancid chamber, but if she's come to learn anything about these apes by now, it's to reserve judgment on their odd behaviors. Close to evening, when the trio finally emerges, the kitten weaves first between Daeo's luminous calves.

"Better luck next time finding your word," Tagi smiles knowingly at the girl.

"I will find it," Daeo assures him, stumbling over Eeao.

"You better hurry back to *momo*," Bowi sighs. "It's almost nighttime."

"Yes, yes, run along now," Tagi ushers Daeo off into the misty evening. He doesn't notice Eeao slip out after her.

Every sunset, twilight plunges the *Uyi* into gray-green gloom, an hour-long cusp between day and night during which the jungle's bioluminescing crust revs to life. While Daeo descends like a purple firefly into a world of verdant shadows, the trees around her glimmer awake, their lichen coats blinking into neon bloom.

Daeo doesn't notice Eeao following her either.

Inspired by the child's courage, the kitten is feeling adventurous tonight. She maintains an altitude twice Daeo's height, slinking along her own protracted trail of disjointed tree branches, feeling excited just to venture out into the forest again. As they travel, she studies her new alpha's movements, tailing several tree-spans behind to remain incognito—she respects the child, but she doesn't trust it the way she does the old man. Not yet, anyway.

Meanwhile, the trees supporting her weight are her true enemies. Sick of being treated like advertising puppets (the cecropias in particular have an already low tolerance for avian volatiles), they've compiled chemical intel and are sending a distress signal down to their fungal underlords, alerting them of their operation's stalemate. The exterminators are here, yet the pest remains. The trees have broadcast more faux-pheromones than the *Uyi* has produced in millennia, yet the war against Eeao's gut bacteria continues ravaging the swamp's fungal biome. It's time to formulate a new plan. Something more radical, something more extreme. Deep beneath the *Uyi*, ranging far and wide, a vast, hydraulic network of mycelial intelligence festers, becoming angry.

"I told you to stay here!" Nyno is livid when Daeo returns.

Eeao gets comfy overhead, hidden within the foliage encircling Nyno's *capku*.

"I just went to stretch my legs," Daeo insists. The sun is long gone, but creeping ribbons of lichen glitter around them, radiance crawling from fissures and crags, places that would otherwise remain shadowed in daylight. "I did not go anywhere dangerous."

"You were gone all day!" Nyno yells. "I told you to mash ants! I told you to stay here! You disobeyed me!"

"You have kept me prisoner for days!" Daeo yells back.

"You're not a prisoner," Nyno scoffs.

"Then why am I never allowed to leave?"

"It's dangerous out there! I'm keeping you safe!"

"It is not dangerous!"

"You could get hurt!"

"I am fine!"

Eeao perks her ears, thoroughly invested in the exchange. In her eyes, the little girl is asserting dominance over the unwilling, larger woman. Ingredients for a bloodbath. Eeao flexes her claws, eager for any reason to pounce in and fight alongside her alpha.

"You cannot control what I do anymore," Daeo pushes past her mother to drink from the water basin.

"Tell me where you went!" Nyno continues ranting. She knows she's lost her grip on the girl—after today, the *paen-aemo* are more of a joke than a threat—but she won't accept defeat without swinging her own weight around first. "I searched all afternoon for you! I'm your *momo*, you're my *babo*, I deserve to know where you went!"

Daeo takes a deep gulp from the basin. When she comes up for air, she grins at her mother, "I went inside the mountains." She feels cryptic and smug with her answer. Water dribbles down her chin, staining the front of her tunic like a bib.

Nyno sneers. "Don't mock me with riddles."

"It is not a riddle!"

"Tell me the truth!"

"I am!"

Nyno winds her arm back to slap the girl again, but then she stops herself. *What am I doing?*

Daeo darts beneath her mother's extended arm and disappears inside the *capku,* excited for sleep—now that life is returning to normal, she anticipates she'll need a full night's rest to repeat her journey tomorrow.

Meanwhile, overlooking the scene, Eeao remains perched on her balsa branch for a little while longer. She watches the grown woman sulk beside the dying fire pit, kicking dirt aimlessly with her toes. She watches tears glimmer in the woman's eyes, and then spill down her cheeks. She watches the woman sink to the ground, sobbing.

Eeao thinks the woman is having an allergic reaction to something. And the girl has clearly gone to sleep inside the fungal abode. So the kitten steals off into the night, back toward the old man and his cave, enchanted by the little girl's supremacy.

Chapter 42
"Paelo"

Revenge?

Paelo has considered several options.

Given a lifetime of ridicule and abuse, retaliation fantasies are only natural.

But that's what they've remained: Fantasies.

Until now.

Because Paelo is smart.

She knew as a child that if she ever took revenge on her mother—whether by dripping *cananeero* nectar into the water basin or setting their *capku* ablaze in the middle of the night—her aunts would simply volunteer her for it. She knew as an adolescent that if she ever took revenge on one of her brothers—whether by driving a *mabato* stake through his heart or slitting his throat with a length of *areemo* wire—her other brothers would simply volunteer her for it. And she knew as an adult that if she didn't conceive a non-*Patummal* child, the *punteeku* would most definitely volunteer her for it. *Kamaruna* awaits any wrong move. Her people consider her less than human—that's why her *momo* allowed her *tynji*s to practice *Kosharuna* on her throughout her girlhood. No one ever considered her *Patummal* body worth anything.

Revenge.

For as long as she can remember, Paelo has known her day of vengeance would have to coincide with her day of death. Since birth, it's been her only possible outcome. She's had a lifetime to prepare. And now, her carefully-plotted victory is nearly here; she's just waiting until the very end to make her move.

"Like a viper waiting to strike," Paelo mocks the *punteeku* who surround her *capku*. They've come this morning to escort her down to the *Aeo* for *Kamaruna*—it's time for her to join the other volunteers and eat her assigned mushroom. Three bristly men step toward her. Armed with flintstone machetes and sharpened harnesses, they mean to apprehend her. But beneath their weaponized exteriors, Paelo can see their eyes twitching. "Afraid I'll bite?" she scoffs—they must've heard rumors. "Here, take me, I'm ready." She holds up her arms in a show of faux obedience, smirking as they seize her bare, unharnessed body.

They march her down to the *honk!*-infested *Aeo,* and then around the shoreline to a small orchid field, where the other volunteers are gathered. First come the ropes—each volunteer is bound by the ankles. Next come the *Kamaruna* mushrooms—Paelo is handed a fungal pearl by one of her very own brothers, now a respected member of the *punteeku.* She wonders if he even remembers her. She wonders if any of her *tynji*s do. Or is she the only one who remembers their torture and shame?

"Finally, you're giving me something I want," Paelo says dryly, taking the ritual mushroom from his open fist. He doesn't respond. He doesn't even make eye contact. Figuring he must've heard rumors about her too, Paelo decides she can at least feel satisfied with that. She pops the mushroom into her mouth and chews. Fruit transformed from soil. What a sweet, refreshing flavor. She's hungry for this psychedelic reprieve.

Next come the stones—a female *punteeku* binds one to Paelo's already bound ankles. Dusty, jagged, and studded with small calcite crystals, the rock is larger than Paelo's head. She's never thought about it before, but now, testing its weight with her legs, she realizes this is probably the reason *punteeku* don't waste *areemo* twine binding volunteers' hands: No amount of arm-flailing will keep her buoyed so long as she's tied to this slab of ore...

As morning shifts to noon, the day remains clear and bright. Both the sun and half-moon hang visible on opposite sides of the *Aeo*'s wispy, celestial dome. Everyone present for the ceremony, plus bobbing multitudes of flagrant *paen-aemo*, Paelo is glad at least to see the *una* and *aruna* in the sky together, one last time.

"xxxxxxxxxxxxxxxxxxxxxxxxxxxxxxxxxxxxxxxx"

The approaching *Fae* horde ruins the scene. They materialize over the northern mountains, at first just a few dark specks against the sky, and then the entire pyramidal formation all at once. To Paelo, who's just now beginning to peak on her *Kamaruna* mushroom, the oncoming insectoid formation looks like a single head floating through the atmosphere, its face constantly shifting and morphing—her brothers, her mother, her cousins, her child. Everyone she's ever known is coming to take her. One last time.

But this time, she's ready.

Further down the shoreline, Nyno stands among the assembled throngs. Daeo is present too, but somewhere along the outskirts, apart from her *momo*. Peering through the crowd, Nyno realizes that all six of today's volunteers are *Patummal...* She already knew Paelo and Veetri were on the list, but why the other four? None are old. None appear ill. She can't see any obvious handicaps among them, or anything else that would warrant early volunteering. Other than their overgrown *patus...*

Daeo? Nyno instinctively reaches beside her, but the little girl isn't there.

"XXXXXXXXXXXXXXXXXXXXXXXXXXXXXX"

"HONK! HONK! HONK! HONK! HONK!"

Like synchronized swimmers, the *paen-aemo* part while the *Fae* descend over the *Aeo*. Amplified off the lake's acoustic surface, the animal cacophony is hellish, apocalyptic, offensive.

Among her fellow volunteers, Paelo stands with arms flung wide, face upturned, chest thrust open for oncoming annihilation. "EAT MY *KAHTOPO!*" she roars at everyone around her. "EAT MY *KAHTOPO!*" It's all she can say. All she can do. In her mind, colors and feelings are now grossly entwined, and everything is tinted a color she's never seen before—some vicious, enthralling shade of infrared, like a thunderstorm of blood burst over the *Uyi.*

Somewhere close, Haelo is screaming too, but in another *momo*'s arms.

"XXXXXXXXXXXXXXXXXXXXXXXXXXXXX"

Tethered to his own boulder, Veetri glares at his brother and the other *punteeku.* Revenge? He'd never considered a need. Born into a position of relative privilege, Veetri learned to overcome his *Patummal* blemish by working hard to impress his superiors. But now, his superiors are all gone. And he's realizing too late that he never put in the same effort to develop bonds with his younger kin. He's always been wary of Maetri, but he never imagined his younger *tynji* could usurp him like this.

"XXXXXXXXXXXXXXXXXXXXXXXXXXXXX"

Wind gusts at Nyno's face, slapping her over and over and over again. Tears stream down her cheeks. She can't take her eyes off the line of *Patummal* volunteers. She can't look away from her cousin, standing there, screaming uselessly at the *Fae*, at the *punteeku,* at her—"EAT MY *KAHTOPO!*" Nyno keeps reaching for Daeo, clawing her arms through empty air, but her last child is already gone.

"XXXXXXXXXXXXXXXXXXXXXXXXXXXXX"

Daeo doesn't even notice the commonality among today's volunteers. She just wants the ceremony to end. She's standing among the outer ranks of assembled humans, eager to leave the scene as soon as possible and scurry off to the cave. The more time she spends with Bowi and the *Teerta,* the more unnecessary all these monthly rituals seem.

"XXXXXXXXXXXXXXXXXXXXXXXXXXXXX"

"EAT MY *KAHTOPO!*" Paelo shrieks, lifted in the air alongside Veetri and the other radiant victims. Weightless, her heart fills her throat. Her body sings with release, arms outstretched and soaring. Chitinous *Fae* fingers grip her shoulders with crushing force, but she doesn't feel any pain. She doesn't feel any fear. She can't feel anything but surging, boundless joy, a oneness with the infinite sky. Flying over her people, euphoric and screaming, they all look as powerless as ants.

Isn't that what they've always been?

All of them. Ants.

"EAT MY *KAHTOPO!*" Her revenge has begun.

"*XXXXXXXXXXXXXXXXXXXXXXXXXXXX*"

Nyno is weightless too. For a moment. Then she's crumpled in the sand, crying.

"*XXXXXXXXXXXXXXXXXXXXXXXXXXXXX*"

Daeo slips away before the volunteers even hit the water. But she's walloped by a wall of sickening odor—is something in the jungle burning?

"*XXXXXXXXXXXXXXXXXXXXXXXXXXXXX*"

Suspended directly beneath the buzzing horde, Paelo's eardrums burst.

"EAT MY *KAHTOPO!*" she screams one last time, deaf to her own voice. And then the fingers around her shoulders release. And she truly weighs nothing. Falling, plummeting, the space of time between her body and the *Aeo*'s rolling surface seems to expand beneath her feet, a neverending pathway to the end. She's not afraid. Looking straight ahead, out over the *Uyi*, she can see two plumes of smoke billowing over the distant trees—she timed her fires perfectly!

And then she hits the water. Her lungs fill, solid. Her vision washes black. But she's unhurt. She's unafraid. Paelo spends her last conscious moments imagining the glorious mess she's left behind for all the other ants to clean up.

"*xxxxxxxxxxxxxxxxxxxxxxxxxxxxxxxxxxxxxxx*"

Noticing Paelo's revenge before anyone else, the *Fae* are quick to depart.

Those left behind in the *Uyi* aren't so lucky. The afternoon remains clear, allowing the fires Paelo built to rage long into the evening. Two columns of putrid, green-black smoke fill the sky, one spewing from her *capku*, the other from her waste pit. All day, noxious flurries of ash fall like snow from a nuclear winter.

Only when the *punteeku* finally manage to temper the blazes, covering their faces with *hympano* canvas to combat the revolting stink, do they realize what the *Patummal* woman had done: Unbeknownst to all, she'd spent the morning prior creating a strategic trail of *cananeero* petals, laced with staggered amounts of ant-jelly to coax gradual burning, linking her *capku* to her waste pit, which resulted in the slow development of two equally odorous bonfires at both locations (inside her *capku*, before decorating the soiled mess in flammable petals, she'd defecated all over the harness and soft-clothes Nyno had made for her).

For several days afterward, the *Uyi's* atmosphere is clogged with the stench of Paelo's *kahtopo*.

No one can escape her revenge.

Chapter 43
"Unkoma"

Somehow, instead of washing the smell away, rainfall only makes it worse.

That first night after *Kamaruna*, a drizzly monsoon bathes the *Uyi* in Paelo's charred fetor. And over the following days, scattered showers and cloying humidity foster an ideal, swampy environment for the odor to fester; it permeates the jungle in lethal pockets, which drift and dance invisible between breezes, whiplashing the desensitized, rendering nose-blind tolerance impossible. Many fall ill in response, somatically sickened by the inescapable stench. Maetri spends several days locked inside his *capku*, plagued with migraines.

Up at the *Teerta's* cave, the fetid reek spares no mercy—Bowi wakes the next day choking on his own vomit. Even Eeao finds the air too unpleasant to sniff; she's switched entirely to mouth-breathing since the smoke began, which (annoyingly) keeps triggering an evolved impulse to hack a nonexistent hairball. As is his habit, Tagi continues to study his panoramic view of the *Uyi* each morning, observing the sky, air quality, temperature, etc. But ever since Paelo set her fires, the atmosphere has been ladened heavier with haze than he's ever seen in his life.

Another catastrophe, another drama.

Oko mee-uyisa?

"Human waste," Tagi wrinkles his nose. "What an unmistakable stink."

By now it's been four days, and though the odor has grown staler, it hasn't diminished. They're sitting around Tagi's fire pit this morning, just he and the boy, trying to eat seared grasshopper legs the old man over-seasoned in an attempt to awaken any sort of appetite—so far, everything he cooks just ends up smelling like Paelo's *kahtopo*.

"I hate my *unko*," Bowi mutters the word for *nose*, giving up on his grasshopper leg. He hasn't vomited again since waking up to the stench that first morning, but his body feels tense, his esophagus wrung tight, like he might regurgitate at any moment.

"You don't hate your *unko*," Tagi tells him. "It's your most crucial sensory organ."

"Yeah right," Bowi scoffs. Sure, he's learned by now that whatever the *Teerta* says is generally correct, but this convenient piece of information just sounds obnoxiously contrary. "I hate my *unko* and you can't change my mind," Bowi resolves. "I wish I never had one at all."

A muffled cough alerts them of Daeo's arrival. Soon, she parts a tangled curtain of vines, joining them in the clearing around Tagi's fire pit. Lately, beneath her *patu* sheen, her dark complexion has been tinged green, one nostril fixed askew—these stagnant fumes are turning her everyday hikes into misery. Today, in order to free her hands to cover her nose, she wears her feather blanket tied over one shoulder like a satchel; wrapped inside, she carries her chunk of petrified wood like it's her own baby.

"You're here early," Tagi observes. Day by day, his feelings for the girl average toward indifference—meaning, she still hasn't found her word and has, so far, remained dutiful to her task.

"How are *momo* and the baby?" Bowi asks, noticing her likeness at first glance.

"They are well," is Daeo's automatic response. "How are you?" she deflects, dropping her blanket-satchel on the ground. She then collapses onto the log beside her brother, utterly exhausted—she woke up extra, extra early this morning, just to buy herself more daylight to spend at the cave.

"Terrible," Bowi laments. "I hate my *unko* and I wish I never had one."

"*Ugh*, me too," Daeo commiserates. These past few nights, just to fall asleep, she's had to stuff her nose into her baby blanket and breathe slack-jawed. "This *unkoma* is the worst ever," she says, using an umbrella term for *scent* or *sense of smell.*

"It'll pass," Tagi finds their melodrama overblown and misplaced—a child's idea of *oko mee-uyisa.* "Just because you don't like today's *unkoma* doesn't mean you should cut off your *unko* and never smell anything again. That's absurd."

"But it has smelled like this for days now," Daeo complains.

"When will it end?" Bowi groans.

"I do not remember what anything else smells like," Daeo realizes in a panic.

"The foul *unkoma* will dissipate soon enough," Tagi rolls his eyes. "The air circulates. In time, the atmosphere will flush away the stink. Maybe a moon from now, maybe sooner? Who knows. But when it does finally vanish, it'll make you appreciate all the wonderful *unkoma* you'd otherwise miss if you didn't have your *unko.*"

"Like what?" Daeo is desperate to remember any other scent.

"Well... Like the smell of a pan-seared grasshopper leg," Tagi holds up his half-eaten stick. Bowi and Daeo grimace—the food's aroma has long been neutralized. "Or the smell of the *Aeo* on a sunny day. Or the smell of rain on fresh soil."

"You can smell rain and the *Aeo?*" to Daeo, the idea of sniffing water sounds like something her bullies would make her do.

"Of course!" Tagi exclaims. "Can't you? *Tsk*—it rains so often you probably haven't taken the time to notice. But trust me, the smell of precipitation is marvelous. It's a shame you've never appreciated it. Once this terrible *unkoma* fades, I want you to step outside after the next thunderstorm and breathe deeply through your *unko*. Take time to linger in the atmosphere's scent. The jungle speaks via smell, you know. *Unkoma* is the most fundamental sensation—it's what guides all animals to food, to energy, to life. And when given fresh water, the *Uyi* sings a song you can only hear with your *unko*. Try it sometime—you'll be amazed by all the wonderful, subtle fragrances you can detect just after rainfall..."

"Sure."

"Okay."

Both Bowi and Daeo intend to forget this conversation by tomorrow.

"You don't believe me!" Tagi gasps. "Get up." Their blatant disregard offends him. "Come on, get up. Follow me." He has something to show them. "And Bowi, fetch a bowl of fresh water from the basin above the cave."

"Where are we going?" Daeo asks.

"*Heersu.*"

Following a tunnel-like trail, enshrouded between leafy walls of foliage and bouldering mountainside, the short walk to the *Teerta*'s garden is purposefully overgrown and tricky. Logistically, it's situated nearby, within a rocky alcove directly adjacent to the cave. But Daeo would've never found the *heersu* on her own—she's awed when Tagi pulls aside a flourishing, multicolored sheet of *wykyno* at the trail's end, only to reveal a roundabout path switchbacking up to the hidden garden.

Eeao tails the trio all the way there. Consciously, she's curious about their business—the old man generally makes his trips to the garden alone. Subconsciously, the combination of *paen-aemo* reek and Paelo's revenge compels her to remain within the humans' proximity, where at least their familiar odors water down the *Uyi*'s pervading stench.

"What is this?" Daeo marvels at the garden. It's small—just a square plot of black soil and twenty-or-so rows of plants. But she's never before seen vegetation cultivated into such organized simplicity. Up until this point, she considered flora nothing more than an ambiguous force, an enmeshed plurality that grows like hair across the *Uyi*. But now, to see the garden's distinct sequencing, the way every plant is afforded its own berth—she's baffled by the individuality of each, single sprout.

"It's called a *heersu*," Bowi loves feeling smart.

"How did it happen?" Daeo imagines it might be similar to the *montada-yryku*.

"Generations of duty," Tagi says. "Long, long ago—longer than you can even imagine—a very wise *Teerta* discovered how to tame plants, and that's how this *heersu* came to be. But enough about that—I didn't bring you here to learn about *renomo* and *talapako*. I've brought you here to learn how to appreciate your *unko. Bowi,* give me that bowl of water."

Full to the brim, Bowi hands the bowl to Tagi. Then, choosing one of the *heersu*'s empty corners, Tagi crouches low and pours the water onto a patch of unoccupied soil. A dark spot wells, blacker than the ground around it. Without giving the water time to settle, the old man plows his fingers into the earth and scoops up two handfuls of moist, crumbly dirt.

Overhead, Eeao quirks her ears. Perched on the lichen-skinned arm of a balsa extending laterally across the garden's cavity, the kitten presumes the humans must be hungry for earthworms or something.

"Smell this," Tagi encourages them, holding the damp soil close to his nose. "This is the *unkoma* of fresh rain."

The children mimic him, dubious—how good could wet dirt possibly smell? Yet they're immediately mesmerized by the soil's chemical bouquet. Organically, they smell the water-activated effusions of microorganisms, mycorrhizal spores and thirsty tubule roots, decomposed bits of plant and leaf matter, as well as the underlying, earthy scents of silt and moistened black humus. But words dissolve as the complex fragrances transport both children into their own respective memories:

Bowi remembers a day long ago, back when he was a much smaller boy, his *momo* once went searching in the rain for a *pomaeo* melon to soothe his stomach; she returned later that afternoon with two of them, emerging from the storm like a battered hero.

Meanwhile, the scent causes Daeo to remember the drizzly day her baby sister died.

"Doesn't this smell exquisite?" Tagi savors the soil's rich aroma.

"I love it," Bowi agrees.

"I hate it," Daeo says. Her hands feel empty, her arms nonexistent—she left her baby blanket back at the cave! Before Tagi or Bowi have time to react, she's gone, sprinting back down the trail, racing to reclaim her swaddled bundle, to feel it again in her arms.

Eeao admires the girl's speed.

Chapter 44
"Nyno"

In contrast to the widespread malaise afflicting everyone else, Paelo's revenge sends Nyno spiraling into an evermore agitated state of mania. Each whiff of the reek saturates her brain with cortisol—a propulsive hormone that ignites her sense of danger, making sleep impossible.

Everything is wrong.

Muscles tense, spine rigid, Nyno lives in a tunnel-visioned state of high-alert, periphery clouded by unnamed urgency and paranoia, as though mortally threatened by the invisible stench itself. She seals herself inside her *capku.* She surrounds herself with piles and piles of work. She refuses to let herself think about anything else. She only ever steps outside her home to bathe in the *Aeo*—but even these trips are becoming more and more infrequent...

"It smells terrible in here," Daeo comments one evening, returning to her mother's *capku* after having been gone all day (again).

"It smells terrible everywhere," Nyno retorts, padding the shoulder straps of yet another new harness with leathery *hympano* lining. Sweat pools on her brow, her armpits, the backs of her knees. Around her, half-made apparel is strewn everywhere.

"Yes," Daeo concedes. "But it smells worse in here."

Nyno glares. Enveloped in her own gaseous bubble of bodily effluvium, she pulls herself to her feet, biting back shame. Bits of *areemo* twine and *hympano* fluff rain off her lap like dandruff. Her vision goes black for several moments, brain thirsty for blood—this is the first time she's stood up in almost two days.

"Do you need help?" Daeo is alarmed, watching her mother teeter.

"So much help," Nyno grimaces, wringing cramps from her legs and fingers. Daeo steps closer to assist, but Nyno swats her away, "No, stop it, I'm fine. I don't actually need help. Not from you. I just need to go take a bath. Excuse me." She dons her spined harness and departs.

Daeo isn't disappointed to see her go.

As though lying in wait, a wall of Paelo's odor assaults Nyno as she steps outside her *capku*. She squints, fighting back a rush of tears. Albeit stale, the stench of burnt feces remains unmistakable in the air. Nyno holds an *areemo* kerchief over her nose as she scurries down to the *Aeo*, anxious and queasy.

The atmosphere tonight is deceptively serene; furling blankets of fog reflect the *Uyi's* nocturnal glow, forming abstract configurations of fluorescent vapor, luminous nebulae transcending forest and sky. Shadows loom from misty curls of negative space—airflow tunnels, the stench channeling pursuit.

How do I escape the wind?

Overcast, the sky glares silver as fuzzy light from the near-full moon refracts and scatters across billions of intermediary air molecules. The *Aeo* itself is like a spacious breezeway beneath the muggy dome—a place of intermittent reprieve and vicious crosswinds. Nyno holds her breath through the worst pockets of odor.

At least the paen-aemo *are quiet tonight.* Diurnal, the giant geese float silently around the lake's mid-perimeter, each sleeping beast the size of a paddle boat. From Nyno's perspective, they look like humongous lily pads, unconsciously teeming for space. Making her way down to the water, Nyno notices several *punteeku* patrolling the shoreline, their silhouettes angled and spiky against the luminous trees—a rotating guard against the invaders, Nyno figures. Still, their overseeing presence doesn't give her much comfort. She approaches the lapping water.

Several *momo*s are currently in the lake, bathing their respective broods. Each child sits dead-quiet in the sparkling, black water, terrified, all of them just one *splash!* away from waking the ferocious birds. Stepping into the gentle, tepid waves herself, Nyno figures most people have probably switched their bathing routines to nighttime, given the invaders' sleep schedules. Those who own harnesses continue to wear them, even in the water. Better safe than sorry—or worse, handicapped. So far, even excluding Veetri, the number of *paen-aemo*-related casualties has surpassed thirty.

"*Nyno?*"

"*Huh?*" Nyno looks up. She'd sat down in the shallow water at some point and then lost track of time, allowing the lukewarm pull-and-tug around her torso to soothe her body into numb reverie. Now she blinks, recognizing Kleeo's face above her. *How long have I been here?* Wiggling her toes, they feel waterlogged and wrinkly.

"Are you okay, *Nyno?*" Kleeo repeats. "We've been watching you for a while. *Syno* thought you might have fallen asleep out here or something." She gestures over her spined shoulder. Behind her, Nyno can see Syno and several other *punteeku* watching from the shoreline.

"I'm fine," Nyno shifts—there's a rock digging into her tailbone. *How long has that been there?*

"You don't look fine," Kleeo observes. "How's your productivity?"

"I've finished twenty-three harnesses so far, including twelve with *hympano* in-lining, and ten with attached machete sheaths," Nyno lists immediately. "I still have one hundred and fifty-eight more to make, along with all the soft-clothes, satchels, and quilts the birthing *momo*s have requested—I haven't even gotten started on those yet—but I think if I split work between harnesses and soft-clothes, and then maybe relegate some tasks to *Daeo*, I could probably—"

"Okay, *Nyno,* slow down," Kleeo interjects, grabbing her by the shoulders—at some point while speaking, Nyno had begun pacing through the knee-deep water, manic. Kleeo holds her squarely, "There's no need to split work or relegate tasks, you're doing great. These latest harnesses you made are your best yet. We want you to keep up the good work. But as your *ameema,* first and foremost, I want to make sure you're taking care of yourself."

Ameema. An intimate word meaning, *friend.*

Nyno can't recall a single point in her life when someone called her that.

"*Ameema,*" she repeats the word, relaxing into Kleeo's grip.

"If you don't take care of yourself," Kleeo continues, "the quality of your work will suffer. As your *ameema,* I care about you, *Nyno.* And it doesn't look like you're taking care of yourself. Whenever I come to visit, you're always holed away inside your *capku,* working nonstop. But are you taking time to eat? And when did you last sleep? Seriously, you look terrible."

Nyno sags with guilt—these are things she knows she needs to do, but simply, inexplicably cannot. "I don't remember the last night I slept..." she admits, sinking in on herself.

Kleeo supports her weight. "Come on, *Nyno,*" she says. "You're a Chief now. You need to be stronger than this. You need to take care of yourself. No one's going to do it for you."

"I don't know how to take care of anything anymore," Nyno feels herself beginning to cry. "I feel so alone. I've tried to ask *Daeo* for help, because she knows how to work with *mabato* spines, but she's never around anymore and—"

"Don't bother with her," Kleeo frowns. "Children are nothing but unripened adults. Useless for the time being.

Especially *Patummal* ones. No, *Nyno,* you don't need to offload work to anyone else."

"But there's so much work to do."

"And you have plenty of time to do it," Kleeo smiles—at least, Nyno thinks it's a smile. "There's no rush. In fact, feel free to slow your productivity. Let go of the stress. The nest needs you more than you need them. Take a day or two off and just relax. Sleep is important. Especially for someone as important as you."

Nyno rubs her eyes. The idea of relaxing for an entire day despite her workload seems sinful, indulgent. Yet simultaneously luxurious. She sighs, imagining the pleasure of sleep—but then she gags on a whiff of tainted wind.

"Stinking *Patummal,*" Kleeo mutters while the breeze passes. Lately, for whatever reason, everyone's been attributing the stench to Paelo's skin condition. *Dirty snakes.*

"I don't know how to fall asleep anymore," Nyno's eyes twitch. She feels hopeless, cornered by everything.

"Here, take this," Kleeo reaches into one of the *areemo* pouches tied to her belt. In her fingers, she withdraws a pearly *Kamaruna* mushroom, no bigger than a thumbnail. Nyno takes it from her discreetly. "This will help you pass out. Just eat it, lie in bed, and think of sleep. You'll be out before you know it."

"It'll work like that?" Nyno hesitates—last time she ingested this forbidden fungus, she severed her umbilical cord to reality.

"Mhmm," Kleeo nods. "I do it all the time. And when you awake, you'll feel completely reborn."

Reborn? Right now, if Nyno could be reborn as anything, she'd want to be reborn as a mushroom—something cold and inanimate and colorless and responsible for nothing. After swallowing the one Kleeo handed her, Nyno trudges back to her *capku.* She lies in her bed as instructed. She listens to Daeo snore just an arm's length away, her little nose buried in the old baby blanket Nyno barely remembers making. She tries to quiet her mind. She tries to think of sleep. She tries to forget about everything. Eventually, as the mushroom's psychoactive chemicals travel from her digestive tract to her brain, she succeeds.

And then Nyno sleeps for three days straight.

Chapter 45
"Bowi"

Hoping for a line of patients, Tagi forbids Daeo visit the day after *Kosharuna.*

"If we're lucky," he tells Bowi the night before, "there'll be so many women lined up outside the cave tomorrow, we won't even have time to go crawling around inside the *ynsyna* cavern. Won't that be nice for a change?"

Bowi continues to find Tagi's attitude toward *Kosharuna* confusing. If the old man is so keen on treating injuries, why not go down to the nest regularly and seek them out firsthand? Surely there are plenty of people in need. Why wait until only the full or new moon to help? And besides, what's so awful about crawling around inside the *ynsyna* cavern? Bowi has come to genuinely enjoy his subterranean studies—the last *Teerta* he read, number eighty-one, another expert on *momyna,* provided a shockingly detailed account of a time she reached inside a laboring mother's birth canal to unwrap her baby's umbilical cord from around its neck. Clutching at his own throat while reading, Bowi felt almost transported to the scene, holding his breath as the old *Teerta* un-strangled the newborn...

"*Bowi!*" Tagi's voice always jerks him back to reality. "Wake up! There's a line!"

Indeed, as Bowi sits up in bed, he feels the eyes of several people peeking around the cave's mouth. Eeao is already hiding in her dark cranny, miffed. Throwing on his tunic, Bowi follows Tagi outside to begin helping. It seems last night's *Kosharuna* was a particularly active one—women cluster in two's and three's, generally sisters or cousins carrying whichever one's bloodiest. Some suffer broken noses or severed lips. Others nurse swollen ankles or dislocated shoulders. Several bleed from between their legs. They all come this morning because the *Teerta* is the only human in the entire *Uyi* with reliable access to *teeho, reewo,* and *harapo* (three medicinal herbs Tagi regularly harvests from his private *heersu).*

"*Bowi,* begin administering *reewo*," Tagi instructs. "I'll handle the *teeho.*"

"*Reewo* is the pain-reliever," Bowi recalls under his breath, "and *teeho* is the antiseptic." He recites aloud the information he's learned as he retrieves the respective clay jars. Green and oily, Bowi uses a small, wooden spatula to spoon daubs of crushed, sappy *reewo* beneath the upturned tongues of those in pain. Those who aren't already sitting or lying on the ground kneel so Bowi can reach their mouths. It's not a difficult job, but Bowi feels important as he works his way down the murmuring line—the medicine in his jar, a natural numbing and anti-inflammatory agent (as well as a mild stimulant), offers patients near-instant relief.

Meanwhile, the antibiotic *teeho* formula Tagi uses to clean wounds functions as an autoimmune steroid. The old man works quickly, sending those who won't require stitches home immediately after applying the poultice.

"*Meh,* you'll be fine," Tagi tells a young woman whose scraped ribs continue to dribble blood. "I know surface wounds when I see them. Next." In general, for the sake of efficiency, he never commits to stitching more than six injuries in a given day—today's lucky, preselected bunch are already waiting for him in their own separate line. "*Bowi,* prepare the *harapo.*"

"*Harapo* is the disinfectant," Bowi recites. A fermented solution made from pickled *harapo* root, it's stored in a larger jar than the other two remedies, requiring both Bowi's hands to lift it. He lugs it out to Tagi, who's already busy with a long *camraea* plume, combing out its shimmery, fibrous strands into separate, individual threads. The needles he'll use for today's stitching—scoured, sterilized quills, similar to the type used for Bowi's intravenous infusions, but shorter and thinner, easier for weaving in and out of flesh—rest steeping within a cauldron over the fire pit.

"Here," Bowi offers Tagi the jug of *harapo* solution.

"Perfect," Tagi says, immediately dipping one of the delicate, blue strands into the distilled liquid. Sterilized and lubricated, the coated fiber glides easily into the sheath of Tagi's quill needle. "First in line," he motions to a young woman with a split lip. "*Bowi,* continue administering *reewo* as needed. And pay attention."

Bowi does as instructed. The woman's lower lip is bisected laterally down the front, exposing her bloody gums and teeth. Whether chewed open or sliced clean with a blade, Bowi can't tell how it happened, and it seems Tagi doesn't care enough to ask—the old *Teerta* gets promptly to work, nimble fingers aflutter, daubing the wound clean and then deftly sewing it closed. The work is over before Bowi realizes it's begun.

"Five stitches, easily done," Tagi pats the woman's back, prompting her to stand and leave. She smiles weakly in thanks, lower lip tied snug with glistening blue fiber. "Don't smile. Keep your mouth still. Your healed skin will push the stitches out within two moons. Next."

The second woman in line presents a deep gash in her right shin, embedded with blood-soaked dirt and pebbles. As Tagi begins scouring the wound of debris, sanding it over with an *areemo* cloth soaked in *teeho* poultice, Bowi gives the woman an extra spoonful of *reewo* and embraces her hand with his own. He knows the hand-holding gesture isn't medicinally prescribed. But he understands the medicine of comfort.

The woman seems to appreciate his gesture. She returns the squeeze of his fingers.

"I remember you," she says to Bowi, wincing as Tagi inserts his thread-bound needle. Bowi looks up—the woman's face is vaguely familiar, her freckles a pattern he almost recognizes. But her eyes hold him as if focused on a memory; given his *Patummal* condition, Bowi can't help being more distinguishable than most other children. "You're *Nyno*'s boy. Or, at least, you were."

"He'll be *Teerta* soon," Tagi says, eyes glued to his work. *Four moons.*

"You know my *momo*," Bowi smiles, figuring the woman must be one of his *momo*'s fellow birthing mothers—a cousin, or possibly an aunt of his; birthing *momo*s exist within a loose, quasi-codependent social circle, wherein more exist further than nearer to one another. "Have you seen her recently? How is she?"

"She's well..." the woman says, wincing between Tagi's needle-strokes. "Very well, actually. She's a Chief now."

"Really?" Bowi is confused—has he given this woman too much *reewo?* Daeo never mentioned this news. "Chief of what?"

"Textile sourcing."

"Hmm..." the position sounds credible enough to Bowi. But his *momo?* Appointed Chief? From what he remembers, she barely eked out survival for her own brood.

"You look well," the woman says to Bowi. "You were always such a sickly child."

"I've been feeling better," Bowi nods, his mind stuck on his mother.

"I've been seeing to that," Tagi takes credit. "Hold still."

"Is my *momo* a good Chief?" Bowi asks while Tagi stitches. "Is she doing a good job?"

"So far," the woman shrugs, struggling to keep her leg steady. "Although I still haven't gotten my satchel yet. Or my soft-clothes—*ouch!* Oh, and there was that incident with the *Meemmal.* But no one blames her for that anymore."

"What *Meemmal?*" Bowi frowns.

"*Ayee-ayee!* Help!" a cry interrupts their conversation. Bowi whips his head around. Clambering up an overgrown shortcut from the nest, three women crash into the clearing, one pregnant and stumbling between two others. Brambles clutch at their legs. Vines snag their arms and harnesses. Several of Tagi's waiting patients move to assist them, but Bowi beats everyone to it, hurrying to disentangle the women from the grasping foliage.

"What's wrong?" Bowi asks, taking the pregnant woman's forearms to hold her steady. Her womb crowds the space between them.

"*Kyn ree-larro!*" the woman cries, face contorted, streaming sweat. *It's coming!*

Bowi's heart skips a beat—has he been here before?

"Our *tynjo* is giving birth," explains one of the assisting women, "but she's only seven moons pregnant."

"It's too early," Bowi knows this much, even without his recent *momyna* studies. "The baby isn't ready, it can't survive outside the womb yet—"

"Then why am I in labor?" the woman groans, compelled to the ground by another contraction. Bowi and her sisters support her landing, guiding her to a cushioned patch of *wykyno*. Onlookers gather in a circle; even Tagi quickens his work, eager to tie up his current stitch job just so he can come over and investigate. Meanwhile, Bowi refrains from panic, fielding the situation without the old man's guidance; at least it's a situation he's studied.

"Has your water broken?" Bowi skims through his mental notes, all while maintaining eye contact with the pregnant woman.

"No," the woman pants through another cramp.

"We already told you, it's too early for that," one of her sisters says.

"Who even are you?" the other shoots Bowi a suspicious glare.

Bowi gulps, floundering for words.

"He's my assistant," Tagi calls over the crowd. "Soon to be your new *Teerta.*"

No one seems to like this information.

"He's just a kid," an onlooker complains.

"And *Patummal,* too," another sneers.

"What does he know?" a sister huffs.

"*Kyn ree-larro!*" the pregnant woman writhes on the ground.

"He knows more than the rest of you," Tagi snaps, still tying the final stitch on his patient's shin. "Now hush and let us do our jobs—you're lucky there are two of us right now instead of just one!"

His remark silences everyone—even the pregnant woman bites her quivering lip.

Bowi takes her hands in his own, massaging her fingers the way his mother used to whenever she found him vomiting. He can't tell if the woman finds his touch as soothing, but at least the manual stimulation helps him think. "So you're only seven moons pregnant, your water hasn't broken yet, and you're having contractions... How regular are they?"

"How regular are what?" one of the sisters.

"Her contractions," Bowi clarifies, and then, turning back to the pregnant woman, "What's your name?"

"*Seero,*" the woman pants.

"*Seero,*" Bowi says, "How regular are your contractions?"

"I... I don't know," Seero's fingers feel like boneless, wriggling worms, her tri-toned face a clammy pallor. Sweat drips down her *patu* hairline. "They come and they go... They were worse earlier today."

"She had four contractions this morning," the older of the two sisters says. "Three more on our hike here. And then a big one right as we arrived."

"It's too early for this," the other sister keeps saying. "She shouldn't be in labor."

"*Seero*, is this your first pregnancy?" Bowi asks.

Seero nods, fear alight in her hazel-flecked eyes.

"And the pain," Bowi continues, recalling fragments of *ynsyna* he's read, "is it more concentrated in the front of your abdomen? Or do you feel it in your back and sides as well?"

Seero takes a moment to think. "It's mostly in the front," she says.

"I have learned about this," Bowi says, holding the woman's gaze as he holds her hands. "Your body changes in the months leading up to birth. Sometimes, along with the changes, you might experience false contractions. They feel similar to labor, especially to a first-time *momo*. But it's just your body preparing in advance. Real contractions will come with increasing regularity. And probably more pain."

"How would you know?" one of the sisters says.

"Look at how much pain she's in!" the other points.

"She managed to hike here," Bowi figures pain is the reason most women don't travel all the way to the *Teerta*'s cave to give birth. Seero's fingers tense around his. "But fear can be just as painful as pain," he says, turning back to her. "This is your first pregnancy, right? Your first experience with these sensations? I wouldn't be surprised if you're panicking, *orynam*, and that's what's making these cramps feel more intense."

"Really?" Seero takes a deep breath, allowing her legs to relax on the ground. Through their interlaced fingers, Bowi can feel her pulse steadying.

"You're saying it's all in her head?" the larger sister sounds offended.

"Where's the real *Teerta*?" the other demands. "If we wanted advice from some *Patummal* boy, we wouldn't have come all the way up here."

"I'm coming, I'm coming," flustered, Tagi breaks through the encircling crowd, blood and *camraea* plumage smeared across his face. "What's the problem?"

"This child doesn't know what he's doing," a sister points at Bowi.

"Our *tynjo* has gone into premature labor," the other tells Tagi. "She's only seven moons pregnant. She needs your help or the baby could die."

After shooing away the onlookers (all of whom simply return to waiting in line for stitches) Tagi kneels beside Seero to examine her condition. Bowi watches while Tagi inspects between the woman's legs, unfazed. "You're not dilated," he says after a thorough examination. "Nor effaced. I see no physical signs of labor."

"We checked her too before we came," a sister explains. "We thought she would've progressed by now from all the walking and—"

"Well, by now nothing has progressed," Tagi says. And then to Seero, "Describe your pain for me."

"It's..." Seero takes a moment to think, still clutching Bowi's fingers. "It's a tight, cramping sensation, in the front of my pelvis, right here," she releases one of Bowi's hands to touch the underside of her womb.

"Did you participate in *Kosharuna* last night?" Tagi asks—though he knows as well as anyone that she would've had no other choice.

Seero nods.

"Were you injured?"

Seero shakes her head.

"Just... Jostled around a bit?"

Seero nods.

"Any stabbing pain?" Tagi asks. "Bleeding or other discharge?"

Seero shakes her head.

"And the cramps, are they irregular?"

Seero nods. "Actually... I think the boy might be right," she says. "If these cramps aren't labor contractions, then I think I've probably just been panicking and making them worse in my head."

"Probably?" both sisters turn on her. "Worse in your head? You scared us half to death with your screams! What do you mean, probably just panicking?"

"I was scared," Seero admits. "You both said I was going into labor."

"Because you said you were having contractions!"

"Well that's what I thought!"

"*Oko mee-uyisa,*" the oldest groans.

"It's fine, it doesn't matter, I've seen this before," Tagi cuts in, glancing over at the line of injuries still awaiting his needle. "Stay here and rest for the remainder of the afternoon. *Bowi* will administer *reewo* and continue to monitor your cramps. If they remain irregular, you'll be fine to return home by this evening. If they progress to full-blown contractions, then I'll step in and assist. Can we all agree to this plan?"

Seero and her older sisters nod.

So Tagi returns to stitching, and Bowi flies into action, first dragging his wooden bed frame out of the cave so that Seero can recline in comfort, and then daubing poultice beneath her tongue to ease her pain. Indeed, her cramps lessen as the afternoon transpires. By the time evening falls and Eeao pokes her head outside the cave, exhausted after hiding all day from visitors, Seero rises to her feet. "I think I'm ready to go home now," she tells her sisters, sounding more embarrassed by the ordeal than anything else. Her sweat and tears have long since dried.

"Are you feeling better?" Bowi asks—it's been so long since her last cramp, he'd begun dozing beside her.

Seero nods. Face at ease, Bowi realizes for the first time that she's not a woman at all, but a girl. Barely older than himself.

Chapter 46
"Maetri"

Elsewhere in the *Uyi*, later in the current moon's cycle, Maetri is officially appointed Chief *raea* wrangler.

There isn't a ceremony for him, nor even a public gathering. It happens on a cloudy morning, several weeks after Veetri's final *Kamaruna*—which, to Maetri, feels long overdue. He's out tending his *raea* flock in the eastern field (just forty-five birds left) when two of the nest's other Chiefs (the Chief birthing *momo* and the Chief of food sourcing) come to deliver the news.

"You're just the obvious next choice," Dynjo explains. Her spiked harness is adorned with vibrant beads and feathers, along with dyed *hympano* tassels signifying her elevated rank among *momo*s. "You basically saved the *raea* from extinction."

"Plus," Toti concurs, squat and toad-like between the other two, "no one will shut up about how you barbecued that first *paen-aemo*. After that spectacle, there'd be a riot if you weren't honored with the position."

"Well thank you," Maetri doesn't even smile. This whole meeting feels perfunctory, if not condescending. But at least they'd chosen a pleasant enough morning to do it; blue-tailed *camraea* soar peacefully over his grazing *raea* herd, warbling back and forth without rhyme or care. The sky is serene, the field's *unkoma* light and floral, the *paen-aemo* contained within the distant *Aeo*—the atmosphere, refreshed, sighs in dreamy ignorance once again.

Wasn't the world just ending?

Meanwhile, human competition never sleeps.

"There's just one stipulation," Dynjo says—she's always loved drama.

"Of course there is," Maetri doesn't care. He'll do anything, won't he?

"As Chiefs," Toti says, "we schedule *Kamaruna* volunteers eight moons in advance."

"Okay..."

"So we'd like you to deliver news to someone," Dynjo explains. "*Tapati* is a high-ranking *punteeku*. Popular. Well-respected. Been around a while. Older than the rest of us. You're his cousin, yes?"

Maetri shrugs, gaining interest. "Sure."

"*Tapati* has eight moons left," Dynjo says. "Deliver this news to him. Temper his reaction. Ensure he agrees. This is your first official task as a Chief. Can you handle it?"

Maetri can't wait. "Sure."

He finds Tapati later that night, gathered around Dynjo's own fire pit, enjoying her signature fried mantis legs with Kleeo, Syno, and a horde of other nighttime revelers. He pulls his older cousin into privacy—not to spare the man any dignity, but to control the conversation more easily.

"What do you want?" Tapati is currently peaking on a *Kamaruna* mushroom, one from his own privately well-known stash, and he doesn't appreciate getting yanked into the jungle behind Dynjo's *capku* before his first bite of mantis-crunch. Around them, oxyluciferin casts everything in a sickly, chartreuse luster.

"You have eight moons left," Maetri pretends to be unhappy, delivering the news without any hint of smarm or glee. "I've been selected among the Chiefs to tell you. I'm sorry, *Tapati*."

"Oh yeah? And whose idea was that?" Tapati slurs, apparently too intoxicated to feel the gravity of Maetri's words. "Was it your idea? Mister newly-named Chief? Well guess what? I don't care! I'm not scared at all! I welcome *Kamaruna! Ha!*"

"You're comfortable volunteering?" Maetri raises an eyebrow. "You aren't afraid?"

Tapati shakes his head.

"Well then, I admire your *ynsyn-eera,* cousin," Maetri dons a phony smile. "All those *Kamaruna* mushrooms have truly prepared you to become one with the *Uyi, eh?*"

"I suppose..." Tapati grumbles, his consciousness meandering through several, nameless realities at once. He's dreamt of this moment, hasn't he?

"But you know, I wouldn't blame you..."

"Blame me for what?" Tapati snaps to attention.

"I wouldn't blame you for feeling afraid of *Kamaruna,*" Maetri clarifies. "It's hard to say goodbye. I know I've grown attached to many things in my life..."

"*Hmm...*" Tapati sighs. "Many things..."

"No one really knows what it's like afterward," Maetri continues. "They say you become a new lifeform after this, underneath the *Aeo,* but who knows? Anyway, it's good that you aren't scared. It's good that you're ready. Besides, you still have eight moons left. That's a long time to enjoy, when you think about it..."

"Yes..." Tapati frowns. "A long time..."

"Plus," Maetri continues, "everyone hates *Patummal.* Especially now more than ever. It's easy to get them volunteered. Who knows? With the way things are going, I bet your *Kamaruna* moon will get delayed as more of them get sent to the *Aeo...*"

Tapati scowls. "Stinking *Patummal.*"

Act 4

Chapter 47
"Daeo"

Good things never last.

"Die *Meemmal!*"

Daeo doesn't intend to get caught.

"Die, die, die!"

But of course, no prey ever does.

It happens on a stormy morning. Having rendered her regular shortcut a choppy, unnavigable river, flash floods force Daeo to hike the main trail to the *Teerta*'s cave. Thunder and rainfall mask the sloshing footsteps of her pursuers. She's tackled face-first into mud before she even realizes what's happening; her first instinct is to protect her baby blanket and its enwrapped fossil, but the ambush sends them flying off her shoulder.

"Stinking *Patummal!*" cackles surround her.

"Thought you'd escaped?"

"Not for long!"

"Pull her up!"

Daeo is dragged to a standing position, propped up and held in place by three stronger children. She can't see anything past her mud-caked brow, but she can recognize all their voices. And that's when she realizes they're right: She truly had thought she'd escaped. Crying despite herself, she gropes blindly for her lost blanket—until another captor restrains her arms.

"What should we do to her?" a boy's voice leers.

"It's been so long!"

"We need to punish her for all the days she escaped!"

"Let's take her to the swamp!"

"Wait, she dropped something—look," a girl's voice trails into the foliage. Daeo can't see, but the girl is pointing to her blanket-wrapped bundle, which rests intact beneath a thrusting corsage of poisonous *canaeero* blooms.

"What is it?"

"It looks like a baby blanket!"

"Aww, the stinking *Patummal* lost her baby blanket!"

"Pathetic!"

Daeo is whiplashed between tugs and taunts. She tries to wrestle control of her arms, but to no avail. It's only after stinging tears push enough muck out of her eyes that she's able to make out the vague, watery impressions of her encompassing captors. They leap up and down. They hit and they kick. When she tries to shy away from their blows, they shove her face into mud again to gunk up her vision. And then they drag her off-trail, through the drizzling rain and scratchy foliage, in the direction of the swamp.

Their clashing voices ricochet off one another, cruel ideas whizzing back and forth, too jumbled and shrill for Daeo to track. She can't guess with certainty what kind of torture they'll inflict on her today. But she can feel all their pent-up aggression, the hatred they've bottled up for her over the last few weeks. From where it comes, Daeo has no idea. But she knows today they'll spare no mercy.

So neither will she.

Tucked inside the waistband of her skirt, a whittled *mabato* shard clings to her hip. A dagger. Her only friend. It's waiting for action. It wants to help. Today is the day.

She just needs to free one of her hands...

Chapter 48
"Eeao"

As far as Eeao knows, inanimate objects don't have wants or desires.

She sinks her claws into mossy tree limbs without fear of repercussion. She treats bark like pavement, navigating twisted branches and taut vines like systems of interlocking highways. By now, she's practically scratched out her own treetop thoroughfare between Tagi's cave and the swamp. She shreds. She tears. She tunnels through foliage. And the trees are none the wiser; to them, her scurrying weight is imperceptible, her claw marks no worse than natural weather erosion.

On a large scale, the kitten is innocuous. For now.

Because microscopically, she's a bioterrorist.

Her menagerie of gut bacteria continues its assault on the swamp's fungal biome. Each fecal pellet she drops is a living bomb, a capsule glutted with toxic, foreign parasites hungry to colonize and feed. Outside the symbiotic confinement of Eeao's intestines, her companion organisms plunge into the *Uyi*'s soil, gliding on their own mucus excretions, penetrating deep into the rainforest's terrain. They feast on native mycelial networks, and then use the stolen energy to reproduce and spread like unfettered cancer cells. Underground, the *Uyi* is falling into distress. Channels that once funneled mineral and fossil nutrients up to the jungle are collapsing, their mycorrhizal pumps infected and inoperable.

Above-ground, the rainforest is only beginning to feel the impact—a mild strain on phosphorus levels. Although as far as the trees can tell, the atmosphere's inundation of avian pheromones is their primary crisis—cecropia leaves continue to wither, repulsed by their own effusions. Why is fungal demand still ringing when the *paen-aemo* already answered the jungle's call?

If only the trees could move autonomously, or somehow understand the full scale of their predicament, the massive beings could easily end the infection themselves. One good swat with a branch would break every bone in Eeao's body, if only a kapok could swat at the impish kitten the way Tagi swats at gnats. Or would trees be more inclined to pounce and claw with their twigs, as felines do?

Alas, inanimate within the animal scope of existence, a tree's preferred method for exterminating kittens remains unknowable. So the rainforest continues following orders as only it knows how: Diffusing pheromone mimicry into the wind.

Meanwhile, Eeao advances her reign of terrestrial terror, victimizing the *Uyi* further each day.

Lately, her trips to the swamp have become especially gratifying. The *paen-aemo* no longer peruse the area, apparently dissatisfied with the bog's bubbling water quality. And now that stampeding herds of human children are nothing but a rarity, Eeao feels more uninhibited than ever. She free-roams through the swamp's reedy *wykyno* thickets, relieving herself as she pleases, brutalizing the land in happy oblivion.

One morning, however, in the midst of a downpouring monsoon, her business is rudely interrupted by one of those rare children-stampedes. Dry and shrouded beneath dripping foliage, Eeao wrinkles her nose, smelling the humans before hearing their approach.

"Let's shove algae up her nose!"

"Worse!"

"Let's dunk her head in the swamp and count to one hundred!"

"Worse!"

"Worse?" Daeo whimpers—Eeao recognizes her alpha's voice immediately. By now, the kitten can see the gang gathering around the swamp's spongy edge, holding Daeo captive in their midst. Compared to the other children, all spry and clear-skinned, Daeo sticks out as tiny, overpowered, overrun by *patu* and people. Eeao feels her fur prickling, but she stands frozen, too frightened to aid her alpha.

"I have an idea," a large girl says. "Instead of algae, let's shove worms up her nose!"

"No," says a tall boy with striped freckling across his face. "That's too easy."

"Please," Daeo cries. "Just dunk my head in the swamp. I can hold my breath."

"Shut up," the tall boy sneers. "We don't want you to hold your breath."

"What are we going to do with her then?" a reluctant-looking girl stands off to the side, passive yet present. In her arms, she holds Daeo's fallen baby blanket—and the chunk of petrified wood still wrapped inside.

Smiling wickedly, the tall boy turns to face everyone. He holds out his hand. "Let's make her eat this," he says. And then, unfurling his fingers one by one, he reveals a single red flower crushed in his palm.

To Eeao, a flower is a flower.

But to Daeo, a *cananeero*'s lethal beauty is unmistakable.

Chapter 49
"Cananeero"

What does death taste like?

This is the first time Daeo has ever wondered.

And even now, she figures it should probably taste something like the *Aeo*—isn't that how humans are supposed to die? One last taste of water's life-giving bitterness? Wasn't that what her sister tasted?

Would that be better than this?

"Open up, *Patummal*," the tall, stripe-faced boy dangles the *cananeero* blossom in front of Daeo's face, holding it by its wilted, crimson stem. "Maybe this will cure your stink."

His companions giggle and snicker, fifteen or so in total. They surround Daeo like a pack of ancient howler monkeys. Scanning the circle, Daeo can't see a friendly face among them. But she can see hesitation in a few of their eyes—particularly the girl holding her baby blanket. None of these children have ever seen anyone eat a *cananeero* flower before. But they've all been thoroughly warned. If any of them object to murder, now would be the time to speak.

"Please," Daeo tries to make eye contact with the girl. "Do not let them do this."

The girl averts her gaze. "Come on, *Nomi*, let's just dunk her head in the swamp," she tells the tall boy, wringing Daeo's confiscated blanket in her hands. No one realizes, but she and Daeo are actually half-sisters, two of Maetri's sperm cells deposited in different birthing *momo*s. But, of course, only one of them inherited their father's *patu*.

"That's so boring," the stripe-faced ringleader sneers. A blundering second cousin to both girls, Nomi doesn't care what either of them really wants. He's just here for the thrill—like the rest of them. Only since he's tallest, his threshold determines everyone else's. "Haven't you ever wondered what actually happens when someone eats a *cananeero* flower? I heard it makes a person's lips puff up and turn all purple. Don't you want to see?"

The four boys holding Daeo snicker, inspired by the imagery.

Daeo gulps. She can smell the flower, its sweet aroma wafting in the misty air as the tall boy circles her, prowling with glee. Its fragrance isn't sweet like honey or *pomaeo* juice; it's a luxurious sort of saccharine, sublime in a foreboding sense, alchemy to indulge from a distance, never to taste. She used to love the scent—even now, it evokes memories of her *momo*, their fire pit, the sweet-smoky fragrance of dawn.

"But we might get in trouble for poisoning her," the reluctant girl warns, still shifting nervously on her feet. Back and forth, back and forth. Yet she makes no movement to help. No one does.

"Yeah right!" someone snorts.

"She's *Patummal!*" another chuckles.

"No one cares about her," says Nomi, the tall ringleader, staring directly at Daeo. "None of us will get in trouble."

"My *momo* is a Chief!" Daeo cries, still struggling against the four sets of hands holding her in place. "She cares about me!"

"Oh yeah?" Nomi leers. "Then where is she now?"

Daeo has no answer. Everyone laughs. Several hands loosen grip.

Seizing the opportunity, Daeo yanks free one of her sweaty hands. She pivots to escape, throwing her weight in the now-open direction—until someone punches her in the gut. She reels, breathless. The pack swarms to reclaim her freed arm. When Daeo regains her senses, she finds her number of restrainers has increased to six: A boy at each shoulder, a boy at each elbow, and a boy at each wrist, all working together to twist her arms behind her back as painfully as possible.

Yet a secret weapon remains at her hip—why didn't she reach for that first?

"Keep struggling, dirty *Patummal* snake," Nomi towers over her. "It's funny to watch."

Everyone laughs. Grips tighten.

Daeo squirms in pain—though the *mabato* dagger strung to her side aches most. It's right there. Her only friend. Ready and waiting. Why didn't she pull it out when she had the chance? Really, she's afraid to use it—she doesn't want to use it—she didn't build the weapon with intent to wield against fellow humans. But now, captured and powerless, her regret terrifies her more. Tears and sweat stream freely down her face; a bitter taste trickles around the corners of her mouth.

Is this death?

"We'll still get in trouble if she dies," the hesitant girl warns. "*Atrypa:* Every *Patummal* has value as a *Kamaruna* volunteer," she recites one of her father's talking points, as though offering Daeo a mercy.

"So what?"

"So," the girl explains, "the adults will be angry if we waste her life."

"The adults won't know how it happened," Nomi laughs—and then, straightening his composure to glare around the circle, "because no one's going to tell, right?"

Slowly, everyone nods agreement—although glances fly back and forth, each child gauging everyone else's commitment to the pact. Yet even the reluctant girl finds herself nodding along. In her hands, she fidgets ceaselessly with Daeo's baby blanket.

Daeo hates her for it.

"HELP ME!" she screams. "HELP ME!" she cries. "HELP ME!" she pleads.

No one does anything. Even the rain stops, as though bored of Daeo's plight—dragonflies the length of logs emerge to hover ambivalently around the swamp, dodging the occasional frog tongue or gas bubble.

"HELP ME!" Daeo can't stop screaming.

"Shut up," Nomi shoves the *cananeero* flower into her mouth.

Everyone gasps—no one helps—it all happens so fast.

Bitter-sweetness stuns Daeo's tongue, followed by an acrid tingle. She tries to spit, but gags as the boy forces his fingers between her teeth, pushing the flower further down her throat. Oozing nectar coats her uvula, her gums, the insides of her cheeks—she chokes, snorting the blossom's toxin up into her sinuses.

This is death.

"Look, her lips are turning purple!" Nomi leers.

Several laugh—someone's grip loosens—no one thought he'd actually do this.

Writhing, Daeo can barely see through her tears—she whips her head backward, desperate to pull her mouth away from Nomi's prying fingers, but he just lunges his hand further, forcing the petals deeper down her esophagus. Daeo can't breathe. She can't think. Panicked, her body begins to do things beyond her control—she heaves, gagging, her stomach pumping upward in a desperate attempt to repel—to fight—to survive—but resistance only causes more pain—

"*...eeao...*"

"Hey, what was that sound?" a hand releases one of Daeo's wrists.

"Look, it's that thing again!" someone else points upward.

Overhead, Eeao is now perched upon the knotted juncture of two drooping willow branches, observing her alpha's quagmire from mossy comfort. No, she isn't compelled enough to pounce down and help the little girl herself. But she's riveted nonetheless—her claws ache, kneading anxiously at the bark beneath her toes. She can't help the uneasy chirps escaping her mouth.

"*...eeao...*"

"Who cares!" Nomi barks, wrestling his other arm behind Daeo's neck to hold her head in place. "Keep her still!"

"I want a closer look!" another hand loosens.

"I'm scared—what is it?" the girl holding Daeo's bundled blanket raises it over her head like a shield, as though afraid Eeao might leap down and claw at her face.

"Let's catch it!"

"Come on!"

"Wait—hold her still!"

Daeo erupts.

She doesn't know how, but in a frantic burst of energy, a sudden jolt of fiery, unconscious force, she seizes the opportunity to jerk an arm free, swipe out her *mabato* blade, and plunge it into the ringleader's gut.

Nomi gasps.

His hand falls from Daeo's mouth, retracting the flower with it.

Someone screams—another hand loosens—no one knows where to look.

Without thinking, Daeo whirls around, shoving shocked witnesses aside—still holding her dagger, she rips it free from Nomi's belly as swiftly as she'd driven it in. Released, he falls to his knees in the mud, seeping blood down his front.

"H—how?" is all he can say. His freckle-striped face is shocked—horrified—betrayed.

Beside him, the red flower slips from his fingers, soggy with saliva and nectar.

Two girls rush to his aid. A boy charges to intercept Daeo, but she deflects, slicing his hand with her *mabato* shard. He howls—bright-red blooms between his thumb and forefinger. Several more boys scramble at her, but Daeo pivots again, swinging her dagger around in a wide arc to ward them off. In her head, no one is human anymore, not even herself—they're all just animals, clawing for survival.

This isn't death. This is life.

Eeao flicks her tail, invigorated by the action.

Numb to everything but the *cananeero's* spicy flavor still tingling her tongue, Daeo scans the circle of children, searching for her next course of action. Her eyes find her baby blanket. Dictated by adrenaline, she charges at the reluctant girl holding it. She swings her arms around the girl's neck. She presses her *mabato* blade against the girl's throat. Standing from behind, she holds her half-sister hostage, turning her around to face everyone else. Stunned, the girl drops Daeo's baby blanket; it falls to the ground, hidden fossil still a perfectly-wrapped secret.

No one knows what to do. Not even Daeo.

"WANT TO SEE SOMEONE DIE?" she screams at her bullies.

Trapped in Daeo's clutches, the girl's hesitation melts into tears.

"Please!" she sobs to her friends. "Please, please, help me!"

No one moves.

"DO YOU REALLY WANT TO SEE SOMEONE DIE?" Daeo keeps screaming. Her pulse thunders through her body, ricocheting around her fingertips; with each heartbeat, she digs the *mabato* shard deeper into her half-sister's throat. Soon, it punctures skin, producing a vibrant bead of blood. "DO YOU EVEN KNOW WHAT DEATH IS?"

"Help me!" the girl shrieks, choked between Daeo's arms and the blade.

"Help me!" Nomi cries from the ground, panicking in his own blood puddle.

"NONE OF YOU KNOW ANYTHING!" Daeo's voice shudders nearby foliage. She drools acid—her body's automatic effort to rid itself of *cananeero* toxin—but her words resonate loud and clear.

"I HAVE SEEN DEATH!" she roars.

"I KNOW DEATH!" blood glistens on her hands.

"AND I DO NOT WANT IT!"

Everyone cowers, equally shocked and terrified by her rage.

"SO LEAVE ME ALONE!"

Daeo releases her half-sister, shoving the girl away.

"LEAVE ME ALONE!"

The girl scurries to rejoin her friends, blood dribbling down her neck.

"LEAVE ME ALONE!"

Several boys rush to help Nomi, hoisting his weight between six of them.

"LEAVE ME ALONE!"

Everyone scatters, repelled by Daeo's sonic force.

"LEAVE ME ALONE!"

Daeo doesn't stop screaming. She can't. Not for a long time. Even after all the children are gone and she's left to herself, surrounded by the swamp's buzzing dragonflies and humongous bullfrogs, Daeo continues screaming.

"LEAVE ME ALONE!"

"LEAVE ME ALONE!"

"LEAVE ME ALONE!"

She finds comfort in the repetition, the breath between each cry. She screams until her voice gives out, eventually more irritated from overuse than toxic nectar. On the ground, her baby blanket lies bundled beside the soggy, red *cananeero* flower. In her hand, she still holds her blood-stained dagger. Gradually, her breath steadies. She spits a wad of saliva, the tingle in her mouth and throat dissipating. But as her heartbeat slows, reality comes racing to catch up.

What has she done?

And what will her punishment be?

"...eeao..."

Overhead, a silver, symmetrical face rustles within a willow's drooping greenery, still watching.

Eeao and Daeo gaze at one another.

Reverence? Empathy?

Through the leaves, Daeo thinks she sees a tear in one of the kitten's glittering eyes. But then, without warning, quick as a rolling droplet of water, Eeao slinks down the branch and plops herself on the ground before Daeo. Face to face with the kitten, Daeo smiles; Eeao isn't crying at all, but gleaming. She purrs, sidling up alongside the girl, who crouches down to pet the kitten's damp, silky fur. No touch has ever felt so familiar.

And then Eeao is gone, darting off in the direction of the *Teerta*'s cave, a striped blur.

Daeo retrieves her baby blanket, tucks her bloody dagger back into her waistband, and races to catch up.

Chapter 50
"Tagi"

Three moons.

It's only as he ponders his own whittling remainder of time that Tagi begins to notice Eeao's growing distance. The kitten used to follow him everywhere he went. She used to purr between his ankles, and paddy-paw along his shoulders. She used to sleep every night on his chest, the two of them respirating in sync.

But nowadays, Eeao attaches herself to the little girl, Bowi's *tynjo*, whenever she visits. She follows the child's shadow everywhere but the *ynsyna* cavern. She purrs between the girl's ankles with animated delight. She leaps into her lap whenever they sit around the fire pit. The two are bonding quickly—*a bond that will last for life, no doubt...* Yet how many more nights does Tagi have left with the kitten? How much longer will he be able to enjoy his own bond with the creature he named *Eeao?*

Three moons.

This morning, Tagi wakes to an empty chest. He feels cold, the center of his body hollow. Squinting down at himself, he finds a piece of her left behind: A single gray whisker, resting on his sternum. He holds it with care, twirling the delicate, conical strand between his fingertips. When did she drop this? Had she slept on him last night? Or has this whisker been stuck to his chest since yesterday, or even longer, waiting here all this time just to mock him?

Tagi doesn't spend much time speculating; a growl in his stomach prompts him to rise. He discards Eeao's whisker to the cave floor, imagining its eventual decomposition into dust particles. And then a strange thought strikes him: *How much of myself will I leave behind as dust?* Not much. Even if he pulled every hair out of his body now and sprinkled them throughout this cave and the *ynsyna* cavern, it wouldn't seem nearly enough...

Suddenly, Tagi envies the kitten. She's the one who will truly inherit this cave. She's the one whose body will join the fossil record, the *montada-yryku*, while his, Bowi's, and all the other *Teerta*s who came before and will come after are doomed to dissolve at the bottom of the *Aeo*... The irony disturbs Tagi. This cave is his home. It's his habitat. Sure, he'll leave behind his knowledge through *ynsyna* etchings, but what about his physical self? His bones and cartilage? His *patu* and *kataka?* He's never before considered it, but now, watching Eeao's whisker spiral to the ground, he realizes that if he has to die somewhere, if he has to lay his body to rest in one final place, he wishes it could just be here, in his cave. A place he loves.

Three moons.

Southbound storms make for a wet and sticky morning. Steam emanates off every leaf and frond—the rapid warming of northern, high-altitude precipitation swamps the clearing outside Tagi's cave like a sauna. Wading through vaporous tides of mist, he collects several damp, nectar-covered *cananeero* buds; wet or dry, flame-flowers possess all the necessary chemicals to create fire, provided the addition of suitable kindling and fuel. Now, he sets to work readying his fire pit for a new day, first raking it clear of all charred, soggy refuse, and then constructing a fresh teepee from strips of dried *areemo* bark. Soon, despite the rainy weather, Tagi manages to stoke a smoky, coughing fire to life.

"*Mmm...* The smell of a new day," he sighs, expecting to find Eeao beside him.

Of course, she's nowhere to be seen...

"Want to split a mantis?" Bowi yawns, emerging from the cave right on cue. "I'm hungry."

"*Ra meerr-ymaeka sae,*" Tagi nods, calling Bowi something akin to *mind-reader*.

They're halfway through roasting their meaty, skewered mantis when, also right on cue, Eeao and Daeo crash onto the scene, tearing through the jungle as if pursued.

"What's wrong?" Bowi senses his sister's distress.

"Alright, alright, that's enough, your game of chase ends here and now," Tagi will not tolerate any such antics this near to the *Teerta*'s cave.

Daeo skids through the mud, halting just before the fire pit. She collapses hands-to-knees, winded, while Eeao's cave-bound trajectory continues; Tagi watches her curly-q tail disappear into the dark.

"What's all over your hands?" Bowi notices the blood next. His first assumption is that she's been crushing *sokeeto* berries with their *momo*—heaps, by the look of it.

"I stabbed a snake," Daeo lies.

"Why?"

"To save *Eeao*."

"One snake?" Tagi raises an eyebrow. Considering the amount of blood on her hands, he imagines she may have gotten a bit overzealous. "I think *Eeao* is perfectly capable of defending herself from a single snake."

Daeo just shrugs. She feels charitable with the amount of truth she's told.

"Are you done eating yet?" she asks them. "I want to go look for my word." Really, she just wants to hurry up and disappear. She suspects her injured victims and their *momo*s will arrive at the *Teerta*'s cave shortly—seeking some combination of poultice, stitches, and/or justice—so her current plan is to simply hide inside the *ynsyna* cavern all day. Maybe all week. Or forever.

"Go clean up while we finish *tyrkuna*," Tagi tells her. "Those hands are unsightly."

Daeo scuttles toward the water basin inside his cave, wringing her fingers nervously as she walks. By now, the splattered blood along her right elbow and forearm is beginning to dry, but humidity retains its slickness in both her palms. Ladling fresh water from the basin, Daeo splashes one hand, then the other. Crimson residue trickles to the cave floor, blood from three different people. Daeo wrings her hands clean, scratching at the tougher stains with her fingernails.

"H-how?" She keeps hearing Nomi's cry in her head. She keeps seeing the shock on his striped face, the betrayal in his eyes. The former she understands; the latter makes no sense. He tried to murder her. Why shouldn't she fight back? She drenches her hands again. What do people expect from her? Meanwhile, Eeao slinks affectionately between her calves, dodging each drip.

Tagi watches the girl splash around haphazardly. "Please don't waste my fresh water," he calls. "Unless you want to take on the job of transferring more from the filtered basin above?" He gestures up to his mycofilter, the water trough perched atop the cave's mouth. Bowi and Daeo both give him a wary look; they know it's a precarious chore. Tagi doubts the children are even strong enough to lift the stone basin themselves yet—*but don't they need to be?*

Three moons.

Visitors arrive a short while later, just after the trio enters the *ynsyna* cavern.

"Tagi!"

"Teerta!"

"Ugh, what now?" Tagi hates surprises. *It's not my time yet, is it?*

Daco clings fondly to a stalagmite, grateful to have hidden in time.

"Tagi!" outside, it sounds like a mob is gathering.

"Stay here," Tagi tells the children, figuring this unexpected visit must have something to do with his own dwindling timeline. *Three moons? Bah—why wait?* He can easily imagine the Chiefs rescheduling his *Kamaruna* to an earlier half-moon, simply for the convenience of someone more important. "Begin your *ynsyna* lesson," he tells Bowi. "I'll go see what the people want."

"*Tagi!*" urgency rings.

It's not like the punteeku *are known for patience.*

Tagi hurries outside to meet the crowd, pulling hairs from his forearms and sprinkling them as he goes.

Chapter 51
"Atrypa"

"I am scared," Daeo knows she's in trouble. "Do not go out there," she grabs Bowi's shoulder to prevent him from following Tagi.

"Why?" Bowi just wants to procrastinate—the one hundred and sixth *Teerta* was an expert on mushrooms, *arunan,* the *Uyi's* most abundant fruit, and Bowi finds the mycological rhetoric uniquely tedious. He can't imagine his sister wants to hear him read the lesson aloud either.

"The *Teerta* told us to stay here and begin your lesson," Daeo says.

"No, why are you scared?" Bowi clarifies his confusion.

Daeo gulps; her tongue is still tingly from *cananeero.*

"Remember when I said I stabbed a snake this morning?"

Bowi nods.

"It was not a snake."

Bowi quirks.

"It was *Nomi.*"

"Who?" Bowi has crammed so much new information into his head over the past five moons, he barely remembers the names of the children who used to torment them. "Wait, you mean stripe-face? That tall kid who used to throw us in the swamp?"

Daeo nods. "And a few others..."

Bowi gasps. "You stabbed multiple people?"

"They would not leave me alone," Daeo is hyperventilating, experiencing the panic all over again. "They tried to make me eat a *cananeero* flower—they were forcing it down my throat—I thought I was going to die—"

"It's okay, it's okay, you did the right thing," Bowi hushes his *tynjo,* pulling her into his arms. The terror she describes sounds unimaginable—but to him, her story is all but surprising. "What did you use to stab them?" he asks, reluctant to envision the scene.

Slowly, Daeo lifts the side of her skirt, revealing the bloodstained dagger hidden in her waistband. Bowi eyes it for a moment, feeling suddenly complicit. When did his sister start carrying around a weapon? Then again, he's glad she did...

"*Atrypa*," he mutters the word for *luck*. "It's a good thing you had that."

"I did not want to hurt anyone," Daeo is hyperventilating again. "I did not want to—"

"*Bowi!*" Tagi's voice calls from outside. "*Bowi*, I need your help! We have three injuries to mend!"

"It is them," Daeo whimpers, folding herself into her brother's arms once more. "Please do not go out there—please stay here—they are going to kill me if they—"

"*Shh*," Bowi stands her sharply upright. "I can't hide in here with you. I need to go out and help. I'm the *Teerta*, too. But no one knows you're in here, so just stay put, okay? And keep that dagger hidden. *Tagi* and I are going to take care of this. *Wyntiko?*"

Daeo nods, "*Wyntiko*," though tears spill down her cheeks. She knows this won't end well.

Triangulated in her cranny, Eeao watches Bowi hustle outside to help Tagi.

Bowi finds the clearing swarmed with activity; twelve or so *punteeku* form a murmuring, bustling semi-circle around three bloody children and their worry-stricken *momo*s. Tagi is center stage, already equipped with his various poultice jars and bandages, mending the bloodiest first: A boy seeping red from his abdomen. Nomi. To Bowi, knowing what he knows, the injury looks almost like a *cananeero* bloom sprouting from his belly. The wounds on the other two children don't appear nearly as bad (a cut finger and a scraped neck) although, judging by their *momos'* fussing, all three children may as well be in equal peril.

"Help my *babi!* His hand is severed!"

"Help my *babo!* Her neck is sliced open!"

Each woman, so focused on her own child—Bowi swallows a wave of nausea. He recognizes everyone. The three children who used to bully him. The birthing *momos* who never offered any aid or sympathy to his own. The same *punteeku* who carried him up here just five moons ago.

"*Bowi!*" Tagi's voice grips him. "Fetch me a *camraea* plume, and then get to work cleaning those two injuries. I'll handle this one, but I suspect all three will need stitches."

Refocusing on the job ahead, Bowi springs into action. He retrieves a plume for Tagi. He offers daubs of *reewo* to both his assigned patients, and then soaks an *areemo* cloth in *harapo* solution to begin disinfecting their wounds. Onlookers chatter anxiously. The *momos* each give Bowi a wary look.

"Stinking *Patummal...*" one mutters.

Bowi ignores the slur. He reaches to apply *teeho* paste to her son's injured fingers, but the boy pulls his hand away, spitting: "I remember you! It was a *Patummal* like you that did this!"

Beside the boy, his mother gasps: "*Patummal* snake! Get away from us!"

Bowi pulls back, alarmed.

"Hey!" Tagi barks, pausing from his work to glare at the woman. "That boy is your new *Teerta.* Let him do his job."

"But it was a *Patummal* snake that attacked them!" the *momo* protests. "Isn't that right?"

Both injured boys nod.

"No," the injured girl's voice is but a peep. "The *paen-aemo* attacked us, and then—"

"Shut up!" the boy next to her yells. "You're lying!"

"It was a stinking *Patummal* that stabbed me!" Nomi cries from the ground, head cradled in his mother's arms while Tagi prepares to stitch his belly.

"But this boy isn't an ordinary *Patummal*," Maetri emerges among the *punteeku*, pointing at Bowi. "He's training to become the future *Teerta*. It's the only station suitable for someone like him."

"How convenient," Tapati is present too—and technically the father of both wounded boys. He glares at Maetri: "I know you're a Chief now, *Maetri*, but who gave you the power to appoint your own *Patummal* offspring as the new *Teerta?*"

"The boy's appointment has nothing to do with me," Maetri scoffs. "It was decided six moons ago."

"Five moons ago," Tagi corrects.

"We don't care!" the *momo*'s are angry. "We don't want a stinking *Patummal* anywhere near—"

"It doesn't matter who stinks or who looks like what!" Tagi growls at everyone. "Just let the damn boy help!"

Murmurs sink to whispers. No one knows what to do or who to trust. Suspicious, albeit painfully aware of their own medical incompetence, the three *momo*s link hands while Tagi and Bowi continue working, as though offering each other a type of medicine beyond the *Teertas*' comprehension. Their children wince and groan while their injuries are mended, but in each case, beneath all the blood, their wounds turn out much milder than Tagi had anticipated; the little girl doesn't even require stitches. Overseeing each operation, the *punteeku* watch in stony silence—except for Maetri and Tapati.

"Are you sure her neck will heal without stitches?"

"Perhaps his hand could use another douse of *harapo?*"

Both are blatantly invested.

"*Nomi* is my firstborn *babi*," Tapati reminds Tagi for the fifth time. "And *Apanati* is my second. They're my favorite boys, they need to recover!"

"They will both recover," Tagi is exhausted—more from reassuring parents than from sewing stitches. "As long as they remain resting until the next *aruna*—and do not pick at their stitches," Tagi swats Nomi's hand away, "they will recoup stronger than ever, ripe and rearing for their first *Kosharuna*s." Tagi knows what these fathers want to hear.

"But look at *Neepo*'s neck," Maetri points to his cherished daughter again, the blood still pooling in her puncture wound. "Are you certain she doesn't need a stitch or two?"

"Her wound isn't deep enough," Tagi explains. "The attacker didn't even nick a vein."

"But who attacked them?" Tapati frowns. "We need to find whoever it was."

"Why?" Bowi's tongue slips before he can bite it.

Tapati frowns harder. "So we can punish them, that's why. This sort of attack is outrageous! It's unacceptable! It's criminal!"

The three *momo*s nod vigorously.

"You're absolutely right, *Tapati*," Tagi concurs, hoping to appease everyone and wrap things up soon—how many more *ynsyna* lessons can he complete with Bowi in just three moons? "Now, why don't you all go off and create a search party so you can find whoever did this and punish them to the full extent—"

"*Kamaruna*," Tapati interrupts. "Whoever did this," he gestures to the three children, all of whom are still seated on the ground, wrapped in their *momo*s' arms, "must be volunteered at the next *Kamaruna*. Without question. That's the full extent, right?"

The three *momo*s nod vigorously.

"Then *Kamaruna* it will be," Maetri agrees. "I'm a Chief, I will make it so."

Bowi's stomach drops out from under him.

"Who did this, *Nomi?*" the tall boy's *momo* prods. "Tell us."

"Yes, tell us," another one urges.

"Go on, boy," Tagi encourages. "Tell us who did this to you."

Nomi winces—more to extort further cuddles from his *momo* than to brace from actual pain; Bowi has given the boy enough *reewo* to tranquilize a full-grown *raea*. "It was a girl," Nomi finally croaks, frail and mincing—the crowd is riveted. "A stinking *Patummal* snake girl."

Bowi flinches at each slur—he's grown so used to formal, academic language.

"She snuck up on us from behind," Nomi continues, milking a narrative into existence. "We had no idea. She stabbed me first. And then the others. We all ran. It was so scary!"

"Which *Patummal* girl?" Tapati sounds almost greedy. "Tell us!"

"It was," he points at Bowi, "his *tynjo.*"

Everyone glares—one of the *momo*s spits—guilt by association.

Bowi's entire body goes numb—which, for him, is at least a welcome sensation.

But Tagi is more shocked than anyone: "Excuse me?" he chuckles at the boy.

Everyone gasps.

"How dare you laugh at my *babi?*" Nomi's mother growls.

"Do you question his story, *Teerta?*" Maetri wouldn't mind if someone did, considering this new accusation complicates his own paternal interests.

"I'm sorry, forgive me," Tagi tries to quell his laughter, "it's just that it couldn't have been this boy's *tynjo* because she's been here with us all morning. *Kahtopo,* she's in the cave right now—*Daeo!*" he calls. "*Daeo,* come out here and clear this up for everyone! *Daeo? Bowi,* go and get your *tynjo. Daeo!*"

Bowi doesn't move. No one does.

"Oh, hurry up now, *Daeo!* Can't you hear me?"

It's only as Daeo comes creeping out from the dark, tear-stained and quivering, that Tagi remembers the state in which she'd arrived this morning: Bloodstained and panting. His heart jolts—*I stabbed a snake—stinking* Patummal—*to save* Eeao—*what have I done?*

Up in her corner, Eeao watches Daeo move unwillingly, a Pythagorean point sliding out of triangulation. She wants to leap down and purr between her alpha's ankles. But the crowd outside overwhelms her sense of duty.

"There she is!" Nomi perks up when Daeo's glowing form emerges. "That's the stinking *Patummal Meemmal kahtopo* snake girl who stabbed us!" All three *momo*s spit in her direction.

Daeo stops just within the cave's mouth, too frightened to step fully outside. She looks only in Bowi's direction, desperate for his comfort. But from Bowi's perspective, she's poised between the cave's rocky jaws, moments from ruin.

"You?" Maetri points slowly at his daughter, drawing out time to think.

"*Ha!*" Tapati exclaims—they all know Maetri fathered more than one *Patummal.* "This is another one of your blemished offspring, isn't it?"

Collective blame pivots to the new Chief.

Maetri stands there, calm and cocky under scrutiny despite the neural firestorm erupting in his skull. "No," he says, mentally tallying each of his fourteen other children. "I did not produce that *Patummal.*" He loves the clean-cut pattern of their *patu*s. "*Veetri* was that child's *kosha-kymara.*" He loves how much they look like him. "Not me."

And who can argue? Even Bowi and Daeo can't know for certain which pair of testes produced them.

Tapati doesn't care much anyway. "Okay then," he says. "The *Patummal* girl is still guilty." He throws his finger at Daeo again, guiding judgment back to her.

"She's a criminal!" one *momo* chastises.

"Volunteer her at the next *Kamaruna!*" another demands.

Helpless, Daeo gazes into Bowi's eyes, searching for hope. He's with her now, right? They're together again, aren't they? Shouldn't he be able to sing all of this away?

But Bowi just feels sick. His brown eyes swim with tears. Where's his voice?

"Wait!" Tagi interjects, annoyed by all the peacocking and politics. "I know this little girl. She isn't violent, and she's certainly not a criminal. Just because she's *Patummal* doesn't have anything to do with the matter. She wouldn't attack another child unprovoked, would you?" he turns now to Daeo, finally offering her room to speak.

"Um—no, of course not," Daeo stammers, surprised by the opportunity.

"Did you stab these children?" Tagi asks.

"I... I did," Daeo admits. "But I did not mean to hurt anyone."

Nobody believes her.

"*Patummal* snake!"

"Stinking liar!"

"We had our backs turned!"

"I am being honest!" Daeo grasps again for opportunity, a chance to speak; she spews her truth in an uncontrollable torrent: "I did not want to hurt anyone! They attacked me! They snuck up on me! I had my back turned! They captured me, and they took me to the swamp, and they tried to make me eat a—"

"YOU'RE LYING!" Nomi is so high on *reewo*, he's going cross-eyed.

"Let her speak," Maetri feels it's his duty, as a Chief, to at least promote justice. "Everyone has a right to defend themself. Even *Patummal.* Go on..."

Everyone simmers. Daeo takes a deep breath. All this attention—isn't this what she wants?

"They have been bullying me for as long as I can remember," Daeo doesn't know where to start. "They throw me in the swamp. They kick me. They hit me. They make me eat things. Today they tried to make me eat a *cananeero* flower. He shoved it in my mouth. He was trying to kill me," she points at cross-eyed, stripe-faced, belly-stitched Nomi.

"And where is this *cananeero* flower now?" Tapati asks. "I presume you didn't swallow it?"

"I do not have it," Daeo shakes her head. "I spat it out and left it at the swamp. But I am—"

"I've heard enough of this *ragran-eena* gibberish," Tapati cuts her off. "I'm not going to stand here and listen to a little *Patummal* girl accuse my son of heinous crimes when she herself doesn't even know how to speak properly."

Someone snickers. Daeo's face burns.

"Volunteer her at the next *Kamaruna!*" Nomi's *momo* insists. "She's guilty! End of story!"

"Our children aren't safe with her around," Neepo's *momo* agrees.

"Wait!" Neepo cries from her mother's arms—a reluctant hiccup. Everyone looks down at her. Daeo wants to lunge at the girl. She wants to scream at her. She wants to fall to her knees and beg her half-sister to just tell everyone the truth. But she's afraid that any of these actions will only make her look worse—aggressive, angry, jealous. And so

Neepo, left to her own tendencies, simply stammers, "I... I didn't have my back turned..."

And Maetri sighs. He sees so much of himself in his daughter, Neepo. Except for her compassion—that's a trait that'll doom her to motherhood. "The *Patummal* girl will be volunteered at the next *Kamaruna,*" he proclaims, sentencing his other daughter to death.

Everyone cheers.

Daeo can't find Bowi's eyes—he's staring at the ground, trying not to vomit.

"Wait!" Tagi is disturbed—more so than he's ever been in all his moons. "Why are you treating this girl like an automatic criminal? Just because she's *Patummal?* Just because her *patu* is overgrown? I'll have you know long ago, long before any of you were even born, the *Teerta* who trained me was a *Patummal* woman. And she was the most intelligent, respectable, magnificent person I've ever known. She went to the *Aeo* at an old age—but just like the rest of us will, she went before she needed to. She could've done so much more as *Teerta* if only she'd been allowed more time... And this little *Patummal* girl right here, she can do so much more with her life if you let her. She's bright and witty and tenacious. Don't send her to the *Aeo* now! Not yet! We need her!"

Everyone blinks.

The old man is leaking tears. He'd said that last sentence for Bowi's sake. Now, aware of himself again, Tagi swiftly wipes his cheeks.

Unused to hearing such words about herself, Daeo just hopes the old man was being honest.

"You're right," Tapati concedes after several moments of thought, "none of us were around way back then. But old times don't matter. Because just this morning, that *Patummal* snake, who you claim to be so witty and compassionate and whatever, stabbed three of our own children. Brutally.

Viciously. She's a monster. She admitted it herself. Now, you're a smart old man, right, *Tagi?* Even you have to admit that such actions require consequences, yes?"

Everyone glares at the *Teerta,* hot and fiery.

"Yes," Tagi grits his teeth—why is he crying?

Three moons.

"She stabbed my boy in the gut," Nomi's *momo* declares. "That's attempted murder."

"And what are the consequences for attempted murder?" Tapati spins the question to Tagi.

"*Kamaruna,*" Tagi wipes his eyes, struggling to stop his tears. "I understand the basic consequences, *Tapati.* But I implore you, please, give this young child some sort of *Atrypa.*"

Atrypa: While generally a word for *luck,* in this formal context it refers to a customary extension of time given to anyone sentenced for early *Kamaruna,* whether due to incontinence, injury, petty crime, ect. A form of mercy, it's supposed to allow the volunteer time to spiritually prepare—or, in legends, physically escape. Tagi's utterance of it now upsets the three *momo*s.

"*Atrypa?*" Nomi's mother spits over the top of his head, aiming at the *Teerta.* "How dare you evoke such a custom in this situation?"

"Please," Tagi positions himself between Daeo and the crowd. "I implore you. She is young. Before today, she's never hurt anyone in her life. And none of your children will suffer lasting effects from their injuries—in fact, I can guarantee they'll be healed within a few moons. Can't you at least give the *Patummal* girl until then? Just a few moons to wait and see? Please, grant her *Atrypa.*"

"Alright, alright, settle down," Maetri steps forward before the *momo*s can start yelling again. He's taken as much time as he needs to devise the perfect ending for this scene.

"You're scheduled for an upcoming *Kamaruna,* aren't you, *Teerta?*" he asks.

Tagi gulps—he knows where this is going. "Yes. Three moons."

"Three moons then," Maetri proclaims. "*Atrypa* for the *Patummal* girl."

Inside their heads, Daeo, Bowi, and Tagi are all screaming—yelling—sobbing.

But Nomi's *momo* is the one who shrieks aloud, "No! That's unacceptable! We can't let her run around the nest for three moons—unfettered—she's dangerous!"

"Then she'll spend her *Atrypa* here, at the *Teerta's* cave, banished," Maetri decides—easy enough. And then he locks eyes with Tagi, stone gray on watery black. "You'll keep her from causing trouble, right?"

Tagi nods silently.

"Good," Maetri morphs his face into a smile. "Three moons from now, both you and the *Patummal* girl will volunteer for *Kamaruna.* Until then, happy *Atrypa.*"

By early afternoon, everyone is gone. The angry *momo*s. The gossiping onlookers. The spiky *punteeku*. Everyone who came to stare and point and condemn Daeo to death leaves shortly after the outcome is decided.

But children aren't psychologically capable of conceptualizing death—especially their own. Life is the purpose of childhood. So when a child is forced to face such doom, how should one react?

Bowi is the one who cries. Daeo is the one who disappears. He follows her into the *ynsyna* cavern, where he hugs her as she hugs their old baby blanket and the lifeless fossil inside. They hold each other all day and all night, just their two bodies glowing in the dark. Daeo exists silently in her brother's arms while he rocks her back and forth, singing songs through his tears—both to help her feel better and to keep himself from vomiting.

Tagi remains in the cave's antechamber, allowing the siblings time and privacy to process the day's trauma together. Though he never had siblings of his own, he recognizes and deeply respects the bond between Bowi and Daeo. He doesn't know how, but he wants to find a way to help them. *They need each other.* Lately, he's begun to view the two children almost as his own—*if any man can ever truly know what that feels like...* He doesn't want them to suffer like this. He wants to die knowing they're both safe and together, with long lives ahead of them. He wants to devise a plan of action, instructions to help them escape this mess—or, at least, provide them with a semi-relevant story to give them hope.

But there is no hope. There are no alternatives. And there is only one plan: *Kamaruna.*

So the old man sits alone within the mouth of his cave, listening to the boy sing on and on, late into the night. Sure, he could sit here and fret about fate. But he'd rather focus on something he enjoys. And right now, he enjoys listening to Bowi. Tagi follows the boy's voice intently, up and down across an endless sea of melody, envisioning each note he sings as a uniquely inspired ripple upon a multidimensional, aural plane. There's no end to each of Bowi's songs, it seems. No conclusion to his ongoing exploration of lyrical sound. *But doesn't there have to be an end?* There's always an end.

Three moons.

At some point, as Bowi's voice finally tires and another rain storm rolls across the sky, washing the *Uyi* in heavy black mist, Eeao hops down from her cranny and sits next to the old man. They pose side by side for a while, pretending to ignore each other while the rain trickles. But before long, the kitten crawls onto Tagi's lap. She makes herself comfortable. She begins to pur, twitching her whiskers as rain cascades outside the cave. On and on, on and on. Tagi doesn't smile, but he does breathe a sigh of relief.

Eeao wishes the little girl would emerge from the smelly cavern. She misses her alpha. She wants to purr on her lap.

But for now, the old man and the rain will do.

Chapter 52
"Nyno"

Word of Daeo's crime spreads fast.

By the next morning, almost everyone in the *Uyi* knows of the scandal. An already infectious story, the tale mutates moment to moment, evolving entirely new offshoots and variances as it escalates from person to person, mouth to ear. By the time Nyno hears the narrative, apparently her own daughter coordinated with *momo* parrots to echolocate and hunt down three child victims, whom she then ruthlessly savaged with a flintstone machete she stole from the *Teerta*.

"WHAT?"

"Relax," Kleeo scowls. "No one died."

"But *Daeo* wouldn't do that!" Nyno reels, leaning against the trunk-like pole in the center of her *capku*. The two women are standing inside Nyno's home this morning, the floor around their feet strewn with half-woven *areemo* straps and half-assembled harness frames. Kleeo has just arrived, first to deliver a new list of work orders (out of nowhere, demand is skyrocketing for *kynaea* feather ponchos, the type that tie with *hympano* tassels around the neck), and secondly to share the outrageous story with the culprit's mother herself (Nyno just woke up from another three-day nap, and so hasn't yet heard). "*Daeo* isn't that type of girl!" she insists, flustered by the dreamlike haze from which this story seems to have materialized. "She's not a monster! She'd never hurt anyone!"

Off to the side, Nyno's unmade sleeping mat looks like a sweat-soaked, disheveled, slovenly nest while Daeo's remains neat and tidy, as though never utilized.

The baby cradle is there too. Vacant as ever.

Why is that still here?

"She's *Patummal*," Kleeo is tired of having to explain this. "They're all dirty snakes."

"But not *Daeo!*" Nyno sobs. Everything hurts. She squats on the ground, holding her face in her hands. "How could she have done that? And why? She wouldn't! I know she wouldn't! I know her!"

"Calm down," Kleeo rolls her eyes. "Why are you panicking?"

"Because she's my *babo* and I—" Nyno chokes, unable to say more. Maternal instinct? Mother-daughter bond? Post-traumatic stress? How can she explain this?

I love her I love her I love her I love her I love her I—

"It's not your fault," Kleeo says. "No one blames you. Stinking *Patummal* are always dangerous. It can't be helped. They belong with *Meemmal,* if you ask me. *Kamaruna* is a grace they don't deserve. But oh well. *Tarma-ako.* We all benefit in the end."

Kamaruna. That one long ago, when she was a child. Watching her own *momo* plunge into the *Aeo,* everyone had told Nyno how normal it was, to see a parent go.

"But she is my child," Nyno says, looking up at Kleeo. "I can't watch my child die." *Again.*

Kleeo stares down at her, confused. "Why do you care so much? I told you before, children are just unripened adults. Like fruit, you either prune them or nurture them for the benefit of the bush. Or, in this case, the nest. Just because you pulled a stinking *Patummal* out from between your legs one day, doesn't mean you owe it anything. Cut the loss. Discard the bad fruit. Start over. It's no big deal."

Nyno blinks—she can't find anything human or recognizable in Kleeo's eyes.

"You have a new life now," Kleeo continues. "You're a Chief. It's the perfect opportunity to start fresh, produce better. You've already done a fantastic job with all the harnesses and satchels you've made. I keep telling you, everyone loves your work. You're a major asset to the nest. Your craft is your greatest strength. So lean into it. Forget your past as a birthing *momo;* it was a brief journey in the wrong direction. But you're heading in the right direction now. Don't turn around. Don't look back. *Ynsyn-eera.* You know I'm right. Want a mushroom?"

Nyno doesn't respond.

"If anything," Kleeo pops a *Kamaruna* mushroom into her own mouth, "you should feel grateful the girl will be gone soon."

Nyno stands. She's sick of Kleeo. She's going to find Maetri.

We're both Chiefs now, aren't we?

She locates him toward evening, upon a *wykyno*-wreathed bluff overlooking the eastern *raea* fields. He stands alone within the flowery, multicolored foliage, studying his herd from above. Below, the massive birds peruse a weedy, luminous field; Nyno sees resentment harbored within their bulbous, black eyes. Overhead, as though complimenting the *Uyi'*s terrestrial iridescence, the setting sun splashes vividly below the western horizon, spraying the last of its light up and over the sky's domed arc in oozing, gradient cascades of liquid, celestial fire.

"*Maetri,*" Nyno feels strange—she's never willingly approached him.

"*Nyno,*" Maetri has been wondering how long she'd take to come find him.

"Haven't you heard?" Nyno hardens her composure. *Of course he's heard.*

"Heard what?" more concerned with his birds, Maetri doesn't even look at her.

"About *Daeo!*" Nyno knows him to be cavalier—*but now?* "Our *babo!*"

"Your *Patummal* girl?" Maetri has been planning this conversation for days. "That's your *babo,* not mine. You had that one with *Veetri,* you whore."

"WHAT!"

"Everyone knows," Maetri says, eyes still roving the field below, long assuaged with his calculated loss. "I don't have any *Patummal* offspring."

"WHAT!"

"What?"

Nyno doesn't know what else to say. Blindsided, she's too bewildered to consider anything but the most basic interrogatives. Who is this man? What is he saying? Why is this happening? And why does she suddenly feel every mark and bruise he ever left on her body, all the *Kosharuna* scars he gave her, the motherhood he inflicted—she feels it all gravitating toward her chest, a painful, crushing tightness around her heart, her diaphragm, her throat.

Liar liar liar liar liar liar liar—

"LIAR!" she screams. She imagines herself charging at Maetri, barreling him into a nearby tree, knocking the wind from his lungs as she bashes his head against its hard, crusty trunk. She wants to cut him—bruise him—stab him—break his bones. Instead, she crumbles, sinking to her knees on the mossy ground, too aware of her own weakness and pain to do anything else. "YOU'RE LYING!"

"Why would I lie?"

"*DAEO* IS OURS!" Nyno pounds her fists into the dirt. "WE NEED TO SAVE HER! WE CAN'T LET THEM—CAN'T LET THEM—"

"Can't let them what?"

"KILL HER—" Nyno's voice cracks, shredded. Deltas pour from her tear ducts.

"No one's killing anyone," Maetri sneers at her hysterics. "The girl is a criminal and we're volunteering her for *Kamaruna*. It's routine justice. That's all. Don't worry, no one blames you—"

"I don't care, I'll take the blame!" Nyno screams. "I want the blame! I deserve it! Please! Volunteer me! I'll go instead of her! Just please, I can't do this anymore! I can't watch another one of my children—"

"SHUT UP!" Maetri charges at her suddenly, scaring her into silence. While he could maul her into the mud if he wanted, he settles instead for intimidation, towering over her, the jagged outline of his spiked harness cutting into the twilight sky. Nyno is technically a Chief now; equals, he'd get in trouble if he manhandled her the way he used to.

"You're not giving up, *Nyno*," he commands. "You're a Chief. You're important. You matter. And do you remember why? Because of ME!" he growls the pronoun. "I'm the one who lobbied so that you could become a Chief—so that we BOTH could become Chiefs! I'm the one who worked hard to ensure WE live for as long as possible! I'm the one who made YOUR *babi* the future *Teerta!* And now, you want to just give up and throw it all away over your useless, criminal, *Patummal babo?* Get a grip, *Nyno!* We're positioned perfectly! If you give up, we all lose leverage! If you give up, I look like a fool! Don't you understand that? Don't you see the full scope of things? You need to get your head out of your own *kahtopo* and stop being so selfish for once!"

For once? Nyno feels like she's never done anything for herself in her life.

"Oh come on, stop crying," Maetri snaps his fingers in her face. "You should be happy. You never liked *Kosharuna* anyway. I'm giving you everything you want. Is there no pleasing you?"

Nyno stands. She doesn't know what to think or say. She doesn't know who's right or who's worked harder or who's pleased whom, if ever. She just knows two things: One, she's sick of Maetri and doesn't want to see him ever again; and two, she needs to save her daughter this time, no matter the cost.

Maetri watches her walk away. He smiles—a strange sensation on his mouth, but he allows it nonetheless. He's glad she acquiesced so easily. That's always been his favorite thing about Nyno, why he always preferred her over his other *Kosharuna* women.

He thinks she's giving up.

Chapter 53
"Tynjo"

Bowi loves his sister more than anything.

Three moons.

Shouldn't he be panicking?

Feelings continue to vex him. Emotions. Sensations. Conditions. To him, they're unrelenting forces, cyclones of perception that twist and churn his stomach until he has no other choice but to vomit the energy outward. These forces control his experience of life, dictating his days and physical health on drastic whims. He's so sensitive, he used to feel his mother's terror every *Kosharuna,* and sense all her aches afterward. He used to feel Daeo's own misery beside him, each day they'd spend together in the swamp. He's always been aware of life's compounding pressures, multiplied by the feelings of those around him, squared.

So why'd he stop crying over Daeo's death sentence?

Sure, he knows it's scheduled to happen. He's well aware she'll disappear with Tagi in a few moons. He just can't conceptualize that reality yet. He's felt many things in his life, all flavors of pain and suffering. But he can't imagine the sort of loss to come. He can't imagine Daeo disappearing forever. He doesn't yet know what it's like to lose a *tynjo...*

Confounded, Bowi's brain opts to remain thoroughly in the present moment. He becomes happy over the following weeks. He's glad Daeo is banished to the cave—it just means she's moving in with him, right? Giddy, he cuddles with her every night, insisting they share the same bed, just like they used to.

Tagi doesn't mind this arrangement, as it blocks Eeao from sleeping with the little girl. The kitten still clings to Daeo whenever given the chance, of course, but at least she's returned to sleeping on the old man's chest every night. *Enjoy it while you can,* he thinks, wondering whether or not the kitten will stick around when only Bowi is left. Perhaps they'll become friends? Or will she go searching for another cave to inhabit? He can imagine Eeao journeying far across the *Uyi*, ever exploring, ever wandering. *Will she go looking for me?* In his wildest fantasies, he envisions Eeao scaling the caldera's sheer ring of cliffs, clinging cranny to cranny, crag to crag, up and over, escaping the *Uyi* altogether on her endless pursuit of him. *If any wingless creature could climb out of this sinkhole,* he thinks, pleased with her weight on his chest, *I'm sure you could manage it.*

Eeao purrs.

Daeo doesn't feel much at all. It's like her brain won't allow her to. She's never once considered fleeing the *Uyi*, but now, every night, she dreams she has wings. She dreams she can leap into the air and run on currents of wind. She dreams she can soar high over the mountains and graze her feathered wingtips through wispy, rippling clouds. Sky. Space. Heaven. *Fae* formations and *honk!*ing *paen-aemo* don't exist in Daeo's visions. Only freedom and expansion, her own boundless self, her lavender *patu*, everything aglow. She looks up into her own eternity. But when she gazes down again, beyond the mountains, as far as she can see, the ground is littered with massive pockmarks, craters, identical *Uyi*'s everywhere, each with its own *Aeo* graveyard marking its center.

Is that what truly lies beyond? Graveyards everywhere? Or is she just replicating the only landscape she knows?

When Daeo awakes from these dreams, her joy and exhilaration all vanish. She's left feeling empty, mellow, detached, depleted—aware only of the baby blanket in her arms and Bowi's arms around her. *Tynjo.* Numb to all other elements of the waking world, this is where her heart resides, sheltered and beating. The baby blanket is her tether to life, its enwrapped fossil an anchor, Bowi's embrace a reminder that right here, right now, she's safe.

She rises with Bowi each morning, and keeps him company in the *ynsyna* cavern during his lessons. Equipped with her blanket and her brother, Daeo isn't afraid. She continues to look for her word, *patu,* as he reads—one of them has to stumble across it eventually, right? How much time do they have left?

"*Myrkuna* is ready!" outside the cave, Tagi announces *lunch*. Today, he's hard-boiled an entire *raea* egg for them all to share (yesterday, Maetri delivered several eggs from the herd in a vainglorious show of recompense for treating Neepo's neck wound). Peeled from its cloudy shell and membrane, the cooked spheroid is larger than Tagi's whole head, with a solid core of velvety, golden yolk.

Eeao prances to greet the children as they emerge from the *ynsyna* cavern, making straight for Daeo's ankles. She purrs and she weaves. She chirps and she chortles. Daeo barely notices—even when she sits beside Tagi's cauldron and the kitten hops onto her lap, she's concerned with only the baby blanket in her arms.

"*Hmm...* How shall we do this?" Tagi holds the steaming egg in both hands, bouncing it between his fingers so as not to burn himself. He has no idea how to divide such a singular, gargantuan piece of food among multiple people. "Why don't we pass it around and each take bites?"

The children don't mind.

"*Momo* would've mashed it into mush, and then spooned it equally into bowls for us," Bowi says, only after they've already eaten half the egg via Tagi's communal, bite-and-pass method.

"Yes, well, I'm not accustomed to feeding an entire family," Tagi grimaces, his fingers coated in crumbly yolk. "Nor keeping giant *raea* eggs on hand."

"*Momo* used to cook *raea* eggs all the time," Daeo says distantly.

Tagi wonders if he'd even heard her.

"Where is *momo?*" Bowi says suddenly.

Tagi quirks, doubtful again of his hearing. "She's in the nest, of course," he says.

"No, I mean, where is she?" Bowi turns to his *tynjo*. "*Daeo*, why hasn't *momo* come to check on you since..." He imagines surely their mother must've heard of Daeo's exile by now—or, at the very least, noticed her absence over the past few nights. Isn't she worried? Isn't she devastated? Doesn't she want to come and see Daeo? See both of them? Doesn't she care? Bowi left his *momo* to become *Teerta* over five moons ago, and he hasn't seen her since. "Why hasn't *momo* come to check on us?"

Daeo says nothing. She stares down at her lap—on her left side, she clutches her bundled blanket; on her right, Eeao sits in loafed devotion.

Tagi takes a bite of yolk, and then proceeds to chew awkwardly.

"She's probably getting ready to come visit," Bowi decides. "She's probably preparing the baby's satchel so they can make the hike up here," he paints the scenario. "We have another *tynjo*," he turns to Tagi. "She's just a baby, so our *momo* spends a lot of time taking care of her," Bowi smiles. "But they'll probably come and visit any day now. Right *Daeo?*"

Daeo can't look at him. Is that really what he believes?

"I hope she brings our baby *tynjo*," Bowi is still talking—primarily to Tagi. "She's so cute. I can't believe it's been almost six moons since I last saw her. I wonder what she looks like now. *Daeo*, what does the baby look like? Has *momo* named her yet?"

Daeo stands and walks away.

Eeao scrambles to follow.

Chapter 54
"Eeao"

Right now, the kitten couldn't be happier.

She lives with all her best friends. She has a daily routine. She's primped and groomed her claws to near-adult maturity. She's regrown all her whiskers and resharpened her sense of hearing. Her meals are completely catered—the old man always has a raw scrap of something on hand.

She has no unmet needs, no outstanding expectations.

Really, Eeao has only two responsibilities in life: Personal hygiene, and stalking her alpha. The latter has become extraordinarily easy, now that the little girl lives in the cave full-time and rarely ever leaves. Eeao naps in her cranny throughout the mornings, when Daeo disappears into the smelly cavern. And then, usually in the afternoons, they've created a habit of visiting the old man's garden together.

Really, Daeo only started visiting the *heersu* because it's the only other place in the *Uyi* she's allowed to exist. Banished from the jungle at large, her range is more limited than ever. Sometimes, she walks to the secluded garden when she wants to stretch her legs. Other times, she visits when she needs a break from squinting at *ynsyna*.

Today, she goes to escape things she can't talk about yet.

The *heersu* isn't Daeo's idea of a fun place—it smells oppressively of soil, mint, and saturated rainwater. But as she continues her daily visits, sitting peacefully with Eeao, her baby blanket, fossil, and the silent, ever-present plants, Daeo decides that she likes the garden, for what it's worth. It has a purpose. Each plant sprouts with intention. She can see them all nurturing each other, their interlacing branches an above-ground reflection of their deeply entwined roots.

Everywhere else, the *Uyi* is wild and ambivalent.

But here, in this lithic alcove, the *heersu* is safe.

Eeao prowls the rows of vegetation, pawing at imaginary enemies. She pretends any crinkly, fallen leaf is a rogue spider, skittering around in the breeze. After having exterminated all the real ones that used to burrow near the *heersu*, she can't resist pouncing at lookalikes—one anticlimax after another. Endless pursuit. After some time, as the afternoon's heat turns balmy, Daeo slips away from the garden without Eeao noticing. Only when the breeze settles does the kitten track the girl's scent back to the *ynsyna* cavern.

Around early evening, as per her daily routine, Eeao ventures off to the swamp by herself for some personal, me-time. She's tried to entice the girl to join her on several occasions, figuring her alpha might appreciate the swamp's clumpy sand too, but, so far, it seems the child either isn't interested in going or just isn't interested in going with her... Regardless, Eeao doesn't take it personally; she respects the girl's fierce independence too much. Alone, the kitten relieves herself in peace—save for the bog's steamy, erratic belching.

Over the last few days, the swamp's gaseous activity has increased significantly. A minor disturbance to Eeao, who merely flinches her whiskers away from each chemical puff, this increased bubbling is a new symptom of the swamp's internal collapse. Beneath her very paws, Eeao's fecal bacteria has formed an entire colony, many times the size of her own body. Its borders swell beneath the mud, unmitigated and festering, a tumor eating the swamp's mycelial infrastructure from within. Carbon dioxide and methane are the primary byproducts of this fevered, cellular enterprise—the leakage of which now fuels the bog's dancing surface. Like sewage flowing in reverse, the swamp has no other choice but to belch Eeao's waste's waste up into the air—the frantic hyperventilation of an organism in decline.

Meanwhile, some trees have given up on the fight altogether. Cecropias all over the *Uyi* continue to wilt as, in addition to their pheromone sensitivity, the jungle's chemical broadcast is now attracting an invasive moth species that has a particular taste for their leaves. Several other tree families have begun revolting too, rebelling against their fungal underlords by ceasing pheromone effusion. But their mycelial puppeteers are too smart and too desperate to tolerate such dissent—the vast, quasi-omniscient network of fungal intelligence shifts its already depleted mycorrhizal attention to favor trees that are still following orders. Underground, the *Uyi* allocates nutrients based on this bias. Soon, the trees in rebellion begin to yellow and droop.

During the next *Kamaruna,* the *Fae* notice the rainforest's fading color. Antennae-blind to avian pheromones and clueless to Eeao's presence, the insectoids grow suspicious. Ideas and questions buzz amongst the horde, rapid-fire as they soar in formation over the *Uyi*. They don't know what to make of this yellowing phenomenon. They've never seen anything quite like it (at this point of Earth's evolution, ecosystems generally know how to regulate and terraform themselves). Scanning with their million-lensed bug-eyes, the *Fae* soon notice the swamp's fitful temper. Flying lower, they taste excessive gas emissions with their antennae. Collectively, they theorize the swamp's fungal biome must be slipping into depletion—although as to why, none can guess. Some sort of nutritional imbalance?

They figure more food should help.

So during the next *Kunjaruna,* the *Fae* deliver sixty-five *Meemmal* victims instead of the usual fifty.

The *punteeku* consider it a blessing. They celebrate while dumping the extra human bodies into their sacred, bubbling swamp.

Chapter 55
"Babo"

Nyno's *momo* wouldn't let go. The day of her *Kamaruna.* Back when she was a child.

"Please, my babo *is still too young, she needs me!"* her mother cried, holding Nyno's tiny *patu* to her own *Patummal* chest. Standing on her own, Nyno remembers hugging her mother back, desperately wishing for both their tears to stop. But that was the problem: She was standing on her own.

"It's time," one of the *punteeku* said. It took six men storming their *capku* just to pry Nyno's mother away.

"Please, just one more babo!*"* she kept screaming, face red as a *sokeeto* berry. *"Let me have just one more* babo! *Please!"*

"You've already had plenty."

"You're lucky you lived this long."

"It's your time, Patummal.*"*

Nyno's older sisters stood in a circle outside the *capku*, all nine of them, watching idly as the *punteeku* apprehended their aging mother. Powerless—*weren't we all?* Still, for many moons afterward, Nyno blamed her sisters for their mother's demise. She didn't know any better. She never saw any of them cry.

Now, Nyno sees three of her sisters idling outside the Chief birthing *momo's capku*—birthing *momo*s tend to flock in close radius of Dynjo. Well, the ones who are valuable do, at least.

"Nyno?" one of her sisters, *Dymeero,* notices her first. They all turn and stare.

Nyno isn't surprised by their surprise; a popular location for dignified feasts and exclusive parlays, Nyno can't recall the last time she was actually invited to Dynjo's *capku.*

And it's not like she was invited today, either.

"Is *Dynjo* home?" Nyno asks the women.

Nyno was once valuable like her sisters (for a short while, when she first came of age). But obviously, her social economy plummeted as each of her children came out, one by one, *Patummal* or miscarried. Or *Meemmal... No*—Nyno's brain has done its best to erase that trauma from memory.

"Yes, *Dynjo*'s home, would you like me to request a summons for you?" Dymeero offers immediately, head bowed.

Nyno hates the faux reverence. *It's because I'm a Chief now, isn't it.*

"Would you please?" out of habit, she returns her older sister's bow.

Dymeero disappears inside the *capku.*

Nyno refrains from chit-chatting with her other two sisters while waiting. They try to engage her in conversation, but she returns only nods and grunts, preoccupied. Today's sky is downy gray, the sun blanketed beneath endless, overlapping feathers of cirrostratus. Roosting along the staggered branches of a nearby kapok, a legion of *momo* parrots sits congregated, bobbing their varicolored heads in passive interest of the world. Where all their assigned children are, Nyno doesn't know or care—although she wishes her sisters did...

Eventually, after an uncomfortably long waiting period, Dymeero emerges from the *capku,* red-eyed and smelling like *syn-syn* smoke.

"*Dynjo* will see you now," she ushers Nyno through the entrance flap.

Within its *hympano* walls, Dynjo's *capku* seems to maintain its own atmosphere, clogged with smoke and ash particles. Nyno's eyes sting as she enters; she struggles to suppress a cough. Billows plume from the *capku*'s center, where Dynjo sits alone upon a pile of pillows, puffing from a narrow, clay pipe longer than her entire arm span.

Cross-legged, Dynjo reclines, propping the immense pipe against her own pregnant womb. Packed inside the pipe's bowl, tobacco and marijuana leaves smolder. Nyno isn't used to seeing the Chief *momo* casually naked like this, free of her colorful, decorated harness. But the loaded *syn-syn* pipe is no surprise.

"*Nyno,*" the Chief birthing *momo* remains seated, smiling through an exhale of smoke. "I've been desperate to speak with you. Please, pull up a cushion." She gestures to a mountain of pillows off to the side. Nyno selects one from the top of the pile (soft, brown *areemo* fibers, woven to encapsulate what feel to her fingers like plush *camraea* plumes—*this is a pillow I made, isn't it?*), and then sits beside Dynjo.

"Congratulations on joining the circle of Chiefs," Dynjo converses while Nyno gets settled, her tone casual, almost intimate, as if she and Nyno speak regularly. "I was the one who granted final approval for your appointment. I knew you'd be perfect for the role. And you've already done such lovely work. I just received the first new batch of satchels, along with some pillows and extras goodies. The children all love them." She pauses to take a long draw from her pipe.

"Thank you," Nyno says automatically, stifling another cough as Dynjo exhales.

"Please, help yourself," Dynjo offers, angling her pipe's mouthpiece toward Nyno. Nyno declines. "*Sokeeto* puree? *Arumato* wedge? Fresh *pomaeao?*" She draws Nyno's attention to a wide platter of food, propped on a wooden pedestal behind her. Lush berries of every color, ripe melons—a pyramid of stacked *pomaeo* rises like a monument. "Please, help yourself to a treat—just between us Chiefs," she winks.

"No thank you," Nyno declines again.

Where were all those pomaeo *when* Bowi *was sick?*

"Suit yourself," Dynjo truly doesn't care. "We all have our own ways of rewarding ourselves," she takes another long pull from her lavishly long pipe. "And after all the hardship you've overcome, *Nyno,*" she continues, her voice velvety and unaffected by the smoke, "I just hope you're rewarding yourself as you deserve."

"I want to talk to you about my *babo,*" Nyno cuts right to the point.

"*Mmm...*" Dynjo has been expecting this. "Yes, the *Meemmal* baby. What a difficult and traumatic situation. As a fellow *momo,* I admire your strength for doing what needed to be done. *Ynsyn-eera.*"

Nyno freezes—wrong *babo.*

"I just don't understand one thing," Dynjo releases another smoky exhalation. "If you were having trouble lactating, why not bring the baby to me? I produce more than enough milk—I'm still nursing five of my own, plus this precious one coming along," she adjusts her pipe to caress her womb. "Why not come to me for help?"

Nyno's brain scrambles, parsing words from emotions, fear from shame.

Why is she acting like we're friends?

"If you had come to me instead of going to that *Patummal* snake for milk," Dynjo continues, "your *babo* would've never become a *Meemmal.*"

These words are an accusation.

"This isn't what I wanted to talk about—"

"I would've helped you," Dynjo interrupts with another puff. "I'm the Chief birthing *momo.* I've weaned eighteen children from my own breasts, all strong and healthy and violet-capped. Why didn't you bring the baby to me? I could've saved her, you know."

Where were all those pomaeo *when Bowi was sick?*

"I just don't understand why you took her to your stinking *Patummal* cousin," Dynjo shrugs.

This is why.

"I came here to speak with you about my other girl, *Daeo,*" Nyno grits her teeth to keep from screaming.

"Oh... Yes... That one..." Dynjo has been expecting this too. "What about her?"

What about her? Nyno doesn't know how to quell the panic. "My *babo* is innocent!" her voice cracks. "She's been wrongly accused!"

"Wrongly accused?" Dynjo frowns. "According to numerous eyewitness reports, she admitted to the crimes herself. What do you mean, wrongly accused?"

"I know my *babo!*" Nyno breaks—between all the smoke and frustration, her tears are unstoppable. "*Daeo* would never attack anyone! This is all a mistake! A misunderstanding! Please, you have to listen to me, *Daeo* is not a criminal, I'm sure of it—"

"*Shh...*" Dynjo coos, waving her lengthy pipe in front of Nyno's face. Nyno gags on the odor. "Poor thing," the Chief *momo* sighs. "You sound so scared."

"I AM SCARED!" Nyno screams. "Please—I can't do this again—I can't lose another *babo*—"

"*Shh... Shh... Shh...*" Dynjo creates smoky figure-eights in the air between them. "There's no reason to cry, *Nyno;* you're not losing anything," she says in a tone practiced for children. "You're a Chief now. You're a person of high esteem. Yes, unfortunately your *Patummal babo* is a criminal, as they tend to be. She committed a heinous attack, and she needs to be punished for it. No one blames you. But we need to do what needs to be done. You understand, right?"

"Of course I understand," Nyno struggles to lower her voice, to match Dynjo's carefree composure. "But surely you understand how well a *momo* knows her child, right? Well, I'm the one who raised *Daeo*. I put her to sleep every night, and I cooked her food every morning. I taught her to speak, I taught her to laugh, I taught her to explore... I love my *babo,* and I know what she's capable of. I know she would never, ever hurt other children. Please, you have to believe me, you have to understand. I know my *babo* is innocent." Her words flow articulately—surprisingly so. Taking a deep breath, Nyno feels proud of the compelling sentences she managed to string together.

"Oh, I understand, *Nyno,*" Dynjo's hand reaches to find hers. Her fingers are fiery hot, slick with hormonal sweat. "Trust me, as Chief *momo,* I understand how conniving and duplicitous children can be. They'll run circles around you if you let them, telling you whatever you want to hear, just to get whatever they want from you. Savages. I learned to stop trusting mine long ago. You give them what they need, not what they want. And, unfortunately, sometimes, as in your *babo's* case, what they need is *Kamaruna.*"

Nyno coughs, sputtering out of control.

"Let's face it," Dynjo continues puffing, "you were never an adequate *momo* to begin with, *Nyno.* Add a mutated *Meemal* and a troublesome *Patummal* to the mix and it's no surprise your brood turned out this way."

Nyno can't breathe.

Will no one listen to me?

"But don't worry," Dynjo continues. "None of it matters anymore. We found the one skill you're truly great at. And we made you a Chief for it, remember? You have a new life ahead of you."

Heaving, Nyno tastes bile.

"Just wait a few moons," Dynjo says. "Once the girl is gone, you'll feel much, much better."

Nyno runs outside to vomit.

In the interim, Dynjo signals for Dymeero to slip back inside her *capku.*

"Keep an eye on her," the Chief *momo* sighs. "She might do something crazy."

Chapter 56
"Patu"

Meanwhile, Daeo commits her eyes to the *ynsyna* cavern.

Determined more than ever to find her word, *patu*—that distinct pair of letters Tagi carved over the cave's entrance, just for her own perpetual reference—she's meticulously scanned more than ten thousand lines of characters so far. But it's not like she's counting. Nose to endless etchings, she's focused not on the task's tedium, but on the satisfaction she feels after completing each row. She doesn't know the words she's reading, of course. But she knows the word she's not. And she knows that each line she inspects to completion only leads her closer to the one containing her prize...

If it's here at all, of course. But it must be. Isn't the *patu* significant? Hasn't anyone ever studied it? Daeo's obsession mounts daily. How much time is left?

Two moons.

Tagi is more aware than anyone of time's waning passage. The lunar cycle's magnified significance on his remaining existence is practically all he can think about. Increasingly, he hears his old *Teerta*'s voice in the back of his head, like a drum keeping tempo, constantly reminding him of all the things he has left to do, and what little time remains.

Two moons.

Why hasn't he shared his own *ynsyna* with Bowi yet?

It's not like Bowi has begun to wonder. The boy seems to have forgotten his companions' peril altogether. He bounds happily into the *ynsyna* cavern after *tyrkuna* each morning, eager to cram as many lessons as he can into the span of each single day. *Aruwyna,* the study of trees. *Onynsyna,* the study of insects. *Heersyna,* the study of horticulture. Tagi appreciates the boy's ambition for knowledge. But at this point, the long-dead *Teerta*s seem to interest Bowi more than anyone else. It's almost like he doesn't realize Tagi has an important lesson to teach him, too. *Perhaps the most important lesson of all,* Tagi is unashamedly biased.

Today, it's another lesson on *momyna* that's captivated Bowi's attention. Technically *Teerta* number two hundred and fourteen, Bowi's really only keeping track of the handful who devoted their research to the science of motherhood. His enthusiastic voice echoes through the subterranean darkness, reaching Daeo's ears in dissipating waves.

Skimming *ynsyna* with only one objective in mind, Daeo has raced far, far ahead of Bowi's own, rudimentary reading pace. She's currently ventured so deep into the cavern she can barely see her brother's glow anymore; they're both just two pinpricks of violet amidst deep, chasmal black. Although between her blanket-wrapped fossil and hip-bound dagger, Daeo feels perfectly accompanied.

"During the first several moons of pregnancy," Bowi reads in sloppy, run-on sentences, too enthralled to slow down, "the developing human fetus looks little different from a big-headed *raea* chick forming inside its own eggshell this leads us to determine a close relationship between humans and *raea* or at least close in the sprawling context of reproductive life at large which includes trees shrubs flowers fungus and the like—*phew,*" Bowi pauses to catch his breath. "Isn't that amazing, *Daeo?*" he calls to her luminous, far-off speck. "We all start life looking like *raea* chicks!"

Daeo only pays attention because he forces her to. "Amazing," she agrees, maintaining *pa-tu-pa-tu-pa-tu* in her mind's eye. But then a thought strikes her, "How do they know what a baby looks like before it is born?"

"The same way we know what *raea* chicks look like before they hatch," Tagi says. "Break the egg." He's sitting within the angled corridor between the *ynsyna* cavern and the cave's antechamber, shaving his own scalp with a flintstone razor. Though the *Uyi*-wide custom of *wakar* is generally practiced in social settings, it's *Teerta* tradition to perform the ritual alone and in the dark, to better appreciate the *patu*'s increasing glow as obstructive hairs are removed.

"But human babies do not hatch from eggs," Daeo argues. "I do not understand."

Bowi understands.

"Sometimes a baby dies early in utero," Tagi explains, swiping the blade across his prickly head. Around him, the cave's damp, glittering walls reflect his amethyst radiance. "Eventually the placenta breaks, which is really just the human version of an egg, and then we see the miscarried fetus when the *momo* pushes it out."

"Oh..." Daeo tries to picture it.

Bowi feels sick. He sees blood—death—panic splattered across his mother's face.

"Does that make sense?" Tagi feels like he's talking to air.

"Yes."

"Absolutely."

"Good," Tagi's tolerance for wasted words is thinner than ever. *Two moons.* "Keep reading, *Bowi.*"

Silence...

"*Bowi?*"

That invisible, ever-present *drip! drip! drip!* fills the cave's sonic vacuum.

"*Bowi!*"

"I miss my *momo*..." Bowi finally says, unable to see *ynsyna* through his tears.

"What?" Tagi nicks an earlobe.

"I haven't seen her in six moons," echoing, Bowi's voice cracks. "Why hasn't she come to visit? Why hasn't she come to see us? I miss her. Doesn't she miss us too? Doesn't she want to see us again?"

"Who?" Tagi is lost. "Are you talking about your *momo?*"

"Yes!" Bowi sobs, pounding his fists into *ynsyna* etchings. "Where is she? Why hasn't she come to see us? We need her!" Coping, floundering, his brain can no longer hold the weight of this present moment.

"I FOUND IT!" Daeo screams. She has no idea the information she's stumbled upon, but she recognizes without doubt the two shapes before her—a squiggly, inverted triangle and a polka-dotted square: *pa-tu.* "I FOUND MY WORD! I FOUND MY WORD!"

Startled and only half-finished with his shave, Tagi scrambles into the cavern, assuming an emergency. Bowi follows as quickly as he can, blotting tears from his eyes.

"What's the matter?" Tagi finds Daeo deep inside the cave, unharmed and beaming.

"I found my word!" Daeo exclaims. "*Patu!*"

"Really?" Tagi steps up to the wall for better scrutiny. Indeed, the little girl has completed his impossible task. "Well done," he gives her a smile, impressed. "I never thought you'd actually find it..."

Two moons.

"I know," Daeo grins, twirling her blanket-wrapped fossil through the air.

"What's the word again?" Bowi steps forward, still sniffling. "*Patu?* Why *patu?*"

"Can you read about it for me?" Daeo ignores her brother, turning to Tagi. "Please?"

"Alright, alright, I'll read you this block of *ynsyna,* just from here to here, *wyntiko?*" Tagi points at the group of lines encompassing her word. The children sit side by side—Bowi still teary-eyed, Daeo enthralled. Combined, the amplified light of their *patu*s allows Tagi to read with ease. "Alright, these are the words of the eight hundred and sixty-fourth *Teerta:*

"Case number four in my study of rare and inexplicable illnesses. During my early days as Teerta, *I was presented with a child marked by a diminishing* patu. *It would recede to* Meemmal-*like absence and then regrow across the scalp, slowly, like algae blooming and receding with the changing moons. I have seen no prior research on this subject matter, so I wish I could provide further information. But I can't. This was a one-of-a-kind case, indeed. The child was unhurt by his condition, and clearly not a* Meemmal, *as he was conceived lawfully by the Chief birthing* momo *herself, so I deemed it* kantru-pyndara. *The child is now a full grown man, with all the same strengths and abilities of his kin—though his* patu *continues to disappear on occasion. None of his offspring are marked with the affliction...*

"Alright, that's it, there you have it," Tagi concludes. "Any questions?"

Silence.

drip! drip! drip!

"What does *kantru-pyndara* mean?" Daeo asks.

"Harmless, insipid, benign," Tagi says. "Much like this topic. Why don't we play the game again, shall we? This time, think of a compound word, something like—"

"I never want to play games again," Daeo cuts him off. "Never."

Tagi blinks. Bowi's mouth falls open.

"Wh-why not?" Tagi stammers—amused, if anything, by her stubborn indignation. *What could possibly be the matter now?*

"Because winning is impossible," Daeo frowns. "All of these games are rigged."

"All wh-wh-what games?" Tagi stammers again, worried she's onto his own.

"This cave, the *Teertas*, the kids in the nest," Daeo grimaces. "*Kamaruna, Kosharuna, Kunjaruna. Meemmal* and *Patummal. Atrypa.* What is the point of anything? None of it is fair! We are the ones who are betrayed!"

"Now, now, I know things have been difficult recently..." Tagi just wants to quash her tantrum.

"Even *momo!*" Daeo turns to Bowi. "She betrayed us too!"

"What?" Bowi recoils. "How can you say that?"

"Have you not heard what happened to our *tynjo?*" Daeo feared she'd cry if she ever spoke about this. "Do you still not know where she is?" But right now, she's too furious.

"What are you talking about?"

"*Momo* volunteered her for *Kamaruna!*" Daeo erupts. "Our baby *tynjo!* Just because of her *patu!* Just because they thought she was turning into a *Meemmal!* But she was not! She never was! She was just like the child in that *Teerta*'s story! Harmless! She should still be alive right now! She should not be in the *Aeo! Momo* let them kill her for nothing!"

Daeo throws her baby blanket to the ground; its enwrapped totem *clunk!*s emphatically on the limestone floor. Tagi and Bowi shudder from the sudden, echoing thunder. It's so loud the resounding vibrations even startle Eeao, all the way out in the antechamber; she bolts from her cranny, darts outside—a flawless execution of feline evasion.

"What do you have in that blanket?" Tagi gawks.

"I do not want *momo* to visit!" Daeo is still yelling. "I never want her to visit! I do not miss *momo* at all! She does not care about us! Only herself! I never want to see her again!"

Enraged, Daeo whizzes like a firefly through the dark, lunging to scoop up her blanket and then dashing out of the cavern altogether. Her crashing footsteps recede like fading rain. Bowi and Tagi watch her *patu* disappear, both of them wide-eyed and stunned—Tagi because he can't imagine what made that *clunk!*ing noise, and Bowi because now he knows the truth.

"*Tynjo...*" Bowi whispers, reaching after his sister.

"It's alright," Tagi puts a hand on the boy's shoulder. "Give her some time. She's just angry."

"She's not angry..." Bowi shifts his eyes toward the old man. "She's sad. I'm sad." He shakes Tagi's hand off his shoulder. "How could you let this happen? Why don't you ever go down to the nest to help anyone? You have access to all this *ynsyna*—the answer to every problem—you know everything there is to know! You could have saved our *tynjo!* But you didn't! And they killed her for nothing! And it's all because of you!"

"Because of me?" Tagi is amused again. "Don't be absurd, boy."

"I'm serious!" Bowi yells. "I remember now—*Daeo* mentioned our *tynjo*'s *patu* moons ago! You could've helped way back then, but you didn't—"

"Enough!" Tagi snaps. "I've already told you, the *Teerta* cannot be held responsible for every single individual down in the nest." He seizes the boy's shoulders, both hands this time. "It's just not feasible. As *Teerta,* we care for those who are brought to us. That's it. If your *momo* truly cared for that baby, she would've brought it here herself, at any point in time. But she didn't, did she? No. It's her fault, not ours. So we wipe our hands clean of it. Do you understand me? Have I made myself clear?"

He has Bowi backed against a block of *ynsyna*. But the boy is unconvinced.

"My *momo* does care for us!" Bowi growls, fighting the old man's grip. "And she cared for my baby *tynjo* too! You don't know her! My *momo* always does whatever she can to take care of us! You don't know anything!"

"Oh, I don't know anything?" Tagi guffaws. "I thought you just said I know everything there is to know! Now it's the opposite?"

"You don't know anything about *momo*s!" Bowi roars in his face. "My *momo* always does whatever she has to so that—"

"Listen to me, boy!" Tagi rams him against the limestone wall. "In all the moons I've been alive, I've seen *momo*s commit atrocities you couldn't even imagine! So don't tell me what I do or don't know! Maybe someday, if you ever get all the way down to the end of the *ynsyna*, you'll read the scrawls I left behind, and learn what my own *momo* did to me when I was born. Have you ever heard of *saeryn-eptek?*"

Begrudgingly, Bowi shakes his head, ignorant of the term for *castration.*

"When I was born, my *momo* destroyed my body in a way I can never repair," Tagi lowers his voice. "She hated males—an understandable result of *Kosharuna.* I was her first pregnancy, her first child, her first product of the ceremony. She went crazy the day she birthed a boy. She mutilated me as I nursed, my most vulnerable stage of life. I didn't even realize I was deficient until I was old enough for my first *Kosharuna.* And then, when the entire nest found out, my only options were to volunteer for *Kamaruna* or train to become the new *Teerta.* Thank goodness the old *Teerta* of my day took pity on my condition. She saw potential in me where everyone else saw waste. She gave me a use after my own *momo* had taken mine away. My *momo* destroyed me, but my *Teerta* saved me. And is that not what I've done for you?"

Silence.

"Was your *momo* even part of the *punteeku* entourage that brought you here?" Tagi recalls the scene. "Six moons ago? When you were vomiting and could barely walk on your own? Was she here that day? Did she come with you on the hike? Did she hug you goodbye? No?"

drip! drip! drip!

"Why didn't your *momo* bring you to my cave sooner? Every day when you were sick, why did she never bring you here for *pomaeo* infusions? Why did she always make you wait for the convenience of my *Kunjaruna* visits?"

Bowi feels his stomach emptying.

"Listen," Tagi sighs. "I'm not telling you all of this to make you feel bad," he loosens his grip on the boy's shoulders. "I'm telling you this to help you understand *Daeo*'s perspective. Your *momo* isn't perfect. Sure, she may have tried her hardest to take care of all her children. But she failed. She failed miserably. She failed all three of you. One of your *tynjo*s died because of it. And now, *Daeo* needs you to acknowledge her pain before it's too late."

Bowi feels everything emptying.

"She needs solidarity with her *tynji*," Tagi says, thinking now of the people he wishes he could see in his final days. *Two moons.* "She needs to know that you hear her. She needs to know that you understand. She needs to feel justice from someone, and I think maybe you can be that person for her..."

The old man's voice trails off into the deep. He releases his grip on Bowi. They remain together in the dark for a while, face to face, two violet flares in an underground vignette. *drip! drip! drip!* Eventually, the stale smell of Tagi's breath overpowers the cavern's dank, moldy odor, forcing Bowi to slip away.

Outside, Bowi finds Daeo at the *Heersu*, crying into their old baby blanket. He joins her.

They cry together for the rest of the day, their tears dissolving into the garden's black soil.

Eeao watches from overhead, perched within an *arunaea* nest she just pillaged. She remains bewildered by the humans' frequent, allergic reactions.

Chapter 57
"Ameema"

Nyno has a plan.

No, it probably won't save Daeo's life.

But she figures she can at least leverage her own to buy her daughter a bit more time.

Given the sheer amount of work she's produced these last few months, Nyno reasons she's garnered enough political power that if she were to flee to the *Teerta's* cave now, pledge her fate to her daughter's, and then demand extended *Atrypa* for the two of them (to complete her workload, of course), the other Chiefs would have no choice but to oblige.

Yes, Nyno is prepared to use her own life as a bargaining chip. At this point, she knows *Kamaruna* awaits every human. And if she has to volunteer herself someday, she'd much rather do it alongside Daeo than slave away making satchels and soft-clothes alone in her *capku* for another hundred moons (or, at least, until whenever her knuckles calcify). Anyway, who knows. Perhaps if the Chiefs are feeling generous, she'll be able to secure an extra six moons for the two of them, or even eight—she'll make as many harnesses as the *punteeku* want, so long as they allow her to spend her final moons with her children.

Too little too late? Never.

She plans to leave for the *Teerta's* cave tonight, if the weather allows—so far, the day has been heavy with lightning and rain.

"Where do you think you're going?" Kleeo's voice thunders Nyno's *capku*. Poking her head through the entrance flap, Kleeo sees the floor within riddled with all the same half-made satchels and harnesses she saw the last time she came to visit—except now there's also a giant, *areemo* sack in the center of it all, into which Nyno is busy packing her own clothing and tools, as though for travel.

"Nowhere," Nyno lies, rolling up her sleeping mat and stuffing it into the sack. Behind her, rainfall patters her *capku*'s north-facing side, streaming down its sloped *hympano* wall in competing rivulets.

"Looks like you're going somewhere," Kleeo's intuition is trained to kill. "Don't lie to me."

Nyno pauses, disturbed by the woman's tone. "Can I help you, *Kleeo?*" she asks.

"Yes, actually," Kleeo assumes invitation, tracks her muddy footprints inside. "I came to pick up the twenty harnesses you were supposed to have finished two days ago. Remember?"

Nyno grinds her molars. "Yes, I remember."

"I don't see them finished," Kleeo says, sneering around at the clutter.

"I've put a pause on production," Nyno stands, testing the weight of her luggage sack—she has no idea how she'll manage to heave it all the way up to the *Teerta*'s cave, but she's willing to break her back if necessary.

"A pause on production?" Kleeo scoffs. "Who authorized that?"

"I did," Nyno scoffs back. "I'm Chief, remember?"

Kleeo doesn't like that answer. "The other Chiefs will not approve," she shakes her head—a full-body motion that rattles her spined harness. "There's no reason to pause production. The *punteeku* have already waited an extra two days for this new round of gear! Plus the *momo*s still need their soft-clothes, and you haven't even finished the satchels yet! There's work to do, *Nyno!*"

"And I'll get to it!" Nyno pushes her aside to collect a stack of cooking utensils.

"When?" Kleeo grabs her arm.

"When I feel like it!" Nyno growls. She tries to yank her arm away, but Kleeo's grip is locked. "Let go of me!"

"I know what you're doing," Kleeo shakes her. "You're giving up, aren't you?"

"What are you talking about—"

"You're planning to run away, up to the *Teerta*'s cave to be with your children, isn't that right?"

"N-n-no!" Nyno's voice *ribbit!*s out of her throat.

"Don't lie to me!" Kleeo twists her arm. "This is about your stinking kid, isn't it?"

"What are you doing?" Nyno can only scream as Kleeo shoves her against her *capku*'s central pole. "Stop—let go of me!"

"I know exactly what you're trying to do," Kleeo snarls in her ear. "*Maetri* and *Dynjo* both said you're upset about the *Patummal* girl's sentence. Now you're trying to bail out on us, aren't you?"

"You don't know anything!" Nyno tries to wrestle away, but Kleeo is far too strong.

"Listen to me, *Nyno,*" Kleeo relishes their weight differential. "We've come a long way, you and I. When we first met, you were just a dumb, cowardly *momo* hiding a *Meemmal* at your breast. You had no idea what was going on. But now... Now look at you. We made you a Chief. We made you important. We gave you power. I wish I had the power you have. And now you owe it to us, the people who made you, to use that power the way you're supposed to!"

"What power?" Nyno cries, her face smashed into the pole. "I don't have any power! I can't even save my own *babo!*"

Kleeo releases her.

Nyno collapses in a heap, already aware of new bruises swelling.

"*Ha,* you admit it!" Kleeo gloats. "I was right. You are trying to run away, just to save your stupid kid. See, that's your problem, *Nyno.* You have all the right skills to be a Chief. You just don't have the right priorities. They really should've just made me Chief of something instead. I would've done the title justice."

"Please," Nyno cowers on the ground, hands over her head. "Please, stop hurting me." Eyelids clenched, she listens as Kleeo crouches beside her, mantis-like.

"Oh, have I hurt you?" This is the *punteeku* way of sarcasm. "If I did, it's only because I love you and I want what's best for you. I'm your *ameema*, remember?"

Ameema. Nyno hates that this is the only woman who's ever called her *friend.*

"Please, let me see my children."

"*Vu-kopa vu-jo,*" Kleeo smirks. *Too little, too late.*

"Please," Nyno begs from the ground, "I just want to visit them, just for today, that's all I want to do, please?"

Kleeo stands—the clacking rustle of her razor-spined harness fills Nyno's ears.

"Please?" she mocks. "Please? Please? *Pfft*—I thought you were a Chief? Now you're begging me to let you go see your children? Don't be pathetic."

"THEN WHAT DO YOU WANT FROM ME?" Nyno erupts, seething fetally on the floor, desperate, her entire body spasming.

Kleeo folds her arms, mildly impressed by the outburst. "What I want," she says, indulging the moment, "is for you to do your job like the rest of us. You think it's easy being a *punteeku?* You think it's easy keeping my body strong and sharp between each *Kunjaruna?* Trust me, you wouldn't last a moon in my position. My job is grueling. But I do it every day. Just like *Syno* does her job. Just like *Maetri* does his. Just like *Dynjo* does hers. Just like we all need you to do yours. Does that make sense?"

Nyno doesn't respond. Dirt clings to the tearstained parts of her face.

"*Pfft—momo*s are so pathetic," Kleeo scowls. "Unpack all that *kahtopo*," she points to the sack. "And then finish making these harnesses. You have work to do."

"No," Nyno mutters.

Kleeo raises an eyebrow. "Excuse me?"

"No," Nyno repeats, still curled on the floor.

"*Nyno,* come on, get up."

"No."

"*Nyno,* don't make me do this."

"No."

"Get up, *Nyno.*"

"No."

"I said, get up!" Kleeo kicks her in the gut.

"No—"

"Get up!" Kleeo kicks her again.

"No—"

And again.

"No—"

Kleeo keeps kicking.

"No—No—No—"

Thunder drowns Nyno's voice.

Chapter 58
"Bowi"

Now that Daeo is banished to the cave, it's only during *Kunjaruna* that she and Bowi must separate.

"We'll be back at dawn," Bowi assures his sister, squeezing her tight. Sitting together on their shared bed, he doesn't want to let go tonight.

"Have fun," Daeo shrugs out of his embrace. It's not that she wants him and Tagi to leave. She just has a hunch that, in their absence, Eeao will be inclined to sleep on her chest tonight, and she's excited for the experience.

"Come, *Bowi*, we're already late," Tagi stands just within the cave's mouth, beyond which a torrential downpour wreaks havoc. Lightning and thunder strobe from the roiling, moonless sky, a multisensory show of force that shudders the cave itself. Outlined in his billowing, feather poncho and broad-brimmed *hympano* hat, Tagi looks like another lifeform altogether. Beneath the bulky folds of his cloak, the old man carries various medicines and equipment they'll need tonight, all clattering around in little clay jars strung from his belt.

Bowi gives Daeo one last hug; clay jars rattle from his belt too. Then, with a long, drawn-out sigh, the boy pulls on his own feather poncho, dons an *hympano* hat identical to Tagi's, and then follows the old *Teerta* out into the stormy night.

From Daeo's perspective, their *patu*s disappear quickly, washed away behind black sheets of rain. Alone, she lies back on her plush bedding. She pulls her warm, baby blanket up to her chin. She listens as gusting rain batters the outside world. She feels luxuriously safe tonight, dry and sheltered within the heart of a mountain. By the next crash of thunder, Eeao is purring comfortably on her chest.

Meanwhile, the hike down to the *Aeo* is sloshy and treacherous. Slickened by rainfall, the jungle floor this evening is a veritable slip-and-slide, a minefield of mudholes and moss beds hidden beneath wind-strewn debris. Bowi falls on his backside many times in his struggle to match Tagi's skilled pace; the old man clings expertly to vines and *wykyno* tendrils for leverage, swinging like an ancient primate whenever his feet slip out from under him. It's a well-practiced dance, Tagi's ability to move upright through the storm. He cooperates with his surroundings as though in direct communication, maneuvering with the visceral instinct of a feather-cloaked animal born for this type of weather. Squinting through the wind and rain, Bowi can barely keep up with the old man; at this point, he's just glad the clay jars tied to his belt are durable enough to withstand his frequent slips.

As they approach the *Aeo,* drenched and winded, Bowi can see the flickering, green glow of *Fae* descending over the lake's northern shoreline. Their formation seems to crack open the sky itself, a buzzing pyramid around which storm and lightning bend. To Bowi, the *Fae* seem impervious, a species immune to all weather conditions. Of course, the insectoids are just as drenched as everyone else—it's just that their hard exoskeletons are exponentially more effective against pelting rain than feather ponchos and floppy, mushroom hats.

Gathered along the southern lakeshore, the *Uyi*'s human population dances and celebrates while the *punteeku* set off, racing around the *Aeo*'s western half in search of *Meemmal* to hunt. High on *Kunjaruna* psychedelics, no one seems to mind the rain—everyone's *patu* is hidden tonight under an *hympano* rain hat. Even the *paen-aemo* sleep undisturbed, sheltered just beneath the treeline—by now, the birds have grown accustomed to the humans' lake-centered antics, and have only left the water tonight to avoid lightning. In their absence, the lake's open, black surface churns violently beneath the electrical storm.

Festivities are well underway by the time Bowi and Tagi arrive at the lakeshore. Rhythmic drums and fluttering reed flutes organize the storm's thundering clangor into a recognizable, almost inspiring tempo. This is now Bowi's seventh *Kunjaruna* training under the *Teerta*, but he's never seen a new-moon ceremony quite as lively as this. *Momo*s dance in concentric circles, as though electrified by the whirling storm above, rattling their harnesses with synchronized gusto as their children chant and chase each other through the rain. Bowi can't tell for sure, but, by the way some of them are behaving, he suspects his young peers got their hands on a stash of the adults' mushrooms tonight.

"*Bowi,* begin setting up," Tagi instructs as they approach their medical booth. Veiled beneath tall, broad-leaved ferns, the *Teerta*'s *Kunjaruna* station is at least dry enough that they're able to doff their bulky ponchos and untangle their belt-strung jars. "Finish organizing these," the old man says, dropping his entire belt of jars on the ground for Bowi to handle. "I need to go take a leak." He then stumbles off into the dripping foliage, leaving Bowi to manage the station alone.

Feeling like a veteran, Bowi easily organizes the remaining tools and jars into their appropriate cubbies, all while keeping an eye above the medical booth to track the *punteeku.* The hunters are currently amassed on the northern shoreline; obscured through the pouring rain, Bowi sees them as a vague, luminous blob undulating across the lake. He imagines they must be ravaging *Meemmal* invaders right now, splashing around in their foreign blood and entrails. At this rate, it'll be a long while before the *punteeku* return to this side of the lakeshore. Bowi looks up—but, of course, there's no moon to track time tonight. Just the storm's constant, electrical pulse...

"*Kyn ree-larro!*"

Bowi recognizes that voice.

"*Kyn ree-larro!*"

It's coming!

Bowi turns around—the pregnant girl from two moons ago is barrelling toward the *Teerta*'s booth! Supported between the same two sisters who aided her last time, they beeline straight for Bowi the moment they see him. All three are soaked from rain and sweat.

"*Kyn rce-larro!*" she cries again as her sisters hoist her onto the medical booth.

"*Seero!*" Bowi remembers her name. "You're in labor!"

"Great observation," one of her sisters grunts.

"How long have you been in labor?" Bowi clumps his poncho together with Tagi's to create a matted wedge so that Seero can recline. "And has your water broken yet?"

Seero screams, clenching Bowi's hand as another contraction grips her body.

"Her contractions started two days ago," the other sister says. "And her water broke last night. She's been in labor this whole time, but the baby still won't come out."

"Where's the old man?" the first sister looks around, flustered. "We need the real *Teerta!* Something's wrong!"

"That boy is the real *Teerta*," Tagi returns just in time. "But what do you want?"

"She's been in labor for two days!"

"The baby is stuck!"

"*Kyn ree-larro!*"

"*Ah*, I remember you," Tagi squints in recognition.

"I need help," Bowi admits. The sweat, the screams, Seero's immensely pregnant womb—Bowi has been here before, hasn't he?

"Alright, let's take a look," Tagi steps up to the booth. Shaking, Bowi administers a daub of *reewo* sap beneath Seero's tongue while Tagi checks by the light of his scalp her measure of dilation. "Well, you're certainly ready to give birth, that's for sure. I can already see the baby crowning."

"Then what's wrong?" Seero moans. Holding her hand, Bowi can feel her pulse. It thwacks against his palm like an electric shock, prodding his own heartbeat to escalate. Bowi wants to let go, but he can't—her grip is finger-crushing. Panicked, Bowi's imagination conjures images of blood, his mother's face, her failed pregnancies—he's been here before, hasn't he?

Yes. And he remembers each outcome.

"This is your first birth?" Tagi clarifies. Seero nods, writhing. "You're young, and you're carrying a large child, I can already tell that much. Your body is struggling to cope. It's important to relax your muscles so your pelvis can stretch. And breathe, like this," Tagi demonstrates a *pant-pant-blow* exhalation method.

"We've already told her all that," the sisters say. "There's something else wrong!"

"*Bowi,* give her more *reewo,*" Tagi instructs, rubbing his chin. "An extra dose of pain-reliever always helps the body relax—you didn't take a *Kunjaruna* mushroom tonight, did you?" Seero shakes her head, revolted by the idea. "Good," Tagi nods. "Keep breathing, like I showed you, and allow the *reewo* some time to kick in. We'll get this baby out of you before the night's end, I can guarantee you that."

Seero's sisters crowd around the booth, embracing her from behind while Tagi gently pokes and massages her abdomen, feeling for any abnormalities. So far, the pregnancy appears otherwise normal, the baby's twitches strong and eager—*it just seems to be stuck in place...* "*Bowi,* more *reewo.*"

Standing beside her, still cinched hand-in-hand, Bowi feels faint. How can Tagi remain composed while his patient suffers so blatantly? Bowi is terrified of her screams—her pain—the potential for this scene to end in horror. Woozy, he struggles to keep his thoughts present. His arms tremble so much he nearly pokes Seero in the face while spooning another dose of pain-reliever under her tongue. Still, she *thanks* Bowi after the spoonful.

That's when a memory strikes him: Long ago, according to *ynsyna*, *Teerta* number eighty-one solved a similar impasse by reaching inside a laboring *momo*'s birth canal to disentangle her fetus from its own umbilical cord.

Is Seero's fetus caught in the same situation?

"*Tagi*," Bowi's tongue is dry, hardly operable. "I think I have an idea."

"What?" Tagi looks at him. The sisters look at him. Seero looks at him.

Bowi feels himself go pale. Trembling uncontrollably, hand-in-hand with Seero, he's sickened now by the thought of actually reaching inside another person.

"What is it, boy?" Tagi hates repeating himself.

"Um..." Bowi gulps. "Remember *Teerta* number eighty-one?"

"Sure."

"Remember how she..."

"What is it, boy?"

"Remember how she reached inside—"

"Oh, quick, get off the booth, the *punteeku* are coming!" Tagi pushes Seero and her sisters away to make room for the incoming stampede of warriors. Bowi doesn't even have time to process the transition; Seero's fingers slip instantly from his own, and by the time he blinks there's someone else lying beneath him on the booth, some blood-soaked, spine-covered, angry-voiced *punteeku* with no patience for Bowi's surprise.

"Look at my ear!" the man barks, holding up his severed earlobe like a trophy. "Fix it!"

The rest of the night passes in a blur. In total, they reattach the ear, stitch twenty-three more wounds, relocate twelve joints, and tie splints around six fractures. By the time the *punteeku* bloodrush ends, the rain has long since passed. On the eastern horizon, Bowi sees the sun peeking just over the mountains—timid, reluctant, like it doesn't want to see what the night wrought either.

Further down the lakeshore, Bowi sees Seero, surrounded by her sisters. She's shaking. She's crying. She must've given birth out here by the water, sometime during the night. Because now Bowi sees her baby, dead in the sand, tangled in its own umbilical cord.

Hiking back to the cave, Bowi leaves a snaking trail of vomit, unable to rid his head of the horror.

Chapter 59
"Maetri"

Of course, Chiefdom has its perks.

A whole crew of *punteeku* refurbish Maetri's old *capku* at his behest, upgrading his *hympano*-wrapped home into a sprawling new domain, nearly twice its original diameter, complete with feather inlining sewn into the walls for insulation and a retractable smoke vent built into the roof's conical center.

Obviously, Maetri has begun hosting parties—lavish, clandestine events among only the Chiefs and their high-ranking *punteeku* friends, wherein everyone feasts, puffs, and then passes out on *Kamaruna* mushrooms in the middle of Maetri's feather-carpeted floor. No one remembers the debaucherous details when they awake. But they at least retain enough wit to limit these secret soirees to once per week.

All other times, Chiefdom is about duty, reputation, and honor.

"*Wakar*," Dynjo tells him. "Shave your *patu*. You need to look the part."

Respectfully, Maetri shaves his famous, scruffy locks. After all, isn't a clean-cut *patu* something to be proud of?

By now, he spends nearly all waking hours between the two *raea* fields, herding his flock back and forth, forth and back. East to west, west to east. He's devoted himself to these purple-plumed, long-necked, ostrich-beasts, almost like they're his own flesh. They are his father's legacy, after all. Just the other day, Maetri watched closely as two *raea* chicks hatched from a nest of giant, speckled eggs. The sight filled him with (what he imagines to be) the divine elation mothers must feel upon giving birth. New life, how miraculous. He even fed the chicks himself, offering each a grubby, dangly earthworm by hand. Yet immediately afterward, Toti, the Chief of food sourcing, visited to select three adults among the herd for slaughtering—which now brings the flock's total down to forty-four. Still shrinking, Maetri is well-aware that if he fails to regrow the *raea* population soon, he'll go the same way as Veetri.

Am I a birthing momo *now, too?* The irony hits him one day, presiding over his squawking chicks.

"*Maetri,*" Kleeo finds him out on the western fields. It's a dark morning, the atmosphere dense with a misty drizzle that hangs like drapery from the sky—she parts a suspended curtain of dew to join her brother in the tall grass. "It's your turn."

"My turn for what?"

"*Nyno.*"

"Oh yeah," Maetri rolls his eyes.

That's another new responsibility of Chiefdom: Ensuring the Chief of textile sourcing doesn't go rogue. Given all the recent chaos that's befallen the *Uyi,* the Chiefs consider it a top priority to maintain law and order within the nest. They can't allow one of their newly-appointed leaders to just run off and abandon production, or make a scene over her criminal, *Patummal* daughter. No. That would send a bad message to the people. So they've secretly tied Nyno prisoner inside her own *capku* and implemented a rotating guard to ensure she continues her workload. Between Maetri and the other Chiefs, plus Kleeo, everyone's required to work a half-day guard shift twice per week. No one enjoys the chore. But they plan to continue their rotation until the *Patummal* girl is gone—or, at least, until whenever Nyno decides to no longer be a flight risk.

Maetri finds her tugging at her restraints, again.

"Don't tire yourself out," he reprimands, striding into her *capku.*

"You," Nyno spits at him. Bound by her ankles, she's tied with *areemo* cords to her home's central pole.

Organized around the floor, completed harnesses, finished satchels, and ready-for-wear soft-clothes lie folded in burgeoning piles, awaiting distribution. The Chiefs think they've been gracious, leaving her hands unbound so she can continue working...

"Where are the ponchos?" Maetri says, glancing at her finished piles. "We provided you with feathers, why haven't you started work on the ponchos yet?"

"Shut up," Nyno grunts. Crumpled and naked on the ground, she looks like a broken, crash-landed *kynaea* chick, *caw!*ing at anything that comes near. Her typically mismatched eyes are almost the same color today, the lighter one swollen and bruised.

Maetri considers kicking her for the insolence, or slapping her (he loves when he can make that perfect *crack!* sound), but he figures (since Kleeo was last on guard duty) she's probably suffered enough today. "Already tired yourself out then, *eh?*" he closes the *capku*'s flap behind him, sealing them inside together.

"I'll make the ponchos later," Nyno mutters. She repositions her body, shifting onto her other side—both to find a more comfortable spot on the ground and to face away from Maetri. "Can I have a *Kamaruna* mushroom? Please?" At this point, the psychedelic sedation they feed her every night is the only part of life Nyno doesn't hate.

"It's midday," Maetri cocks an eyebrow. "You can't go to sleep now, *Nyno*. There's work to do."

Nyno clenches her eyes, desperate.

"Come on, *Nyno*," Maetri walks toward her. Outfitted in his harness, *hympano* belt, and various machete scabbards, every step he takes is a clattering *thud!* in her direction.

Nyno recoils, curling her body into a tight ball.

"What?" Maetri smirks, towering over her. "Did you think I was going to kick you?"

Nyno doesn't say anything. She remains on the ground, shaking.

"You're so dramatic," he sneers. "This is your own fault, you know."

She tries to make her body as small as possible.

"If we could just trust you to stay here and do your job like you're supposed to," he continues, "you wouldn't have to be tied up like this."

Nyno doesn't respond.

"Come on, *Nyno*, get up," he yanks her. "Take this," he reaches into his belt. "It'll help you work," he pulls out a *Kunjaruna* mushroom. "Open up," he shoves it into Nyno's mouth.

Nyno gags on the unwelcome taste. She tries to push Maetri's hand away, but it's too late. And she's too tired to heave the *Kunjaruna* mushroom back up.

Before long, Nyno's brain mistakes the fungus' psychoactive chemical structure for norepinephrine: She spends the rest of the day in a manic frenzy, weaving feather ponchos at record speed under Maetri's dutiful watch.

Chapter 60
"Aruna"

One moon.

According to ancient tradition, during the *Teerta's* final moon of life, it's customary to ingest a single *Kamaruna* mushroom each morning at dawn. Now, whether this is supposed to grant him supreme wisdom in his final weeks as *Teerta* or merely compensate for all the *Kunjaruna* and *Kosharuna* goodies he's missed throughout his life, Tagi can't be certain. *"The way you're supposed to do it,"* his old *Teerta* told him, on the first morning of her regimen, *"is to collect thirty, and then eat them from smallest to largest, one per sunrise. Except on your last."*

"What are you supposed to do on your last sunrise?" Bowi asks, foraging alongside Daeo beneath the *wykyno* thickets surrounding their cave.

"On my last morning, I'll eat two," Tagi explains. "One on my own, and then a second with the other *Kamaruna* volunteers. That's when you'll take your mushroom, *Daeo.*"

Daeo doesn't respond. Tagi sounds excited, at least for the experiment of it. But she still doesn't know how to feel about their upcoming *Kamaruna* date. How is a child supposed to prepare for death? Caked in soil and leaves, she and Bowi have been scavenging the forest floor all morning, collecting any mushrooms they can find of the *Kamaruna* variety. A saprophytic fungus, unattached to the *Uyi's* deeper mycorrhizal network, they aren't particularly difficult to extract, poking their little pale caps through the dirt like they want to be picked. But they do require a bit of stone-turning to locate.

"Is this a good one?" Daeo holds up another tiny, white knob. Though she's found the bulk of their collection so far, she always double-checks with Tagi to make sure she's not mistakenly dug up one of the other hundreds of fungal species sprouting around the cave's vicinity.

Tagi steps over to inspect her find. *"Size doesn't matter; it's the pearly ones that are best,"* he remembers his old *Teerta* saying, on the last day of her regimen. The one now resting in Daeo's palm glimmers pale and lustrous, no larger than Tagi's own thumb knuckle. "Yes, that's perfect," he tells her.

"We're finished then," Bowi jumps up from behind a furling, red-leafed *wykyno*, holding their foraged sack over his head. "That last *Kamaruna* mushroom makes thirty."

"Well hold on now," Tagi raises a hand. "We still need to find one more—a mushroom for *Daeo*, remember?"

Bowi glares at him.

"I will pick one myself," Daeo says. "When the day comes." She's starting to think the day will never come. Because how can it? The more she thinks about her own death, the more unlikely it seems...

Tagi shrugs. "Suit yourself; they're easy enough to find." And then he waves his hand at Bowi. "Bring me the bag, boy. It's well past sunrise and I still need to eat my first mushroom." Really, this will be the first psychoactive mushroom Tagi's ever eaten in his life. His fingers jitter as he processes the sacred collection.

Organizing the mushrooms from smallest to largest, just as his old *Teerta* instructed long ago, this moment feels to Tagi like an epic rite of honor, like there's some continuous root of never-ending *Teerta*s on which his tiny life-cycle is now only budding to fruition. "Pay attention, *Bowi.* Someday your final moon will come too, and you'll need to pass along this tradition. Remember, smallest to largest."

Bowi continues glaring at Tagi. It's all he's done since last *Kunjaruna*...

"What do they taste like?" Daeo wonders.

"*Hush*, I'm about to find out," Tagi calls for silence.

Sitting beneath the cave's mouth, Eeao flicks her tail in listless displeasure. She doesn't understand why the children have been sniffing through the dirt all morning, no more than she understands why any living creature would willingly eat a mushroom. She's tried to distract each of them with play, but the children keep shooing her away, and now Tagi is busy sniffing through their worthless collection. Vexed, Eeao wishes they'd all move on to a more interesting activity.

Tagi is similarly skeptical of the mushrooms. From what he remembers, the month-long regimen turned his old *Teerta* into a giggling, dithyrambic old wit. *Will my ending begin now, too?* Vacillating between heartbeats, he pops the smallest *Kamaruna* mushroom into his mouth and chews... Odorless and gummy, the tiny, fungal morsel seems harmless enough; he has no inkling of the dopamine-serotonin tsunami soon to flood his brain.

"I can barely taste it," Tagi notes. "Perhaps I should try another."

"Only one per day," Bowi crosses his arms. "That's the custom, right?" By the tone of his voice, the boy sounds like he's trying to make a point.

"I was joking," Tagi is tired of Bowi's new, self-righteous attitude. Overhead, the atmosphere is sunny and warm, the sky a brilliant canopy of light-reflecting vapor—there's no room in such a glorious day for grief. Besides, Tagi has a special *ynsyna* lesson planned for today, and he needs everyone to be agreeable so he can finish teaching before the mushroom hits. "Come children," he leads them back inside the cave. "Today I'm going to show you my favorite *ynsyna* of all."

"Which *ynsyna* is that?" Daeo asks.

Tagi smiles. "My *ynsyna.*"

Bowi scoffs.

Tagi ignores him.

Eeao bristles; the trio is abandoning her for their moldy cavern.

It's a long walk, all the way down to Tagi's block of *ynsyna*. He is the very last *Teerta*, after all. On and on and on and on... Both children are amazed at how deep the cavern goes. An endless tunnel of floor-to-ceiling words, it seems to slope ever-downward, broken only by the occasional pair of calcified speleothems or crumbling, breakaway concavity. Bowi feels ensconced in information. How many moons could he spend down here, researching *Teerta* after *Teerta* after *Teerta?* And how many more *Teerta*s still have yet to come after him? Even when they reach Tagi's etchings, his final lines of human knowledge, the source of that ever-present *drip! drip! drip!* sound is still further off, yet to be discovered in the deep, bottomless dark.

Bowi is disappointed to see Tagi's *ynsyna* block isn't numbered—apparently, the *Teerta*s lost count of themselves somewhere in the ten-to-twenty-thousand range. Tagi's *ynsyna* is unique, however, given the elaborate diagram he's carved beside it.

"What is this?" Daeo swings her blanket-satchel over her shoulder so she can run her fingers around the bizarre, circular engraving. Webbed with squiggly, meandering contours and irregular, looping grooves, the design is larger than her entire body, and clearly a singular emblem, distinct from the run-on striations of adjacent *ynsyna* letters. Their *patu*s illume the round engraving like a subterranean moon.

"This is the *Uyi*," Tagi gazes fondly upon the map. His life's work. He's spent most of his existence toiling on this creative project, both outside in the jungle, re-trekking old trails and tidying lost paths, and down here, alone with his *patu* and a shard of flintstone, recreating exactly what he walked, perfectly to scale (or, at least, as perfectly as he can measure between his own aging knuckles).

"The *Uyi?* What do you mean?" Bowi can't conceptualize the analogy.

"Like, from above?" Daeo gets it.

"Exactly," Tagi pats her head. *"Kyr-aea mae."* *Bird's-eye view.* "See this point, right here?" Tagi draws their attention to the diagram's lower arc, where an asterisk-shape seems to signify something important. "This spot marks our cave. And then this line, branching upward from it, that's the path to the nest. And then this big, shaded area up here in the middle, that's—"

"That is the *Aeo,*" Daeo recognizes the lake's circuitous shoreline.

"Very good," Tagi is impressed by her knack for topography.

"How is that the *Aeo?*" Bowi isn't impressed at all.

Tagi sighs, "Alright, *Bowi.* See this big circle?" he swings his arm to encompass the entire diagram. "This represents the ring of mountains surrounding the *Uyi.* And everything I've etched inside the circle represents all the paths and other geographical features of the land, like the *Aeo,* the nest, the two *raea* fields, the swamp, the different lakeshores, and such. You get the idea?"

"How do you know all these paths?" Bowi squints at the latticework of crisscrosses, more convoluted and abundant than the veins in his own wrists.

"Well, I don't know if you've come across the subject in your reading yet, but for my life's research I chose *Uysyna,* the study of the *Uyi* itself," Tagi explains. "I made it my life's work to tend every trail in the land. Studying from old maps carved by earlier *Teerta*'s, I re-cleared ancient walkways, and charted new paths as well. This, right here, is the latest, most comprehensive diagram of the *Uyi* yet. Above-ground, I've made the trails more navigable than ever. And below-ground, here in the *ynsyna* cavern, I leave for you my life's greatest legacy. I hope my creation serves you well in the future..."

Tagi doesn't realize it yet, but his dopamine receptors are now rocketing at full-throttle.

Bowi glares back and forth between Tagi and the map. "You spent your whole life making this?" he scoffs. "You're the oldest person in the nest, and you spent all your time just digging trails and drawing this picture of the *Uyi?*"

Tagi smiles in rapture, "Yes." He feels himself melting into his map, shrinking down to the proper size and scale so as to fit perfectly inside his own magnum opus.

But Bowi has never disliked the old man more. He turns to leave, trekking upward through the cave's earlier testimonies. He'd rather resume his studies today where he left off—*Teerta* number three hundred and sixty-one, another devotee to the study of *Momyna*—than waste any more time down here studying Tagi's useless research.

But Daeo remains with the old man. She doesn't think his map is useless at all. She's captivated by the perspective he's created, the idea of a bird's-eye view. She's seen this before, hasn't she? Yes, in her dreams. But not in such tangible detail...

So while Tagi sinks into a blissful state of self-actualization beside his masterpiece, Daeo studies his diagram, certain she'll find an escape.

Chapter 61
"Daeo"

No, there's no trail around the mountains. It's just as the old nursery rhyme says: *Ko-ama-mo. No way out.* Even on a map, their world is wholly contained.

But it's not like Daeo ever expected an easy escape. Just a possible one.

She already recognizes much of what she sees in Tagi's diagram. The winding path between the *Aeo* and the nest. The arduous, uphill hike from the nest to the *Teerta*'s cave. She even imagines she can place her own *momo*'s *capku* on the map, not far from the looping trail between the *Aeo* and the swampgrounds. An explicit correlation between this simple, albeit detailed depiction and her intuitive understanding of spatial reality seems to pop out from the cave wall itself, an abstraction she can't unsee. It even depicts mountain elevations around the caldera, including the lowest point along the southern rim. Analyzing the map now, Daeo thinks Tagi must be the smartest person ever.

"Oh my, the floor is all squishy, isn't it?" Tagi teeters on wobbly legs. With each passing moment, the *Kamaruna* mushroom he ate earlier warps his senses until he can hardly balance upright, let alone walk all the way back to the cave's entrance on his own. He remains alongside Daeo in the cavern's depths while she absorbs as much of his map as she can (she'll return later of course, it's just such a long walk), and then when she's satisfied, they hike out of the cavern together—although Daeo has to guide Tagi by the elbow just to keep him from tottering off into random chasms.

"What's wrong with him?" Bowi notices the old man's state as they emerge from the dark.

"Oh my, look at all the colors," Tagi stumbles toward the cave's mouth, dazzled by the sunset beyond. "What is this?" he passes his hand through a beaming ray of daylight.

Daeo shrugs at her brother.

Tagi wanders outside, unattended.

From her nook, Eeao yawns, just waking up for the evening. She eyes each human, mildly irritated. And then she plops down to settle herself between Daeo's ankles.

"What's for *kyrkaruna?*" Bowi calls out to the old man, hungry for *dinner.*

Tagi stirs at his voice, as though briefly roused from a dream. And then, "Oh, just throw a mantis on to boil," he sighs, slipping back into breezy delirium. "What is this substance?" he keeps fluttering his fingers through the sunbeams. Somehow, to him, each lightwave feels slippery—*But to differing degrees!*

"What a fool," Bowi mutters, rising for the chore.

"He is not a fool," Daeo says. "He just sees things we cannot right now."

Bowi sneers. "He's a bad *Teerta, Daeo.* He has all the knowledge in the *Uyi,* and look how he's wasted it. I'm going to be a better *Teerta* than him."

"I am sure you will be..." Daeo says.

But will she be there to see it?

"Come on," Bowi can't think that thought. "Help me fill the cauldron."

Bowi ends up doing most chores over the next week, as Tagi continues his *Kamaruna* regimen. And he has to do virtually all the work over the following *Kosharuna* and *Kunjaruna,* too. Each new day is a new episode of erratic behavior. The mushrooms cause the old man to cycle from trance-like pensiveness in the mornings to euphoric ecstasy by evening time, and the children learn quickly what to expect from him during his psychedelic trips: That being, not much.

As Tagi frolics between his cave and *heersu,* jabbering nonsense to the wind, Bowi spends most of his time reading in solitude while Daeo memorizes the old man's map. Lost in his own head, Tagi soon falls out of interaction with the children altogether. Even Eeao finds she's unable to sleep on his chest anymore, as serotonin levels in his brain cause him to babble while dreaming.

However, about halfway through his second week of daily dosing, something begins to shift in Tagi's brain. A subtle acclimation of neurotransmitters. An evolution of mind. Gradually, the dopamine isn't so disorienting, the serotonin no longer so befuddling. He remembers who he is, and what he still has left to do.

One moon.

And though colors continue to vibrate his eyeballs, Tagi realizes one balmy morning after *tyrkuna* (boiled mantis, since that's all Bowi knows how to cook) that he's able to speak in coherent sentences again.

"I'd like to walk my trails today," the old man says. "One last time." A tear glitters down his cheek.

The children join him—which means Eeao tags along too. They meander as a quartet through the dewy jungle, traveling along the lush, bouldering foothills in a northwestern direction, away from the nest so that Daeo isn't spotted outside of exile. She's grateful to be included on the excursion. After two moons stuck inside the cave, to be out exploring the *Uyi* once again, armed with her secret dagger, beloved baby blanket, and hidden fossil, Daeo feels like she's returned to her element—but this time, she has Tagi's map in her head as well.

Will this be her last hike through the jungle, too?

Eeao has little concept of conclusion; she stalks Daeo through the trees, wondering why they don't do this more often.

"Oh my, look at this succulent *arukono,*" Tagi keeps getting distracted by random oddities of flora. He's generally familiar with the scenery along most of his paths, but this blood-orange *wykyno* stalk seems to be a new growth.

"Notice how its conical leaves curl inward? Look at them. Aren't they unique? *Arukono wykyno* don't usually grow this close to the mountains."

"Why do you think it is growing out here then?" Daeo asks.

"Space from relatives, perhaps?" Tagi shrugs.

"It's past noon," Bowi notices the sun's position through the treetop canopy. "We should start heading back to the cave." Really, he just wants to return to the intellectual comfort of *ynsyna*. All this chatter between Tagi and Daeo keeps forcing him to remember their deadlines...

"Just a little further," Daeo insists. "Up to that next hill!" she points forward, through the tunneled vegetation. "Please?"

Eeao is already trotting ahead.

"Yes, just up to that next hill," Tagi agrees. "Come, *ado-aeo*, I'll race you!"

Daeo pauses. "*Ado-aeo?*" Why did the old man just call her *after-water?*

"Yes, come," he waves his hand excitedly. "Don't you want to race?"

Bowi halts alongside his sister. "Why did you call her that?"

"Call her what?"

"After-water," Bowi is annoyed—has the old man lost his mind again? "Why did you call her *ado-aeo?* Her name is *Daeo.*"

Overhead, watching from the forked limbs of a rubber tree, Eeao hopes the humans have only paused to course-correct in the direction of a nearby *kynaea* nest.

"*Ado-aeo...*" Tagi repeats slowly, hallucinating the letters across his visual field. "It's the symbological meaning of her name, spelled out. *Daeo. Ado-aeo.*"

"What does that mean?" Bowi snaps.

"It means... Exactly what it means it means," Tagi says. "*Daeo* literally means after-water."

"What?" Bowi is confused.

"Your name has an ancient meaning too, *Bowi,*" Tagi jumps with glee. "Would you like to know what it is?"

"What are you talking about?" Bowi is angry now. "How can a name mean something that it's not?"

"It's based on the alphabetical symbology of *ynsyna,*" Tagi raves. "Every letter has a coded meaning. There's a chart somewhere in the cavern, I believe around *Teerta* number one thousand and—"

"Shut up!" Bowi erupts. "Shut up, *Tagi!* Just shut up! Her name is *Daeo!* And *Daeo* means *Daeo!*" he points to his sister. "That's what *Daeo* means! Don't tell me her name means anything else! You don't know what you're talking about! You never know what you're talking about! So just shut up!"

Tagi sees each word as an explosion—rockets of lava spewing from the boy's mouth—but, thanks to his current neurochemical state, the fiery comments glance off his spirit like heat off fire-proof *hympano*. He remains doe-eyed and smiling.

Bowi, however, is feeling all of his worst emotions at once. He knows what's coming. He sees it all now: Death, fear, conclusion. How many nights does he have left with Daeo? What will it be like when both she and Tagi are gone? How can he possibly live the rest of his life alone? In a cave? With a cat that doesn't even like him? Sobbing, Bowi can't take these thoughts anymore—he bolts back in the direction of the cave, terrified of the nausea roiling his gut.

Eeao considers his departure a win for the group.

"*...eeao...*" she hopes to now coax her companions in the direction of *kynaea.*

But the humans don't notice her. Watching her brother storm off, Daeo thinks she knows why he's upset...

"I do not blame you," she says to Tagi.

He looks down at her; shrunken by age, he's only a head taller than the girl. "Blame me? Blame me for what?"

"For telling everyone I was in the cave," Daeo believes it's as simple as this. "You outed me to everyone when I was hiding. I could have hidden in the cave forever, but you made me come out. That is why *Bowi* is mad at you. You should not have told everyone where I was. But I do not blame you. You did not know better at the time. It was not your fault. I do not hold it against you."

Tagi is surprised—his eyes spring with tears. Why does her voice sound exactly like his old *Teerta's*? "Well, thank you," he says. "And... I'm sorry for outing you... I guess?"

Daeo smiles up at him. She tells him not to worry. He thanks her again. She tells him to stop wasting words.

In the sun's angling light, they walk together back to the cave, trailing Bowi's footsteps. Disappointed, Eeao follows—but they'll go exploring again soon, in the future, right? The kitten comforts herself with this hope. Now nearly a full-grown cat, Eeao has a firm grasp on object permanence, the expectation of tomorrow, the stability of family...

A thought occurs to Daeo as they walk: "You said names have hidden meanings, right?"

Tagi nods.

"Well... What does *Tagi* mean?"

Tagi pauses mid-step. "I'm glad you asked," his face beams so bright even Daeo, sober though she is, can see his figurative radiance. "*Toa-gyh-i.* It means *across-familiar-ground*. I chose the name for myself. Isn't it nice?"

"You chose your own name?" Daeo feels conned. "How is that possible?"

"I didn't like the name my *momo* gave me," Tagi shrugs, laughing now as he remembers—*Umpati*. "I changed it to *Tagi* when I became *Teerta*."

"What was it before—"

"I don't remember," Tagi lies.

Daeo believes him, considering all the things she wishes she could forget about her own life. Like the taste of *cananeero* nectar. Or the blood on her *mabato* shard. Or the petrified weight inside her blanket. If she could erase all thoughts and feelings for such objects and people, would she? Right now, Daeo isn't sure.

But her name? Could she at least change that? Before it's too late?

Daeo is going to brainstorm some options.

Chapter 62
"Eeao"

By now, Eeao sees herself as the quartet's second-in-command.

And she may as well be. She patrols the *heersu* alongside their alpha. She guards the cave's antechamber whenever the primates disappear into the deep. She always brings back prized cuts of meat from her nocturnal hunts (although the humans often overlook these raw, feathery offerings as garbage). She's resumed her midnight throne upon the old man's chest, yet again, despite his sleep-talking (she's learned to brave the spook). And she's clearly several rungs above the boy—certainly by any scalable tree's metric.

Truly, the kitten wields power.

Of course, she's also destroying the entire *Uyi* from within. But Eeao would never give herself that much credit. She's just here for a good time with her friends. That's all. And as far as she can sniff, good times abound.

Although, the old man has begun to smell odd lately. A musky odor, produced by overstimulated sweat glands and some sort of hormone Eeao doesn't recognize. He's been acting strange, too. Energetic and bouncy. More childlike than even the children. They've created a game together, the old man and the kitten, in which he manipulates a strange, wiggling specimen (a strand of *areemo* twine, which Tagi drags across the cave floor) and she must execute the perfect pounce in order to halt its creeping invasion. Eeao purrs while the old man laughs—a sound she's grown to expect daily.

They play for an eternity, it seems.

"*Bowi! Daeo!* Watch this!" Tagi loves the game. He insists the children watch one evening; they're always holed away inside the *ynsyna* cavern nowadays.

One night.

Bowi and Daeo come moping out—Daeo exhausted from poring over Tagi's map, Bowi evermore irritated by Tagi's voice.

"What's wrong?" Bowi asks.

Tagi blinks up at them, pupils dilated. "Nothing's wrong," he smiles, cross-legged on the floor. "But watch how *Eeao* plays with this string! Look!" He slithers it along the floor, eliciting an immediate wiggle-pounce from Eeao—she barrels it into the dirt, maintaining her one hundred percent success rate.

Daeo giggles. Bowi grimaces.

"Isn't it cute?" Tagi exclaims. "It's like she thinks it's a snake or something!"

"*Aww,*" Daeo kneels to pat Eeao's round, little head. "I do not think *Eeao* could handle a real snake."

"Doubtful," Tagi agrees with a smirk. He gives the string another wiggle.

Eeao believes everyone is impressed with her prowess. Careening across the floor, she gives her pounce an extra swivel-kick, just to show off.

"Is that all?" Bowi can't believe Tagi interrupted his studies for this—he'd been finishing a lesson on the *Aeo*'s salinity, and the various fungal organisms that live within...

"No!" Tagi can't get enough. "Watch, she'll do it again, see!"

Eeao springs, a nimble savant.

"She goes for it every time!"

"Don't interrupt me again," Bowi mutters. He turns to resume his studies.

"Wait," Daeo stops him. He doesn't look at her. Why doesn't he look at her anymore? "Why not take a break from *ynsyna?* Just for tonight? We can all play a game!" Really, she's considering giving up on Tagi's map altogether. Their deadline is tomorrow, after all. Maybe *ko-ama-mo* really does mean *no way out.*

"I was just reading an important lesson," Bowi argues. "I need to finish it. *Teerta* number four hundred and eleven was an expert on—"

"Come now, *Bowi,*" Tagi insists, still waving the string. "*Teerta* number four hundred and eleven will still be there tomorrow, and the next day, and the day after that, and—"

"I really need to study," Bowi stammers, painfully aware of his stomach.

"*Ba-owo-i,*" Tagi sees the letters of Bowi's name splayed as freckles across the boy's face. *Beneath-ancient-ground.* "You can always study later, *Bowi,* but you can't always play right now."

Bowi tastes bile.

"Come on, have a seat," Tagi waves his hand. "Join me! It's fun!" He twirls his wrist again, which sends Eeao backflipping through the air.

Daeo drops her blanket-satchel to sit on the floor beside Tagi, eager for a turn with the string. She doesn't want to think about tomorrow. She doesn't want to think about anything. And why should she? Their final night together isn't a loss.

Right here, right now, they can all win.

"*Ugh,*" Bowi groans, bracing against the lurch of his esophagus. He wants everything to stop—he can't bear these sensations. "I need to lie down."

He stumbles into bed. Lying on his side, curling away from the pain, Bowi watches while the other three continue their antics in the middle of the cave floor. Daeo is ingenious with her string-maneuvers, but Tagi is quicker, and therefore better at driving Eeao into a state of fluster. Bowi tries to find humor in their game, but eventually all the string-twirling aggravates his nausea further, and he has to close his eyes to keep from retching. Instead of vomit, he expels tears. He falls asleep listening to them play, weeping softly to himself.

Tagi's game lasts well into the night. But, of course, he and Daeo inevitably tire out before Eeao does. Soon, Daeo carries her baby blanket to bed with Bowi, Tagi vanishes beneath his own feather coverings, and the kitten is left alone in a motionless cave. She twitches her ears as the three apes begin snoring around her. Obviously, Eeao doesn't stay long. She has her nightly duties—it's part of being second-in-command.

First, she pays visit to a familiar *kynaea* nest—the stupid mother keeps hatching babies in the same spot.

Then, she returns homage to the cave—the bulging, green-feathered head of a fresh *kynaea* chick.

Last, she steals off to the swamp for one more piece of business—the fungal biome is near another tipping point.

And then Eeao returns to sleep one final night on Tagi's chest.

Act 5

Chapter 63
"Tagi"

"Bring *Eeao!*"

The sunrise pulls Tagi awake on his last morning, just as it's done every other day of his life. But this time, the old *Teerta* startles from one bizarre, final dream.

"Bring *Eeao!*"

The kitten leaps from his chest, furious he evoked her name via sleep-talk.

"*Tagi?*" Daeo hurries to his side. She's been awake for a long time already, just breathing silently beside Bowi, absorbing time. Now, she tries to steady the old man's shoulders as he jerks awake.

"Bring—bring—bring *Eeao!*" he keeps stammering, barely cognizant.

"What's going on?" Bowi regrets waking. He's been dreading today for how long?

"*Tagi* is having a bad dream," Daeo says, struggling to hold the man.

"*Daeo, Daeo,*" he repeats her name as consciousness hits. Holding her face in his hands, he understands what to do. "*Daeo,* you need to bring *Eeao* to *Kamaruna!*"

"What?" Daeo tries to picture what he means. Would they bring Eeao just to watch from the lakeshore? Or does he intend to drown her with them?

"I saw it!" he says. "I saw how to survive!"

What had he seen? It's already fading. But for a moment, a glimpse, a snap of unconscious, neurological harmony, his brain finally identified the one letter in their *ynsyna* puzzle that doesn't belong. "We need to bring *Eeao* to the *Aeo!*"

"Please, stop yelling," Bowi groans, still in bed. This is exactly how he feared today would begin—nausea, pain, dread. Will he spiral into vomiting once they're gone?

"But I saw it," Tagi insists, squeezing Daeo's cheeks. Her radiant face, just like his old *Teerta*'s. "You will be alright, *Daeo.* You will survive. The *Aeo* will spare whoever brings *Eeao,* and it has to be you!"

"Why me?" Daeo has no idea what he's dreamt, or why she should be so special.

Tagi kisses her cheek, "Because you still have so much life to live, *Daeo!*"

Chapter 64
"Bowi"

Here's the irony: All this time, Bowi's been getting yanked around by the sun too.

Already susceptible to external sensations, his body is like an exposed rung, a snag in the Earth's crust, a gravitational point of leverage by which the celestial beast swings up and over the horizon each morning. Its solar tug warps his waking experience. It's what nauseates him each morning, propelling him to empty his insides—what good is a mere esophagus against the sun's relentless gravity?

Freefall. Whiplash. Somersault.

Again and again and again and again.

The sun. The old man. The boy.

Identical sensations, opposite reactions.

Fitting, then, that Bowi and Tagi, on their final morning together, are further away from each other than they've ever been.

Paralyzed in bed, Bowi struggles to keep his stomach inside. Outside, Tagi is preparing a quick, steamed breakfast—"just because it's our last morning doesn't mean we skip *tyrkuna*"—and the smell of boiled grasshopper is only intensifying Bowi's urge to retch. He won't let himself, of course. Not until they're gone. Not until he's alone.

But still, the pressure has to go somewhere.

"*Bowi,*" Daeo returns to his side.

Lying flat, shaking and sweat-soaked, Bowi feels like his chest is rupturing, ripped open by the sun—his sister—today—their deadlines—

"*Bowi,* I want to give you something," Daeo is saying.

Bowi can barely see through his tears. Her luminous face ripples and streams before him, filling his visual field. He blinks. He wipes his eyes. This is the last time he'll ever see his sister, and he wants to memorize every detail of her.

He wants to capture her in his mind forever, steal her away into the safety of his imagination, his songs, his stories. But now he's crying again, and it's like he's viewing her face submerged beneath the *Aeo.*

"I can't let you go!" Bowi tries to launch himself from bed, to stand between his sister and the entire world, but his stomach convulses. He collapses back into his pillows.

"Do not worry about me," Daeo says. Through his tears, she almost looks like she's smiling. Is she? "Here, take this." She slips her blanket-satchel off her shoulder, and then unwraps its contents. A skull-sized chunk of petrified wood spills from its feathery folds, but Daeo is quick to catch it. She places it on Bowi's chest. He gawps down his nose at it. The fossil's blunt weight, at first startling, settles like a warm compress over his heart. Somehow, its gravity seems to counterbalance the sunrise.

"What is this?" Bowi runs his fingers over its pockmarked surface.

"*Atrypa,*" Daeo says. Empty, the old baby blanket now feels weightless and unfamiliar in her hands. But she doesn't care. The baby needs to be unwrapped. "I'm giving it to you."

"But why?" Bowi can't tell if it's a rock or a chunk of stalagmite she found inside the cave. "Is this what you've been carrying around in that blanket all this time? What is it?"

"It is me," Daeo says. Through his tears, her face magnifies, stretching at its edges.

"What do you mean?" Bowi can no longer parse pain from comfort. He tries to take the fossil off his chest, to get a better look at it, but Daeo won't let him.

"Hug me," she says, unfurling their baby blanket to wrap around them both.

Bowi doesn't hesitate; her words have broken the sun's power. He throws his arms around her, pulling her into his chest, squeezing her, the fossil between them, the blanket around them. He feels a rush of freedom, a lightness—he no longer cares if he cries or vomits. Holding Daeo, Bowi sobs. He rocks back and forth with her. He squeezes her until neither of them can breathe. He cries until his voice finds a gasping melody, and then, suddenly, they're both heroes in one of his songs again. Running. Flying. Singing.

"Please, don't leave me," Bowi says after an eternity of tears.

"I will never leave you," Daeo says, her voice gentle, content. "As long as you have this," she presses the fossil into his chest again, "you have me."

"But how—"

"You will feel sad at first," Daeo continues, interlacing their fingers. "You will feel alone. And you will feel scared. But you will not give up. Because you will not *be* alone. And you will not *be* scared. Because you have me. Right here. Always." She caresses the fossil between them. And then she pulls herself away.

Bowi has no idea what she means, but he's too overwhelmed to ask questions. He begins sobbing again, this time without any grace or melody. He reaches to hug Daeo once more, but she's already drifting off to join Tagi outside the cave. To Bowi, it looks like she's being swept away by his deluge of tears. He clutches her offering to his chest, scratching his fingers along the fossil's craters, but he no longer finds comfort in its dense, jagged weight.

Is she the one submerging, or is he?

Chapter 65
"Daeo"

On one hand, by now, marching straight into her final sunrise, Daeo figures she should feel scared.

But on the other hand, what does *should* even mean? It's such a fickle word.

Her mother *should've* prioritized her children's wellbeing over social taboos. But she didn't.

The *Teerta should've* intervened on her baby sister's behalf. But he didn't.

The Chiefs *should've* given her a fair trial. But they didn't.

No one ever does or feels or thinks what they *should*. Only what they *expect*.

And maybe, on her final day, this is what Daeo is learning: To let go of all expectations and imperatives. Life is flux. Divergence is law. Reality is chance. And *should* is a meaningless word.

"Worse, it's a wasted word," it's as though Tagi heard her thoughts.

"*Huh?*" Daeo squints into the blood-red sunrise, joining Tagi beside his fire pit.

"Here, eat this with your *tyrkuna,*" he offers her a pale *Kamaruna* mushroom, along with a steaming bowl of grasshopper broth. "I'd rather you take it alongside me than the others." Daeo takes both and sits beside him, draping her empty baby blanket across her lap like a giant napkin.

"How's your *tynji?*" Tagi asks reluctantly. He'd hoped Bowi would be well enough to join them on their walk down to the *Aeo*. But now, judging by the moans emanating from inside the cave, Tagi thinks, *Have I made any progress with the boy at all?*

"He'll be okay," Daeo says. "I'm not worried."

Blinking, Tagi looks back and forth between the little girl and the cave's dark mouth. Daeo usually speaks in a quick, anxious manner; pleading, childlike, desperate to be believed. *Ragran-eena.* But that fluid statement, delivered without any hesitation or stammer, is perhaps the most believable thing Tagi's ever heard her say.

"Yes, he'll be okay," Tagi agrees, relaxing into her certainty. "And so will we." At this point, his brain is so thoroughly plasticized by *Kamaruna* mushrooms, he can be convinced of anything.

Daeo doesn't feel any fear as she and Tagi eat breakfast, nor as she nibbles on her *Kamaruna* mushroom. Willing. Curious. Excited, even. The open blanket across her lap unfurls like a massive petal. Each woven feather is a healed scar. Positive emotions well like dewdrops on the surface of Daeo's heart.

Meanwhile, tucked inside her waistband, her hidden *mabato* shard now feels like an unnecessary encumbrance. Friend? Foe? She pulls it out, bloodstained and whittled. A dagger. A knife. Has it always been this sharp? Tagi doesn't notice Daeo stake it into the ground behind her. She intends to leave it there. What was once a tool became a weapon, and Daeo has no use for weapons anymore. She'd rather accept fate than challenge it, rise and meet it no matter the cost.

Because really, that's still all Daeo suspects *Kamaruna* to be: A big bluff.

Her life can't just end... Can it?

"*Eeao!*" Tagi summons once they've finished eating. "*Eeao!*"

The kitten comes lumbering in from the surrounding foliage, dragging behind her yet another small *kynaea* offering (no one seemed impressed by the hatchling's head she left last night). A conspicuous trail of bloody, pink feathers marks her repeated path.

Daeo winces, alarmed by the sudden vivacity of each color, each feather, each molecule of blood. When did the world start looking like this? Nothing appears stable. Visible light warps and congeals as it funnels into her pupils. Magnified, intensified—photons trampoline off the backs of her retinas, one by one by one, each a micro-dimensional bit of information. Distortion or clarity? Daeo can't tell. But after eating that mushroom, she's certain she now has the eyes of an entirely new animal.

"Is this how you see the world, *Eeao?*" she giggles down at the kitten, who blinks up at her, bug-eyed and ballooned in Daeo's perception. Now nearly a full-grown tabby, Eeao fits perfectly in Daeo's lap; she jumps up as soon as the girl sets her empty bowl aside to make room. Purrs ripple across Eeao's blood-smattered fur.

"That'll work perfectly," Tagi observes, watching Eeao settle herself upon Daeo's feathered lap. "Wrap her up in your blanket."

"What?" Daeo twirls her finger through Eeao's tail. "Why?"

"So you can carry her to the *Aeo,*" Tagi explains. "Fold the corners of the blanket around her and tie—"

"No," Daeo recoils, pressing Eeao against her chest. She'd assumed the old man's earlier ramblings were nothing more than sleep-gibberish. "We cannot actually bring *Eeao* to *Kamaruna.*"

"Why not?" Tagi flips the question.

Daeo free falls into his mirror, his reflection, the way his ideas bounce into hers.

"Why not?" she repeats. "Why not? I... I do not want *Eeao* to die."

"Do you believe you will die today?"

Daeo bites her lip. "No," she admits, feeling guilty—somehow, despite full confidence in her own survival, she knows today will be Tagi's last.

"Then take *Eeao* with you," Tagi insists, more certain of his dream than even his own map. "She won't die today either. I'm sure of it. And if the two of you stay together, your odds of survival will multiply."

"But..." Daeo looks down at Eeao, who's begun to knead gingerly at her knees. The idea of entrapping such a free-spirited, aloof creature inside a blanket seems cruel to Daeo. Inhumane (though their language has no equivalent word). She already unwrapped one baby. Isn't this a step backward?

"Are you sure this is a good idea?" Daeo and Eeao make eye contact.

"I'm not sure of anything," Tagi chuckles. "So why not try something new?"

"But—"

"Stop asking questions," Tagi smiles at her. "You already know the answers."

Chapter 66
"Eeao"

The alpha is acting strange today.

Well, this whole morning has been strange.

First, the old man's rude awakening. Next, the boy's heightened musk (though Eeao typically finds Bowi's smell repugnant, today he reeks of the sharpest fear-odor she's ever sniffed, like his entire endocrine system simmered overnight). And now, after venturing off for an early-morning hunt, mainly to put some distance between herself and the acrid boy, she's returned to find her alpha smelling just like the old man—that strange, earthy, chemical scent he's adopted lately.

Those unremarkable white growths they keep plucking from the ground... The alpha has eaten one, hasn't she? Hmm. Surprising. Eeao feels it's her responsibility to investigate, evaluate, maybe emulate. She wouldn't dream of mimicking the old man's behavior, nor the foolish boy's, but the little girl is an animal she admires. Perhaps those odd, tiny fungi are tasty?

The kitten hops onto Daeo's lap. She sniffs at the feather blanket, nosing around for a mushroom. Nothing. She looks up to assess her companions, but both humans seem tense. Are they even breathing? Flexing her claws against Daeo's lap, Eeao looks her alpha straight in the eye. She senses something is about to happen, something unexpected, another surprise...

And then she's folded up inside the little girl's blanket like a bagged *pomaeo*.

Snuffed, Eeao succumbs to black feathers. Whiskers, tail, ears, eyes—everything disappears in a blink. Eeao doesn't realize what's happening at first—her paws slip out from under her as Daeo wraps her, round and round, like a bundled baby—so her first instinct is to panic. But she can't even thrash, her limbs are so tightly wound. She opens her mouth to *eeao!* but downy fibers clog her throat. Sure, she can breathe through them. But she's ensnared nonetheless. And the sensation of paralysis triggers a traumatic memory:

This has happened before.

Predator, snake, trap—Eeao doesn't know words, just instinct.

"*Shhh... Shhh...*" Daeo squirms against the kitten's thrashing. "It is okay, *Eeao*, do not worry."

The kitten seizes, desperate to escape.

"Here, let me help you," Tagi plucks the blanket from Daeo's hands, cartwheeling Eeao's orientation yet again. Claws extended, Eeao manages to nick Tagi's hand through the woven-feather barrier. "*Oww!*" Tagi flips the blanket around, tying its four corners in a knot to bind Eeao's four paws. Then, flipping the bundle upside right, he carefully creates a small hood in the blanket's upper folds for Eeao's head to poke through.

"There," he struggles against the kitten's convulsions. "Oh come now, *Eeao*. At least you're comfortable. You don't even have to walk."

Eeao glares out at them through the hood of her straightjacket.

"Here, I can calm her down," Daeo reclaims her baby, settling Eeao's swaddled form in the crook of her elbow.

Indeed, the transfer helps. Daeo's scent neutralizes Eeao's flashback—she realizes she's wrapped in feathers, not snake scales; and better yet, these feathers smell like the hands of the girl who rescued her. Moons flash in rapid succession. The snake is long dead. Nothing hurts. Eeao's mind catapults forward through time, arriving back to the present moment.

She stills. She purrs. She sinks into her alpha's arms.

Why be afraid?

Right here, right now, Eeao knows she's safe.

Better yet, her height tripled and she didn't even have to jump for it.

Aloft, pressed against Daeo's chest, the kitten settles hesitantly, side-eyeing everything through her hood. What does this new position mean? Eeao has never been carried like this.

Docile. Tended. Babied.

She doesn't remember the day Tagi found her, almost twelve moons ago. She doesn't remember the way he scooped up her little body with his own hands, or the way he nursed her back to life with *raea* formula. She doesn't remember her birth on the moon. She doesn't remember her mother or littermates. She doesn't remember the spacecraft or fireball. She doesn't realize how much she's grown. Or why she's here.

But she remembers what it's all felt like—life, trauma, gravity, hope.

And here she is again. Suspended in the arms of the creature she trusts most.

What could possibly happen?

Anything.

"Ready?" Tagi asks. His cauldron is empty. The fire is out. He's already tidied his cave, stocked and organized his medicinal tools for Bowi to manage—he even filled the water basin with an armload of fresh *pomaeo* yesterday, though he has no memory of doing so. What's left?

Today.

"Ready," Daeo nods. Her baby is light; she hugs Eeao to her heart, and then takes Tagi's weathered, old hand in her own.

Fingers entwined, slipping into psychedelia, Tagi can't tell if she's Daeo, his old *Teerta*, or somehow both.

"Will you keep me?" he asks without meaning to. "After I'm gone?"

His question sends ribbons of light rippling across Daeo's visual field. Tree trunks bend and sway as though underwater, influenced by his stream of language. In her arms, Daeo feels Eeao shift within her swaddled pouch.

Breathing. Everything is breathing.

"Keep you?" Daeo giggles at Tagi's question. "I do not have a choice. *Braeam* is forever..."

The word for *love* tastes fizzy.

Cocooned, Eeao tries to get comfy as her carriers embark into the jungle, straight toward the sunrise. To her, the morning is misty and unremarkably gray. But to Daeo and Tagi, the forest around them writhes with seemingly new colors. Braided cords of fuschia and teal *wykyno* frame their path, climbing all the way up the forest's arched canopy; their flowery, ruby-veined leaves unfurl in early-morning bloom. Elsewhere, pale streaks of lichen glimmer like malachite, half-extinguished in the emerging sunlight.

Airborne scent molecules drift past Eeao's whiskers, which poke and twitch beyond the lip of her hood. *Kynaea* directly overhead. *Camraea* further down the path. Her litter-box swamp bubbles from the opposite direction. Eeao can even detect the amphibious odors of mud-burrowing toads and newts just underfoot. Tantalizing chemicals pop and sizzle from all directions—yet she can't pursue any. She's a passenger. A willing prisoner. She surrendered her autonomy to the nose-blind humans, and now must go wherever they take her.

Oh well.

This is the first time in her life Eeao has ever taken a day off.

Why not enjoy the luxury?

Chapter 67
"Aeo"

Geologically speaking, the *Aeo* is a fairly boring lake.

Freshwater, it exists in volumetric equilibrium.

Drawing from a deep, continental aquifer, which rests like a kettle upon a sprawling bed of heated magma (the source of Yellowstone's ancient supervolcano), the *Aeo* draws hot water up through a narrow, geothermal fissure in its lowest point, evaporates excess steam off its surface, and then tops off again with cool water whenever it rains. Its shoreline is stable, only ever spilling over its northeastern bank during the worst typhoons. Its ecological niches are monopolized by a handful of robust species—one type of fish, one type of crustacean, one type of amphibian, one type of water snake, one type of algae, one type of plankton, one type of lily, one type of reed. Sure, the *paen-aemo* patrol is new, but, if anything, the competition they provide, along with their nutrient-rich guano, only serve to stabilize the lake's ecosystem further.

Really, the *Aeo* hasn't seen any actual change in almost a million years.

Not since it formed in the aftermath of Yellowstone's last eruption.

Built from the scar of that ancient doomsday, the *Uyi*'s igneous foundation is solid and unchanging, the *Aeo* regulated to hydrothermal perfection, Yellowstone's volcanism tempered and repurposed for ecological symbiosis.

At this point, the place is more of a terrarium than a naturally occurring biome.

And that's due, in large part, to the collaborative efforts of fungi and insectoids.

Beneath the lake, feasting off the corpses that sink to its bottom, a massive network of aquatic mycelium regulates the basin's health—if the nearby swamp is a fungal city, the *Aeo* is a fungal nation. Distinct from the swamp's mycelium, however, which sprout from the cuticle yeasts already present on its *Meemmal Kunjaruna* victims, the *Aeo*'s superorganism proliferates directly from the human *patu*s it consumes every *Kamaruna*.

A special, semimonthly diet, genetically manufactured one million years ago.

Deep beneath the water, decomposing around the fissure, human skeletons feed a luminous entity.

The *Fae* are willing caterers. Attuned to most chemical languages and intelligent enough to realize the benefits of what they're doing, the insectoids feed their fungal nurseries whatever finely-tuned diets they require. Elsewhere on Earth, across all seven continents, similar terrariums exist for similar purposes. *Fae* enjoy the chemical byproducts these massive, underground fungi produce and siphon into the soil, the water, the atmosphere; the entire planet hangs in the carbon-tapered balance of these symbiotic superorganisms. And together, fungi and *Fae* have maintained their optimal, global hothouse for hundreds of thousands of years.

Meanwhile, humans, their original creators, are now their most coveted prey.

Genetic Revolution?

Genetic Insurrection.

Hyphal roots hold Earth by its crust, spanning tectonic plates and ocean chasms alike, regulating each continent to biogeological perfection.

But *Homo sapiens* are their mothers.

Humans harbor their spores. Humans germinate their colonies. Humans sacrifice their bodies in various ways as fertilizer—their skeletons populate the *Aeo*'s rocky floor, each one encrusted in dense, violet hyphae, parasites intelligent enough to first incubate their hosts' skin before rationing the marrow in each bone for hundreds of years at a time, only to then channel the nutrients back into the soil, the water, the air.

The system works. Earth loves it.

And do humans know any better? One million years later?

Of course not.

When it comes to remembering, humans would rather forget. They don't like their histories, and they're afraid of the future. They see trees as objects, and hear only silence from the ground; the language of mycorrhizae far surpasses their scope of intelligence. They'd rather eat mushrooms and rationalize everything as something meaningful to their own senses. Something solipsistic. Self-serving. Human-centered.

As always.

They have no idea how biology has surpassed them.

They don't even realize the freedoms they've lost.

They all succumb to the same enemy: Their own creation. Over and over and over and over again.

They just do it in different ways.

For example: Tagi and Daeo willingly join today's *Kamaruna* volunteers while their *punteeku* overseers cackle and make bets on which ones they think will scream first. The rest of the *Uyi*'s human population is already gathered along the *Aeo*'s southern treeline, where the towering jungle hangs over the lakeshore like a verdant tidal wave, petrified mid-crash.

No one seems to care that Daeo brought her baby blanket to the ceremony. The man who ties a rope around her ankles lets her hug it while he cinches. Folded inside, Eeao's hooded face is barely perceptible. At one point, Daeo thinks she sees a female *punteeku* eying her bundle suspiciously, narrowing her eyes at her like Kleeo used to, but then the woman proceeds to swat at a fruit fly buzzing around her ear.

Pupils fully-dilated, Daeo hones her vision on the nimble insect. She's never taken time to examine a fruit fly before. Let alone one in motion. But in her current state of mind, its flight trajectory paints a visible trace through the air, a gleaming ribbon of recent travel; she predicts and follows its movements with ease. Delicate legs fold beneath its body like silk eyelashes. The fly's translucent wings don't seem nearly strong enough to do what they're doing—and yet they are. Lift. Propulsion. Thrust.

The large woman swats blindly as the fruit fly loops around her head, but Daeo has it locked in her sight. She admires the little pest. Compared to the mobility of a fly, humans are a subdimensional species, trapped on a single, flat plane. How maladaptive. Life is afforded so much space, and what has the human species done with it? Daeo wishes she'd been born with wings. Feathered. Membraned. Any type would do.

Is it too late to grow some?

Speaking of trapped, Eeao is beginning to fidget in Daeo's arms. The kitten had been comfortable the entire trek down to the *Aeo*, wedged gracefully against Daeo's heartbeat. But now the luxury of the experience is wearing off. This game isn't fun anymore. Eeao can smell their proximity to the lake, and it's making her nervous. Why would they travel all the way out here? Unusual behavior. And where did all these extra humans come from? Eeao knows she's safely hidden, inconspicuous in her alpha's arms, but she still feels surrounded. Today has been so strange. Why is any of this happening?

Eeao tries to wiggle a paw free, but her ankles are bound as tightly as Daeo's.

"Hold still," the man is back, this time with a huge chunk of sediment to tie around Daeo's feet.

Daeo flips her blanket around, depriving Eeao's outward view.

Now, nose pressed against the girl's heart, Eeao begins to relax again. No scent can overpower her alpha's. No vibration can compete with her pulse. Everything else melts away. Caressed in feathers, Eeao lets her body go limp.

Naptime.

Beside them, tied to his own heavy rock, Tagi smiles. Though his mushroom-addled mind wavers in and out of focus (remember, he's eaten two mushrooms this morning), he's fully aware of Daeo and Eeao, their close presence, the way they're embracing each other. Unbidden, his thoughts flow back to that first day he found the kitten, a precious gem extracted from fiery wreckage. Burnt. Scarred. Alive. She fell asleep against his chest so quickly that first night, so naturally, they made a habit out of it. *Has she grown at all?* In his mind, they're all babies once again, helpless, bound to new umbilical cords...

"*Aruka-om-uka,*" the old man muses. *Some things never change.*

Yet right now, the *Aeo* is changing.

Finally.

After ages of stagnation, the *Aeo*'s mycelial entity is waking from its pampered, multi-millennia-long stasis. Warning signals from its sister entity (the swamp) have been buzzing around the lake's perimeter for several spore-cycles now—minor nuisances that keep adding up. The two fungal entities evolved to function in harmony, but major mycorrhizal hubs (underground channels through which the *Aeo*'s fungal bed exchanges nutrients with the swamp) have fallen inactive. On the other side of the *Uyi,* the swamp is suffocating beneath Eeao's gut bacteria, and the *Aeo* is only now hearing its screams. What had at first seemed like a minor problem that would fix itself is now a full-blown emergency.

The swamp is dying. The *Uyi* demands aid.

Ugh, drama.

Thus far, the *Aeo* has done its best to remain undisturbed. But today, it detects a new infochemical bleeding through the daily mycorrhizal chatter: Allelochemicals. More bite than bark, fungi reserve these agents for combat against only the most extreme pests. Unlike the failed defense chemicals and faux-pheromone signals the swamp utilized earlier, allelochemicals have one purpose: To exert physiological damage on the surrounding environment. Potentially suicidal, this offensive tactic hinges on the fungi's ability to exterminate its pest before exterminating itself.

A gamble. A risk. Death versus survival.

Earlier this morning, in one final gasp of vitality, the swamp's fungal body ejected a stream of these potent molecules into its mycorrhizal channel. Like *pomaeo* juice infused into a vein, the message now circulates throughout the *Uyi's* underground network.

Tree roots slacken. *Wykyno* leaves curl. Though cryptic, the jungle understands this warning.

PREPARE TO ABORT

But the *Aeo* is annoyed. Allelochemicals haven't been employed on this side of the continent in hundreds of thousands of years. At this point of evolution, they're ecologically taboo.

Radical. Dangerous. Mutually catastrophic.

The swamp intends to uproot the entire *Uyi*.

And now, the *Aeo* sees the swamp as the pest.

Chapter 68
"Nyno"

The only upside to sustained torture is that eventually, over time, torture becomes comfortable. A natural ebb and flow arises between cycles of pain and recovery, tension and release.

How long does a kick actually last? Mere moments. The pain afterward is uncomfortable, but that's all it is. Pain. Memory. It's nothing dangerous. The punch happens, and then it's over. Impact occurs, and then the body does what it needs to do to heal—or, at least, prepare for the next one. It's like a dance. Any length of downtime in between blows makes the chronic bouts of suffering feel worth it.

Outright slaughter implies apathy between predator and prey.

At least abuse mirrors the cyclic nature of symbiosis.

Imprisoned inside her own *capku,* Nyno's days pass like grueling endurance tests. But at least nighttime offers the sweet, satisfying reward of sleep. Plus *Kamaruna* mushrooms. She can always count on receiving one of those before bed.

"Shut up and sleep," last night, Kleeo had been the one to administer the hallucinogenic pearl. She's still here this morning, presiding over Nyno like a resentful prison guard.

"Enjoy your beauty rest?" Kleeo scowls as Nyno pulls herself awake—still tied to her *capku's* center pole, Nyno sleeps in a small nest she's clawed into the ground while her sleeping mat remains mercilessly out of reach. Scabbed and speckled with welts, she flinches away from Kleeo, expecting a good-morning kick.

"Eat a *Kunjaruna* mushroom and get to work," instead, Kleeo extends a tiny, brown morsel toward Nyno's nose. Nyno grimaces—*pick your poison*. Ever since Maetri forced her to eat one, the Chiefs added a mandatory *Kunjaruna* dose to her morning regimen; cluttered around her *capku*, newly-made harnesses and satchels outnumber the *Uyi's* entire human population.

But by now, Nyno has lost count of everything. She's lost track of the moon's cycle. She can't even appreciate how productive she's been. Lost in a swirling, nightmarish miasma, Nyno barely remembers who she is. She just works and sleeps, sleeps and works. The routine is far from fulfilling.

But at least it's a routine.

"But it's your turn to watch her!" Kleeo snarls.

"I'll be back after the ceremony," Maetri's voice.

When did he arrive? Nyno looks up, startled to find both a new person in her home and a newly-woven satchel already assembled in her lap. *Did I make this?*

"I spent the whole night here!" Kleeo rants. "My shift is over! It's your turn!"

"I'm needed at the *Kamaruna* ceremony," Maetri towers over his sister, easily dwarfing the already-large woman. Beneath them both, Nyno feels like a newt in a boiling pot.

"You're needed?" Kleeo scoffs. "Why? Just because you're a Chief?"

"You know the rules," Maetri shrugs. "Stop being jealous."

Kleeo's eyes bulge; Nyno flinches, expecting one to pop out of the woman's skull and pelt her in the face.

"Besides, you should be grateful," Maetri continues. "I only stopped by on my way to the ceremony to give you these," he proffers a handful of ivory *Kamaruna* mushrooms.

Kleeo snorts. "*Tapati* is my source. I don't need contraband from you."

"Do you have any on-hand right now?" Maetri cocks an eyebrow.

Kleeo rolls her eyes. "Only *Kunjaruna* ones, for her," she points down at Nyno, the animal they're keeping alive. "Here, eat another one," she jams a second, fibrous spore down Nyno's throat.

Nyno gags, swallows, and then begins work on another satchell.

"You'll want these today," Maetri extends the offer again, side-eyeing Nyno. And then, in a lower voice, "Once the *Kamaruna* ceremony begins, she'll be able to hear it. She might freak out. Better tranquilize her with a mushroom. Give her the day off. Understand what I mean?"

"What's so special about today's *Kamaru*—"

"Her *babo* is volunteering," Maetri hisses.

Nyno looks up. *Babo?*

"Finally!" Kleeo exclaims. "About time! This stupid drama has gone on long enough. Once the *babo* is gone, everything can go back to normal, right?"

"Shut up!" Maetri snaps.

Babo? A synapse fires again in Nyno's brain, inducing a cascade of neural reactions. Her fingers stop moving. Her vision tunnels—Daeo's glittering face materializes at the end of it, a bright focal point in a sea of black ambiguity. And then the baby comes into focus, side-by-side with Daeo, a tiny, non-luminous figure cloaked in feathers. *Patummal. Meemmal.* How did her daughters end up looking so different from each other? *So different from myself?*

"Eat this," Kleeo's fingers invade Nyno's mouth again.

Nyno sputters, but the welcome flavor of *Kamaruna* abates her gag response. *Is it nighttime already?* She chews and swallows, eager to pass out.

"Well, now she's had both *Kunjaruna* and *Kamaruna* mushrooms this morning," Kleeo snickers. "This should be interesting. Got a *Kosharuna* mushroom? We could give her the full trifecta."

"Encourage her to sleep," Maetri dismisses the idea, making his way to exit the *capku*. "*Aevi* double-dipped on mushrooms once and flooded my place with vomit."

"Eww..."

"Just don't let her die," Maetri says. And then he's gone.

Babo. It's the only word from their conversation Nyno understood. Now, she believes she can see them, her daughters, her girls—they're at the end of this long, black tunnel that's materialized around her. But whenever she tries to reach for them, the tunnel lengthens. Daeo is dark and glimmering. The baby is freckled and patchy. They both look scared.

But Nyno's arms aren't long enough. *Were they ever?*

"Get comfy," Kleeo is kneeling beside her now. "You're in for a long day."

Somewhere outside the *capku*, beyond Nyno's hallucination, a hollow drum *boom!*s in the distance. Soon another joins its rhythm. And then another. A ceremony is beginning...

Kamaruna!

All at once, Nyno sees the rock tied around Daeo's ankles. She sees her baby choking, drowning. Her daughters are both submerged. It's happening again. *It's happening right now!*

Boom! Boom! Boom!

"NO!" Nyno springs to her feet.

Kleeo kicks out one of her knees, knocking Nyno to the ground. Nyno struggles to get up again, but Kleeo is already on top of her. "Where do you think you're going?" she cackles, straddling Nyno's chest, crushing her lungs beneath her weight.

Writhing in the dirt, Nyno believes her *ameema* has morphed into a giant snake—and it's squeezing her to death! She tries to punch at its green, angular face, its beady eyes, but it recoils too quickly, deflects, bites her hand. Fangs pierce flesh. Nyno screams.

"Calm down," Kleeo snickers, rattling her spiked harness. "You're going to hurt yourself."

"N-no!" Nyno gasps for air. She swings at the serpent again, but this time slices her forearm. "*D-Daeo!*"

"Shut up and sleep," Kleeo bashes Nyno's head into the ground.

The moon erupts before Nyno's eyes. Shards of silver burst in all directions. The entire lunar sphere disintegrates outward in shimmering ripples, undulating shockwaves against the blackness of space, until only a belt of reflective debris remains, a silver ring orbiting a deep, whorling void. What was once the moon is now a black hole so intense Nyno can't bear to look straight into it.

But she has to.

It's that tunnel. Her daughters are inside. She needs to reach them! She forces herself to look.

Only this time, the girls are gone.

Instead, her son fills the focal point.

He's inside an unfamiliar cave. Alone. Folded over himself. Crying.

Bowi. Nyno has seen this before. Not the cave. But Bowi, like this. Strings of snot, saliva, and vomit dangle from his mouth and nose. He's sobbing. He's heaving. Behind the *capku,* every morning before dawn. In the waste pit, that day he found her miscarrying. And then the next time. And the next. Should he have seen all that? *He was the only person who helped me.*

Soaked in sweat, Bowi's arms encircle his abdomen. He's hugging himself, holding himself, bracing himself.

Nyno feels herself suffocating.

And then Bowi vomits. Everywhere. Again. And again. And again. And again.

Alone. Always alone.

Why is he alone! Why hasn't the Teerta *healed him!* Nyno tries to leap into the void, dive straight through, but the vacuous space-tunnel lengthens. *"Bowi!"* she screams into it. *Can he hear me?* She sees him so clearly, his whole body aglow, shaking and retching—*he's right in front of me!* Why can't she cross the void? Traverse the tunnel? Hold her *babi?*

When did I lose my children!

She can't remember the exact day, the exact moment, the exact reason she lost them. But here they are. All of them. One by one. Her whole family.

Alone.

"Please," Nyno hears Bowi crying to himself. "I just need the pain to stop."

Nyno feels the pain too. In her heart. A crushing tightness, a sputtering wail. *What did* Bowi *look like as a baby?* She can't remember. Her firstborn was such a blur, such an overwhelming rockslide of events that only ended with her getting pregnant again. And again. And again. Eight miscarriages. Three babies. *Was he ever my baby?*

YES!

"BOWI!" Nyno screams. She feels time rushing around her, wispy currents of light coursing into the tunnel, photons succumbing to the void's immense gravity. *Why can't I?* She longs to be sucked through the portal, delivered to her son. But something's anchoring her in place. *"BOWI!"*

"I said shut up," Kleeo groans, bored of sitting atop her deranged prisoner. "Don't make me tie you upside down."

Nyno hears the snake hissing, tightening its scaly muscles around her abdomen.

And that's when she realizes something: Bowi *has been feeling my pain this whole time.* Purging. Heaving. Desperate to undo what's been done. With nowhere else to go, his pain harbors in his stomach, a churning typhoon that floods his esophageal barrier. Nyno knows this pain. Not the exact type. But she knows the way it cycles, the way it hijacks the body, the way it kills all hope.

Torture. Injustice. Trauma.

"Please," Bowi continues laboring in the cave. "I just want the pain to stop."

"Give it to me!" Nyno cries, clawing for her son. "You don't deserve it! It's my pain! It's been my pain this whole time! Let it go, *Bowi!* Please! Let me hold it for you! Let it go! Give it back to me!"

The tunnels warps around Nyno, tightening like a vice. Her window into Bowi's cave blinks once, twice, and then he's gone. Vanished. Eaten by darkness. And the moon's final, orbiting shards evaporate into empty space.

"What are you babbling about?" Kleeo is now sprawled across Nyno, pinning her arms and legs to restrain her thrashing. "Hold still, you're only going to hurt yourself." She's sick of playing *momo* to this tantruming child.

That's when the nausea hits.

Inexplicably, without warning, Nyno and Kleeo lurch in opposite directions, both spewing vomit across the *capku*.

Chapter 69
"Uyi"

Bowi feels better.

He doesn't know how. He doesn't care why.

Wiping vomit from his lips, he jumps to his feet and races toward the *Aeo*.

With one hand, he carries Daeo's fossil: *"Atrypa,"* she'd said. With the other, he grabs a *pomaeo* on his way out of the cave: *"Never skip* tyrkuna," Tagi sings in his mind. Heading toward the nest-bound trail, a bloodstained glint catches his eye—something staked into the ground, near the charred fire pit. Daeo's *mabato* dagger. Acting on impulse, he picks that up too, tucking it into his waistband.

Has *Kamaruna* started? He imagines he can hear the distant, ceremonial drums.

Boom! Boom! Boom!

Bowi runs.

As usual, Tagi's trail is clear and broad, offering Bowi a stretch of ground wide enough to gallop. The day is misty and temperate, the morning only beginning to grow warm. Bowi maximizes his lungs with each breath, determined to maintain his running pace.

Where did this strength come from? His stomach feels relaxed. Numb almost. And there's barely any hint of vomit on his tongue. He slows for a moment, but only long enough to puncture the *pomaeo* with his thumb and take a quick swig; his stomach welcomes the electrolytes. And then he doubles his pace, imagining Daeo and Tagi at the end of the trail, waiting for him, their faces beaming. He needs to see them one last time, to memorize every detail, to hear their voices, to touch their hands, to keep them forever in his mind—he'd wasted so much time—he didn't even speak to Tagi today—he needs to give Daeo one more hug goodbye—sing her one more song—then he'll be happy—or at least content—slightly proud—less ashamed—not a complete failure—

"Please!" he screams into the trees. "I need the pain to stop!"

An immense ache swells in his heart, like its four chambers are brimming with tears. But at least, compared to nausea, Bowi finds this pain tolerable. At least he can run.

Beneath his feet, allelochemicals surge even faster.

The *Uyi* is preparing for something, though it doesn't quite understand what. A victimized bystander in the ongoing saga between the swamp's mycelium and Eeao's fecal bacteria, the jungle has weathered (albeit painfully) the underground storm thus far and considers the introduction of allelochemicals as more of an overdue blessing than a final death blow. The *Uyi* doesn't mind tanking some damage. Anchored by its own deep, interconnected root system, the rainforest knows it can easily reproliferate off whatever microorganisms survive this fungal catastrophe.

Sure, some roots will tear. Some trees will fall. Some landmass will flood. And most animals will die. But the jungle itself is widespread and well-drained, built upon the fertile, geothermal graveyard of its fossilized ancestors, flora buried one million years ago beneath magma and ash. Land animals are a mere luxury as far as this biome is concerned. Pretty, but expendable. Useful, but also pretty useless. They can be replenished over time. And from elsewhere.

No, the *Uyi*'s plant life isn't worried about the oncoming war.

It knows the only real casualties will be the oblivious land animals colonizing its terrestrial skin.

Like Bowi. And everyone else.

But Bowi feels strong—stronger, perhaps, than he's ever felt in his whole life. Powered by adrenaline, love, and pure rage, he tears through the rainforest, eager and free. Something about his movement, his rhythm, the interlacing melodies of his breath and heartbeat—something about his presence causes leaves to open toward him.

Newfound inhibition. Tectonic drift.

Unburdened, untethered, Bowi emanates his own gravity. And as he races past, *wykyno* blooms slowly, imperceptibly unfurl in his direction.

The *Aeo* and the swamp are at a stalemate. But the *Uyi* is eager for war. The rainforest welcomes change. It loves change. It demands change.

And now, Bowi does too.

Too little too late?

"Wasted words," Tagi tells him.

Bowi runs faster.

The *Uyi* breathes.

Chapter 70
"Fae"

Insectoids: The final piece of this biological puzzle.

"XXXXXXXXXXXXXXXXXXXXXXXXXXXXXX"

Yet just one million years ago, they didn't even exist. An infant species on this planet, they're absent from the fossil record. Detached from the family tree. Still just a blip on the harrowing, multi-billion-year-long timeline of life on Earth.

They didn't even evolve.

Manufactured. Synthesized. Spliced.

Life's perfect, little amalgamations.

Fae.

Their genetic code is so crisp, so durable, even nuclear radiation can't crack its double helix. Equipped with the optimized genomes of each species that went into their creation (dragon fly, wasp, firefly, ant, and, of course, human), *Fae* are the death of evolution.

There's just no room for improvement after them.

Their skeletons are lightweight and biodegradable. They produce zero body waste, and use their own regenerating exoskeletons as building materials. Convergent biology at its finest. If they were to go extinct tomorrow, all traces of their society would decompose and disappear from the face of the planet within a century. No fossils. No ruins. Certainly no petroglyphs. They've ruled Earth for nearly an entire megaannum with fine-tuned precision, but they don't do it for selfish reasons. They don't do it for their own science or philosophy or history or art. They just do it for life itself. Simple as that. They do it because it feels good. It feels right. It feels fun. And when your biology is as supreme as the *Fae*, you can trust your feelings.

Anyway, it's not like the insectoids are going anywhere.

This planet is theirs, and, frankly, everything else on it is lucky to live alongside such an immaculate, peaceful species—fungi especially. Today, the *Aeo*'s mycelium is hungry for its scheduled feeding. The lake has been shoring up its nutrient reserves all day, readying its mycorrhizal channels to subdue whatever underground chaos the swamp may try to unleash. Meanwhile, allelochemicals saturate the *Uyi*'s root network, radiating from the swamp. Clearly, the swamp is angry—which only makes the *Aeo* angrier. Why all the drama? Why now? Currently, the lake is amassing a barrage of defense chemicals to shoot in the swamp's direction—a firm rebuke. But first, it needs to eat.

The *Fae* arrive exactly on time.

"*xxxxxxxxxxxxxxxxxxxxxxxxxxxxxxxxxxxxxxxx*"

"Line up!" the *punteeku* prod today's volunteers onto the lakeshore, Tapati and Syno calling orders. Maetri presides over the procession, impassively standing atop a large boulder, watching—though he purposely avoids eye contact with his chained daughter below. Just over the northern mountains, the *Fae*'s pyramidal formation rises into full view. *Let's get this over with,* Maetri thinks. Except for the old *Teerta,* all of today's volunteers are *Patummal.*

Tagi and Daeo shuffle alongside the others, dragging their bound feet through the sand. Hugging her baby blanket, Daeo can feel Eeao waking from her nap. She presses the kitten's face into her chest, and then cups a hand over her pointy ears, shielding her from the oncoming noise.

Already, people crowd the southern shoreline. Dynjo and her entourage of *momo*s hoist their infants. Armed *punteeku* fan out amid the trees. Adolescents linger near the water's lapping edge, fingers pointed skyward. *Kamaruna* is well underway. And now, for the first time in his life, Tagi realizes this whole ceremony only exists to ensure everyone gets a good view of the horror, the sacrifice—the fate that hungrily awaits each and every one of their *patu*s.

"XXXXXBoom!XXXXXBoom!XXXXXBoom!"

Typically, around the lake's halfway point, the static roar of approaching *Fae* drowns out the humans' ceremonial drumline. But today, Daeo hears every beat, every vibration, every *Boom!*—sonic waves crash through the air and bombard her body, competing frequencies, seismic force. Overwhelmed, Daeo's eardrums quake as her brain scrambles to interpret each wavelength, each tone, each cascade of electrical impulses orchestrated by the maelstrom coming to kill her. In her arms, Eeao whines. Daeo hugs herself, squeezing the kitten tight.

"XXXXXBoom!XXXXXBoom!XXXXXBoom!"

Absorbed, Daeo feels weightless, adrift in a sea of noise.

"Do you think you will die today?" Tagi's voice creates melody from din.

But when Daeo looks beside her, the old man is slack-jawed and mute, staring straight into the sky, his face streaming with tears.

Daeo hugs her baby tighter.

From the *Fae's* perspective, the humans gathered on the lakeshore are easy, welcoming targets. They practically advertise themselves. Their purple-glowing *patu*s attract the insectoids' UV-sensitive eyes like flowers ripe for pollination. What was once a benign, fungal species bioengineered for fad-fashion one million years ago is now a prime indicator of edibility for dominant life on Earth. The *Fae* drone toward the *Aeo's* southern bank, sight locked on their glittering prey.

Still, elsewhere, the *Fae* can't help but notice the rest of the *Uyi's* prevailing dullness. Once-towering *wykyno* stalks now wilt around the lake's perimeter, drained of color and form, phosphorus and magnesium. Cecropia trees are faded yellow, and typically-broad philodendron leaves exhibit curled, brittle edges. The stench of *paen-aemo* certainly isn't helping. This biome is ill, dysfunctional, dying—all the *Fae* agree.

But why?

Several ideas circulate through their ranks, communicated via rapid-fire antennae chatter. Flying low over the *Aeo*, the *Fae* observe the lake itself to be normal, its acidity balanced, algal blooms tempered—they can tell just by tasting steam off its surface that the lake is as healthy as ever. Harbored within their digestive tracts, *Fae* host a variety of microscopic fungi, derivative yeasts cultivated from mycelial nurseries like the *Aeo*, which optimize their digestion by converting intestinal waste into absorbable sugars. Reciprocal influence. It's impossible for insectoids to starve. In return, *Fae* neuroanatomy allows their brains to communicate with their intestinal mycelium via sympathetic, hormonal impulse. Like breathing, like sleeping, like digestion itself, this intimate, symbiotic relationship between *Fae* and their own internal mycobiota is subconscious. A power they don't realize they possess. But it's powerful nonetheless—powerful enough to influence behavior, society, ecosystems. Even real-time diagnostics.

Yes, the *Fae* know in their gut the *Aeo* is fine.

As a group, they decide, once again, that the *Uyi's* diseased organ must be the swamp. Another problem for another moon. Oh well. Today, their duty is to the *Aeo*, and the *Aeo* is perfectly healthy. Business as usual. Next *Kunjaruna*, they decide, is when they'll investigate (meaning they'll increase the swamp's diet to one hundred *Meemmal* and then reassess the situation from there). Nowadays, they expect ecological problems like this to fix themselves. Isn't that how symbiosis is supposed to work?

Really, the *Fae* are just as lazy and clueless as every other species.

No one understands what's actually happening.

Homo sapien. Mycelium. *Paen-aemo*. Feline.

No one sees the full picture.

The gulfs between each creature, each lifeform, each individual cell inside each individual body—the chasms between self and other—are too wide. They all think they're communicating, listening to one another, herding each other, living together on the same planet.

But really, no one is.

They're all disparate, atomic configurations spinning out of control.

Like the Earth. The moon. The sun. The cosmos beyond the atmospheric shroud.

Daeo is as far from her mother as she is from her brother as she is from herself.

But maybe that's the safest place to be.

Cradled in her own arms.

"XXXXXBoom!XXXXXBoom!XXXXXBoom!"

Then again, occupying that same cradle-space, Eeao feels extremely unsafe. To her, it sounds like the sky is exploding with nonstop thunder. She squirms. She whines. She kicks against the blanket binding her body, desperate for escape. She just wants to be alone. To be by herself. To go take a shit alone in the swamp by herself. Everything here is too loud. Daeo is squeezing too tight. Nothing feels good. Everything is scary. Nothing is safe. Something terrible is happening!

"XXXXXBoom!XXXXXBoom!XXXXXBoom!"

The *Fae* are directly overhead. Their buzzing formation whips the lakeshore into a gusty sandstorm. Tapati, Syno, and their fellow *punteeku* back away from the six volunteers. Maetri shields his eyes from dust and flying debris.

But Daeo keeps her eyes open. She glares up at the formation descending toward her. She frowns at the six insectoids who break rank, each honing in on a volunteer.

She squeezes Eeao, herself; one of the identical, winged creatures singles her out.

She's never been so close to a *Fae*.

Now she's afraid.

"XXXXXBoom!XXXXXBoom!XXXXXBoom!"

Its wingspan consumes Daeo's visual field. Its unblinking eyes swallow her face. Chitinous fingers knuckle-lock around her shoulders. The creature smells like *cananeero* nectar and stomach acid. In her arms, a baby shrieks. Daeo looks beside her, but Tagi is already in the air, hoisted by another massive set of dragonfly wings—he's looking back at her, eyes ablaze, mouthing something.

"Ynsyn-eera!"

Daeo loses her footing—no, the ground falls away—no, she's in the air too, wrenched by her shoulders, up into the sky.

Flying. Isn't this what she wanted?

"XXXXXBoom!XXXXXBoom!XXXXXBoom!"

"Eeao!" the kitten finally manages to wiggle her head out of Daeo's blanket.

Alerted by a whiff of strange, feline odor, their *Fae* captor pauses midair while the rest continue ascending. It glances down at its cargo. Its bulbous, tessellated eyes narrow and widen, narrow and widen, scrutinizing the baby blanket in Daeo's arms. Its silver-green face, just a sheen of translucent skin stretched over interlocking muscles and veins, seems to frown.

Eeao rotates her face and frowns back.

"YNSYN EERA!" Daeo screams at her captor.

And then she releases hold of herself. Her baby blanket unravels. And out jumps Eeao, straight at the insectoid's face.

"EEAO!"

Stunned, its dragonfly wings sputter; Eeao sinks her claws into its forehead.

"XEXEXEXEXEXEXEXEXEXEXEXEXEXE"

It's a noise Daeo has never heard before. No one has. Even the other *Fae* are startled by their cousin's unfamiliar, unnatural-sounding scream. The formation glances down to assess this rogue behavior—only to see an ancient, long-extinct mammal perched on their cousin's head.

"XEXEXEXEXEXEXEXEXEXEXEXEXEXE"

Punctured by kitten claws, the insectoid's skin bubbles in allergic reaction.

Panicked, Eeao rebounds, diving groundward, claws damp with some sort of bluish, bodily fluid.

"XEXEXEXEXEXEXEXEXEXEXEXEXEXE"

Looking up into her captor's face, Daeo thinks she sees a humanlike expression of fear. Or is that her own reflection in its bulbous eyes? Behind its head, hovering in formation, the entire horde is now shrieking.

"XEXEXEXEXEXEXEXEXEXEXEXEXEXE"

Eeao lands comfortably on her paws (the *Aeo*'s sandy bank is soft enough), and then she darts off into the jungle, disappearing from sight. The *punteeku* gawk. Dynjo and several other *momo*s scream. Children run after the kitten in pursuit. No one knows what they've just seen.

Except the *Fae* know immediately what Eeao is. An alien bioweapon. An invasive parasite. Something that doesn't belong on Earth anymore.

It's been eight hundred millennia since insectoids finished exterminating most mammalian life from the planet (they're allergic to fur), but *Fae* still have strict protocol for this. Evolved instinct. Generational trauma. Biological memory. This situation is now a dire emergency. The entire *Uyi* is compromised. New plan. Time to uproot.

The injured *Fae* releases its contaminated cargo.

And Daeo freefalls toward home.

Finally, weightless.

Chapter 71
"Tagi"

The sun and half-moon hang on opposite sides of the *Aeo* today.

But Tagi is in the middle of everything, suspended between earth and sun, water and sky.

Yes, he dangles alongside four other volunteers beneath a billowing swarm of insectoids. But none of them matter to him. He's only ever had enough room in his heart for just a few people. And right now, the fact that neither Daeo nor Eeao are beside him anymore means they've escaped *Kamaruna*. His dream came true. He saved them. Maybe just for a day. Maybe a moon. Who knows. But at least for today, he can die knowing he used the rest of his life to give back to those he loves. He's on this death-bound voyage alone. And this knowledge, at least, gives him joy.

You're not alone, you know, his old *Teerta* reminds him.

The sound of her voice makes him both laugh and cry.

I was never alone, was I?

No one ever is.

"XEXEXEXEXEXEXEXEXEXEXEXEXEXEXE"

Tagi's eardrums implode.

The lakeshore diminishes as he's shuttled silently out over the *Aeo.* He sees Eeao spring away into the jungle. He sees Daeo plummet back to the ground, discarded by her *Fae* captor—though her arm appears to snap beneath the force of her fall. Everywhere else, people scatter, alarmed by the *Fae*'s panicked behavior. *Punteeku* trample children. *Momos* duck and cover. *Paen-aemo honk!* furiously at all the noise.

But Tagi hears none of it.

Run! Run! he watches, hoping to see Daeo rise. But she doesn't. She lies motionless where she's fallen. Rolling blue *Aeo* spreads beneath Tagi's feet—high in the air, they're nearing the lake's center—but now Daeo is just a faraway speck, sprawled in the sand, helpless and injured. *Better than sprawled in the water;* the stone tied to his feet swings like a pendulum.

Look! Tagi's old *Teerta* says in his useless, right ear.

Tagi's eyes follow. He squints. Far across the water, on the other side of the lakeshore, he spots a skinny boy crash out of the jungle and sprint down the shoreline. His entire body glows radiant. Yet even from this distance, faceless and blurred, Tagi knows without doubt the boy is Bowi.

Yes! Yes! Tagi has never felt such elation, such euphoria. Sure, he's ingested thirty-one *Kamaruna* mushrooms this month. But right now, witnessing Bowi storm onto the scene, just in time to aid Daeo, not a moment too late—Tagi feels his entire life's work budding to fruition. He gave himself to Bowi, and now Bowi is giving himself back. He trained a new *Teerta.* He renewed the legacy. Imparted the honor. Now, dangling high over his own grave, Tagi knows he's finally ready to go.

And yet, there's so much more he doesn't know. For instance, he doesn't know that he's just been doused with potent pheromones—volatile organic compounds excreted by his *Fae* captors. A mimicry of allelochemicals, concocted by their own mycobiota and secreted through vestigial sweat glands, this is the *Fae's* natural, autoimmune response to a bioterrorist like Eeao. The entire formation is fumigating. By now, all five *Kamaruna* volunteers are thoroughly coated in the vaporous substance. And once dropped into the lake, the *Aeo* will recognize the chemical agents added to its meal as its own allelochemicals.

It will then react accordingly.

It's been nearly three millennia since *Fae* last aborted one of their own mycelial nurseries (a fungal virus mutated and rampaged through an *Aeo*-like colony beneath the former Loch Ness, forcing insectoids at the time to intervene), but knowledge of this rare procedure is practically their lore.

Just as Eeao nuked the swamp with her own gut bacteria, the *Fae* will now nuke the *Aeo* with cargo coated in their own bioweaponry. Their signal will hijack the *Aeo*'s mycorrhizal brain, impelling it to self-destruct along with the swamp.

But to all participating parties, this bombing is not an annihilation. It's a call to action. Fungal intelligence is easily transferable across continents, even around the globe—they've practically formed their own high-speed, mycorrhizal internet, full of impulse avatars and chemical realities, a worldwide web of DNA databases more complex than quantum computing. The entire planet is a permeable, semi-aqueous nursery for these diverse and plentiful superorganisms; its crust teems with hyphal sentience several miles deep. The specific mycelia within the *Aeo* and swamp will survive the *Uyi*'s decimation, as will most trees and *wykyno* species. Anything with escape-hatch access to the mycorrhizal internet will be fine. The goal for these nukes, of course, is to kill everything else.

Anyway, it's fitting, then, that Tagi feels like a bomb. He's ready to crash into the waves. To meet the *Aeo*. To find out what's really down there. To experience the full cycle of life, all the way to its universal fruition. Yes, he's ready to meet his fate, even if it means dissolving his own flesh in the process.

Ynsyn-eera?

Braeam, Tagi's old *Teerta* corrects him. *Love.*

Then his *Fae* captor releases him.

And Tagi falls.

Wind passes slowly up his body.

The Earth is so blue and round beneath him.

What a beautiful view.

Across the lake, he can still see Bowi running, a luminous streak of violet.

And there's Daeo—she's standing up! She's on her feet! She looking out at him!

Yes! Yes! Tagi waves to her.

And then he hits the water.

Everything vanishes. Blue washes black. Tagi holds his breath. And then he begins to wonder why...

Through the murky water, he can see his four other companions by the light of their *patu*s. They're all sinking together at similar rates. One is thrashing. Another is spewing bubbles. Another already looks dead. Tagi smiles, feeling each emotion spread across his chest the way Eeao used to. Looking down, he can see the lake's floor coming into view—a litterbed of radiant human skeletons, thousands upon thousands of his ancestors, luminous fuzz blanketing everyone in a singular, sprawling *patu.*

Breathe, his old *Teerta* looks up at him, her face emerging from endless glitter.

Tagi opens his mouth.

And then his spirit—his soul—that immortal spark of his molecular energy—is severed from his umbilical body.

Come with me.

He's pulled from the *Aeo,* yanked off the planet, and sucked straight into the sun.

Chapter 72
"Oko Mee-uyisa!"

No, the world still isn't ending.

Just this current iteration.

Tumbling midair, Daeo braces her limbs for impact. Nowhere near as nimble as Eeao, she lands on her side—arm extended, her left shoulder absorbs the brunt of her fall, *POP!*ing clean from its socket like a twist-ripped *mabato* spine. She's too shocked to scream. Her baby blanket flutters down after her, landing spread-out across her chest.

Dazed, she lies in the sand, half-deaf and paralyzed from pain, her left arm ratcheted at a severe angle, her feet still tied to a rock. Around her, everyone else is screaming, running in all directions, abandoning her fallen body in mass confusion. Thank goodness. She'd rather they leave her like this. She isn't ready to face the crowd. Not yet. In a way, she feels like she still hasn't landed on the ground, but is suspended in some post-conscious limbo.

Not quite safe, but no longer in danger.

Alive, but not completely.

Staring skyward, the open dome over the *Aeo* looks to Daeo like a massive, blue eyeball; the roving *Fae* horde is its dilating pupil, scouring the ground, searching to reclaim her body.

Yet slowly, the eye looks away...

"xexexexexexexexexexexexexexexexexexe"

With it, Tagi and the other volunteers disappear beyond her visual horizon.

The *Fae* are leaving. *Kamaruna* is ending. And she's still here.

That's when Daeo knows she's free—from scrutiny, from expectation, from death. The *Fae* took her, and she overcame them. *Kamaruna* challenged her, and she called its bluff. Triumph. Now all she has to do is find Eeao, bring her to every *Kamaruna* ceremony henceforth, and then, theoretically, she should be immune from the *Fae* forever!

Right?

Lying in the sand, Daeo breathes...

How will the Chiefs punish her now?

"*Daeo! Daeo!*" a familiar melody emerges over the chaos. "*Daeo! Daeo!*"

Somehow, the voice sounds like Bowi's, Tagi's, and her mother's all at once.

With her uninjured arm, Daeo pulls her baby blanket off her chest and leverages herself to roll over. Sand coats half her body and face. Tiny, shelled organisms flake off her skin and scatter away as she rises to her feet. The sun is so bright, the half-moon crisp against the wispy, sapphire sky. Blinking, disoriented, Daeo gazes out over the *Aeo*—the *Fae* are hovering in the distance, directly over the lake's center.

And then, one by one, five figures plummet into the water.

Four *Patummal.* One Tagi.

"*xexexexexexexexexexexexexexexexexexexexe*"

"Thank you, *Teerta,*" Daeo whispers, unaware of her own tears. And then the *Fae* depart, ascending once again over the northern mountains, succinct and casual, evidently satisfied with today's five victims (really, they're evacuating this half of the continent). Holding her baby blanket over her heart, Daeo promises: "I will keep you forever, *Tagi.*"

And then she hears his voice:

Run!

Deep beneath the sand, the *Aeo* is flexing its mycelial limbs. Already, even as its meal sinks to its maw, the *Fae's* chemical alert has entered the *Aeo's* awareness. Everything makes sense now. Volatile organic compounds seep like allelochemicals through the lake, altering its chemistry just enough to convey a clear message to the fungal entity beneath:

ABORT!

Alright then.

Caught between the swamp's incessant pleas and now a direct order from their insectoid caretakers, the *Aeo* has no choice but to comply. It rapidly converts a portion of its reserved nutrients into allelochemicals, and then disperses its warcry into the *Uyi*'s mycorrhizal system. On a timescale too small to measure, the message escalates like an autoimmune takeover. Catastrophic mutualism. A necessary reset. Painful, but quick. The jungle will be fine. The *Uyi* will recover. Even the mycelial entities beneath the *Aeo* and swamp will equilibrate and restructure the land to their liking within a century or two. This is just a brief illness. A minor transformation. In time, the rainforest's organisms will recover like nothing happened.

But the animals aboveground? With no roots for anchorage? Foolish evolution.

Pain immobilizes Daeo's left shoulder. But at least her fingers and legs are working—using only her right hand, she unties the rope around her ankles, freeing herself.

That's when the ground starts to shake. Beneath everyone's feet, allelochemicals cascade into a biological symphony powerful enough to shatter elemental physics—all at once, cracks splinter across the *Uyi*'s tectonic crust, ruptured by miles and miles of unfurling hyphal roots. Seizing, engorged with water, mycelial veins swell underground like tentacles to ten, one hundred, even one thousand times their normal size, thrusting land and mountains apart like puddy. Uncorked, Yellowstone's deep, geothermal aquifer gushes up through these new fissures, propelled both by the mycelium's hydraulic network and the superhot bedrock underlying the caldera. Overhead, the jetstream circulates, whipped by the sudden upheaval into a violent, *Uyi*-wide whirlwind.

But Deao, she's the fire, the catalyzing ignition.

"Oko mee-uyisa!" someone shrieks.

No. This is how life starts.

Turbulence. Action.

Unbound, Daeo runs.

That's when the ground explodes: *WHOOSH!*

Bodies soar, flung skyward by an immense jet of scalding water. Daeo dodges the geyser, pivoting in the other direction, only to face another eruption—the entire lakeshore is disintegrating! Pockets of sand sink into the ground while geysers flood the spaces in between—in a blink, the once-familiar lakeshore dissolves into a disjointed archipelago, the land fractured by colossal fountains of jettisoned debris, some soaring as high as the clouds. The entire *paen-aemo* population takes to the skies, but not quick enough—pelted by airborne rubble, most of the winged monsters are forced back into the roiling lake.

Honk! Honk! Hon—WHOOSH!

Following a beam of solid ground, Daeo continues running. Back toward the jungle. Away from the *Aeo*, the water. Anywhere but here. Over her limp shoulder, she hears several *punteeku* scream—a sinkhole opens beneath Tapati, Syno, and a legion of other harnessed warriors. They disappear into the earth—and are then belched straight into the sky a heartbeat later. Hydrothermal spray sears Daeo's face, but the pain is no worse than her injured shoulder. She continues running, wrapping her baby blanket around her arm like a sling.

"Daeo! Daeo!" The melody sounds like rain trickling beneath thunder.

That's when she sees him: Bowi is here, running across the shoreline from the other direction! She pauses, tears streaming, trickling around specks of sand plastered to her cheeks—but then another geyser explodes to her left, shooting Dynjo and a group of shrieking *momo*s into the clouds—the volcanic force of it knocks Bowi and Daeo to their knees.

One hundred paces and four giant geysers now separate the siblings. But Bowi feels only adrenaline—he springs back to his feet, identifies a clear path to Daeo (though he'll have to brave a narrow dash between two crumbling sinkholes), and then continues his pursuit.

Around them, bodies and boulders rain. Infants. Mothers. *Punteeku*. Chiefs. Huge *raea* birds launched all the way from the geyser that opened beneath their western field. Chunks of unearthed igneous pour from the sky like hailstones. Ancient blocks of hardened magma—the charred crust of Yellowstone's last eruption—are throttled into daylight, only to crash back to Earth like rejected meteorites; the planet is strong, but its gravity is stronger. People land on their heads. They land in the water. Those that land on solid ground leave craters. But most plummet into widening gorges, sinkholes, chasms formed from hyphal convulsions, and simply disappear forever.

Everything screams—wind, earth—rockets of water whistle into the atmosphere.

But Bowi and Daeo don't hear the commotion anymore. Only their own syncopating energies. Hearts. Lungs. Neural impulses fire against their eardrums, harmonizing the chaos. Bowi feels Daeo's pain like gravity pulling his stomach—he increases velocity, hurtling like a comet toward his sister, impending, unstoppable, nothing exists but the two of them, destined for impact—

WHOOSH!

Another geyser torpedoes from the ground, erupting right beneath Bowi's feet as he runs—the force of it, combined with his momentum, propels him forward—he catapults through the air, clears the remaining space between himself and Daeo, and tumbles into her headlong.

They careen together across the sand.

But Daeo doesn't mind his impact. "*Atrypa!*" She's pleased to see he's still clutching her prized fossil between his hands. Its luck must be working; they're together again, alive and intact.

Well, almost.

"Your shoulder!" Bowi notices Daeo caressing her arm like a detached appendage. Her left shoulder cuff looks like a bruised, deflating *pomaeo*.

"I am fine!" Daeo insists. "We need to keep running!"

And then—*WHOOSH!*—the ground ruptures again, flinging them both to their feet, thrusting them onward—they run simply to absorb propulsive shock. Galloping, pumping their legs, they sprint headfirst into the jungle, perfectly prepared for the world around them to end.

Chapter 73
"Maetri"

Maetri ran the moment the ground rattled.

Up until that point, he'd been calm.

The appearance of that unidentified species (Eeao) hadn't alarmed him. Nor had the *Fae*'s bizarre, sonic response. He didn't even blink when his own *Patummal* daughter plummeted the height of a kapok tree and landed on her shoulder. He only became concerned when her designated *Fae* captor neglected to retrieve her. He watched with mounting apprehension as the horde continued *Kamaruna* with... Only five volunteers?

"You dropped one!" he yelled angrily over the ensuing raucous. But no one seemed to care. The *Fae* left, and everyone else devolved into bedlam, bickering, and speculation.

Something's wrong. Very wrong.

Once that first tremor pulsed beneath the *Uyi*, Maetri took off, back to Nyno's *capku*, responsibilities be damned. He didn't want to stick around just to watch the ground regurgitate his fellow *punteeku*. He didn't care to see his remaining seven brothers blast into the sky, nor did he care to waste time watching Dynjo and all her babies catapult into the *Aeo*. He didn't even consider checking on his doomed *raea* flock.

No. Maetri chose to avoid all that drama because, frankly, Maetri hates drama.

The moment he senses something's wrong, he vanishes. Until he can figure out a way to exploit things.

It's a survival strategy. A way of life. And it's why he's still alive right now.

"*Kleeo!*" Maetri barges into Nyno's *capku*, ripping the entrance flap off its binding cords. Behind him, outside, trees sway back and forth, gyrated by the ground's rippling surface. But inside, the abode is a wreck. Vomit everywhere. Furniture in disarray. Nyno isn't even tied up anymore! Both women are occupying opposite sides of the floor, each keeled over with strings of bile dangling from their mouths and noses. "*Kleeo!*" he roars. "What's going on here?"

"We've been poisoned!" Kleeo gags on her own voice.

"What? Why did you untie her?" Maetri points at their prisoner.

"We need help!" Kleeo dry heaves.

"The whole world needs help!" Maetri retorts. "Don't you see what's happening outside? Can't you feel the ground?"

"I know, I know," Kleeo moans. "*Oko mee-uyisa!*"

"Then pull yourself together!" he yanks her to her feet. She spews a fresh stream of bile across his chest. Maetri gags, nearly vomiting himself. He slaps her face instead. "Come on, *tynjo!* Now is our moment! Our chance! This situation is perfect!"

"Our moment? Our chance for what?"

"*Oko mee-uyisa,*" Maetri repeats. "And when everything ends, something new has to begin. That's how the world works. This is our chance to be that something. To escape our dying society and start a new one in its place. The mountains are crumbling. The *Aeo* is flooding. People are disappearing into the sky. We'll need to start over fresh. Recreate social ranks. Repopulate. But it's new life regardless. New life, *Kleeo.* Don't you understand how great this is?"

Kleeo opens her mouth to respond, but then—*WHOOSH!*—the clearing upon which Nyno's *capku* is situated erupts. The home and its occupants are flung into the towering foliage. Everyone screams. The structure's *hympano* walls cave inward, enwrapping the fragile humans within its soft, leathery cushioning; they crash into the side of a Dinizia tree, and then tumble back to the forest floor, all three of them bundled like babies inside the home-turned-satchel.

"*Ayee kahtopo!*" Kleeo curses—she's landed face-first within the heap of rubble, her arms wrapped by her sides, but her ribs cushioned nonetheless. "What happened?" Overhead, a newly formed geyser sprays furiously into the clouds, white and steaming.

"*Oko mee-uyisa,*" Maetri groans, sick of this whole process. Beside him, Nyno is snuggly wrapped and soundly unconscious. *Good.* He begins tearing himself free of the wreckage.

Suspended above him, Kleeo watches her brother wiggle loose, too sick and tired to unbind herself. "You're the one who poisoned us, aren't you?" she spits down on him.

"WHAT?" her yellow saliva splats across the back of his shaved *patu*. He writhes angrily.

"Those *Kamaruna* mushrooms you gave us!" Kleeo rants. "You laced them with something!"

"I didn't lace them with anything!" he yells up at her. "You're delusional! Now be quiet and let me concentrate on getting myself out! Then I'll help you! *Wyntiko?*"

Kleeo mutters something, but Maetri can't hear her over the rumbling ground—the entire *Uyi* reverberates the cacophony of its own demise. Or is this the sound of new birth? The earth recreating itself anew? Vicious. Guttural. Liberating. Maetri thrashes once, twice, and then tears himself free. Simple enough, though his spined harness is ruined. He crawls out, and then spins around to assess the state of his companions.

Nyno is easy to extricate—she's practically as light as a child, and only bound by a single *hympano* knot around her waist. Kleeo is a different story. The ground quakes as Maetri struggles to untangle and hoist his heavy, harness-bound sister from the wreckage; her spikes come out all broken and askew. But at least the geyser that created this mess was short-lived—it's now just a massive, steaming sinkhole in the ground behind them—and their elevation proved too high to flood. They're safe where they are. For now.

"What! Has! Happened!" Kleeo gawks around at the carnage. "My harness is wrecked!"

"Everything's wrecked," Maetri leers. The earth continues shuddering beneath their feet, making it difficult to stand. He and Kleeo drag themselves (and Nyno) away from the sinkhole, clambering up the side of a scraggly *wykyno* thatch. Insects and newts scramble anxiously beneath their limbs, just as desperate to survive this catastrophe as they are. Around them, massive trees groan against their roots as they bow into the newly formed crater; vines dangle sideways off their branches like eviscerated entrails. Maetri wonders how long it'll take for the huge, immortal trees to snap their roots and succumb to this new terrain. Already, resident *kynaea* and *camraea* disperse from felled branches, abandoning the safety of their former nests in favor of airborne turbulence; most of the birds drop within eyesight, blighted by hailing debris.

And then—*WHOOSH!*—the sinkhole erupts again, spraying another brief but powerful geyser into the sky. Steam wallops Maetri and Kleeo; they gag and cower away from the heated blast. But wedged between them, facing the surge, Nyno watches from deep within a coma, her face expressionless and glistening wet.

"WHAT! IS! HAPPENING!" Kleeo screams over the gurgling roar.

"THE BEST DAY EVER!" Maetri roars back.

Chapter 74
"Eeao"

Today isn't real.

None of this is happening.

That's what Eeao decides, scampering through the jungle, away from that awful, insectoid drone:

"XEXEXEXEXEXEXEXEXEXEXEXEXEXEXE"

The noise drums inside her skull, even after the *Fae* are long gone—phantom signals looping between her brain and traumatized eardrums.

What were those creatures? Pure imagination.

"It went this way!"

Of course this hell includes rowdy children, too.

Are they following her? She feels pursued from all directions. Trapped.

Unless she can manage to wake up.

Because all of this is just a dream. A bad dream.

That's what Eeao decides, clinging to the side of a yellowed cecropia while the ground explodes around her. *WHOOSH!* She's lucky the plant's roots don't tear. She's lucky the geysers spawn on either side of her, rather than right beneath. Nearby, tree trunks and solid stone blast skyward, launched by writhing, fungal roots and hydrothermal pressure. Half of the children who followed her into the jungle are ejected into oblivion, while the other half are left scalded and screaming. Eeao has no other choice but to hunker on her flimsy, shivering cecropia branch and wait for the shockwaves and tremors to pass.

Except the shockwaves and tremors don't pass.

They intensify.

That's when Eeao decides, pivoting in the direction of a tall, sturdy kapok a safe distance from the floodwaters and remaining children, that she isn't in any real danger at all. She never has been. This whole day is just a nightmare.

Vivid, yes—but don't nightmares often seem that way? All she has to do is outrun her own legs, or else find somewhere to defecate, and then she'll wake up. Either course of action should rouse her from a dream... Right?

WHOOSH!

Even flying through the air, launched head over tail, Eeao is still convinced she's asleep. It's just the simplest explanation for all of this. Everything she's witnessed today—the *Fae*, the noises, the carnage—is just an ongoing fever dream. And when she considers her situation like this, her terror becomes so much more tolerable.

The noises will disappear when she wakes up.

The ground will stabilize when she wakes up.

She'll land on Tagi's chest when she wakes up.

Falling, swiveling, Eeao whips her tail around her body, positioning her feet for impact. But rather than the old man's oscillating chest, she lands squarely in a pile of leafy balsa branches, the tree itself uprooted and thrown aside by a separate eruption.

Tangled, cratered within foliage, Eeao struggles to claw her way up and out. Spiders and flightless *kynaea* chicks skitter around her, too vulnerable to flee the timber. But the spry kitten escapes—aided partially by the quaking ground, which helps jostle her upward through the criss-crossing branches. She bolts as soon as she's free, this time in the direction of her beloved swamp.

Awake or asleep, Eeao's internal compass is infallible.

She trusts her gut.

And when your microbiota is as potent as Eeao's, you do whatever it tells you to.

Somehow, the children are still following her—well, the ones who are still alive, at least. Most of them are Daeo's former "friends" (Nomi and Apanati, along with Daeo's half-sister, Neepo). Of course, to Eeao, all hominids look the same. Especially the small ones. But to them, the striped kitten is a familiar omen, a mysterious pattern, the cause of this chaos.

"KILL IT!"

Out of all the creatures in the *Uyi*, it's the children who are on the right track—

WHOOSH!

The remaining children are ejected.

Eeao appreciates the timing. Alone again, save for the ongoing exodus of panicked insects, birds, and reptiles desperate to escape the *Uyi*'s deteriorating understory alongside her, she anticipates the joyous seclusion her clumpy swamp is sure to provide. She's confident its sand alone will jolt her from this terrible nightmare.

Except when Eeao arrives, the swamp is gone.

Completely gone.

A gaping cavern consumes its place; disoriented, confused by the sight of the massive, bottomless sinkhole, Eeao can't fathom how a cave can exist vertically in the ground like this. Should she jump in? Will she reorient to its sideways gravity? Or perhaps wake from this dream? Poised on a broken root jutting out over the enormous chasm, Eeao approaches the sinkhole's crumbling lip.

Is this sheer cliff the cave's floor or roof?

No... It's a tunnel. A free-fall. Death.

Hydrothermal heat gusts from its depths—a growling wind—hungry or nauseous?

Eeao scrambles backward, away from the wide-open maw, which continues to expand, bit by bit, as the earthen crust encircling the swamp's former perimeter continues to dissolve. Mycelial roots, once microscopic, now protrude through the broken ground like lazy tentacles, myriad and engorged to their absolute maximum; the sinkhole's encompassing walls teem with them, like the baleen-packed mouth of a long-extinct whale.

Gone is the clumpy sand.

Gone is the comfort-and-ease.

Devastated, Eeao—*WHOOSH!*—goes flying.

She lands unharmed, again (of course). This time in the vine-tangled mass of a fallen rubber tree. But she has no idea where she is. Or how far she's been launched—the mega-geyser that ate the swamp is the most powerful one she's encountered yet, and now it appears far in the distance, rocketing into the sky. Her whiskers are frayed. Facial fur seared. She's been here before, hasn't she? Taking inventory of herself, Eeao knows these wounds are temporary, but still... Her face stings with pain.

Odd.

Dreams are supposed to be painless... Right?

Oh no. Today is real. Everything's happening.

Oh well. Time to find a new swamp.

Following her gut, Eeao bolts free, this time in a direction she's never taken.

Chapter 75
"Bowi"

"One, two, three—"

POP!

Bowi relocates Daeo's left shoulder—he's seen Tagi perform the trick so many times, he can do it even while the world's ending.

"Great, all better, now keep running!" Daeo attempts to leap to her feet (her brother forced her to lie flat on the ground for this operation), but Bowi presses her down again.

"Careful!" he warns. "You need to keep your arm in a sling from now on. Let me tie you a proper one—this baby blanket won't do."

"Give it to me!" Daeo yanks it back with her good arm.

They're alone in a tiny clearing, encircled within a battered pocket of jungle that's finally fallen silent—save for the mournful shrieks of injured birds and frogs. Beyond the gnarled, buckling trees, floodwaters splash and gurgle from all directions, indicating their plot of forest might be no more than an island marooned amidst an archipelago of whatever's left of the *Uyi*'s surviving landmass.

Though the ground continues to shudder, the tremors are weakening, and becoming more infrequent. After running madly through the jungle all morning, dodging superheated jets, raining debris, and ensuing tsunamis, Bowi and Daeo only intended to pause here long enough to relocate her shoulder. But now, surrounded by raging floodwaters, it seems they've run out of places to run.

"Fine," Bowi retains grip on the baby blanket, holding it taut between them. Discarded on the ground beside them, their *atrypa* fossil is a dormant observer. "But let me tie it in a sling for you. If you don't tie it right, it'll strain the injury."

Daeo huffs, releasing the blanket. Now that her brother is officially the new *Teerta*, it's kind of annoying. But she appreciates his wisdom. They're both exhausted. And even reset, her shoulder remains swollen and excruciatingly sore. Who knows when (or where) they'll be able to rest next? Considering the extensive damage around them, both she and Bowi fully expect the *Teerta*'s timeworn cave to have collapsed during the quakes.

All that *ynsyna...*

How many people disappeared today? Only Bowi understands the full extent.

And even then, he'd only read a few hundred of them.

Working fast, Bowi wraps their old, soggy baby blanket into a makeshift sling, and then he helps Daeo slip it around her arm and shoulder. "There," he says, helping her stand. "Now try to keep your arm still."

But it's time to move again.

Overhead, struggling to absorb the *Uyi*'s hydraulic temperature shock, the upper atmosphere swirls like a vortex. Cross winds pummel the terrain. Competing gusts circulate, propelled by ongoing steam rockets. Hunkering against the cyclonic gale, Bowi grabs their *atrypa* fossil and scrambles with Daeo back into the trees. They find refuge beneath fallen ones: Inside nests of toppled branches, within great balls of upheaved roots, slapdash caves exhumed from the underworld. Somehow, demolished as it is, the *Uyi* abounds with ready-made shelter. At any moment, exploring the limits of their flood-locked island, the siblings need only dive into the nearest pile of vegetative rubble to escape climatic threat. Even wounded and vulnerable, the *Uyi* wants only to give. To protect. To home.

The children are scratched and bruised, but they're alive and moving.

Fallen tree to fallen tree to fallen tree to fallen tree.

Is their *atrypa* fossil lucky? Or is petrification an unchangeable fate?

"So what happened?" Bowi doesn't even think to ask until later that afternoon. As the day-long devastation finally settles, they're afforded a period of respite within a muddy alcove of exposed roots, the tree's capsized trunk extending behind them.

Daeo doesn't know how to answer his question. Earthworm refugees writhe around her feet, peeping their blind heads through the newly excavated soil. Every now and then, distant geysers spout off at random, but these episodes are becoming few and brief—the bedrock's underlying kettle seems to have reached a comfortable simmer.

"I mean, how did you escape the *Fae?*" Bowi clarifies. He's relieved she did, of course—ecstatic even. His sister should be dead in the *Aeo* right now.

But Daeo still doesn't know how to answer.

"Did *Tagi* escape too?"

This question pushes too far.

"No," Daeo bites, glaring at her shoulder. Slung within her re-repurposed baby blanket, her left arm is streaked with bruises, subcutaneous blood cascading from the severed vessels inside her shoulder cuff. Her entire limb tingles. Even her fingers feel fragile. "I am the only volunteer who escaped."

Bowi swallows; the information burns like bile on its way down. Unwillingly, his brain conjures an image of Tagi, blue-faced and drowning. Wrenched by competing gravities, his stomach flips—the return of an all-too-familiar sensation. The ground has been quaking all day, but only now does Bowi feel motion sick.

"How?" he stammers.

Daeo shrugs—and then winces. She tries to explain everything to Bowi: How she carried Eeao all the way to the ceremony, and then how the kitten attacked the *Fae* while the other volunteers were taken, and then how she fell and broke her shoulder while Eeao ran away. But she still can't fathom *how* any of it actually happened. Or why...

Bowi doesn't know what more to say. He's afraid that if he speaks, he might retch. Are they lucky enough to be stranded with a *pomaeo* patch nearby? Doubtful. Dusk is falling, and though the day's chaos dwindles, Bowi feels an internal dissonance brewing.

Facing eastward, housed within their giant, overturned root ball, the siblings watch the sky swirl with dark clouds. Displaced tubers dangle and twist around the alcove's opening, framing their view like hundreds of fingers curled around an empty palm.

For a moment, Daeo feels like she's being held.

Just beyond their tree-hollowed shelter, the muddy ground dissolves into oozing floodwater, a languid river engorged with detritus; plant matter, animal remains, mangled chunks of earth stream past in an endless funeral procession. Human bodies and entire kapok trunks mingle in the surging flow. Beyond the river, further than a stone's-throw, another solid, tree-dotted landmass protrudes from the watery wreckage, and then another one off to the left. Each speck of jungle is a surviving chunk of *Uyi.* And separating the islands, chasms stretch like fault lines from sinkhole to sinkhole, creating an interconnected web of floodwater and floating debris, subterranean viscera seeping up through the cracked earth.

Or is the water more like a salve?

Either way, it looks like someone took a sledgehammer to Tagi's map.

Even off in the distance, beyond rising curtains of steam, the siblings notice the caldera's once towering ring of mountains are now fractured and jagged, riddled with newfound valleys and flooded gorges.

"Ko-ama-mo," Daeo smirks, now seeing countless ways out of the *Uyi.*

"We're stuck here until the floodwaters drain," Bowi reminds her.

"We can swim," Daeo smirks again.

"Look at your shoulder!" Bowi scolds. "You're not allowed to move."

"Until when?" Daeo hates feeling pain. Can't they just ignore it?

"Three days," Bowi gives an arbitrary number, too busy managing his own nausea right now to give Daeo's injury any further assessment. "Just stay still and try to fall asleep early tonight, *wyntiko?* We can look for food in the morning." *And a* pomaeo *patch,* he pleads with the *atrypa* fossil in his hands.

"We need beds!" Daeo can't imagine sleeping in the mud like this. "And pillows!"

It takes the rest of the afternoon and evening, but Bowi eventually convinces Daeo to remain in the muddy tree-hollow while he scavenges their island for *wykyno* fronds, soft vines, broad sheets of *hympano*—anything pliant to craft into bedding. Really though, he just wants time alone in case he starts vomiting. Ever since they stopped running, his adrenaline has soured into nausea. He's never let his little sister see him get sick. As far as he knows, she's completely unaware of his chronic illness. He'd like to keep it that way. *Teerta*s can't be sick, can they? He brings their *atrypa* fossil with him, rubbing it vigorously between his palms.

But Daeo knows where her brother is going. She's known all along the illness he hides. His songs. His heroes. His stories. It's all a salve he's developed to nurse the constant, recurring pain of existence. Sometimes he can pull himself out of the agony. Other times, he succumbs. Sometimes he's strong enough to share his strategy with her. Other times, he only has enough strength to save himself.

Now, Daeo has her own pain to nurse. But she's done this before, hasn't she?

Sitting alone in their earthen alcove, Daeo watches Bowi stumble off into the jungle. Everywhere, streaks of exposed lichen glimmer to life, roused by twilight to oxidize and glow. Across the flooded gorge, Daeo sees their neighboring landmass twinkle alive as well—layers of neon green saturate the nighttime verdure, illuming the island like a radiant bubble, a fist of resilient flora jutting up from the sea of geological carnage.

But the jungle isn't all that glows anymore.

Paen-aemo. Above-and-below. Water and sky.

Between fragments of floating rubble, plant and animal carcasses alike, Daeo notices that the entire river emanates a faint, violet glow, like there's some luminous superorganism lurking beneath the flooded gorge. Something the same color as her *patu...*

And then above, across an expanse of darkening sky, the depleted atmosphere sucks itself into a void over the *Uyi*, revealing a once-in-a-millennium glimpse of the cosmos beyond.

Daeo reels, dazzled by the horror of space.

Look up.

Bowi hears Tagi's voice. Slogged over himself, searching for either a *pomaeo* patch or somewhere to puke, Bowi tilts his face skyward and, for the first time in his life, sees stars.

Chapter 76
"Nyno"

The moon shattered, and now its remnants glitter across the sky.

This is what Nyno thinks, lying in the mud, staring straight up through a gap in the forest's tattered canopy. Twinkling pinpricks pierce the night's black dome, shards of lunar dust embedded into heaven's great, cave wall.

If only she knew how deep space goes.

How ancient those stars are.

How intact the moon remains.

She's been unconscious all day (that first geyser knocked her flat-out) and she feels like she's missed something crucially important.

As usual, she thinks, *I sleep through everything.*

Now, blinking awake into a searing headache, everything feels broken—her timeline, her surroundings, her body. She feels like she's missing half her brain, and just to her left, half the jungle is now a raging river.

Granted, she's still feeling the double-effects of the *Kamaruna* and *Kunjaruna* mushrooms she ingested earlier today. She doesn't trust anything she sees—or hears, for that matter.

"I still don't think it's a good idea."

"What other choice do we have?"

The voices belong to Kleeo and Maetri.

Predictable, at least. Considering everything else.

Still, Nyno can't help but groan.

"She's awake!" Kleeo notices first.

Nyno hears them race at her; their *THUD-THUD*ing feet kick dirt onto her face.

"Don't touch her!" Kleeo barks.

"Relax!" Maetri roars back.

Nyno goes rigid.

"Wh-what's happening?" she manages to croak, her voice parched and sandy.

Kleeo and Maetri tower over her body, both of them still clad in their broken harnesses. Silhouetted against luminous trees and a star-filled sky, the pair no longer look like spiky warriors, but mangled ghosts emerging from a spectral reality.

"You slept through everything," Kleeo confirms.

"How are you feeling?" Maetri asks.

His uncharacteristic question makes Nyno suspicious. *How am I feeling?* She narrows her eyes at them, but her vision is still a foggy patchwork. Maetri appears to be holding something in his hand—in her state of mind, the mystery object must be something dangerous. A sharpened *mabato* spike? A dagger of whittled flint? Nyno can imagine anything. She tries to crawl away from them, crablike, but her hands sink into sodden mud.

Kahtopo. She's cornered between Maetri, Kleeo, and a sea of floodwater.

"Where are we?" Nyno formulates another question—last she remembers, she was supposed to be jailed inside her *capku.*

"What's left of the *Uyi,*" Maetri says, opening his arms as if to show off something impressive. He sounds... Happy?

"*Oko mee-uyina,*" Kleeo sounds annoyed. *The world ended.*

Nyno deflates, collapsing again in the mud—her violet head *splop!*s into the soggy ground. But at least it's comfortable. She figures she should go back to sleep, and then hopefully wake up once this hallucination is over. She's eaten more mushrooms than food these past several months, and she knows better than to panic over phantom sensations. All of this destruction, Nyno concludes, is just a mirage fabricated by her double-dose of *Kamaruna* and

Kunjaruna. Really, she's still tied inside her *capku*, comfortable and safe.

But really, the sacred mushrooms have nothing to do with this.

Kamaruna, Kunjaruna, Kosharuna—jailed for eons within Antarctic ice, the three fungal species now thrive worldwide, fruiting copiously across ecosystems and continents alike. Innocuous and shallow-rooted, the spore-bearing bodies function entirely separate from the *Uyi's* greater, mycorrhizal networks. Saprophytic. Off-grid. Nobody minds them. Plants. Mycelium. *Fae.* Humans, especially.

If the *Aeo* and swamp are data servers within the world's greater mycorrhizal internet, the fun, psychedelic *aruna* mushrooms are no more than aberrant pixels on their generated screens. Flashy, but superficial. Distracting, but insignificant on their own. They have no agenda, no sentience, no will. Each budding spore is just a tiny bit of genetic information, an aimless symbol of decomposition sprouting from the omniscient bionetwork beneath. Infinite and innocent—and packed with psilocybin-like compounds!

No, the mushrooms aren't responsible for any of this.

If anything, Nyno is starting to like them.

"Don't make her eat another one," Kleeo's voice.

Nyno feels Maetri seize her shoulders. She's yanked upright.

"Any broken bones?" his voice interrogates while his hands swivel her body; hardened mud flakes off her naked skin. "Pain anywhere?"

Nyno winces, "My head hurts."

"We know," Kleeo sounds bored.

"You got knocked out," Maetri says. "There's a huge lump on your forehead."

"Great..." Nyno is bored of this hallucination too. "Now can I go to sleep? I'll get back to work in the morning—"

"Forget work!" Maetri laughs. "You've been demoted back to birthing *momo* status."

Nyno cocks her head, still unable to focus her vision—yet she knows Maetri is flashing his signature grin. "Y-you can't demote me," she stutters. "I'm a Chief."

"There are no more Chiefs!" Maetri laughs harder. "They all died!"

"Look around us, *Nyno*," Kleeo folds her arms. "*Oko mee-uyina.* Did you think I was joking?" The tone of her voice makes Nyno feel incriminated.

"B-but you can't demote me," Nyno struggles against Maetri's grip. "I'm not a birthing *momo* anymore. You can't make me—"

"Everyone's dead," Maetri says, forcing Nyno to face him squarely. "The *Aeo* erupted and flooded everything. There are no more children. No more *momo*s. No more Chiefs. Not even a single *raea*. Nothing. We're the only humans left in the whole world. You. Me. And *Kleeo.* Get the implication yet?"

"B-but how you do know there's no one else left?" Nyno still can't tell if this is even real. She's had countless hallucinations more vivid than this shoddy situation. Nothing about this scene makes sense. "How do you know we're the only survivors?"

"Everyone was at the *Kamaruna* ceremony, down by the *Aeo,*" Maetri says. "I saw them all drown. I barely escaped myself." He then points to himself and Kleeo, "You're lucky we saved you after everything flooded."

"Yeah," Kleeo chimes. "Why haven't you thanked us yet?"

Nyno refuses. "What about the *Teerta*'s cave?" she asks. "Have you tried going there? It's at a higher elevation. Maybe someone else survived?" Really, she hopes this idea will invoke that void-tunnel to return so she can alter this hallucination and see her son again.

Nothing changes.

"We're surrounded by floodwater," Maetri's face is all she sees. Clean-shaven, *patu* beads gleam within the hair follicles of his scalp and chin. "We're trapped on this island, maybe forever. This is our new home now. And we're the only ones here."

"Which means we have to start over," Kleeo says. "Completely."

Nyno says nothing.

They all know the legends—*Kamaruna* represents sacrificial death, *Kunjaruna* represents vigorous survival, but everything stems from *Kosharuna.* The beginning. The great organization. The funneling of chaotic energy into something new and worthwhile. Long, long ago, on the very first *Kosharuna,* the *Fae* planted two humans in the *Uyi,* one male and one female, and instructed them to multiply...

"Here we are again," Maetri is still holding Nyno's shoulders. "Alone in the *Uyi.*"

That's when Nyno's eyes finally focus: Wedged between his fingers, Maetri's mystery object is a pair of *Kosharuna* mushrooms. Their tawny, elongated caps brim with spores.

"He's not doing it with me," Kleeo doesn't sound sorry.

"B-but it's not *Kosharuna,*" Nyno is stunned, baffled—*what kind of hallucination is this?* Monthly, non-consensual intercourse is bad enough. But the idea of doing it beneath a moonless sky disturbs Nyno in a way she never imagined possible. She tries to jerk away, but between psychedelic overdose and a severe concussion, her motor coordination is virtually nonexistent.

"Look at the sky!" Maetri scoffs, easily forcing her. "The moon is gone! It exploded too, just like the *Aeo!* There is no more *Kosharuna,* or *Kamaruna,* or any *aruna!* We're free from those binding forces! We're free from the ceremonies and rituals! Don't you see? We can procreate whenever we want! We can do anything in this new world!"

Nyno shakes her head. *I'm hallucinating. I'm hallucinating. I'm hallucinating.*

"You still shouldn't make her eat another one," Kleeo points to the mushrooms between Maetri's fingers. "She's already done *Kamaruna* and *Kunjaruna* today. If she eats a *Kosharuna* mushroom now, she'll experience the full trifecta."

"So?" Maetri just wants Nyno drugged and unconscious so he can rape her. Despite his perpetually cool demeanor, today has been exhausting. He's itching for this release. "Don't we all need to blow off some steam tonight?"

"You're disgusting," Kleeo sneers. Still, she watches idly while her brother forces a spore-laden *Kosharuna* bud into Nyno's mouth.

The full trifecta.

Nyno retains a vague sense of consciousness while Maetri begins their ceremony. His heaving body is outlined by stars rather than the full moon tonight. It's a strange sight—one that only aids Nyno's belief that this is all just a terrible hallucination. She clings to that hope. To that notion that her current pain isn't real. Because if this whole scene is imaginary, then she should be able to imagine it into a new one, right?

With ease, Nyno slips out of her body. And then she sees everything from above. The wreckage. Their island. The mishmash of floodwater and debris, the entire *Uyi* split by its seams. Her body beneath Maetri's, their *patu*s writhing against the dull, muddy ground. Kleeo leaving them, venturing off by herself into their patch of jungle to do who knows what. And Maetri eventually tiring out, collapsing in a heap upon her unconscious body.

"*KOSHARUNA!*" he howls like he's won something.

Nyno feels nothing.

Unbidden, her hallucination tugs her slowly through the air, across the flooded gorge, over to an adjacent island. There, she sees her son on its shoreline, his entire body a beacon, brighter than anything else.

Bowi!

He's alone, kneeling on the ground, knees in the mud, body swaying back and forth, back and forth. Nyno recognizes his stance, the furrow in his brow, the paleness of his lips.

Why is he always sick?

Uncured illness. Endless suffering.

It's not your pain, Bowi!

And now, Nyno realizes it isn't her pain either.

It never was.

"KOSHARUNA!"

This pain belongs to Maetri. All of it.

Give it to him! Give it back to Maetri!

Chapter 77
"Kosha-kymara"

Nausea is a state of mind.

Bowi hasn't eaten anything all day, yet his stomach feels ready to explode.

Tension. Build-up. But what's there to build?

Having long drained the electrolytes he drank this morning, Bowi drags himself across their water-locked landmass, stumbling through tangled nighttime verdure, hoping desperately the *atrypa* fossil in his hands will help him find a *pomaeo* patch...

No luck.

Panic hits as he scours the island's opposite bank.

He falls to his knees, dizzy beneath the starry, alien sky. If he starts vomiting now, how will he rehydrate? He has no access to medicine, let alone the tools needed to create an intravenous drip. He'll dehydrate within a day or two. Snarling beneath his ribcage, Bowi's stomach urges him to retch—but he can't let himself succumb.

He knows it's a rigged ultimatum.

Emesis is the body's natural solution to nausea; a good upchuck or two generally rids the stomach of any parasites. But when the nausea's origin is psychosomatic, induced by anxiety rather than physical disease, vomiting works only as a compulsory comfort. A temporary release. An escape hatch from the constant pain of psychological trauma.

Except behind that escape hatch is another escape hatch.

And another. And another. And another.

How many inversions can the esophagus sustain before rupturing?

No. Bowi won't let himself do that tonight. There's a difference between release and remedy: One is a deadly spiral, the other is an uphill journey, a quest he has yet to solve, a song he has yet to sing. Yes. In order to remedy this pain, Bowi knows his only option right now is to endure. Press forward. Remain calm.

But how?

Crouched in the mud, he caresses his sister's *atrypa* fossil, pressing its jagged surface into his abdomen. In a way, its pressure helps alleviate some of his nausea, but he has to keep rotating it, pressing different sides of it into his belly in order for it to work. If it's even working at all...

Ahead of him, the foliage falls away into another flooded gorge—indeed, their island is ringed by three intersecting rivers. But at least the geysers have ceased, and the floodwaters abated to a slow-moving ooze. Radiating its own mysterious, violet glow, the river before him is so clogged with rubble, it barely sustains its own current. Upstream, a massive pocket of drifting *raea* carcasses forms a levee along one of the chasm's forking curves, further staunching the floodwater's movement, limbs and feathers braided together like massive *areemo* cords tying the gorge shut. Now, littered with stagnant debris and wreckage, Bowi is mostly just shocked to learn dead bodies float.

He hears nothing but the gently-sloshing river and his own roiling stomach.

And then a voice he'd recognize anywhere:

"KOSHARUNA!"

Bowi scrambles behind a *wykyno* bush, alarmed by the sudden howl—though it clearly came from over the water, he'd rather not be seen. Squinting across the river, following the voice with his eyes, he sees two *patus* glowing on the opposite island's bank. A man and a woman, lying together in the mud like beached newts.

But even at this distance, Bowi can tell who they are.

He knows his *momo*'s creased *patu* and speckle-patterned skin by heart.

And even though Maetri is missing his iconic scruff, Bowi can't help but recognize his own father's voice.

"KOSHARUNA!" Maetri whoops again, delirious and slurred.

Bowi double-checks the sky for a full moon. Nothing. Just infinite stardust. *Why's he screaming about* Kosharuna? Bowi only wonders for a moment before shifting focus to his mother. He hasn't seen her since the day he was appointed *Teerta*, eight moons ago. His entire life with Tagi never included her. It was like she disappeared from the *Uyi* altogether. But now Tagi is gone. And there she is. Lying in the mud across a listless river. Straddled by Maetri.

Why is he always hurting her?

Bowi's stomach lurches. He steps out from hiding. He walks into the water.

He doesn't know what he's doing. Just that he has to do something.

Like earlier today, he's following his gut.

The river is warm; it's like he's swimming through a massive vein, submerged in hot, soupy blood. The sensation is sickening, but Bowi doesn't care. He uses a floating scrap of wood as a raft and paddles across the gorge, balancing his *atrypa* fossil atop its dry surface—including the *mabato* dagger in his waistband, he's equipped with all the tools he'll need for this procedure.

Beneath Bowi, as he swims across the chasm's stretch, something luminous and purple glitters up at him from the bottom: Beneath the floodwater, exposed mycelial roots sprout from the craggy, ruptured depths like lustrous coral reefs. Refracting their glow, the water around Bowi ripples the same color as his *Patummal* skin; he feels like a camouflaged frog, kicking his way across the violet river. Downstream, a lone *paen-aemo* paddles by without even noticing him—although the bird appears just as wary of this new, depopulated world as Bowi is, grinding its serrated beak, keeping its head low.

Are we the only survivors?

"Kosharunaaaa!" Maetri assumes he has the whole world to himself; naked and unharnessed, he's still singing euphoric by the time Bowi docks his raft against their landshelf. Beneath the man, Nyno is just a naked, unconscious body, discarded, barely breathing, caked in mud and dirt. Bowi doesn't want to look at her again. He can't. His stomach might explode if he does.

"She does not care about us... Only herself," Daeo's words replay in his mind.

And isn't it true? She never came to visit. She never defended Daeo. She never said goodbye to either of them. Eight whole moons passed. Did she even notice?

Bowi slicks his own arms, legs, and face in muck before slipping out of the water.

"Kosh-Kosh-Arunaaaa!" delirious, panting, Maetri collapses on Nyno, smothering her in the sand.

Disguised as he is, Bowi approaches like a trick of shadow and starlight. The burly man is clearly drugged, and Bowi has never felt more powerful. Crawling across the riverbank toward his parents, he reaches into his waistband to retrieve his sister's dagger. Still unsure of his own intentions, the only thing Bowi knows for sure is that his stomach hurts. And it's all because of this man.

The dagger is light in his fingers.

It feels hot like a *cananeero* bud.

It wants to help.

And then it's gone.

Disappearing from Bowi's hand, its atomic structure reconfigures through space, willed into Nyno's palm.

"Kosh-Aruna! Kosh-Kosh-Aru-AHHHHH!"

Empty-handed, Bowi watches his mother drive the dagger into Maetri's chest. A torrent of blood erupts over the pair, volcanic and hot. Still pinned beneath him, Nyno yanks the shard out and stabs Maetri again. And then again. And again. She slashes his abdomen. Eviscerates his insides. Opens his heart while he flounders atop her. She doesn't really know what she's doing, or if any of this is even real; she just knows she wants justice for her children, her cousin, her lost babies, herself. A weapon built by her daughter, delivered by her son, returned to their father—but harnessed by *her*. Eventually, Nyno drives the spike so deep into Maetri's upper chest, it gets stuck somewhere between the man's cervical ribs.

He gasps and heaves and vomits blood, drenching himself and Nyno.

Stunned, grossly fascinated, Bowi watches his parents' operation from a short distance away.

Should he help?

Which one?

He's a healer, not a fighter.

Should is a wasted word.

"S-stop!" Maetri sputters blood. Riddled with holes, he rolls off Nyno, soaked in his own gore. Lying beside her, the two of them gaze up at the infinite stars, both petrified and glistening red.

"You stop..." Nyno hisses under her breath. And then she's unconscious again. And Maetri is dead.

But to Bowi, they both may as well be. Brutalized. Strung-out on mushrooms. Leaking blood and bodily fluids. Not even a *Teerta* could save them. But at least Bowi's stomach feels better now, having witnessed his parents settle their differences once and for all.

Action. Turbulence. The funneling of chaotic energy into something new and worthwhile.

For a moment, Bowi feels his mother's psychic pull. He considers approaching her. Waking her. Helping her. But why? It's not like he and Daeo need her anymore. She's not their responsibility. The *Uyi* is a completely new place. She already sold them both, and he doesn't doubt she'd do it again. They don't matter to her. Maybe they never did. Daeo is the only person Bowi trusts now.

"Maetri!" The arrival of a new voice, Kleeo approaching from the jungle, finalizes Bowi's decision.

He allows himself to look at his mother's face one last time, just to ensure he has it fully memorized. Her soft freckles. Her glittering *patu.* Her mismatched eyes. Then he gazes at Maetri; Daeo's dagger protrudes from their father's chest, silhouetted like Eeao sleeping on Tagi's. And then, tears spilling down his own face, Bowi slips back into the river with his *atrypa* fossil and swims back to his sister.

He believes the stone's luck must be working.

Chapter 78
"Daeo"

Given Daeo's age, the effects of the *Kamaruna* mushroom she took this morning last long into the night. Her tiny liver, unused to metabolizing psychoactive fungal agents, struggles to keep up with the flow of foreign chemicals circulating her bloodstream.

But Daeo isn't worried about that.

Actually, she feels pretty good.

Aside from her shoulder, she took minimal damage on her sprint through the collapsing *Uyi*—thanks, mostly, to Bowi. Just a few bruises here and there. A scratch on her right cheek. A sharp pebble in her knee. There was so much flying debris; Bowi had to shove and jostle her a few times, but only to shield her when he could. Nothing critical. All in all, she's pleased with how today transpired.

Except Tagi... She wishes she still had him.

You still do.

"*Ugh*, not the same," Daeo sighs. "And I want *Eeao* back, too."

I can't help you with that. You'll have to wait for her to return on her own.

Daeo pouts. She's confident the kitten survived and is out there somewhere. She just wishes she had her company. The night is late, and Daeo is still alone in a root-ball alcove overlooking a carcass-clogged river. She feels safe enough. She knows Bowi will come wallowing back eventually, hopefully with one of those *pomaeo* melons he's so obsessed with. But right now, the hallucinogenic colors and shifting patterns she's been seeing all day are becoming tedious. Stale, almost. Like there's a lag between her depleted brain and heightened sensations. She's even convinced herself the stars overhead are just part of her mushroom trip—and she's already bored of them. She needs more stimulus to distract her from her shoulder injury...

She won't even look at it.

She just sits there, cross-legged, cradling her begrudged arm in her lap like it's a penalty she's serving while she tries to ignore the pain.

She'd rather think about anything else.

Remember how I changed my name to Tagi?

Sure, Daeo remembers.

Do you still want to change yours?

Daeo frowns. "I did not tell you I wanted to change my name."

Ah, but you thought it.

Daeo rolls her eyes. She's not sure if she likes having Tagi's voice in her head.

But yes, she's still considering a name change. Now that she knows there's another dimension to language, she wants to utilize each letter in her name for maximum potential. *Ado-aeo?* After-water? What a ridiculous name. A true waste. After surviving today, she feels worthy of so much more. She sits with her legs dangling over the alcove's lower lip, staring down at the murky, violet water to avoid looking at the arm in her lap, and ponders what else she'd call herself...

Then again, what do all the letters mean? She only knows the letters of her own name. She'll have to wait for Bowi to return to begin brainstorming—but even then, what if he didn't memorize the *ynsyna* symbology chart? Sure, he knows all the letters and their sounds, but did he learn their symbological meanings? Daeo groans. Out of all the ways Tagi and Bowi differed, Daeo is certain Bowi would've never wasted time on silly symbology.

Oh well. No use worrying about it now. She's already survived enough today, and there are much worse fates than getting stuck with a name like *after-water...*

Over the eastern horizon, now a craggy range of broken mountains, the waxing half-moon orbits slowly into view. It looks odd to Daeo, surrounded by all the sparkling sky-dust. With it, a westerly breeze descends over the *Uyi*, the jet stream above finally recalibrating after today's ecological mess. Cool air glides across Daeo's face. She inhales a rush of ozone, moisture, and airborne geosmin, gleaned from all the fresh, overturned soil.

This smell... She's been here before, hasn't she?

The day Tagi made them stick their noses in the *Heersu.*

The day her baby sister drowned in the *Aeo.*

This smell, so similar to rain... Daeo has kept herself distracted for a long time—from pain, from fear, from grief—but now everything's walloping her in the face, and she can't escape the *unkoma.*

Her shoulder hurts. Too much to ignore.

She's afraid the damage might be permanent.

She's afraid her arm could be ruined forever.

She's afraid that if she looks at all her injuries, they'll consume her.

Physically. Emotionally. Mentally.

But her shoulder hurts. Too much to ignore. And if crying had a smell, this would be it.

Overcome, Daeo looks down at her arm and weeps. She sees her shoulder, all bruised and swollen, even more purple than the purple of her *patu.* She sees her bent elbow, supported within her baby-blanket-sling. She sees her fingers curled loosely around her own empty palm. Each one looks so delicate, so frail.

Yet this is the hand that broke her fall.

This is the arm that saved her life.

And now it's her baby, wrapped in her old baby blanket. Why is she ignoring it?

"I am sorry!" Daeo cries, caressing her arm like it's her sister. "I am so, so, so sorry!"

She heaves and sobs, and her shoulder hurts all the more for it. But the crying feels good, so Daeo lets herself go. She cries about everything. Today. Yesterday. Her life. Her family. She sees her arm as her sister, her brother, her mother, Eeao, Tagi—*All anyone wants is to be loved!*

"I love you!" Daeo cries, burying her face in her shoulder, her baby blanket, her aroma. "I love you! I love you! I love you! I love you! I love you! I love you! I love you!"

This smell. These memories.

After-water. *Ado-aeo.*

Isn't it exquisite?

"This is what makes me who I am," Daeo realizes. "Even the pain."

No, she isn't going to change her name. Like the smell after rain, she decides to love it instead.

Daeo is asleep by the time Bowi returns. A single ray of dawn vaults over the eastern horizon, but other than that, the sky is still dark, once again awash in thick currents of star-blotting atmosphere. Daeo rouses uncomfortably; the reality of her shoulder pain is like a blaring alarm. Still, she mutters, "I love you, I love you, I love you," to her arm as she readjusts herself so Bowi can sit beside her.

"Did you see the sky last night?" Bowi asks. He doesn't appear to have found a *pomaeo* patch, but he seems relaxed. Serene, even. And cleanly bathed. Did he go swimming? "All those dots of light?"

"You saw those too?" Daeo is shocked. Was everything she saw during her *Kamaruna* trip real? The ripples of light? The floating *ynsyna* letters? The earthquakes and geysers? "What even happened yesterday?"

Bowi shrugs, baffled himself. "*Atrypa?*" he says, holding up their lucky fossil.

Daeo shakes her head. "No. We do not need that anymore. Give it to me."

"What?" puzzled, Bowi hands it over. "Why?"

"Because we are the *atrypa,*" Daeo points between the two of them. "Not this."

And then she chucks the fossil downstream.

Stunned, Bowi watches it arc through the air and splash into the river.

"What the—" he gawks at her. "Why'd you just throw it away?"

"Why do you care?" Daeo snorts. "It was just a rock. And it was mine, anyway."

Bowi stares out over the water, imagining their lucky fossil sinking to the gorge's bottom. A symbol of hope? A tool for death? He figures it's probably better that it's gone, lost to the flood like so much else. But still... He'd finally started to believe in luck.

Look!

Daeo and Bowi both hear Tagi's voice. They turn upstream.

And there, clinging to a submerged log, the siblings see a familiar (albeit soggy) creature bobbing in their direction.

Pointy ears. Slinky tail. Striped *patu* beneath bristling, striped fur.

"Eeao!"

To be continued...

Glossary of Terms

- ❖ <u>**Vowel Pronunciation**</u>
  - ➤ *ae:* "ā"
  - ➤ *ee:* "ē"
  - ➤ *o:* "ō"
  - ➤ *y:* melodic "*yih*"
  - ➤ *a:* "ă"
  - ➤ *i:* "ĕ"
  - ➤ *u:* "oo"

- ❖ <u>**Core Words**</u>
  - ➤ *Aea:* Air, sky (broadly, birds)
  - ➤ *Aeo:* Water, lake (broadly, fish)
  - ➤ *Uyee:* Fire
  - ➤ *Uyi:* Earth (terrestrial realm)

- ❖ <u>**Ceremonies**</u>
  - ➤ *Kamaruna:* half-moon ritual; six humans are sacrificed to the *Aeo*
  - ➤ *Kosharuna:* full-moon mating ritual; mushroom-induced orgy
  - ➤ *Kunjaruna:* new-moon *Meemmal* hunt; mushroom-induced bloodbath

- ❖ <u>**Flora**</u>
  - ➤ *Areemo:* type of ficus tree; its bark can be stripped and softened into fabric, twine, and even fine thread
  - ➤ *Arukona:* rare, blood-orange variant of *wykyno*
  - ➤ *Arumato:* melon, cantaloupe-like
  - ➤ *Bareebo:* flowering garden plant; its seeds are edible and often eaten as a snack
  - ➤ *Cananeero:* poisonous red flower; its nectar chemically reacts with formic acid to create fire
  - ➤ *Harapo:* medicinal root; pickled solution used as disinfectant

- ➤ *Hympano:* leathery fungal species; material used for canvassing *capku*s; melted, its organic substance dries into a sticky paste
- ➤ *Hynho:* mint
- ➤ *Keeryno:* tobacco
- ➤ *Mabato:* succulent, spiny plant; its arm-length spines are used to adorn clothing and weapons
- ➤ *Pomaeo:* water-engorged melons developed during the Genetic Revolution in response to a global water crisis; nutrient-rich juice also works as IV fluid
- ➤ *Reewo:* cooking herb similar to basil
- ➤ *Renomo:* garden-grown herb similar to chamomile; generally used for tea
- ➤ *Sokeeto:* a type of berry; cranberry-colored; raisin-like when dried
- ➤ *Syn-syn:* a combination of *keeryno* and *zymo*
- ➤ *Taepo:* a centralized kapok or dipterocarp tree; prominent outdoor gathering point
- ➤ *Talapako:* spicy cooking herb
- ➤ *Teeho:* medicinal plant similar to spiked pepper; its leaves can be pulverized into an antiseptic poultice
- ➤ *Voreeko:* long, gourd-like vegetables; consistency similar to zucchini
- ➤ *Wykyno:* a diverse, newly-evolved group of non-green plants, all of which rely on underground mycorrhizal networks instead of chlorophyll to photosynthesize carbon
- ➤ *Zymo:* marijuana

- ❖ <u>**Fauna**</u>
  - ➤ *__Arunaea:__* white-faced "moon" birds; descendents of screech owls
  - ➤ *__Camraea:__* blue, raptor-sized birds; descendents of hoatzins; calamus can be used for IV tubing, plume fibers for stitching
  - ➤ *__Fae:__* insectoids; human-insect hybrids, bioengineered during the Genetic Revolution
  - ➤ *__Gaeo:__* frogs and related amphibians
  - ➤ *__Kynaea:__* colorful descendents of macaws
  - ➤ *__Lyreea:__* broadly, reptiles
  - ➤ *__Mee:__* *Homo sapiens*; humans of the *Uyi*
  - ➤ *__Meemmal:__* derogatory term (-*mmal* is a suffix for "bad"); humans uninfected by *patu* yeast
  - ➤ *__Momaea (Momo__* parrots): giant, domesticated birds trained for human childcare
  - ➤ *__Mongaeo:__* large, amphibious newts
  - ➤ *__Onynsa:__* broadly, insects and bugs
  - ➤ *__Paen-aemo:__* fanged, web-footed, dinosaurian birds of legend; descendents of Canadian geese; literally translates *"above and below"*
  - ➤ *__Patu:__* a luminous yeast bioengineered during the Genetic Revolution to inhabit human hair follicles; the glowing area of skin covered by violet *patu* yeast [(generally limited to the scalp, armpits, and groin, but sometimes overgrown (see *Patummal)*]
  - ➤ *__Patummal:__* derogatory term; humans infected with too much *patu* yeast

- ➢ ***Raea:*** huge, flightless birds; descendants of ostriches; herded for their valuable, purple feathers and hardy meat
- ➢ ***Syreea:*** broadly, snakes

- ❖ <u>**Common Words**</u>
  - ➢ ***Ameema:*** friend
  - ➢ ***Anun(am):*** (to) breastfeed
  - ➢ ***Aruna:*** moon; fungus
  - ➢ ***Aruwyna:*** the study of trees
  - ➢ ***Arynmo:*** emergency
  - ➢ ***Atrypa:*** good luck; a mercy given to early *Kamaruna* volunteers
  - ➢ ***Babi:*** son
  - ➢ ***Babo:*** daughter
  - ➢ ***Brae(am):*** (to) love
  - ➢ ***Capa(ma):*** alive (life)
  - ➢ ***Capku:*** "home"; a conical abode, generally wrapped in *hympano* canvassing and supported by a central pole
  - ➢ ***Eera:*** hope
  - ➢ ***Heersu:*** medicinal garden
  - ➢ ***Heersyna:*** the study of horticulture
  - ➢ ***Kahtopo:*** derogatory term for excrement; "shit"
  - ➢ ***Kataka:*** blood
  - ➢ ***Kyro(ma):*** eyes (vision)
  - ➢ ***Kyrkaruna:*** dinner, supper (*-yrk* is the root word for "eat")
  - ➢ ***Mankata:*** "late-bloomer"; children who learn to speak late

- ➤ *Meerso:* hurry
- ➤ *Momo:* mother
- ➤ *Momyna:* the study of motherhood
- ➤ *Myrkuna:* lunch
- ➤ *Nunee:* breasts
- ➤ *Lynee(ma):* ears (sound; sense of hearing)
- ➤ *Lyrgo:* mercy
- ➤ *Onynsyna:* the study of insects
- ➤ *Oryn(am):* (to) panic
- ➤ *Otrypa:* bad luck
- ➤ *Param(am):* (to) drink directly from the *Aeo* *ill-advised
- ➤ *Punteeku:* hunter; killer; the class of warriors who fight during *Kunjaruna*
- ➤ *Syn:* joy
- ➤ *Teerta:* doctor; the exiled Chief of science
- ➤ *Tunko(ma):* tongue (flavor; sense of taste)
- ➤ *Tynji:* brother
- ➤ *Tynjo:* sister
- ➤ *Tyrkuna:* breakfast
- ➤ *Una:* sun; day; morning
- ➤ *Unko(ma):* nose (scent; sense of smell)
- ➤ *Urynka:* earthquake
- ➤ *Uyeenka:* volcano
- ➤ *Uysyna:* the study of geography
- ➤ *Wakar(am):* (to) shave; traditional head-shaving custom
- ➤ *Wyntiko?:* "capiche?"
- ➤ *Ymee:* name; identification
- ➤ *Ynsyn(am):* (to) read/write

> ***Ynsyna:*** written language; alphabet
> ***Yryk(am):*** (to) eat
> ***Yrya(m):*** dead (death)

- ❖ **<u>Compound Terms & Phrases</u>**
  > ***Amutee una kotyna-ah:*** literally, "allow the sun to move"
  > ***Aruka-om-uka:*** equivalent to, "some things never change"
  > ***Eejo-o kompu-eptek:*** *Kamaruna* proverb meaning, "no one is useless"
  > ***Fynza-eera:*** "false hope"; named for the tingling sensation associated with *cananeero* consumption
  > ***Kantru-pyndara:*** harmless, insipid, benign; literally, "lock-jawed"
  > ***Ko-ama-mo:*** literally, "no way out"
  > ***Kosha-kymara:*** literally, "sperm donor" (this language has no intimate word for "father")
  > ***Kyn ree-larro:*** equivalent to, "it's coming"
  > ***Kyr-aea mae:*** equivalent to, "birds-eye-view"
  > ***Montada-yryku:*** literally, "death-housed-in-rock"; fossilized remains
  > ***Oko mee-uyisa:*** forbidden phrase equivalent to, "the world is ending"
  > ***Ra meerr-ymaeka sae:*** equivalent to, "you're a mind-reader"
  > ***Ragran-eena:*** "child's tongue"; speech impediment; in this language, contractions are

pronounced by rolling "rr"s between words—a linguistic challenge for some

- ➤ ***Saeryn-eptek:*** castration; literally, "rendered useless"
- ➤ ***Tarma-ako:*** equivalent to, "the greater good"
- ➤ ***Vu-kopa vu-jo:*** equivalent to, "too little, too late"
- ➤ ***Ynsyn-eera:*** "knowledge-hope"; "faith"; belief in life after death

Acknowledgment

Seven years ago I was hospitalized for anorexia. At the time, I thought my life was over. After decades of trauma-related nausea and OCD, I felt trapped inside a body that felt only pain. I feared nothing else existed. Eventually, finding starvation a more tolerable mode of existence, my brain systematically prepared my body to die.

Seven years later I'm proud my preparation failed. I'm proud of the joy I found beneath the pain, and the life I'm creating around it. I'm grateful for the doctors who saved my body, and the friends who showed me it's safe to trust others again. I'm grateful for my intuition, my gut instinct—that I've learned to channel my sensitivity into novels like *Petrichor* and *Cryfest*.

Pain can be horrifying, and PTSD a lingering nemesis. But like all the best horror stories, it's usually worth it to fight for survival and stick around until the end. Because then you get to bask in all the beautiful carnage.

About the Author

Jonathan D. Robbins is a genderqueer author from Phoenix, Arizona, with a Bachelor's degree in Psychology from Arizona State University. He wrote and published his first novel, *American Cryfest*, after breaking his spine during the 2020 pandemic. His latest novel, *Petrichor*, is the first installment in an upcoming sci-fi trilogy exploring family structures, linguistic evolution, and the geothermal ecosystem(s) of the Yellowstone caldera.